PILGRIMAGE

❧ *of* ❧

LOVE

A Tale of Romance, Heartbreak
and Meeting 'The One'

ANAIYA AON PRAKASHA

ANAIYA AON PRAKASHA

anaiya@pilgrimageoflove.com

www.pilgrimageoflove.com

ISBN 978-1-4467-8863-9

First published 2011

Text © Anaiya Aon Prakasha 2011

Cover design, text design and typesetting by

David Andor / Wave Source Design

www.wavesourcedesign.com

This book is dedicated to all Beloveds, everywhere.

Pilgrimage |·pilgrəmij| An arduous and often harrowing journey towards that which is greater than your mortal self.

ACKNOWLEDGEMENTS

This whole journey would not have been possible, or even imaginable, without the powerful loving presence of my Beloved, Sananda Gabriel. He is a private person by nature, but unfortunately that privacy ended the day he met me! I thank him with the whole of my heart for his encouragement to share with you all so openly our journey into the path of the Beloved.

To my parents, Dinah and Patrick Cuddihy, for seeding within me this inextinguishable fire of love, and bringing me into this world in the first place.

To Carolyn Billingham (Chloe) for standing by me every step of the way as I went heart first into this wild and crazy adventure. You are a true 'best friend'.

Heartfelt gratitude to Damien Nola (Darren) the one I would often turn to in the moments of much needed clarity and understanding.

I must also extend a huge wave of gratitude to Audrey and Don Wood, who supported this book by placing it in the right hands at the right time.

To my passionate and magical midwife/editor, Heather Strang, who would sit up at all hours of the night and day making sure that only the very best manuscript would be birthed. At the end of it, she was left with no choice but to go on this journey with her guns blazing! Way to go, Heather!

To David Andor, whose visionary talents created the front cover and layout of this book you are holding, his passion for perfection continued to be paid off as his thirst for this project spilled over into the creation of the *Pilgrimage* website days later.

Finally to Gangaji and Eli, the teachers who brought me to my knees in the humble realization that Love is Truth.

Thank you all for helping me bring this story to the world.

May you all know how deeply you have touched me, and that this touch reverberates throughout the entire cosmos.

INTRODUCTION

Pilgrimage of Love is a story based on similar events that happened to me a few years ago. Only the names have been changed; everything else remains untouched and exactly as it happened.

Scarlett O'Shea is a wild haired, hot-blooded, young (ish) woman who is determined to find "The One" just one year before her fortieth birthday. This is the story of how they met just nine months after she called him in from the top of a mysterious, sacred mountain deep in the heart of Southern France. This is her personal, ruthlessly intimate, and hilarious tale of finally meeting her Beloved in person and their journey back into the enormity of love, along with the many (and let me tell you, there were many) trials and tests along the way.

My sole intention in sharing this story is to dispel the myth that true love belongs in fairytales (I never believed it then, and I certainly don't believe it now), and the notion of "The One" being something we grow out of after our school days. This story fiercely demonstrates a woman who took hold of the reins of her life, at the age of forty, by saying "yes" to love—no matter the cost.

Fortunately, I have left nothing out, making sure I confess all of the ways I protected myself from being hurt, so you can have a few giggles on me, as you say, "Ah ha, that's what I do!"

Only your heart knows if this is the path for you.

Anaiya Aon Prakasha,
14th February 2011

Beloved Journey Warning

Make sure you are seated comfortably, and your seat belt is securely fastened before we take off. Please pay no attention whatsoever to the emergency exits, as they won't open in time. However, an oxygen mask *may* drop down above your head in the extreme case of an emergency. There are no life jackets under your seat, as I do not find value in safety, but rather encourage all passengers to freely jump into the eye of the awaiting storm.

Are you ready?!

You are about to enter the roller coaster of Love, the most wild and dangerous of all rides that will send you heart first into a labyrinth of the most inflamed passion and rapturous love.

Everyone may have a Beloved, but whether they meet him or her in person is an entirely different matter. It used to be said that only a handful of people at one given time would meet their Beloved. Most of the time one of them would be incarnated on Earth, while the other would be a million galaxies away, guiding the other through life's challenges. There was, however, a price to be paid for those who met in person. That price was that they would only be together for a tragically short amount of time. Yet these Beloveds would stand out and mark the significant times within our history. I'm sure you're familiar with many of them: Solomon and Sheba, Jesus Christ and Mary Magdalene, Anthony and Cleopatra, Helen of Troy and Paris, and more recently Romeo and Juliet.

Now, all of this is changing.

You will know, like I did, whether you are destined to meet your Beloved or not in this lifetime. I also know that by reading this book the vibration of its message will align and awaken within you the powerful magnetism that it takes to discover either your Beloved or Soul Mate. We'll cover both, as they are gifts from the heavens whose chance meetings are filled with grace.

The moment you meet, you know.
The moment you know, you meet.
When the time is ready, no one can prevent it.
    Not even you.

Below are my 'spiritually serious' (insert serious, straight-laced voice here) descriptions of the words Soul Mate and Beloved, so you can understand for yourself and navigate where you are in your current relationships. Please note: this journey is not for the faint hearted or the weak in spirit, as it takes balls and bravery, gentleness and genuineness to walk this path. When you pick up the gauntlet I have laid down for you, you may experience a love beyond words, a love that wipes clean all and every disappointment. You will discover the quality of love and intimacy that inspires the realization of all realizations, *"Oh, so that's what it's all about…"*

If I were to tell you now all of the twists and turns—all of the drama, all of the new and varied ways of making love—it would ruin your read. So I'll just say this: the chances of finding "The One" are increasing, and that's where *you* come in. By the end of this book you are going to be invited to embark on your own personal pilgrimage. And I have no doubt that you're ready for this, because you would not be reading this book if you weren't.

Sit back, relax, and enjoy the journey that is about to unfold, because soon it will be your turn...

Below are the definitions for both Soul Mate and Beloved. Let these definitions guide you, so you can feel into the possibility of merging with your Soul Mate(s) or Beloved in this lifetime.

You're being called... can you hear it?

Just say, "yes!"

SOUL MATES

Soul Mates are souls that have been created within a soul family, so there is a family-type feeling of coming together. When you meet one another there is recognition, a familiarity that brings with it a wondrous joy and feeling of 'belonging.' Soul Mates are in each other's lives to offer support, love, and richness. There is a timeless feeling when together that is often acknowledged through the words, "feels like I have known you forever." All Soul Mate relationships are for the purpose of spiritual growth, and the deepening and expanding of all spiritual attributes. Soul Mates teach each other how to love themselves and then how to love each other, thereby creating the most ideal situation for a conscious family. Not all Soul Mate reunions are sexual; there can be a genuine experience of having a purely platonic relationship where one actually places the needs and wants of their Soul Mate before their own. They can literally serve one another for years as they learn to embody unconditional love. Soul Mates prepare us for union with our Beloved, either in this lifetime or the next.

HALLMARKS OF A SOUL MATE

A warm and comfortable feeling when together. A slow start with less intensity and conflict. Feelings of support, friendship, family, and familiarity. A strong attraction, you may adore and love the way they look, enjoying their entire being. But you will always be two, keeping your separate identities very much intact. No desire to merge; happy and content to enjoy individuality and two-ness.

BELOVEDS

Now, Beloveds are a whole other type of relationship. First, let's take a closer look at the word Beloved. Watch this: Be *'love'* d. Yes, that's right, the Beloved will do everything and anything to push and pull you around your so-called neat, safe, and organized life, until you simply become LOVE. This is no walk in the park ladies and gentleman, this is The Full Monty. Only those prepared to 'bare all' will come out on top! But, don't be scared—the payoff is worth every bit of it.

Beloveds are two halves of the same soul brought together for the purpose of making an obvious difference in the world. For those meant to join with their Beloved, the incessant throbbing of desire and longing for the other is never far beneath the subconscious. They constantly crave a deeper, more meaningful love and will settle at nothing to find it. Beloved love is always steadfast and enduring. They are unable *to not* love one another; their love is eternal and continues way beyond their human experiences. They unite when there is important spiritual work or collaboration to be done, and there is a readiness and willingness to understand the full breadth of human connection. Both will carry out a mission together for the benefit of mankind.

When Beloveds come together, similar to Soul Mates, they act as two mirrors. But unlike Soul Mates, Beloveds reflect back each other's "shadow self" for the ultimate goal of perfect polarity integration, or ultimate unity. This can be a huge task for human beings, as we have learned so many ways of staying safe and protecting ourselves from being hurt. But this is the gift of the Beloved. The Beloved frees you from the controlling powers of the mind and sends you heart first into the ecstatic joys of the liberated heart, *once* you have faced and gone through a few select initiations (more on that to follow!).

Those who live lives of emotional detachment often do so when they are unable or unwilling to face their Beloved. It can be an overwhelming, life-altering experience to come face-to-face with the other half of your soul. Many people flee in emotional terror and allow emotional baggage to destroy the process. But when they accept this beautiful opportunity, it can be the most intensely transformative and powerful experience a person can have. Whatever the case, there is no force on Earth that can keep Beloveds apart—but emotional soul injuries can injure or even delay a reunion lifetime after lifetime.

HALLMARKS OF A BELOVED

It is usually intense, challenging, light and dark, polar opposites of each other, with near Hollywood style showdowns happening within a highly attracting energetic field that you cannot fight against or deny. Every type of duality (pairs of opposites) will be played out, until there is nothing left but love, and an incredible desire to merge and become one. The idea of being two is completely repelling. Beloveds yearn to merge into one. It is their natural state.

Some people say that a Soul Mate is the starter, while the Beloved is the main course. I say they both taste good to me!

Are you ready to begin?

The minute I heard my first love story
I started looking for you,
not knowing how blind that was.
Lovers don't finally meet somewhere.
They're in each other all along.

—RUMI

CHAPTER ONE

SHAMBALLA URBAN RETREAT

The Metropolitan Hotel,
Park Lane, London. October 2007

I NHALE deeply, and exhale completely. Allow your breath to dissolve all the stress and tension from your shoulders and neck; let it all go. Breathe out all your worries, anxieties, and fear. As you begin to breathe in, experience the possibility of something new being born within you…"

I smiled as I watched this small group of people get comfortable as they left behind their high maintenance lifestyle, six-figure salaries and twenty-four seven careers, and drifted into a world of carefree peace and harmony; a place free from demands, free from their everyday identity, and full of new possibilities. In normal life they were high-flying international peacekeepers for the United Nations. Here in this moment, they had become *the peace* they were *keeping* as their deep purple fleece blankets emblazoned with the gold Metropolitan Hotel logo covered their blissed-out bodies. I watched from afar as all traces of stress dissolved from their faces, and smiled inwardly knowing the magic was working.

I had been teaching yoga for twelve years all over the world, and my clients read like a who's who in the latest copy of *Hello* magazine. I was now a private teacher for The Metropolitan Hotel in Park Lane, London, perhaps one of the trendiest and most expensive hotels in one of the most expensive cities in the world, the home away from home of the of A-list. This enviable position magically placed in my hands a year-long VIP pass for The Met Bar, the chic, glamorous hang out of the young and beautiful "it" crowd, along with a free room at the hotel whenever I wanted, discounts worldwide throughout their chain of hotels, free membership at London's infamous Yacht Clubs, and of course teaching the most high calibre guests at their sister resorts in Mauritius, the Seychelles, and Bali.

Celebrities and millionaires weren't the most grateful of students as I reflected back on the many divas and gangstas I had worked with over the years, like the Iranian Princess, who lived on the entire top floor of the Halkin Hotel, in London's Hyde Park Corner. She moaned and complained her way through every session, often getting up in the middle of class to answer her mobile and then have a complete hissy fit with the person on the other end. She had everything going for her and it didn't look like it was about to run out. She was young, beautiful, infinitely wealthy, and healthy. Yet her attitude towards life was that of a spoiled, pain in the ass teenager.

Then there was the cast of *American Pie*. These guys were hilarious to teach, just like their characters in the film, cracking jokes at anything that even hinted at having a possible sexual association. "Inhale and lift up your breastbone, exhale and squeeze your anus, bend over all the way," became the green light for an all out side-splitting, pant-wetting frenzy. And of course, there was a certain American actress, who we all know as the star on the TV series *Dallas*. She would come to class totally made up, not a hair out of place, resulting in her refusal to do anything that messed up her hair, made her sweat, or go red in the face.

Why did these women and men who seemingly had everything come to me? Because I shared with them a feeling of joy, of freedom that their bulging bank accounts couldn't buy. I guided them to places deep inside themselves where they finally found some inner peace and felt waves of love that didn't have conditions attached to it. My classes were renowned for my dynamic style and love of music. My clients would enter a world of sound, magic, and movement that stimulated their every sense. Their ears would soak up the most exquisite soundscapes while their noses would draw in the delicate scents of hand-rolled Balinese incense.

All my classes were in candlelight, as I whispered out the words that guided them to that tangible peace, that place where their true selves could be felt and relaxed into, and then taken into their hearts where they could rest forever more, and slowly over time forgive all past grievances. Over my twelve years of teaching, I did this again and again; and the people just kept on coming as my reputation reached the furthest shores. My email inbox was full, my mobile glowed red with messages, and invites kept on appearing. But I left one person out, someone who came to every single one of my classes.

Myself.

I was not free. I was not at peace, because I knew I was living a lie. Like my A-list clients I had it all, and in the end it meant nothing. This lie was the pretense that I was content. As I climbed the ladder of success and prosperity, slowly my dreams of finding "the one" began to subtly diminish. I was beginning to accept that maybe we would not meet one another, that I had fabricated the whole thing. That is what I was telling myself, but I knew deep down this was untrue. I couldn't understand why we hadn't met yet, and to be honest I was more than a little pissed off with God for not orchestrating the answer to my prayers.

So, I transformed my frustration by teaching yoga, and giving all that I was in the process. I left absolutely no space to even receive love. Every waking moment of my life was consumed with service, which worked brilliantly for a while until one day I realized I had sold out on my quest and settled for second best. I had been living with this lie for over twenty years, and as every week passed it grew stronger, its voice louder. I had taken a role in life I knew was for someone else, and I had woven myself so tightly into this life that I did not even know how to begin to unravel myself. By the time I was thirty-eight, I was comfortably stuck, nicely trapped, and absolutely stagnant.

Great!

Life ends (or does it begin) at forty? From where I was standing I had little more than a year to go until it was over—unless I did something radical to change my life…

"Slowly begin to come back into your bodies, inhaling deeply and exhaling completely. Gently start to rotate your fingers and toes as you inhale and stretch out your whole body. When you feel ready, come up into a seated position as you slowly bow your head over to end the class."

After a few minutes an ocean of smiling, radiating faces

beamed back at me from inside the Shamballa Urban Retreat. The group was made up of four men and two women. One of the women was a gorgeous African American lady named Prudence. Imagine Oprah meets Dolly Parton. She was athletic, warm, beautiful, full of happiness, and possessed that certain star quality which Oprah and Dolly exude. The moment I saw her, I was hooked. She was fantastic, and no doubt the United Nations prize negotiator. She would win my vote any day. There was a certain sense of trust about her; she bestowed good feelings to all around. I watched her move around the room as she rolled up her mat and placed it in the corner. I felt as if she had something important to tell me, like I knew her from… before.

"Scarlett, say you will stay and have drinks with us tonight honey?" she crooned in her southern belle accent.

My eyes widened excitedly, as an, "I'd love to," tumbled out of my naturally glossed lips. I rolled my yoga mat up and pushed it inside my Prada bag, pulled on my Donna Karen ankle length cashmere cardigan and released my hair from its topknot. I glanced at the floor length mirror as we left the room, and ruffled my golden tumbling curls over to one shoulder. We all went straight downstairs to The Met Bar; it was early evening so we had the place to ourselves. I made sure I sat next to Prudence as the guys went to order drinks.

"I so loved your class," she eagerly told me. "It reminded me of a feeling I had when I was on vacation three years ago…"

She drifted off for a moment. I watched her eyes move away from mine, as she glanced out the window. She brushed her fingertips against her lips as if she was contemplating something important. She hummed to herself and turned back. The guys came back with the drinks and the table sprang to life, as they chatted busily about their upcoming meeting tomorrow in the city. I had no idea what their meeting was about; all I could gather was that the very best men and women had been sent to seal the deal. Prudence kept including me in the conversation, asking my opinion on how they could compose themselves before the meeting. How to remain centered and focused, yet powerfully clear with their colleagues. After an hour or so, I started to think about getting home.

I was beginning to get my things together when Prudence dropped the time bomb, "Scarlett, are you married? Or do you have a partner at home?"

It's the question of my life right now, I thought to myself.

"Yes, I am in a relationship," I told her, "but it's nothing terribly serious. I don't really have any time outside all my teaching hours, plus I'm often traveling."

I tried hard not to let my voice give away my bottomless pit of emptiness, revealing the truth of my seemingly perfect existence. Although surrounded by people, and adoring ones at that, nothing could fill the space that ached to meet my Beloved. I knew I was missing a massive part of my purpose. After years of half-hearted relationships and lively conversations into the night with girlfriends, at the end of the day they all seemed to point towards the idea that 'The One' does not exist. It was as if I was the only person alive who felt that 'The One' was still a possibility.

One spiritual teacher after the other would tell me that this longing was for the love of God, that what I really wanted was to return to the Source. Return to the Source?! "I am the source!" I would humbly yell, realizing yet again that no one could understand unless they had met theirs. "What do they know?" I muttered to myself as I left their white washed angelic sanctuaries behind, closing the door on their spiritual advice.

I knew I had to go it alone. But the question was, where?

"Mmm… that doesn't feel right to me sweetheart, a woman like you needs to find her Beloved, she needs to find The One…"

Prudence's eyes shone like torches straight into mine. It could have been the candles flickering on the table between us, or quite possibly the wine she was drinking. But she had suddenly transformed into a modern day goddess before my very eyes. Her eyes glinted with knowingness, and suddenly I was all ears.

This was the first time in my life that someone suggested that they knew my plight. It was as if she could see straight through into my soul. The tension mounted, and I had to seize the moment. I could feel that a special turn of events was about to unfold. This one sentence alone was causing a chain reaction inside of me that was beginning to challenge me to find 'The One' by listening to that place in my heart that I had silenced by settling for second best.

"Do you ever have that feeling, that there is one who searches for you, as much as you search for him?" she asked.

My heart began to beat wildly; I pulled up my seat to get even closer to her. "What do you know about this?" I demanded—in the nicest possible way, of course, without actually kidnapping her and holding her hostage until she told me everything.

She looked around at her colleagues, making sure they weren't listening to our conversation. She moved closer to me, as our backs began to turn ever so slightly away from the others.

"Three summers ago I was in Montpellier in the South of France with my girlfriend," she whispered. "One night we were at a local restaurant, and the owner came over to our table and began to speak about the area. He told us that this part of France had a legend that had many flocking to the region for centuries," she continued.

I drew closer still, casting one more look over my shoulder at the others who were in the process of getting up to order another round of drinks.

"My friend Jenny was in the beginning stages of romance with her boyfriend and was constantly outside on the mobile. She got a call just then. Maybe he felt sorry for me sitting alone, I'm not sure, but he pulled up a chair and sat down."

"He told me there was a mountain, and the path up that mountain was known as The Pilgrimage of Love. The Mountain was called, Mont de Coeur—The Mountain of One Heart. At the top of the mountain, was a cave, called The Cave of The Beloved. The legend continues that whomever walks up that mountain, reaches the top, goes into the cave, and sincerely prays to find The One, will do so within one full year." Prudence took a few sips of her wine, as if dying of thirst. "Not only that, I remembered what the old man said, and decided to go."

Prudence excitedly picked up the pace as she told me how she climbed to the very top, climbed inside the cave, and shouted out. God knows to who or what she was shouting out to, but she demanded with all her power to meet "The One" she had been waiting for her entire life! She loved telling this story, I could tell. I wonder if she loved telling it as much as I adored listening to it.

"Go on, go on, what happened? Did you meet him?" I nearly stood up and called for silence in the bar. My heart was pounding with anticipation.

"Oh yes, I met him. Within six months to the day that I took that hike," she breathed like air escaping from a deflating balloon, as her voice got lower and quieter.

Whoa. I slumped back into my chair.

"The legend continues to say that whoever climbs the mountain, must tell one other of its existence, but only ever one. You have to know exactly who to tell, or the mountain will lose its power," she looked down into her glass, slightly frowning.

"How do you know who the right person is to tell?" I asked.

"You have to know that the person you tell is ready to hear, and willing to climb within nine months of being told. If the story falls on deaf ears, then the legend is lost to story books and fire side magic," she said, brushing the stem of her glass as she looked sideways at me.

My mind raced; images, memories, feelings, emotion, heart beating, beating, beating…Get your diary! Nine months time, tell one other, Mont de Coeur, near Montpellier, South of France. Who do I know there? 9 months, 9 months, I worked it out in my head right then—it was July. I must be there by the middle of July!

I had this feeling all night that Prudence had something to tell me. How did she know? How could she know?

"I promise to go!" I swore to her.

She took my hand and whispered in my ear, "I knew you would!"

We exchanged emails, and I vowed to keep her posted on all that happened as the future began to unfold. I hurriedly said goodbye to my new one-off friends, yet knew that Prudence's influence on me would last a lifetime. I took the stairs down to the underground parking, to where my cute little red MG Roadster was waiting to take me home. Home? I don't have a home, I thought to myself. Home is where the heart is, that warm, comforting, nest-like place that is your sanctuary, where you share your life with the one you love.

But I didn't have a home. I had a house, a place where I lived with my thirty-five year-old boyfriend, who had been gifted with the emotional capacity of a twelve year-old. Danny was a great guy, but we seemed to have our roles back to front. I worked all day, every day while he sat "at home." I am driven and focused, he is confused and lazy. I want to grow and explore myself; he would rather not know what lurks "in there." I have had enough of sex and was now ready to explore the depths and mysteries of actually making love; whereas he would rather I put on a fluffy pink bikini and crawl around on all fours.

Of course, appearances can be deceiving. Looking in from the outside you would see a gorgeous rambling old renovated barn in the rolling hills of the English countryside. Soft willow trees flanked the entrance, birds at the windowsills, horses in the next-door field, where they also bred dogs and furless cats. Yes, it sure did look like heaven, but the moment I entered that front door, the dream fragmented into a million pieces, as did my heart. Oh, and the renovated barn? Well that belonged to his parents, adding yet another reason why it could never quite feel like home.

I unlocked the door of my car and jumped in. I turned the ignition, and nearly blew my ears off. I'd taken to playing my music loudly to drown out my problems, often forgetting to turn it down. I had to sort that out—either the problem or the volume. Which one would it be? So far, I had decided I would stick to the volume. But after my discussion with Prudence, things would have to change.

I drove up to Hyde Park Corner, past the Iranian Princess palace and took the road towards Harrods. It was a beautiful evening, the golden street lights gracing the stores and welcoming bars. The traffic was slow; it was a Friday and everyone was out on the streets making the most of one of the last warm autumn evenings.

"Louder, louder, as if you have a choice, even if you cannot hear my voice I'll be right beside you dear..."

Snow Patrol's soothing tones filled the car and tore at my heart. This singer knew about my pain, he knew about the yawning black hole I was heading towards; he knew I couldn't bear it much longer.

"And to think that I won't get to see those eyes, as we say our last goodbyes..."

A huge wave of contracted heartache moved up through my throat and escaped from my mouth as I felt an inner wail of separation and loneliness. The roof was down on the car, but I didn't care as I turned the volume up loud enough for the whole of London to hear. "Please find me!" I pleaded."I know you can hear me!"

I had been twisting and turning in a space that was too small. My life felt like sand falling through my fingers, with my heart losing the last shreds of hope. The weight of it all began to pull me under. No one knew how I felt; my best friend just thought of me as extremely fussy, while my mother was sure no one could ever keep me interested.

"You'll get bored in the end, you always do darling," was her latest nugget of wisdom.

Inside I felt so unmistakably miserable, so unsatisfied and distant with my boyfriend, my life was empty, and I was absolutely terrified it would stay this way forever. All I knew was that I missed someone so badly that it constantly ached inside my heart. The MG stretched out onto the M4 and purred as she headed west out of London. As the three-hour drive loomed in front of me, my mind began to drift back to my early childhood and teenage years.

I had my first heartbreak at the age of thirteen. I was only a child when I discovered that my handsome, older and blonder boyfriend, also known as the "be all and end all" of the teenage years, had another girlfriend. I found out by looking through his bedside drawer one Sunday afternoon, whilst he was having a row downstairs with his sister. I was bored, so I began to look around at things to amuse myself. I opened the drawer and saw some handwritten letters on pink paper that smelled of perfume. I continued on into territory, that even at thirteen, I knew I shouldn't. I opened the letters and began to read.

Bang. In that moment the world and my place in it ended.

I remember rereading again and again, as I was so sure I had made a mistake. It couldn't be true, it just couldn't be.

It was.

That was the moment when everything changed. My childlike love, which was so full of trust and innocence, changed. It turned into something that became protected and safe. I had no idea how unbelievably painful heartbreak could be. From that moment on, I never felt safe to fall in love again. I would cry in my mother's arms, asking her how long it would take for my sadness to go away.

She would gently smile, and deliver yet another priceless gem, "You're too young to be in love. It's just a schoolgirl crush. You will be over him in a couple of days. Just you wait and see."

And in a way she was right. Not because it was a crush, it was. But, because I began to return to my Beloved in my dreams, retreating into my imagination and sharing with him all that I was experiencing. It had been about three years since I last connected with him. As I went through pubescence I felt like I ought to grow out of all the imaginary, soul love stuff. So, I had left him behind and stopped reaching out to him in my dreams. Hormones—what crazy ideas they can put into your head!

To him three years was three seconds. He held me into the night as I cried and cried into my pillow. Once I finished crying, he looked straight into my eyes and asked whether I was ready. "Ready for what?" I asked. He took my hands and placed them on either side of his head and begged me to bring him to life. He said that if I kissed the top of his head and made that promise then I would be given the power to make him real. By my tears and love for him I could create a way for us to meet when we were older.

I slowly bent towards him while mustering all the love within me. I gently kissed the top of his head as I whispered the words out loud, "By this kiss I shall bring you to life so we may find each other when the time is right." The next morning I woke up with a secret smile knowing I had done something very magical. I reached over to my bedside table and grabbed my diary. Hiding under the duvet I began to scribble down words as I began the process of creating "The One" in my dreams. And boy, did the outside world have a fine act to live up to.

I literally "designed" him exactly as I wanted him to be. He was dark, adventurous, funny, athletic, had a beautiful smile, loved animals, and was very kind. He also believed in magic, and things you couldn't explain. He was mysterious, and he lived in my kind of world. Yet even within my perfected dreaming, there was still one thing I couldn't control.

I intuitively knew I could not be the one who decided when we would meet. That had to be left to the great unknown. I had to let go and let faith engineer the perfect time. In the meantime, we would grab every possible moment to meet in my sleeping hours. I would dream of him running towards me. We would meet in the woods, playing in the streaming sunlight as we noisily laughed and danced together. The dream would always end in the same way, with the dream growing quieter, and the quietness triggering a surge of dread in the pit of my stomach. The silence meant he was going back, away from me.

He would stop whatever we doing together and look over his shoulder as if someone was waiting for him. He would then grab both my hands as if time was running out. Eyes wide and full of sadness his eyes searching mine, he would whisper that it was time for him to leave. His hand reached for my cheek as he stroked the outline of my face. He would always tilt his head to one side as held the tip of my chin. He would mouth in silence, "One day we will be together again, I promise you…"

Even as I remembered this over twenty-five years later, my eyes turned upwards, gazing into the night sky—looking, wondering, and searching. I came back into the present moment, remembering Prudence as I passed Stonehenge on the infamous A303 road between the Wiltshire/Dorset borders. As I looked to my right at England's most legendary monument, I nodded my head in confirmation. Yes, I will go to France. I will climb that mountain and I will call out with all my might and strength to bring him to me.

This inner resolution filled my heart with a warm tumbling happiness. I felt like I was finally making good on a promise my younger self had made, that my older, more cynical self had broken. I was ready to believe in love again.

I took her in my arms and flew her to paradise

Fame and fortune surrounded her

She conquered the hearts of men

Pride shone in her eyes for a moment

And then it died

"I have no joy in you," she cried

My woman of sorrow

Days go by and she cries

"Tell me what is it you want?"

and she said "When will my lover come,

the one with the unknown name,

when will my lover come to me from the heart?"

—RUMI

CHAPTER TWO

FAIRYDALE BARN

Dorset, England, May 2008

LIFE CONTINUED on the way it does when you don't create too many waves. Since that legendary meeting with Prudence I had slowly but surely begun to put things in place for my soon-to-be adventure. I had found out where the mountain was located, where to stay, how to get there, and had allocated a month off from teaching so that the pilgrimage could begin. It had been six months since my meeting with Prudence and I now had three months to put all the pieces in place to call in my Beloved.

The only thing that currently stood between me and my search for true love was my current toy-boy boyfriend known as Danny, a half Spanish would-be actor. My friends referred to him as, "the Spanish Peacock," as he was good looking, but hardly husband material. Although we had been living together in an idyllic picture box countryside house for almost a year called FairyDale Barn, it was far from a happy home. My life was driven by passion and determination to teach everyone and their dog about yoga, whilst Danny continued to dream of being a bohemian artistic performer and was more than happy to lay about the house all day, accepting hand outs from his parents.

As I neared forty, my respect for him had almost dwindled to zero. I was now only interested in a red-blooded man, throbbing with life, full of love and passion, willing to knock down all the obstacles and safe zones that stand between the human experience and love, hungry for a lifetime of adventure. I was interested in a real man, one who was ready to live outside of the box, not someone who virtually needed a babysitter. And this is where I now find myself, not knowing how to approach the rut I am obviously in. I know where I want to go. I know what I want to do, but for the life of me, I just do not know where to start.

I have been back at the barn for two days since returning from my regular three-day stay in London where I taught yoga every week. I have been doing my best impersonation of myself, going through all the motions and responding in the most agreeable ways to ensure smooth sailing. All the while, I've been searching, or rather hunting, for the most appropriate moment to break the news that I am currently sitting on. Danny is being his usual self, threading chop sticks through his hair to hold it all in place while he surfs the Internet for the festival listings happening in the U.K. that summer. He is in the process of deliberating between setting up a raw food sauna teepee, or starting a band with a bunch of friends while doing a series of gigs over the summer. Either way outrageous costume, nudity, and intoxication will be top of the bill.

It was a little under three years ago when we first met. There was a huge attraction between us although I never imagined we would last this long. Like life-long friends, we immediately gelled and were instantly comfortable in one another's company. Many people thought we were brother and sister; we were often told that we looked very similar in appearance. It didn't bother me that people said this, in fact we both rather liked the idea. For me being with Danny was like being with someone from my family. We both suspected we were Soul Mates for each other, hence the instant attraction and sense of tremendous well-being in one another's company. Like most Soul Mate connections, I knew the relationship was not meant to be "forever." While Danny and I had never talked about this, I knew in my heart that the time had come for us both to move on.

I continued to pace back and forth in my mind of how to broach the subject in the best possible way. I knew I had to strike while the iron was hot so not to lose the momentum that was already clearly in place. My heart whispered the advice I longed to hear:

It starts right here. Just speak of how you are going to France for ten days. Go downstairs and begin to talk honestly with him. The longer you delay, the more you deny the change that will set you both free.

I took a deep breath, wandered downstairs, and found Danny in the kitchen blending up the latest concoction of raw superfood smoothies. This is one thing that can be said about Danny; he truly is one of the world's best raw food chefs. Without fail, he would prepare delicious food for me, which resulted in a welcomed loss of weight and glowing complexion. For a moment I faltered...

"Good morning babe, I got a super elixir ecstasy bomb smoothie ready for you!" he cheerfully announced as he spun around wearing a bright pink t-shirt with a cute cat on the front.

"Thanks D.... I'll have it in a while. Could I speak to you for a moment? I need to talk," I uneasily mumbled.

"Sure babe, what's up?"

Danny is four years younger than me, but dresses and behaves even younger than that. His dark brown cork screw hair tumbles to his shoulders, framing a near perfect body. His slender form is the result of intensely healthy living and crazy stunts that he throws himself into on a weekly basis. Since I have met him he has been a trapeze artist, stilt walker, fire eater, semi-erotic model, night club dancer, and now, the latest craze that rocks his boat—being suspended by hooks as a form of macabre performance for a weird alternative arts crowd. This is Danny. The Peter Pan of performance.

What attracted me to him was his "who dares wins" approach to life. There was nothing this guy would not do, nothing too risky, nothing too outrageous; apart from being real, authentic, honest, open, and present. At a drop of a hat his clothes would be off even in the middle of so-called normal society. I loved this side of him; it was like having my own private performer on hand. He reminded me of Johnny Depp, outrageously camp and indefinable. There was always a slightly twisted show inside Danny waiting to leap out, even if he so much as suspected there may be an audience.

Also, I had this strong fascination for opposites. I found Danny so compellingly different from me. Because of our warm and sincere friendship I felt I could let go and trust more, happy to go along with his way of life for a while so I could explore my more wild and creative nature. Nine times out of ten, he would leave me standing alone as he carried on way beyond what I was comfortable experiencing. My intuition indicated that spending some time with him was good for me, as I was eager to be with this character who I found so unusual and thrilling. He introduced me to so many outrageous people who lived outside of the usual, societal box. And I must admit I loved to watch and marvel at his extreme antics imagining he was completely fearless, although later I found out this was not the case.

Without the audience, there was only a shell that paced around the house frantically dreaming up new ideas of how to risk losing his life. Minus the adrenaline buzz, he would become wired as if trapped inside his own cage. Depression lurked around every corner unless he invented ever-new versions of himself. Danny was your typical extremely high eccentric artist who was terrified of being nothing and no one in particular. Whenever I attempted to speak with him during these depression days, he would protect me from knowing what was really going on. He said he didn't want me to know how dark his thoughts were. But I knew. I knew what he was capable of. It's only a matter of time when being with someone one-on-one that you get to clearly see what makes them tick.

With Danny, his high antics veiled a great gapping hole that would show itself every now and again when the winter months began to appear. For days and nights on end he could become completely paranoid and irrational, working himself up into a right huff. I put it down to artistic license letting him know that I was here for him if ever he needed me. He never did.

So he never did meet me there, in the deeper chambers of the heart, because if he did, I would have shown him that there was nothing; no darkness, no demons, simply more entertainment. The entertainment of his own mind. He knew that, so he shielded himself from me. Slowly, over time, our relationship morphed into *only* behaving like brother and sister, and that is where we were now.

We walked outside onto the patio where the cats were playing. It was a beautiful May morning, as the crocuses I planted began to bud, pushing and heaving their way up through the earth. Nothing could stand in the way of nature once she received the warmth of the sun. I reflected on that for a moment as I was also in the process of emerging from the dark as I pushed my way up through the earth. My sun was the inner candle that flickered with love, teasing me to surrender to its flame.

With that reminder, the words tumbled out. I spoke of having to go to France, the meeting with Prudence, the legendary Mont de Coeur, and this agonizing restlessness that was eating away at me. He knew all about my obsession of what he called, "weird Love stuff," and he felt the fire of this incessant passion from me on a regular basis. Whenever I got close to this place within me that *knew* about the possibility of meeting my Beloved, I would succumb to tears, as nobody ever seemed to understand. This love that I knew could exist between two people frightened many; it was so wild, untamable, and did not have a place in normal society.

I was denying this love, keeping it quiet, keeping everything nice and reasonable as I suppose, in one mad way, I wanted to fit in. There must have been a part of me that thought I could live this way, only allowing little bits of my true nature to leak out every now and again. In my quiet moments, I was consumed with this love of my Beloved and all I wanted was to find him, so that we could live in this ecstatic way together. And then one day use our love to invite others who felt the same to join us.

Teaching yoga was my saving grace throughout all of this, as it greatly relieved the tension that was with me on most days. For an hour and a half I could be my true self, not caring what people thought, using love to inflame the people, to break through anything that got in its way. I was mad, totally wild with love when I taught, but right outside the door of the yoga studio was the betrayal, waiting for me to pick it up where I had left it. It was not only the relationship that was a lie. I was a living lie, and I was now becoming hell bent on destroying the lie that veiled this love. I explained all of this to Danny one more time, as he simply listened with a worried look on his face.

With the last words of my monologue, all done in one exhausted breath, I said, "I just have to go, D; I just have to go…"

Admittedly, I kind of side-stepped the bit about the entire trip being based around meeting my Beloved at some point in the future. I simply said that this trip was more of an inner quest. Some time alone to meditate and open myself up to the deeper aspects of love. It was an easy conversation in many ways because it was obvious that our relationship had been on hold for so long now. In a way I guessed that he may have been hoping that this trip could be our saving grace, taking sanctuary in that old adage: "Absence makes the heart grow fonder." For me, I was the living truth that absence makes the heart grow stronger. Just look how long I had been waiting to meet my Beloved!

I witnessed a flicker of sadness in his eyes. He knew he was not invited, and I sensed that he may also suspect that this could be the beginning of the end. For the whole of our relationship we had never, ever argued. I tossed a few sharp words around every now and again, but he never retaliated, not once. He let me set the pace and dropped in sometimes beside me, but more often than not behind me. In this exchange, he was doing it again. He was taking in what I had to say and not challenging me further in any way. I too felt a pang of guilt. I did not wish to hurt him. Yet, the truth remained that we were living a fantasy, a lie based on the idea that our life together was comfortable, that we got on great, that we had a laugh together. All this was true, but I wanted to go deeper with someone. I was ready to dive into intimacy, to reveal the soul, to stand in the fire of life, and surrender all boundaries, all limits to the power of love.

This love that I speak of is not solely the love of a person, although that person is naturally included. I am referring to the very nature of love, allowing a wild "Yes!" to emanate with the compulsion and madness of love to drive the lives of those who surrender to it. The Beloved is this essential love that animates one into absolute union together by tearing down all sense of self, wants, needs, and ideas; releasing them from their idea of who they think they are and what they're going to get. Catapulting them heart first into a reality where they do not possess love, it possesses them, an existence that belongs to love, where lovers embrace in an exquisite myriad of ways in every moment, freed from duality, freed from themselves.

He stood up as he collected our glasses and walked back into the kitchen. I was left alone with a beating heart, wondering what was going to happen next. I felt the beginnings of the adventure stirring in my stomach. It was inevitable. I had taken the first step on the Path of Love, and it simultaneously swallowed me up into its current. In that moment, I had already begun to leave all worldly responsibilities, all notions of duty, and any last remaining ideas of sanity. Freedom breathed in me, as I surrendered into being silently drawn by the stronger pull of what I really loved.

Danny appeared around the corner of the patio doors with a

tea towel in his hands as he dried off some cutlery. "I just want you to know that I am all for your trip to France. To show my support, I would love to offer you my trusted steed, Robbie!" he exclaimed elegantly in a perfect English accent, as he took a flamboyant, thespian like bow, brushing the ground cavalierly as he gestured toward his electric blue Mercedes van.

"Wow, D, thank you so much!" I said, as I jumped up and hugged him. We stayed there for a while longer than usual, as a few tears welled into my eyes. It was so natural for Danny to offer me his van. He had always given me so many gifts and was so unconditionally generous with anything that was his. My heart bled for a moment as I searched for something, anything I could give to end the suffering in our relationship, so we could both enter into an untiring peace. But I found nothing.

We broke away and held hands at arm's length as we twirled around in the garden. How can this be? How can I feel so much love for this wonderful soul when I know our time is limited? As I spun around again and again, sensations of agony and ecstasy danced within us both. Our faces changed from spontaneous laughter one minute, into the first stages of our hearts breaking in the next. This was our first authentic meeting, the moment we knew we were in the process of breaking up.

CHAPTER THREE

OPENING THE DOOR

Alchemy Yoga Center, London, May 2008

H
I CHLOE, its Scarlett. I'm calling to see whether I could stay over at your place next week? I really need to see you sweetheart; I have so much to tell you. Anyway, give me a call or text me back, either Tuesday or Wednesday night. I can meet you after work and we can go for drinks. Speak soon, bye."

I left a message on my best friend's mobile, on a break from *The Future of Love* spiritual workshop I was in, knowing that the moment she got it, hell or high water would not stop her from calling me back. Unless of course there was a man involved, and if that was the case, it might take a little longer. Chloe had been my best friend for twelve years, although I was not necessarily classified as hers. This was fine with me, since I was a bit of a hermit. I loved spending time with her, but we never did it on a regular basis. I would see her maybe once a month, or every six weeks. You have to understand that I am not a "normal" kind of woman. I do not have a group of friends that I meet with every week and I certainly do not have a girlfriend that I speak with on the phone every other day. That would drive me crazy! All my time is taken up with teaching and traveling, and when I am not doing that I am at home alone or with a boyfriend.

God bless Chloe for understanding me so deeply; she accepted my hermit-like nature of often disappearing off the radar whenever I needed to, knowing I would always turn up with some amazing news to share with her. Chloe's oldest and truest best friend was Sarah who lived in New Zealand, who I had also met and loved. Chloe had been my best friend since the moment she swaggered into my yoga class so many years ago. The reason I say swaggered is for a couple of reasons. One, she may well of had a couple of glasses of wine before coming to class and two because she had this incredible way of walking, as she swung her hips from side to side, daring anyone to *not* look at her delightfully peachy butt. This lady was all woman and she knew it, and she played the game fabulously well.

I remembered how she plunked herself down on the yoga mat right in front of me, the mat that everyone else avoided as it was too close to my watchful eye. She pulled herself into the most perfect lotus position, winked and warmly smiled at me, as if to tell me she was ready. Before me was a vision of blonde hair, shapely curves, pedicured pink toe nailed feet and a ripped vest that said "Jesus is Coming" on the front and "Look Busy" plastered across the back. Now, this was my type of lady.

Her life was, is, and always shall be centered on all and everything about being a powerful female. She is the living embodiment of Samantha Jones from *Sex in the City*. She set up her own PR agency years ago, and now, thanks to her hard work, she operates a string of offices all over London's West End. I admire her drive and foresight when it comes to business. She may give the impression of being a helpless blonde, but underneath that perfected persona is a feminine Donald Trump. Every moment of her waking existence is sacrificed to her work, which was confirmed when she become one of the first official blackberry addicts, tapping away throughout lunch on not one, but two Crackberry (as they're affectionately known) handsets. She is a star spangled, hard-nosed business Queen. A modern day Empress. Yet underneath all this power and business acumen, the real blonde lies waiting, waiting for when the coast is clear to come out and reveal her incredibly dizzy nature.

I am referring to one time in particular when I was running a yoga retreat in the middle of nowhere. The whole group was meeting at 11pm to climb a holy mountain overnight so we would reach the summit in time for sunrise. I was checking everyone off, making sure they had everything for the five-hour climb that was up ahead. Chloe appeared in the lobby wearing a baby blue Prada Mac, flimsy sandals, and a handbag slung over one shoulder. Not exactly climbing gear. She'll also fight tooth and nail over every new anti-aging treatment and product that hits the shelves. In fact, I cannot actually say how old Chloe is as everyone is still in the dark regarding her real age, including me.

The phone rang, and I dashed out of the workshop. I was so over it anyway. The teachers were talking about love in the workplace and how to create loving marketing. Really? Do you honestly think love can be marketed?? Plleeaassee.

Yay—it was Chloe! She wanted to know what was going on; and was already suspicious as she threw potentially endless possible scenarios at me to see which one I bit into. "Are you pregnant? Has Danny had an accident? Are the cats okay? Is it your parents?" On and on she went, as she dramatically escalated all the possible reasons why I wanted to see her on such short notice. For me, making arrangements spontaneously and out of the blue was natural and commonplace, for Chloe something like this put a severely unscheduled spanner in the works. I could feel her groaning under the enormity of rearranging her diary for the week.

"Barb, stop for a second will you?" I now had to resort to special tactics to grab her attention before she spun off into outer space. I used the nickname that only a handful know her by. "Barb" is a shortened version of Barbie, which (you may or may not know depending on which side of the universe you live on) is a popular plastic blonde haired doll that little girls play with as they grow up. The full name of Yoga Barbie was given to her the day she arrived for yoga teacher training wearing a pashmina meticulously matching the exact shade of her toes. From then on, Yoga Barbie was born. Add to that her certification as a yoga teacher (something she did for fun because she loves yoga)—and it was the perfect nickname for her.

"Let me speak. I want to see you, as I am going on an adventure by myself... to search for my Beloved." I turned the volume down on that last bit, as she probably did not even know what that term meant, and even if she did, it would have meant far too much trouble to handle over the telephone.

Silence. I could hear her mind searching the archives of her subconscious to gather any information on the word "Beloved." As the silence thickened to almost a perceived mist, I reflected back on how Chloe had frowned upon my own change of career from fashion guru to yoga queen. She had been there watching with utter amusement as I turned up to teach yoga after a day in my fashion studio creating the most flamboyant and edgy stage gear for the latest tours by The Prodigy and Bjork. I would often arrive on my scooter already in my yoga outfit, combined with some killer heels and a face full of make-up. Even though she would have preferred that I kept a foot in the fashion world, I was her confirmation that fashion does not die if you become spiritual. She had a little bit of the spiritual in her as well, as Chloe had been practicing yoga since the age of fourteen—way longer than me! I knew she was an authentic being—even under layers of anti-aging products, make-up, and the latest brands—and that's why we were friends, connecting from the very start.

I continued to rant to myself as Chloe proceeded to cognize what I was expressing. Moving my inner spotlight from Chloe to the workshop I had recklessly entered—and was now rapidly exiting—I realized I had had enough of the wafty weekend workshop crowd who dipped in and out of being spiritual as if it had an on/ off switch. I had been part of this crowd, with my Reiki healings, yoga lifestyle, raw food fanaticism, and various other trends that come and go, to be consigned to history's dustbin. My spiritual in tray was always full, but I was tiring of this, and dumping it all on the out tray. Why? Because none of it touched what I knew and felt within me; this endless love burning deep, waiting to be expressed but not knowing how or where to reveal itself.

Spirituality had been turned into the latest trend according to the "What's New?" section of *Vogue* and *Vanity Fair*. This notion was already reaching the international press and TV shows; it was everywhere, infiltrating into the masses with yet another "thing" they could buy off the shelves, along with their matching floating kaftans, Buddha statue, meditation cushions, and incense. Sometimes, I looked at western society and wondered if there was anything that did not have a price tag attached to it. Initially, I had fallen for the spiritual sales pitch, but now I was no longer interested in being part of the subculture, playing around with ways of living from Deepak Chopra or the latest guru Oprah had on her show. I wanted the real thing, the pure transformation, the alchemical process that a handful of beings once spoke of. I was ready to give everything to this force within me, and now at this stage in my life, the scene was being set for exactly that to happen. I had shared some of this desire with Chloe over the twelve years we had known each other, and so she knew that my use of the word "Beloved" and needing to see her right away was about more than a passing phase.

Finally she spoke. "Okay Bare, I guess the sooner the better. Why don't you come straight round to my house after yoga? I will be in by the time you get there."

"Thanks Barb, I really appreciate you juggling things around to see me, you are the only one I can turn to right now," I shared.

I hung up; grateful for her existence, and also giggling at how she had called me Bare, as that was the nickname she had given me. I was named after a cartoon character called Yogi Bear, but for fun (and some inside joke laughter) we had changed around the way it was spelled to imply something entirely different.

As planned, after yoga on Tuesday I mounted my bike (that I carried back and forth on the train from Dorset to London—very ecological of me!) and cycled up to the familiar nouveau riche district of North London. I cycled in and out of the bus lanes until I eventually turned the corner onto her road where I was greeted by a wide, palatial avenue of trees in full bloom bordering either side of her street. I rung her doorbell, and heard the customary turning of numerous locks and bolts as she appeared in front of me holding a glass of wine. We hugged on the doorstep, preening one another as we smoothed down each other's hair, standing back looking at each other at a distance. It was always such a delight to see her, and whenever I did I simply oozed with joy at the prospect of staying over at her house. I loved her place; it was teeming with memories of laughter and many, many good times.

Together in her front room, she had watched me grow from fashionista yoga teacher to a more soulful woman who was authentically looking to live her life as love for all living things. We had shared so many wondrous moments of profound insight. I recognized that we worked well as a team. I would reach for the more soulful, nourishing ideals in life, while she would ground them in "keeping it real." I was a dreamer, a romantic, and an optimist, while Chloe was an adorable realist.

Like Danny, Chloe and I were in many respects complete opposites. I was fascinated by her, wanting to dig deeper to see how she really felt about her place in life. Over time, I realized that going deeper was not what she had in mind. To go deeper involved being open, totally transparent and revealing your vulnerability. There was *no way* that Chloe would do that with anyone *unless* she had vetted them at least ten times over first. Even so, I considered Chloe a Soul Mate, as we gave one another perspective and grounding over the years.

We ate supper catching up on the latest news as the day's sun slowly sunk below the horizon of the infamous Primrose Hill. The mood deepened, as Chloe went around the edges of her living room lighting the floor candles with yet another stick of Nag Champa. "Okay Bare, now your turn. What is really happening in your life?" Chloe pulled up another cushion for her neck as she slouched back into her luxurious oversized sofa, preparing herself like a lawyer for her cross-examination of the witness: me.

I took my place in the witness stand, and for the first time in my life actually opened myself up to Chloe in a way that I had never done before. I had nothing to lose, allowing her to hear, see, and feel the real me. My mind was already made up, no matter how professionally she played good cop, bad cop. I spoke of my early childhood and my fascination with anything that appeared to be love. Any form of feeling, tenderness, kindness, or compassion—be it on TV, in films or cartoons, or in school during story time, even between adults in the street. In fact, any random act of kindness always touched me in such a way that I would be affected for days afterwards.

I ventured on into more dangerous territory as I began to speak of a realization that I had at twenty-one. I lay bare my deepest torment of knowing without any doubt that I was one half of another being. I took a deep breath as I released my intimate secret and held her hand to stop any questions that looked likely to pounce. I continued to tell her how I knew there was another half of my being out there in masculine form, longing for me as much as I longed for him. That this had nothing to do with finding a boyfriend or husband, it was nothing as trivial as that, this was a matter of the Soul, or even greater.

"Scarlett, I just don't understand something. You are already whole; you are the most together person I have ever met. Why do you feel there is this other person out there, you don't need anyone else." Chloe searched deep into her heart to try to comprehend what was being shared with her, as she was not born with this same desire, and so it was difficult for her to understand what I was saying.

"That's true Chloe, but that isn't what I am speaking about." I took some time searching for the words for the clearest explanation before I continued on. I decided the only way to translate this was to keep it simple. "I know that I share my Soul with another!"

That did it! She pulled the cushion from behind her and totally collapsed into the sofa, repeating the words "Oh my God," over and over again. I was not sure she could understand, and for a moment I worried whether or not I had completely overwhelmed her. Still the cat was out of the bag, so I had to carry on. I left her to process that last sentence with her eyes shut for a few minutes before continuing on further.

I then went on to describe how I used to accuse my parents of giving away my brother to an orphanage, and that one time I demanded to see my birth certificate to make sure that I was born alone and not with a twin. I spoke of how I would dream and speak with 'my other' all throughout my childhood. I told her about the promise I made, that I could bring him to life and that one day we would meet in this lifetime. Still I went on, revealing how in my teenage years this connection got stronger. How he came to me twenty years ago, through a mirage of haunting dreams and memories as I danced for him around the desert fire, his eyes tearing into my heart as I moved only for him. The urgent heat of this sensuous love and our tearing hearts would linger with me into the early hours, as I awoke with beads of sweat covering my body and my hair stuck to my tear streaked face. Drenched with passion and desire my longing for reunion was at an all time high. I was ravenous for contact and aroused beyond belief. In my hopeless attempt to hold onto these dreams for dear life, all I could do was witness our sacred reunion slip from my consciousness as night became day.

I looked over at Chloe, propped up on her elbows as tears poured from her eyes. She dried her eyes with a tissue whilst miming for me to carry on. I explained that as I approached my 35th birthday, his presence began to take on a more urgent tone. My dreams became more frequent and easily remembered throughout the day. He was with me in every moment, I sensed him everywhere. I would write to him in my journals, consult with him regarding any decisions and only made those that brought us closer together. He spoke of his promise to find me, that no matter what, we would be together again in this lifetime. I could sense that he was preparing to enter my life, as I too was making haste to emerge into his. I knew that once we found each other a whole process would begin as we integrated together on every level.

Finally I came to the present day and told Chloe about meeting Prudence at The Metropolitan; how she spoke about the mountain in France, how she had been there, that she was a member of the UN, therefore very grounded and real, and lastly how I had no choice, that no matter what I had to go there, and soon for that matter. Meeting Prudence had brought all of this back to life for me, and now I could not forget. I had to go to the mountain to let my

Beloved know I was ready once again for his real presence in my life. Chloe was transfixed, staring back at me with huge eyes hanging on every word, hoping there was more. Which there was, but that was between my Beloved and me.

I could see her struggling with her rational mind and the heart of a woman. She wanted to believe in what I was telling her, because deep inside she knew it was true for me. But there was a strong mind in there as well, which told her that love like this couldn't exist. Especially since she had no desire in this lifetime to experience it for herself. Yet before her stood the living proof of its existence; although she was having an awful time realizing it.

She got up and poured herself another glass of wine. As an afterthought she offered me a glass, which I gratefully accepted. Chloe and I walked outside and sat on the edge of the paved steps overlooking her garden. She must have been retelling certain parts of my story, as every now and again she would start to silently cry, whispering how she had no idea that I was feeling this way. I gently reminded her that this was not just how I felt; this was how I lived. She was beginning to tremble as the cool night air closed in on us, and upon feeling the chill she wrapped her legendary pashmina around her for warmth and reassurance.

After some time she dried her face, cleaned away some unruly eye make-up, patted her cheeks, and took a deep breath. She reached for my hand, and sincerely looked into my eyes as she announced that I had to make room for one more—she was coming to France. I couldn't believe my ears. Chloe was coming! I never imagined that she would want to come too. I was so excited; I jumped up to hug her. We cheered into the night sky, as this was going to be one hell of a wild adventure, especially with Chloe on board. Love and excitement rushed through her house and garden. We were like two giddy schoolgirls. I explained that we were going to travel in Robbie, and that we would most likely camp all the way down to the south of France until we reached our destination.

"Stop right there, don't tell me the details or I may change my mind, you know how I am regarding insects. Just tell me the dates and I will arrange it so work can cover me," she warned.

"We leave on July 18th, in two months time. We have to be Mont de Coeur by July 22nd," I confirmed.

"Why that date?" she inquired.

"Oh, just a hunch," I coyly smiled.

CHAPTER FOUR

ROAD TO NOWHERE

FairyDale Barn, Dorset, England, July 18, 2008

TWO MONTHS sailed by like a kite in the wind, sometimes gliding effortlessly, whilst at other times it felt like I was being pushed and pulled as an invisible hand wrestled with my emotions and my soul. Whenever there was a quiet moment the voice of doubt would creep around my mind endeavoring to put the cat amongst the pigeons, seeing whether I would double-back. Its voice was always the same. Was I doing the right thing? Was I being deceitful to Danny? Why was this restlessness continuing to haunt me? Was I truly prepared to meet my Beloved? What would happen if I did?

At times these fears would really amp up and attempt to smother me in the middle of the night, as I lay awake next to a blithely unaware Danny sleeping soundlessly. As usual, he was not aware of my core feelings and longings. These same fears and questions at other times were my ally, confirming to me that I was on the right track as I neared the inevitable sea of change. In these times of great uncertainty, there was one thing that remained indisputable. I knew without a doubt that the woman who left for this pilgrimage of love would not be the same one when she returned, that is *if* she returned at all.

At last, the day of my departure finally arrived. I had already christened this day as the first day of the rest of my life. I could feel the enormity of this voyage as I packed the final bags into the van. Danny was being good-natured, yet quiet as he helped me secure the contents inside the van. We said our goodbyes as lightheartedly as possible to avoid any high drama, ensuring that we moved through this downright uncomfortable, already over rehearsed scenario with ease.

At the first light of dawn I backed out of the drive of FairyDale Barn, and turned the wheel of the Mercedes van towards the motorway for London, way ahead of the slow slog of commuters. As soon as I was out of sight of the barn I breathed a huge sigh of relief. It felt so exhilarating to be in the driving seat of Robbie as I headed towards the residence of Miss Chloe Kingston. After three hours of driving, I pulled up outside of her house around noon. I sounded my usual toot to announce my arrival, leapt out of the car, and almost tripped over the steps to her front door as I ran towards her bell. I was bursting to use the bathroom as I had stubbornly refused to go on the way, as that would have meant a delay in reaching her. I rushed past her startled form, promising a swift return.

When I reappeared I took a closer look at Chloe. She looked totally stunning in a low cut, blood red strapless Dolce and Gabbana dress with dangerously high spiked Jimmy Choo heels— and it was only lunchtime! Her hair and make-up was immaculate as she twirled on the spot, asking what I thought of her look. It took some time for me to find the right way of handling this delicate situation. As usual, I kept it simple as I told her she looked fantastic, yet highlighted that for the next ten days we were not on the catwalk, nor would we be dining at award winning Michelin restaurants. I asked her if she had brought her Birkenstocks, some warm clothes, and some proper clothes for camping. She huffed as she opened up her bag to show me.

"It may be a good idea to put them on, because for the next couple of days you won't see anything apart from the inside of Robbie and the tent!" I predicted.

"You never know whom you might meet along the way," she remarked as she swanned past, leaving a trail of perfume lingering in the air, while grabbing her matching luggage. I rolled my eyes as I helped her load in the rest of her belongings. I could not have expected anything less from Chloe; she belonged to the world of glamour, and thanks to her impressive health regime, glamour belonged to her world. I laughed at the hilarity of it all. I knew what I was getting into when Chloe decided to join this pilgrimage of love! We climbed up into our destined seats at the helm of Robbie. I switched on the engine, preparing to get into gear and go.

Chloe reached over and grabbed my arm, "Hang on a second, there's just one more thing. It's tradition to have a nip of brandy before the start of a journey, for good luck and safe travels," she gleefully announced.

From within her purse she seductively pulled out a pearl hipflask, unscrewed the lid with nude nails, and placed it at my lips, "Go on Bare, let's raise a flask to our great adventure," she purred.

"You're on," I said as I took a healthy gulp.

To the road we belonged as we headed towards Dover to catch our ferry across to France; listening to music and sometimes singing out loud together as we both became lost in our thoughts. On the boat we decided, as we sat hunched over the map, that we were prepared to drive as long as possible so that we got there sooner rather than later. By taking smaller roads, I estimated that we could do the entire length of France with one sleepover, and if we wanted to we could decide later on to take a longer journey home.

The Aizou Valley, France, July 19, 2008

By early evening, as twilight was shrouding the land, we slowly inched up what seemed to be a never-ending winding hill. We had driven for eight hours flat, and I promised myself that once the road flattened we would pull over and get some sleep. As we reached the summit, a glorious spectacle welcomed us, taking our breath away and instantly bringing us back to life. The landscape was ablaze with soft pinks and ravaging oranges as we looked down into the vast, dramatic folds of the Aizou Valley. We were both moved to tears as we pulled over and parked Robbie, grabbing our purses as we stepped out into the mystery that was revealing itself to us. Unbeknownst to us, we had reached the rocky plateau of Rocamadour, one-hundred kilometres north of Toulouse. This was the site of an ancient pilgrimage, swamped in history and natural beauty.

Rocamadour at this time of night was spectacular, emblazoned with streaks of warm golden russets and veins of indigo purple radiating from the setting sun. It perched on a rocky plateau that protected a complex of religious structures centered on a miraculous statue of the Virgin Mary and the tomb of an ancient saint. Before our disbelieving eyes, this whole panorama transformed into a luminescent landscape, as the walls and structures of the ancient sacred site became the backdrop of projected ancient and modern masterpieces. There was a magical feel in the air; the sense of an otherworldly presence permeating the evening breeze, as an elemental tension mounted all around us.

According to legend, Rocamadour was the home of an early Christian hermit named Zaccheus of Jericho. It is believed that he died in about 70 A.D. and had conversed with Jesus Christ himself. According to some accounts, this Zaccheus was the husband of St. Veronica, who wiped the face of Jesus as he climbed to Calvary. I gasped when I read these words in the tourist information pamphlet we had stumbled upon. I had to reread it a second time to ensure that I wasn't making it all up. I steadied myself as a wave of Shakti (life force) coursed through me, lifting up every hair on my body.

"Oh my god," I said to Chloe as I placed one hand on my mouth in near shock. "The place that we're standing was the fountainhead of another pair of Beloveds." She stared back with innocent eyes, reminding me that she didn't know what all this was pointing towards. And, truth be told, neither did I. But, I had my suspicions.

The Beloveds were Veronica and Zaccheus. Of all the stories I could remember back in the days of my reluctant once a week religious education class at school, it was the story of Veronica that remained steadfast in my memory, as a testimony of love. I learned by heart how Veronica was one of the last people to recognize Christ before he was crucified. She risked her life as she pushed past the Roman guards and knelt at his side to offer her veil to wipe away the blood from his face. This merciful act opened the way for her to finally meet her Beloved soon afterwards in the face of Zaccheus.

"That's it. I don't need to read anymore!" I said as I closed the pamphlet, slamming it on the table. With eyes wide and slightly flushed cheeks I looked over at Chloe in disbelief. "Something is happening! I had no idea this place existed. We are being guided Chloe, it's no coincidence that we are here," I said, lowering my voice as I spoke in hushed tones. I carefully looked around to be discerning and aware in case someone overheard us. I knew something powerful was accompanying us on this journey.

We continued to walk through the winding, climbing, narrow streets towards the Cité Religieuse (that's "Religious City" in French). The closer we got to the top, the stronger I could feel my Beloved; his compelling presence absorbed all of my attention, and it was clear he was here in Rocamadour, now and previously. My heart began to swell as I imagined us being together in the past in this precise spot. His presence clothed me, as I drank his memory in. For some quantum time, I was elsewhere, while simultaneously Chloe and I walked up a stairway of 216 weathered steps to the main grand entrance of the Basilique St. Sauveur. Backed against a natural cliff, the Basilique was built in the Romanesque-Gothic style from the 11th to the 13th centuries. It's decorated with paintings and inscriptions recalling visits of celebrated persons, including Philippe the Handsome (founder of the Hapsburg dynasty in Spain)—need we say more about his looks? They made things *very* clear in those days.

The energy shifted as we approached the doorway of the Basilique. We became saturated in a deep, oceanic sapphire blue that drenched the entire sanctuary. The light from the outside was illuminating the stained glass windows and casting its prismatic reflections throughout the entire nave. We gasped in awe as we unknowingly touched our hearts and with eyes full of wonder we silently entered into this heavenly abode.

We flowed around the inner sanctum with hypnotic fluidity, sometimes together, more often alone, and lost in other realms and dimensions. Words, images, and symbols poured into my consciousness as I glided over the ancient marble floor upon which this Temple of Love was built. My fingers reached out to caress random pillars as I slipped under arches and through ornate alcoves. I became lost in my feelings as I drifted into another world where my Beloved was waiting for me. In this other world he reached for my hand as he whispered words I shall never forget:

We were once here my Beloved, when this gateway was created. This magnificent structure was erected to open the hearts of all who entered its walls. These walls are woven with the essence of the majestic love between Beloveds. This is the Well of Love. Drink from me my love, and be given the moisture that shall bring about my faithful return.

I became submerged by his words, unspoken yet heard everywhere. I steadied myself against a pillar and closed my eyes to linger with him a moment longer. I trailed after these last words, hoping they would lead to him, the one I was longing to see, for just one glimpse of his face had the richness to fulfill my entire lifetime. As with every other time before, the words rose and fell into emptiness beyond measure. I plunged into this emptiness, groping my way around looking for the one whose voice was the reason why I was here. The yawning nothingness threatened to swallow me. "If the heart of your mystery can't be held, at least let me see your face," I whispered, as my last prayer crashed upon the altar of love moments before I lost consciousness.

A steward touched me lightly on the shoulder, whispering to me in French that it was near closing time. I abruptly returned back into my body and opened my eyes. I checked the time on my phone; two hours had passed since being inside the Basilica, while outside twilight had irresistibly merged into darkness. I got up to look for Chloe, but she was no longer inside.

The very first time I passed out was when I was twenty-one. I had pulled off the road and stopped in my VW Beetle in an attempt to sort my head out, as some serious issues around injustice in the workplace seemed to be mounting into areas I couldn't handle. I began to passionately pray to my Beloved to help me navigate through these challenging waters. I truly imagined his face nearing mine, instantly manifesting as if sensing danger. Within a few moments I felt his presence fill the car like a thunderbolt. The whole car was electrified. Like a true flame, his powerful guardianship swirled around me creating a protective force field. It was that moment when I realized that if I even as much suspected that I might be in danger, he would be there. For one brief moment I saw his face in the rearview mirror smiling at me, and then I passed out.

There have been a couple of other times in my life when this has happened. It's as if his presence overwhelms me, the sheer power of reunion with my Beloved blows out all my circuits. It was clear that this same thing happened only a few moments ago in the Basilica. Trying to shake these memories free, I quickly walked down the steps and into the city to find Chloe. I had to focus. As I stepped out into the carousel of light and sound that the local summer festivities around me celebrated, a familiar voice sounded from across the square.

"Scarlett, I am over here!" shouted Chloe.

I looked over in the direction from where Chloe's voice emerged and saw her sitting outside a traditional French bistro. I joyfully waved at her, as her familiar face declared her whereabouts and safety. I hurried across the cobbled pavestones towards her, bursting with excitement, and spilling over with the confirmation that we were in the right place and advancing in the predestined direction.

"Scarlett, what happened in there? You disappeared and I couldn't find you anywhere. There was this strange light…" Chloe gazed up towards the clear night sky as she searched for the words, "…That felt almost heavenly. I have never experienced anything like that before. To be honest I am blown away by the whole experience, and also a little afraid."

My hand reached for hers as I asked what she was afraid of. She explained that maybe we were getting into something that we should not be interfering with. She was worried that we were in over our heads, and that there was an unusual presence in the basilica that might continue to follow her around. She had to get up and leave, as it was getting stronger and stronger, making her feel sick and faint. She admitted it took all of her will to not openly cry in the street as she headed for the bistro. I tenderly asked her why.

"Because there was so much love in that place, as well as the suffering left behind from all of the pilgrims that came in the hope that they would be cured. I can't stand it Scarlett; I am not used to things like this. I live a normal life, this is too weird for me," she cried.

I decided not to tell her what happened to me in the basilica, not tonight anyway, as that would freak her out even more. I felt I had to take this journey one step at a time with Chloe. By looking at her darling face it was clear to me that she had quite enough to contend with already from today. She really didn't need to know that I could potentially pass out any moment my Beloved decided to show up.

"No, not tonight," I whispered to myself as I shook my head, knowing that the time to tell her would arise in the future. I knew that the best thing for Chloe right now would be some nourishing French cuisine, something that brought her back to earth and away from the gnashing jaws of fear. Chloe was experiencing her first encounter with life outside of her perfectly arranged little box. She was entering my world, a place that openly invited the Beloved to consume all that was false and that stood in the way of infinite love.

We had done a few otherworldly things together in the past, where we spent time in nature, meditating, and talking about the richer qualities of life. But this journey was, and will continue to be, something quite different. I felt compassion for her, as I knew the nature of the Beloved was at times rough, ruthlessly tearing away at false pride, and demolishing all and every form of protection from love. Like most people, my dear friend Chloe had built up some rather impressive walls around her heart, not that she would admit it. Yet every now and again, those walls would be penetrated and for a moment she would taste the freedom of innocence once more. She had chosen to come on this trip and from the vantage point of love; she would be subject to its teachings.

I flagged over the waiter as we ordered some food, and I continued to reassure her saying that the best thing to do was, "trust the process." To surrender to whatever happens, to literally see what happens when you trust life completely. I invited her to let go of the reins of her life, to cast them aside and ride roughshod into the oncoming experiences. She looked at me worriedly, not confident in what I was saying. Luckily the food arrived, buying me some time to look for a different tactic. As I took my first bite, an inspiring idea came to light.

"Just think about all the stories you will be telling once we get back. Can you imagine what your clients will say when you tell them that you really went for it? That you said yes to life for ten days? Even now you don't know where that will take you. Its only ten days Barb, surely you have the courage and power to stay with this uncharted adventure?" I cleverly baited her.

I knew she could not resist a well-earned moment in the spotlight at high profile dinners and after drinks parties. She would be a star, one foot in the glamorous world of success, wealth, and beauty, and the other in a world where passionate memories lingered of a time when what mattered was saying yes to love, at any cost. She lightly pressed the crisp white cotton of her napkin against the corners of her mouth as she contemplated what I was saying.

"So, Scarlett, what you're saying is that life presents us with only one simple question—either love or fear? And you're asking me to keep on declaring yes to love? Is that what you are saying?" she inquired.

"Pretty much, Chloe. And what results from that will be your greatest teacher in life," I warmly smiled at her.

After a five-hour drive through the heart of Aix-en-Provence, we eventually caught sight of the towering Mont de Coeur Mountain

Range. Chiseled high up into the rocky peaks, the Cave of the Beloved loomed like a black hole, both welcoming and foreboding. A silence of reverence filled Robbie, as we both stared out the windows with our jaws dropping open. I slowed Robbie down to an almost crawling pace. With sunglasses perfectly perched on our noses, we leaned out the windows as we inhaled our appreciation. Mid-drive-by we both lifted our sunglasses as we narrowed our eyes to get a better, more focused look on our upcoming challenge. I laughed out loud as I shared with Chloe that the way we were driving in such slow motion reminded me of something out of a gangster hip-hop video. Complete with sunglasses and pouting lips, all we needed were two fur coats and a white trilby hat. That eased the tension for a short time, but within minutes it crept back in as I turned into the dense neighboring forest of this sanctified crypt.

I noticed Chloe beginning to prickle as soon as we pulled up. She spun around to face me with burning cheeks. "What are you doing? You don't plan to stay here tonight do you?" she angrily asked.

"Yes, this is where we are being asked to stay tonight. We can't go back into town, as we need to be embraced by the nature of this place, so that we will be prepared for what comes. I require all the help I can get from the natural world if I am to awaken to the energy of this mystical mountain tomorrow," I calmly stated.

She was paralyzed as she recognized that what I was saying was true, yet she was torn because this place terrified her. To Chloe this forest was the epitome of darkness and the dreaded unknown. To me it was the meeting place of energies and etheric beings that shaped and crafted this world. Chloe was petrified of being alone in the woods, being out of sight and out of earshot was her worst nightmare. Not only that, she was now being asked to confront another fear—her utter distaste of insects, especially spiders.

I watched as she covered her entire body in clothes, including her face. It was her intention that every part of her body was protected from any potential intruders. From my vantage point, she was wrapping herself up *from* the Divine that was so evidently here. We finally settled down for the night, with all the windows closed as Chloe stuffed her mobile phone under her pillow in case of an emergency. Every now and again we were able to pick up a mobile service provider, which was an extra bonus considering we were in the middle of nowhere. I hoped this would settle her mind some. I waited until she was asleep before pulling the van door back, to reveal the succulent, moist freshness of the darkened forest and choir of insects. Silently, I tiptoed out onto the fertile earth in my bare nakedness.

Le Mont de Coeur, Southern France, July 22, 2008

It was July 22nd, the date that had been carved into my Soul since the moment Prudence shared her amazing story with me. Her beautiful, joyful face appeared in my mind, as she whispered, *"Go for it girl! You know I am with you every step of the way. You were destined to find this place, and I am damn happy that I was the one that could deliver the coordinates."*

I rolled over and playfully cuddled Chloe in her all-in-one anti-insect suit. Her blonde hair was all over the place as it mightily defied gravity, due to her entourage of hair products that kept her usual coiffure in place. She groaned as she turned over, lifting up her eye mask to reveal two big black panda eyes from yesterday's mascara. I happily smiled at her, asking if she wanted some tea. Over breakfast we again discussed the correct procedure for a) having a wash: jump in the ice cold fresh spring, b) going to the bathroom: find a tree, dig a hole, and squat, and finally c) getting dressed: has to be done whilst standing, therefore out of the van.

Secretly I loved teaching her all this life stuff, as it was indescribably hilarious watching this civilized modern woman get low down and dirty. Eventually, after breezing past all the hurdles of outdoor living, we prepared for our ascent. I had prepped Chloe well and was confident and ready to go, when suddenly a voice pierced our quiet vigil as we stood together holding hands.

"Hey, Chloe is that you? My God, it is!" another woman's voice shrilled across the car park from the whistle stop café where climbers replenished themselves before and after their ordeal.

We turned around to see who it was, when Chloe's arms went up and she too let out a strange squeal that (I think) was some type of excited recognition. As it turned out, it was an old friend from New York who was in France with a group from Australia on a wine tasting tour. As they chatted at high speed, I looked over their shoulders to see what sort of people were in the group. Well, it was no wild guess (this was a friend of Chloe's after all), as the group consisted of mostly men, and young ones at that. Once they saw me looking, they flagged us over to come and join them. Chloe's eyes loomed large when she saw the quality of the goods on offer, and she then proceeded to give me her biggest and best doe eyes, blinking ever so innocently.

I sighed as I looked down the path. I took my time as I debated what to do next. She kept tugging at my sleeve, as her friend coaxed us to join them for a glass of the fabulous wine that they had just discovered down the road. I glanced up, ignoring her New York friend, and focusing in on Chloe. I grabbed both her hands again, like we were only moments ago, right before we were interrupted.

"Chloe, we both know that this pilgrimage was my wild idea, and that you only came along as a way of supporting and protecting me. You don't have to come with me now sweetheart. I really am okay it you want to spend some time here with these guys. I am not upset, and in a way it feels totally natural to be climbing alone."

I squeezed her hands to reaffirm my sincerity. We stood for some time, as she searched my face for any hint of a white lie, and found nothing. In a spontaneous move she grabbed me with both arms as she held me close to her. "I love you so much Scarlett and I am always here for you, no matter what. But you are right, on this day you have to climb Le Mont de Coeur alone. Darling, I will be waiting for you at the bottom. I will stay here until you come back down, I promise," she declared.

Her friend cheered when she knew Chloe had decided to spend the day with them, and for that matter so did most of the lads. It felt right that this was the chosen course of action. I was carved out for a different journey and we both knew this. Even when seeing each other from our opposing vantage points, the love and respect of our friendship deepened as we chose to rigorously enjoy the differences that made us who we are.

Before my ascent, I checked to make sure I was ready. My laces were tucked in on my hiking boots, I had little packets of raisins in the pockets of my cargo pants, and a bottle of water placed into my rucksack. Yes, I was ready to go. I grabbed my red cloak (my trusted accompanying garment on all my adventures in nature and sacred sites) and swooshed it over me completely.

"I'll be back," I boomed in my deepest impression of *Terminator*; waving my staff in the air and lifting up the hood of my red cloak as I stepped onto my pilgrimage of love.

Chapter Five

Pilgrimage of Love

Le Mont de Coeur, Southern France, July 22, 2008

As soon as I stepped foot onto the Pilgrimage of Love, also known as The Path of Kings, I was teleported into a world beyond the usual rules of our third dimensional reality. This otherworldly dimension was a forest where existence was raw and untouched by human hands, with its centuries-old yews and wild apple trees. The path was carved out previously by eighteen kings who made their pilgrimage to the Cave of the Beloved, some in penance on their knees, others on horseback. I trembled in anticipation as my hairs stood on end, sending a cool breeze of ecstatic energy through my body, confirming once again that other energies were around me.

There are two ways to climb to the top to reach the cave. One way is for tourists, a smooth tarmac path that zigzags its way up with wooden benches where you can sit to catch your breath. And then there is the true pilgrims' path—The Path of Kings; a well-worn trek through the forest where little wooded signs are few and far between. The sounds of the forest richly resonated with the regular crunch of my footsteps and deep, almost sensual breathing.

There were no other souls around, so I slowed down, taking my time to drink in the divine nectar of this much yearned for experience. The further I moved into the forest, the more my body and heart began to ache. There were times when I felt I would strip my clothes off, to cast away anything that was between me and this delectable love making that was happening within and all around me. There were times when I leaned against a tree, recounting whether I had taken some kind of hallucinogenic that morning. But I had not; this was a natural awakening of once dormant energies that lived within me.

I came to a clearing within the forest, where the path continued on, up towards the chiseled mountain face, leaving the alluring trees behind. The further I climbed, the more obvious it became that the energy was changing into a darker, more melancholic energy. Now my aloneness triggered off fears that maybe I would not get to the top, that perhaps I had taken a wrong turn, or worse still that I was lost. Damn, why didn't I bring my mobile? I looked all around me, hoping to find a clue that would put a firm stop to the questioning of my navigational skills. Suddenly, I heard his voice.

My Love, keep going. This is part of the initiation. You have to be able to pass through all your fears and desires to reach me. You cannot be swayed by any of them to reach the purity of heart that can open the way for me to be with you once again.

My heart was pounding now with fear and a touch of pure determination. I had to keep going; I must trust that I knew the way. I was already starting to sweat as the midday sun glaringly shone down without the protective shade from the earlier tree coverage. On and on I went, relentlessly climbing up and over the large inhospitable limestone boulders, until I finally came face-to-face with a small handwritten wooden sign with the words: "Lieu de silence, la grotte" (Proceed in silence). The sign included an arrow pointed towards the cave. I was so relieved to see that sign. I wondered how many other people may have been saved by that little wooden plaque. God bless whoever put it there.

Even as I carried on, there was no one else to be seen or heard anywhere near me. I came to a set of well-worn stone steps that zigzagged up the face of the cliff. Because of the heat, I took the steps one at a time, pausing every now and again for a breath as I turned around to look out over the view of an ocean of sunflowers and the distant Alps. There was a wind swirling all around me that seemed to carry sounds of Tibetan chants and drones, the sound growing louder the higher I climbed. Again, there was a heightened sense of awareness, and even though mildly afraid, I stayed present and kept going. I was coaching myself every step of the way, as this was clearly a supernatural experience, and something I had never encountered before.

As I turned yet another corner I realized that after an hour I had finally reached my destination. It was incredibly beautiful, drenched in femininity and a peace beyond words. There was a full-size statue of what was to be Mother Mary carrying the limp, lifeless body of Jesus Christ in her arms. To the world this image was one of unbearable suffering and injustice, yet to me it was just the opposite. It was a beacon of the Beloved, the constant reminder that love has the power to change the world forever. I knelt there and celebrated the courage of love, and its magnificent, ungraspable nature.

As my euphoria subsided, I stood up and breathed in the abundant freshness from the valley down below. I also breathed a massive sigh of relief as I took a moment to reflect on all that I had gone through to reach this point. After three steady breaths I was ready to enter the cave. I was bursting with life, literally pulsating with love as I humbly entered into the dark, damp, musky cave. Crossing the threshold I entered into an enormous grotto, far bigger than I had imagined it to be. Its only light source was from five stained glass windows that depicted the image of Jesus Christ and Mary Magdalene in an obvious rapturous embrace, along with a handful of candles that were already lit. Shafts of blood red and cobalt blue light flooded the entrance of the cave, and the further I entered the darker the colors became. From somewhere towards the back of the cave I could hear the faint sound of trickling water.

I walked around in near darkness trying to figure out the formation of the cave's layout. To settle my curiosity, my hands discovered a pool of water in the far right corner, as well as a flight of steps leading down to a lower level. As my eyes adjusted to the dark, I began to see that the floor was laid with black, red, and white tiles, and that there were actually seven stained glass windows. I sensed that the best place to seek out my Beloved would be beside the stone cistern with both my hands in the pool, knowing that water was a powerful conductor of energy.

I unclasped my sandals and left my rucksack at the door, gracefully moved over to my seat on the side of the pool. I stayed there for a while gently breathing with my eyes closed, as my fingers delicately played with the water. The water cooled my body and seemed to electrify my heart. A profound peace entered me, cleansing away all pain and bitterness from my past, wiping clean all hurt and disappointments. Listening to the silence, all afflictions within me dissolved, as a smile crossed my lips, and my heart opened like a flower embracing all of life everywhere. In the chasm of the cave I spoke out into the penetrating emptiness.

"Beloved, I have come all this way to meet with you once again in the flesh. With all of my might and power I call for you to be with me here once again on Earth. With the entirety of my heart, I command you to be made manifest so that I may hold and love you in the physical form. This life means nothing to me without you to share the glorious experiences of this earth with."

I began to cry as I tapped into the innate pain of our supposed separation. I knew we were already together, that he had never ever left my side; that this was indisputably known and to that knowing I would have happily endured anything. But there was an agony that was deeply felt as a result of not being able to touch him, hold him, see him even with my human eyes. The tremendous power of my longing began to stir, like a ravenous storm brewing in every corner of the world. I could sense the elements building around me, organizing themselves to create an irreversible phenomenon.

I saw him in my inner eye and felt the distance, the vast space that etched itself out between us. With all the authority of my feminine heritage, and the colossal leverage of the emblazoned female spirit when she is aflame with that which she loves, I stood up and opened my arms as if crucified, with the words, "Be with me, be with me, be with me, now!" ringing out from the opening of the cave to reverberate across the land.

After what must have been a little under an hour, I was done completely emptied of all the longing that had steadily grown since the age of twelve. I had done what I came to do; there was nothing more I could give. I felt exhausted; yet strangely light, as if I had removed a heavy burden that I had been carrying around. There was a jubilant sensation within my heart, as a sincere happiness swelled to a level never experienced before.

I slipped on my sandals, lifted my rucksack onto my back, and gave a humble bow to the darkness of the cave, as I slowly turned to walk away, making sure I did not look back once. The blinding sunlight warmed my face as I reappeared on the plateau, breathing in the fresh and perfumed air of Southern France. I felt truly amazing, awesome in fact. With that, I remembered Chloe waiting down below, and could hardly wait to meet her.

"I did it! It is really done; there is nothing more I can do," I dreamily imagined, feeling satisfied and purposeful. "That's it; the pilgrimage of love is over."

I was totally unaware that it was, in fact, only beginning.

I walked back to begin my descent down, laughing as I reminisced over my amateur dramatics on the way up. One minute I was scared to death and now I felt like a victorious heroine. I was still reflecting on the experience as I slipped on my iPod and began to listen to a playlist that I had created called The Beloved. It was a montage of sounds and songs that instantly took me to that place within that yearned for him. As soon as I began listening I signed with relief, as even this music brought such a feeling of connection, a respite from my perceived reality. I merged into aroused feelings; feelings of gratitude, awe, and belonging to this journey. I took my time, taking it easy, using my hands to steady myself against the rocks, when suddenly I heard my name being called out next to me.

"Scarlett!"

This was the voice of a real person spoken so loudly that I could hear it through my headphones. I was incredibly taken aback (as you can imagine) and surprised as I was sure it was only me on the mountain. I removed my earphones and turned around with a, "Yes?" expecting to see someone, thinking that maybe I had left something in the cave.

But there was no one there. I was still convinced there was another person around so I spoke again, "Hello, is anyone there?"

Again, no response.

This is strange I thought to myself, as I carried on walking, only now with the music off. Moments later it happened again. I heard a real human voice at my right hand side as I walked through the forest—but there was no one there. I immediately stopped and sat on a tree stump, looking all around. "Okay this is getting silly. I know you are there, I can hear your voice. What's going on?"

God knows who I was talking to. I started talking to the trees, to the forest, to whatever was out there.

"Scarlett, it is me. I am here to tell you that I will be with you within seven months to this day. You have my word," said my disembodied Beloved.

For some time I sat there, on a tree stump, knowing that this voice was heard with my ears, spoken from outside in the forest, not inside my imagination. I have never heard a voice like that before, in fact I have never heard any voices without bodies full stop. I am not a psychic person, nor claim to be. Yes, I have visions and full-on intuitive foresight. But to actually hear a voice all around me as clearly as I hear other people in the street? No, that was not commonplace. Although, it's exactly what happened. This voice was spoken through a pair of lips! He was there, right beside me, walking with me every step of the way.

I was without words or thoughts after that moment. I was floored; my understanding of the world flew right out the window.

And in the midst of all of this, somehow—within half an hour—I managed to reach the bottom of the mountain in one piece. I must have been wearing a completely clueless expression as I walked towards the table where Chloe and her new friends were obviously getting along great. She looked up to wave me over, as she mouthed the words, "Are you okay?"

I gave her the diver's gesture of "all good" by making an 'O' with my thumb and forefinger. I walked towards an empty chair and slumped into it, kicking my feet up and onto the table, leaning back interlacing my fingers behind my head, letting out a huge sigh of relief.

"Hey Scarlett, what have you been doing? We've been missing you," said some young guy as he pulled his seat a little closer to me.

I turned and stared him in the eye with the most deadpan expression, "Oh nothing much, just been out for a little walk," I said as I winked at him, then looked away gazing up towards the mountain, smiling to myself.

Chloe spontaneously burst out laughing, spluttering her wine all over the table as she tried her best to stifle her giggles, whilst mopping the table.

"Huh?" he commented. He did not understand; in fact no one did as they turned to look at one another, asking if they missed out on some in-house joke. All the conversations at the table died for a moment, and then the chatter began again. I kept my poker face expertly fixed. But inside, the Beloved and I were rolling on our backs holding onto our stomachs as we laughed and laughed and laughed throughout the Universe.

❧

*FairyDale Barn, Dorset, England, a few days later
—July 29, 2008*

It was now crystal clear that I was heading back home to FairyDale Barn to bring an end to my relationship with Danny. As I dropped Chloe off in London, I began yet another solo journey, this time within my own conscience, as I searched my mind over and over for the best way to do this. I felt sick as I imagined Danny excitedly waiting for me at home. Knowing him so well there would be a bunch of flowers and all kinds of welcoming gifts waiting for me upon my return. I groaned out loud as I turned the music up in an attempt to drown out my guilt.

Moments later I resumed listening to my inner voice, which kept nagging at me to come back to this crucial debate. After a deluge of emotional agonizing over which way to turn, I found a neutral and sobering still place, whose voice was profoundly wise. Its wisdom soothed me by suggesting that I should return tonight, not say anything straight away, but wait until the morning to announce my decision. Phew, that feels better, I can drive again in relative safety knowing that there was a plan of action and that underneath all this turmoil, was a wise, rational, and clear-headed woman.

I arrived back at the barn to a flurry of activity. Yes the flowers were there, so were the cutely wrapped gifts, and surprisingly, a house that seemed to have been professionally scrubbed and tidied by the *Queens of Clean* (British TV comedy). I swallowed hard when I realized all the effort he had put into my coming home. He was forewarned of my return as we had kept in contact via regular text messages. And now looking around, I saw how wonderfully he had prepared for it. I had to keep reminding myself to stay close to that neutral wise woman that was in there somewhere, as I sensed he may try to play every trick in the book to win me back. But I was untouchable, I was unwinnable, there was nothing he could do, my heart was now elsewhere and my mind made up.

Early the very next morning, I padded back and forth in the kitchen clasping my cup of coffee, rehearsing my lines before I ventured upstairs to wake Danny; an unexpected text message bleeped in as my mobile burst to life, vibrating and crashing to the floor. Bloody hell, I almost jumped out of my skin, as I bent down to pick up the offending item to see who was texting at this ungodly hour. I tentatively pressed the "Read Message" button to discover the shocking news that a close friend of Danny's named Aaron had died suddenly. The message was coming from a close friend of ours who was currently in India. He went on to say that he had been calling Danny for days, but his calls kept going directly to voicemail, so he decided to send the message to me.

I had met Aaron only a couple of times mostly during my wild hey days when I lived in Brighton, known affectionately as the little San Francisco of the U.K. He was part of the cosmic hippy brigade, another wild stallion the same age as Danny who refused to be placed in any box; a free spirit that ventured outside the boundaries of society, to see for himself what lurked beyond. Aaron was like a brother to Danny; I knew that these guys had once lived together on the outskirts of Brighton and their history was as long as it was colorful. Danny was going to be devastated. The text went on to explain that because he was Jewish the funeral would be within the next couple of days, and to reply straight away if he could come.

This news changed everything. There was no way I could end

the relationship with Danny now. I would have to be there to support him through this, and wait until he was strong enough before I broached the subject again. So this time, I mounted the stairs with a different version of shattering news to break to him.

CHAPTER SIX

DESTINY STRIKES BACK

Shekinashram, Glastonbury, England,
late September 2008

A S I APPROACHED my thirty-ninth birthday (December twenty-second), my Beloved's presence began to take on a more urgent tone. My dreams became more frequent and lingered in my mind throughout the day whether I was at home alone or in London teaching. He spoke of his promise to find me, that no matter what, we would be together again in this lifetime. I sensed he was preparing to enter my life, as I too, was trying my best to emerge into his wherever he may be.

He would come to me in meditation and sit beside me, taking my hands in his. I would drink in his strength as he reminded me to stay strong and keep the faith that everything was exactly how it needed to be. His reassurance washed away my mounting concern and doubts that I was possibly in this world alone. I drew strength from him, and noticed that within minutes of consciously reconnecting with him I morphed from a highly confused emotional state to a still and silent radiance. All I wanted was to remain in this blissful, meditative state with him forever, away from all human suffering—my own included. I rested within his words of love and the energy of his presence. I felt torn in two, telling myself I had to stay strong for Danny so he felt that I was there for him throughout the grieving process of Aaron's recent death. And so, week in and week out, I continued the charade, boarding the train for London to teach yoga for three days, and like clockwork would return again in time for the weekend.

As is common for me, I lived for my work. Nothing out of the ordinary could happen during the weekend, as by Saturday I was often back to teaching yoga again in Glastonbury. Sometimes I would spend the entire weekend teaching if I also had my monthly weekend workshop. It's a wonder Danny was still around, as I hardly had any time left over to spend with him. But I knew my core truth, and I suppose Danny probably guessed it too.

Teaching yoga was far more fulfilling than being at home. This fulfillment drove me on to schedule in even more classes and reserve more week-long retreats away, until my year was full; every moment given to something other than my relationship. Inside I was itching—no pulling my hair out is closer to the truth—to leave him, end our relationship, and begin again at some point in the future with my Beloved. My fiery impatience grew stronger, constantly complaining that it wasn't happening quickly enough.

I kept forgetting that meeting ones Beloved is all about timing. To bring your Beloved through, you have to take clear, directed steps so the Universe receives the message. There cannot be another person posing in the position that is reserved for your Beloved (like, um, Danny). If there is, the Beloved may not manifest. If you miss one another or get consumed in fear and leave the relationship you will simply have to wait until the next lifetime to try again. And who wants to do that? My vote is to get on with it now! Although, it was taking me some considerable time to leave my present situation. I had to continue dropping down into my heart to receive reassurance that staying with Danny for now was the right thing to do and that I wasn't missing my Beloved.

I learned along the way that there is a *very* precise art and science engineering the whole Beloved process. The three steps below are my own contemplations, insights, and system that I created and worked diligently to follow (regardless of how long it took me to get there!). All of this was discovered and developed as I directly experienced each step firsthand, which is always the very best way.

First step: Create the vacuum. There's one thing the Universe can't stand and that's an empty space. Please note, I don't mean a 'dead' space, like, "I can't find my Beloved, so in that case I will turn into a hermit." No, you must create an alive space that's teeming with Shakti (life force). Your life should be more like, "I am having so much fun finding my Beloved, but there is no way that I will get serious until I know he's The One."

Second step: Begin to prepare. Embark on your own personal healing journey, paying special attention to healing all of your past relationships and attitudes towards sexuality. Spend time alone dissipating all energies that are not your own. And last, but by no means least, meditate daily and speak with your Beloved, even if you feel he/she is not there or listening. You may feel as if you are entering a dark night of the soul. Remember to trust the process; you are emptying out all the unnecessary junk from your emotions and subconscious mind. Stuff that will inevitably get in the way when you do finally meet your Beloved. Trust me, it's no good coming together with a wild variety of unhealed experiences. Get rid of as much past accumulation as possible. There is a whole stock of methods located in the Last Word at the end of the book to facilitate this.

Third step: Follow all impulses (Shakti urges) however unusual, as your Shakti will guide you both to collide with each other in a very *big* way! If you hear or feel guided to, "Be at the library at 3pm and wait on the steps." You better be there. At first, all these impulses may not lead to much. But I assure you, you are simply exercising an old intuitive muscle. The more you trust and respond to your inner guidance, the truer and deeper the wisdom will become.

For now, I was teetering on the edge of Step One.

So there I was, at the end of yet another Saturday yoga class in Glastonbury's Shekinashram, one of three spiritual ashram's that nestled into the foothills of the infamous Tor (the supposed entrance to the fairy underworld, Merlin's Tomb, and a whole host of other mystical meanderings). Shekinashram was the home of a small community of vegan yogis, who rented out their six bedrooms and yurt at the bottom of their garden to spiritual seekers. Every week I would teach yoga there as long as I wasn't too noisy, as this place enjoyed its moments of vipassana (silent meditation). Its yoga room was a purple clad landscape with a huge alter in the middle dedicated to Kali the goddess of destruction and dissolution. The room could hold about twenty-five people, which was an ideal group for me to handle safely, making sure that everyone received personal one-on-one attention.

Glastonbury was the heaving mecca of all things weird and wonderful. It was a small town, known within the New Age circles as being the heart chakra of the planet. It was also known for being the meeting point of light and dark energies, as well as a transmitting station that covered the entire British Isles. Whatever was going on in Glastonbury had the potential to color the rest of the U.K., as it was positioned on a powerful ley or energy line that crossed through Glastonbury, Stonehenge, and Avebury. It was for this reason that countless spiritual teachers would flock to its streets to hold their latest offering. These worldwide guru's and teacher's brought with them an entourage of devotee's that kept the streets of Glastonbury paved with gold. Its worldwide magnetism always kept the place exciting and wild, as you never knew who you were going to bump into next.

It was the same with my yoga classes; I never knew who would show up. All types, colors, genders, age ranges, and economic status flocked to Glastonbury, and thus, at times the yoga ashram I taught at. Typically, it was a welcome surprise, yet sometimes I had to get hands on to guide the various crazies that showed up. Like the time a couple of guys turned up for class at 10am still high as kites from the night before. They were exceptionally eager to begin even though they were in fits of giggles. I had to delicately steer them out of the premises as I guided them over the bodies of students who were blissfully unaware and lying in Savasana Pose. So when a beautiful young French woman beaming with excitement rushed towards me as if she had known me forever after class one day, I was not in the least bit fazed.

"Scarlett, I have to tell you about this man I have just come across, you are *so* going to love him!" She brimmed with a certain excitement that intriguingly demanded my attention.

"His name is Sananda Gabriel, he is *just* like you. You both speak about the same things, I am sure that he is you, but a male version." She spoke as if she had way too much coffee that day. Full of beans and excitement, she told me a whole entourage of facts and figures about this Sananda. There was one thing she said that I will never forget.

"I am sure you are the same soul, I am certain that when you meet him, you will feel the same way!"

Suddenly, all the students in the class stopped whatever they were doing to turn and face me with their jaws hanging open. There was a hushed tone that filled the yoga room, as they eagerly waited for what I was going to say next. That did it. It brought my full attention rushing forward, as I inwardly pounced on those last two words. Same soul. A warm smile broke across my lips; as a wave of recognition warmed my heart.

This was not the first time that someone had mentioned Sananda to me. Curiously, she was perhaps the fifth person in the last year that had mentioned to me that Sananda Gabriel was the masculine version of myself. I was told that not only did we have the same passion and the same "energy;" but all of these people instantly thought of me whenever they met him. This was the second reason why I raised one eyebrow while squinting my right eye in contemplation. What was going on?

It was all very strange.

Or was it?

As I picked up the yoga mats from off the luxurious purple carpet while blowing out the tea lights around the Kali (Hindu deity) alter, one by one every student made their way over to say their goodbye's as I hugged each of them. The young French maiden hung around making sure she got my full attention one last time so she could deliver her message properly before she departed and headed back onto the swirling mist-filled streets of Glastonbury.

She called out, "Make sure you look him up, whatever you do don't forget. I have left his website on your sheepskin rug."

Again, I couldn't help but smile.

Driving home that afternoon in my trusted red MG, I reflected on the morning 's events. There was no doubt that there was a certain kind of magic in the way that French woman spoke to me. It's true that every time you go to Glastonbury there is magic in the air, but this was different. I swear the town is caught in-between worlds; one moment it's a thriving modern day city that accommodates hundreds of tourists at any given time. Then in the next moment, it's all Knights of the Round Table and Guinevere's running around on horseback as they ride right through the center of town, down the main high street as if it were Arthurian times.

I mulled over the sequence of events: the way she pressed her case, making sure I received all she was telling me, and the way she waited until everyone was gone so she could warn me not to forget. And then writing down his website! This kind of magic was far from the high antics and chaotic madness that Glastonbury is so well known for. As my MG climbed up and over the undulating Somerset meadows that surrounded the town, I wondered yet again if I really did have the balls to leave Danny sooner rather than later.

I was again in the same scenario, fooling myself that I was a) moderately fulfilled, and b) enjoying a relatively purposeful life that was *mostly* full of contentment. That is, until I went home and climbed into bed, alone. Then the truth came out. As if starring in the leading role of my own version of *Groundhog Day*, every night was a repeat from the one before. I undressed in the quiet stillness of my rose colored empty bedroom, dropping my clothes on the floor. Our vast bedroom was renovated from within the rafters of the barn, so the whole ceiling was vaulted with heavy oak timbers straddling the walls supporting the entire structure. The bedroom mirrored the way I was feeling; wishing I had some oak timbers of my own to support my heavy load, ensuring that I stayed strong enough to see all this through to the end.

After climbing into my clean, crisp, white organic cotton duvet (always alone as Danny came to bed later) I would stretch out claiming the whole bed to myself, enjoying the space and sense of relative quietness as I closed my heavy eyes before switching off the light. Moments later I would fall into the awaiting arms of the eternal pitch blackness of the void (there are no street lamps in the countryside—thank god!) where I tended to hang out these days. In between my first finger and thumb I would delicately hold two rose quartz crystals as if I was in the classical Gian Mudra hand posture that all yogis are timelessly portrayed in. I would begin to feel streams of soft, feminine loving energy flowing through my fingers up through my arms, and permeating into my heart. As soon as I felt the presence of the rose quartz I would begin to pray. Every night since my thirty-fifth birthday I would pray the same prayer over and over:

"Dear God, where is this Beloved that I wait for? How much longer do I have to continue to live without him? Please, I beg of you to engineer the way so we may meet, as my life without him is so painfully silent."

I just knew that my Beloved existed in human form, and I knew he longed for me as much as I longed for him. The burning question was, where was he? I didn't want to meet my Beloved so we could settle down and play happy families together, keeping him all to myself. No, that was not it at all. I yearned for this man, so together we could and would love the world, by creating a radiance that emanated from our union. All who were with us would fall into love and bring that love back into their homes, into their hearts, and into the world. Together we would fearlessly shower life with the same miraculous healing as Beloveds such as Jesus Christ and Mary Magdalene, King Solomon and the Queen of Sheba, and the U.K.'s infamous Diana Dors and Alan Lake.

I once read that Alan Lake died of a broken heart months after Diana passed away. The news report said he gave up the urge to live without her. The autopsy actually found a tear in his heart—a physical tear! I was only fifteen years old when I received the news, reading the *Sun* (famous British tabloid) newspaper with the girls, smoking a furtive cigarette; yet even in my teenage "screw you" attitude, my eyes filled with tears as I felt his broken heart and the life that was torn from him when she closed her eyes for the very last time.

I was so choked up that I had to hide in the girls' toilets for the best part of twenty minutes (because to cry was totally uncool!), until I could reset my black eyeliner and flick the collar of my blazer well and truly up, like a proper British teen in angst. Even so, it was this deep, big love that I longed for, for my entire life. And I knew it existed because I saw it in a few others and felt the desire at the core of my being.

For now, it was back to reality. I pulled into the drive of FairyDale Barn. Surely Danny is emotionally strong enough now after Aaron's death to stand on his own two feet? At this point, I had all but completely tuned out of my three-year relationship; convinced it was my nemesis because the longer I delayed leaving him, the lonelier I felt. This loneliness that I speak of was not the normal kind. It was a loneliness that made my soul feel cold. A loneliness that could never be cured by having other people around, no matter how much they adored and loved me.

No, nothing could soothe this ache to love. Only a glimpse of the Beloved could offer some type of healing balm. But, a glimpse was not enough. Because I knew. Knew with every fiber of my being that we would meet and spend every waking moment together. Soon. Even so, there is nothing worse than knowing you are with the wrong person, and the longer you stay with them, the further away your Beloved is. Somehow I *had* to create that vacuum. I had discovered the process for god's sake, you'd think I could take the action step!

The craziest thing is that Danny also knew of my dreams, and he too wished that I would find the heartfelt happiness I yearned for and deserved. He admitted to me many times that he was not the man I ached for, that he could not meet me on that level, and he was afraid of the fullness of that commitment. He would gaze into my eyes, with tears threatening to fall: "Scarlett, I am not the one that you seek, I wish I was. Even so, I just can't let you go. You are my life and I love you so much. I wish I could be the man you relentlessly seek, but I know that I am not."

In these moments my heart sank. How much more obvious does it have to be before I do something? I felt as if I had totally sold out. It was so clear that I had settled for comfort, stability, security, and left out part of my soul in the bargain. Even Danny realized it. What do you do when you meet that kind of truth face on? When you know that you're living a life that seems impossible to break down and leave? He was making it so easy for me to leave, spelling it out for all to see—he was not "The One." But for the life of me, I couldn't figure out how to begin the process. I fretted over endless minor details that seemed insurmountable to overcome. I agonized over ending our rental agreement before its due date, I fretted over calling it a day with our joint business venture, an online forty-day raw food diet program. I squirmed over losing him as a friend, and I dreaded the idea that I may break his heart.

I have never taken so much bloody time nor agonized over a decision like this before in my entire life. I was sure there was more going on than meets the eye. Whenever I tuned in during meditation I would always get a reaffirming grounded feeling that this type of procrastination, which is totally out of character for me, wasn't procrastination at all. This slow, heavy, long-winded episode that was driving me nuts was a classic sign that the Beloved was nearing. It all went back to timing again. Obviously I wasn't ready, and neither was my other. It wasn't the right time, yet. I had always suspected that Danny was a Soul Mate, therefore this feeling of 'not being ready' suggested that I had more to learn and do before I could be guided to my Beloved. At least that's what I had come up with thus far!

As I pulled into the drive, past the willow tree's flanking the entrance, I took a deep breath and grabbed my bags. I could do this. I stepped in through the front door that opened into the kitchen with accompanying breakfast bar, greeted Danny like a friend, and offered to make him a cup of tea. He had his back to me as he hunched over his desk bobbing his head to the latest dance tracks from iTunes. After making tea for both of us, I pulled up a stool at the breakfast bar and turned to my faithful Mac and went online.

I rummaged through my bag as discreetly as possible, trying

not to cause too much attention as I searched for the web address that was given to me by the young French woman earlier that day. My heart was pounding as I turned my Mac screen in such a way that Danny wouldn't be able to see what I was looking at, while I constantly looked over the top to make sure the coast was clear to check out Sananda's site privately. This was exciting, I felt like I was being dishonest and secretive on one level, and in a way that was true. I knew if Danny caught me looking at Sananda's site he would feel threatened and would sense what was happening. I wasn't going to take that chance, as I did not want to hurt him.

So I did what I could to shield him from Sananda's presence, although on one level, as my Soul Mate, he would have known already. In close relationships partners can immediately sense the presence of a potential threat—I know I can. The propelling urgency to discover Sananda's site was not only seductively thrilling but also streaked with an honesty that was undeniable. I knew that I had to do this. No, change that. I knew I was born to do this. Born to find my Beloved, by any means necessary, and willing to follow those Shakti urges. By the way, this moment right here, right now was a massive Shakti moment. Packed full of life force and vitality. Those are her signals, those are her signs. When a strong impulse appeared, it was critical at this stage in the Beloved path, that I didn't question it (that would be my mind), but to instead follow it with my heart.

The site opened up, and from the pixilated screen of words and images, a face appeared that tore my heart open. My eyes refused to move, as my heart lurched forward and burned into my throat. I gasped, as I realized I was looking into the face of my love. There he was. There was the now mature face of that little boy I played with in my imagination when I was a child. That same face I looked into when I made my teenage promise to bring him to life. The intense eyes that haunted me into my twenties, and the mouth I promised I would kiss forever in my thirties. Finally, after all these years, after all of these phases of life that I passed through—here he was. The moment I laid eyes on his face, I knew it was him. There was no doubt whatsoever.

He was finally here on Earth, and now I knew his name.

I hastily closed the screen as if caught with another lover. My hands touched my mouth making sure no startling noises escaped my lips. I smoothed down my clothes, rearranged my hair and told Danny that I needed to get some air as I went outside barefoot. Danny's "No worries" reply confirmed that he was absorbed elsewhere. I tip-toed across our patio and plunged my feet into the moist dew-laden grass as I breathed in a full, rich, cool breath, and turned my eyes upwards into the night sky. I marveled at the dark silhouette of the oak trees against the soft grey backdrop of mottled stars resting within the shimmering glow from the soon-to-be full moon. I slowly dropped to my knees, as I sank into the earth and exhaled from the depths of my soul, "Thank you. Thank you. Thank you for finding me."

"You okay, babe?" asked a concerned Danny as he poked his head around the kitchen door fifteen minutes later. "You look really strange, like you've seen a ghost."

"That's because I have," I whispered.

You think you are alive
because you breathe air?
Shame on you,
that you are alive in such a limited way.
Don't be without Love,
so you won't feel dead.
Die in Love and stay alive forever.

—RUMI

CHAPTER SEVEN

BREAKING UP AND BREAKING DOWN

FairyDale Barn, Dorset, England, October 2008

TWO MONTHS later and I was no closer to leaving Danny. After the initial euphoric moment when I first saw Sananda come to life on the Mac screen in front of me, I returned to my life routine. There always seemed to be one reason or another why I couldn't leave Danny. The latest one was his mother's sixtieth birthday in September, when I let myself get roped into planning the surprise party in the garden. By that time, France seemed like a vague, distant memory, and even Sananda, the exquisitely beautiful man on the website (who I once strongly felt could be "The One"), now seemed like only a dream, as I read that he lived in Hawaii. It's amazing how strong being comfortable can become. Back and forth I went: Shall I? Shouldn't I? I've got to leave, I can't leave. Even I was getting bored with it all!

Then, suddenly one morning everything seemed to fall into place.

Without any rehearsal or forewarning of "this is your destined moment" it all poured out. Danny and I were in the kitchen one morning slopping around in our dressing gowns as we joined forces to make a smoothie. I was chopping while he was blending, when I accidently cut my finger as I attempted to peel a mango in one piece. The cut wasn't serious, but all the fuss I was making was enough to think I had lopped my finger right off. All the suppressed emotions I had been sitting on had finally found an escape route as months of uncried tears, unspoken sadness, and unshared truths burst through the dam that I had hoped would continue to hold everything back.

In between sobs I found myself telling Danny that I could no longer continue the relationship with him, and that I wanted to move out. He didn't know what to attend to first, my bleeding finger or respond to the time bomb that had just gone off. Understandably, he was shocked at first, then angry, followed by feeling denial, and finally hurt. He paced up and down the entire length of the kitchen and when that was not enough he ventured outside walking around the garden until he came back with his head in his hands chanting the word "why, why ,why?" over and over again.

After half an hour of pacing he began to calm down, enough to pull up a stool as he confessed that he had known all along this day would come shortly after my return from France. It had been three months since I had been back, and apparently he had been counting every single one of them as if they were our last. I had no idea. He held his head in his hands for what seemed like ages before he eventually lifted his head so I could see his face. With tears in his eyes, he said he was strangely relieved that I was leaving, as he knew deep down he could not go on any further with me.

He expressed that he really didn't want to grow up just yet. That he still wanted to have fun and be largely irresponsible, but agonized that his desire would no doubt lead to our break-up. He had, at one time, hoped he could be "The One" for me, and that given enough time he could change, but now he realized he had to be brave enough to stand on his own two feet and let me go. Danny knew he was holding me back by clinging so tightly, trying so hard to please me, but only recently had he finally admitted to himself that he was only buying extra time. Now that this day had come, he felt he could almost breathe again, that he was no longer trying to out run this sense of dread, as the truth finally arrived.

By the time he released all of his regrets and sadness, we were holding hands in our oversized dressing gowns at the kitchen sink as our honest disclosures had dissolved and healed most of the resentments that had built up over the years. We found ourselves innocently open as we met each other in the space of this shared sorrow of parting. Also present in that very moment was an undeniable care for each other and the gratitude that we were somehow able to do this with such maturity and self-responsibility. As soon as all words fell silent we naturally embraced one another.

I could smell his skin and hair; a strange blend of sage and a highly exotic perfume that can only be found in Glastonbury. His softly brushed skin, that he religiously groomed every morning before his shower, was pressed against my cheek. It was as if all the veils and ways we had taken each other for granted suddenly dissipated. In that instant we were incredibly present to one other and the situation we were in, our hearts open and forgiving.

I moved away from our embrace so I could look at him a little deeper. As I gazed into his eyes (something I hadn't done for a long time) I realized that Danny truly was one of my Soul Mates. He was a beautiful being that encouraged me to grow by showing me the areas in my live that needed changing. It was only Danny who could have played this role of openly and honestly telling me he wasn't "The One." His honestly was freeing me in many ways. Anyone else may have hidden the truth and gone along with the whole idea. But not Danny. He was true and honest, even though it felt like a rude awakening, it was what I needed to get moving again.

I now looked way beyond his eyes, feeling that I was looking into his soul, touching the deepest parts of him. It was as if I could suddenly see him so clearly and the role he was playing in my life. Waves of compassion flowed through me, as I realized the true love that was behind it all. Whether he was aware of this or not, didn't matter. I knew. It was now so blindingly obvious that he was one of my Soul Mates. It explained why I found it so hard to leave. With that realization, another wave of sadness fused with gratitude washed over me as I buried my head into his shoulder.

Soul Mates are the ones who prepare us to meet the Beloved. They endlessly join forces with life to mirror back to us the areas and places we need to develop. Together, you lovingly work to become more of the person you truly are. Soul Mates help to define and create your sovereign soul identity, your own independent connection with the divine or flow of life. The nature of a Soul Mate relationship is to push each other towards the deeper aspects of life, so that it becomes second nature to come from this more sovereign place rather than some superficial one. Like a piece of soft sandpaper, the Soul Mate will rub away at those jagged edges so that one day soon—either in another lifetime, or perhaps this one, you will be relatively ready to meet your Beloved.

Soul Mates have no desire whatsoever to merge together and become one. Their focus is on the opposite outcome. They instead yearn for their complete whole sense of authentic independence, and enjoy immensely their meeting with another on that level. The role of the Soul Mate is to create the ways and means for the other to feel a sense of true fulfillment within oneself. As it is only when one is completely whole within themselves that they are ready to meet the Beloved.

As I made sense of all this in my mind, suddenly everything began to fall into place. "No wonder we both knew Danny wasn't The One, this clearly explains the reason why we had no desire to merge," I thought to myself. Suddenly, I was able to relax, releasing the tightly wound up energy I had been creating due to all the confusion and lack of action. After some time of holding onto each other, sobbing into each other's arms, the fires of change began to eat away at the cords and connections of our partnership. We began to shake as the inevitable process of breaking up took root, diminishing any and all lasting ties between us. We knew it was real—our relationship was over.

All of a sudden Danny pulled back quietly asking, "When are you thinking of leaving?"

"What did you say?" I asked in complete bewilderment as the turmoil rolled over me like crashing waves.

"I asked when you will be leaving?" he was almost pleading for my response.

As if frozen with fright, I looked at him searching my internal archives for the answer. I couldn't actually reply at first, because I hadn't technically planned to say any of this so soon on this random Wednesday morning. All this activity was coming from a spur of the moment, spontaneous, and impulsive place that seemed to speak with no warning. But that was all besides the point. Now that this ball was rolling, I had to decide when to leave.

I heard myself say, "November first, in two weeks time."

"Oh God," he groaned, "That's so close. Where will you go?" he asked.

Again, no real answer. I resigned myself to further time spent in a limbo-esque state until the answer arose from within me. "There is only one place I can go, and that's back home to my parents," I answered. Yikes—was I meant to say that? I nervously squirmed at the idea.

Once I said it out loud, the sheer reality of what was happening hit me. Our barn house loomed cold and empty, as a shadowy cloud seemed to descend over us darkening all four walls. The truth was my finances were at an all-time low. I was living well beyond my means, due to increasingly feverish ways that I had been footing the bill for most of our outgoings. The thought of living with my parents brought about a huge sense of failure and a suffocating fear that everything I had accomplished would somehow fall apart and be lost forever. But I could not think about that now, as I first had to get through the ordeal in front of me. The shadowy cloud momentarily lifted, but I knew I would feel it again in the not so distant future.

Danny turned ghostly pale and limply walked away, saying he was going out for a bit to sort his head. As soon as he left, emptiness reached for me as she whispered into my ear that we would get to know one another well all too soon. I groaned out loud sensing the truth of that statement. I had a strong feeling I was heading towards a pretty dark and lonely place before I could meet my other. I had no idea why, all I knew was that this despairing place was a parting gift from my last Soul Mate. Once I got through and out the other end of all this, then I would be ready to be with my One. Some part of me knew that this was the path to the Beloved. We must go through the healing journey alone so we can come out ready to be with our other half. With that realization, I dragged myself into the front room, laid down on the carpeted floor like a corpse, and allowed all the emotion from the previous months to pass.

It was a typical grey and wet English morning, the drizzling rain splattering against the windowpane causing my mood to sink even further. Winter was coming, and now I had to think about getting all my things packed up. I thought about Danny outside wondering whether he was getting wet. Next thing I knew I was opening my eyes and nursing a very stiff body. I had been out for over an hour!

Danny was back, I could hear him upstairs talking to someone on the telephone. It was probably his mum or sister; they were the ones that he usually turned to when we hit a rough patch. I guess this is what you could call the ultimate rough patch. I crawled on all fours towards my handbag, as I reached in to find my mobile to call my parents and ask for their help. What I had started in France six months ago was finally moving forward. I was drained, but relieved. It was my time. Although I had no real idea for what.

Over the next couple of weeks I managed to pack up all my belongings, and together with Danny, we fairly shared out all the furniture and items we had jointly purchased together. It was a somber two weeks. The house was deathly quiet, as Danny would take all his calls in the other room so I would not hear. An unspoken distance began to form between us, as I understood that this was the beginning of the natural healing process. I did not force anything different to happen.

It is such a strange experience to split up with a Soul Mate and remain living with them whilst arranging different living spaces. It's a kind of in-between world; a world caught between the life and death of the relationship. I helplessly watched as someone I loved and cared for deeply became a distant stranger on the human level, as he worked hard to protect his heart from further breakage. I knew at a soul level that we were deeply grateful for all the time we had spent together. Even so, it still hurt like hell to see his once open face become grey and cold as all that we once shared became separated and divided. It was a painful time, like a death, and I had no choice but to face it head on, for there was no going back once the process had started.

Chloe insisted that I stay over at her place weekly whenever I was in London teaching. I graciously took her up on the offer, grateful for the respite from all the upset. In the meantime, I listened carefully to what my body and heart needed to get through this time as lovingly as possible, and I made sure that I was available if Danny needed to share with me. I sensed deeply that this was the most conscious way of breaking up, knowing that something as painful as this could be done in love. This was my Soul Mate, after all.

My parents were incredibly supportive throughout all of it. Mum would call me everyday making sure I was okay, and that everything at home was bearable. And dad? Well, he was over the moon, grabbing the phone once mum had finished, in utter jubilation at the fabulous good luck that I was coming home and there was no fixed date when I would be leaving. As much as he loved Danny, he was openly relieved that we had called it a day. Being a typical Irish father, he was rather keen on the idea of me marrying a millionaire, or at least someone with royal blood. Danny was never good enough for his daughter, in fact looking back in hindsight, none of my boyfriends were, and I sneakily suspected, none of them ever would be. I wondered what he would think of my Beloved once I finally came together with him.

On my moving day, mum and dad offered to help and turned up at the barn first thing in the morning with a rental van the same size as Robbie. It was rather awkward when they first arrived. I felt so sorry for Danny, as he clearly did not know where to look or what to do. It was an absolute farce! Mum did what she does best, which was to cluck around Danny like a mother hen, offering to make him tea and breakfast. I had to intervene to rescue Danny from being force fed to keep up his health and strength. He took his one and only chance to wriggle free of my mum's clutches, announcing that he was going out whilst we packed the van, promising to return before we left.

As soon as Danny was gone, all three of us packed the van at warp speed, and then finally, the only job left was to entice our two tabby cats from under the bed and bundle them into their basket. We decided it would be best for the cats if they went with me. Danny had no idea where he was going next, all he knew was that he had to leave the barn as it was full of too many memories. Last I heard he was heading to Costa Rica to spend some time with a raw food community.

Within half an hour a red-eyed Danny appeared, as mum and dad mysteriously faded into the background. Now, was the moment to say goodbye to my boyfriend and Soul Mate of three years. I was fumbling around in the kitchen, not knowing how or where to begin. I wondered whether I had picked up some sort of compulsive obsessive disorder as I constantly opened and closed cupboards checking to see whether I had left anything behind. After wandering around the breakfast bar a few hundred times, back and forth across the length of the kitchen (something that seemed to be a bit of a theme for us), I reached for my nude leather fringed handbag and walked right up to him, as he stooped over his laptop pretending to be interested in something.

"Danny, it's time for me to leave now," I whispered.

He slowly turned around to face me, as all the futile attempts of trying to keep it together collapsed in one moment. We both cried as we held each other for the very last time. I felt as if my heart was being ripped open, as this genuine love poured out of me towards him.

"Please take care of yourself and make sure you are safe at all times, you promise me?" he begged.

"Safe? With my dad around, that's a guarantee," I hopelessly attempted to joke as a way to lighten the moment.

"I love you so much babe, be happy, and if you need me, I am here. Always," he bravely whispered.

"Me too, Danny, but we have to ride this one out. We have to let some time pass before we speak again. Bye, sweetie. I love you." I choked back the tears as I turned and walked away from our FairyDale Barn, climbing into the passenger seat of the rental van, keeping the door open for mum.

Mum and dad said their goodbyes, both openly crying, which is very strange for mum, who never gives the game away. She is a true Brit through and through, choosing instead to keep a stiff upper lip rather than show a flicker of emotion. However, she always had a soft spot for Danny, and to be honest, I was sure she could sense that he was a true Soul Mate to me. My dad, on the other hand, openly wears his heart on his sleeve and can often be found crying at the drop of a hat. I watched Dad give Danny one of those man to man slaps on the back, marking the end of their shared sentimentality. Dad walked over and climbed into the driver's seat, while mum sat beside me at the front holding my hand, whispering, "Be brave lamb, be brave." Dad reversed the van out of the driveway past the flanking willows. With a deep breath we drove away from FairyDale Barn for the last time. I didn't look back.

Step one—create the vacuum. Done. I now had empty space to fill. But first before I did that, I had to take the fated second step. Prepare yourself and embark on a profound self-healing journey.

❦

My parents house, Newbury, Berkshire, England,
November 2008

I did not speak throughout the entire two-hour ride until we reached the family home, the one I had left over twenty years ago. We pulled up into the drive, and all three of us heaved a huge sigh of relief. In true English style, we immediately made some tea before unloading the van. After downing an entire bucket of tea, dad and I felt ready to start again, and began to unpack all of my belongings, placing half in the loft and half in the garage. All I had with me was one zebra stripped suitcase that I took into my old childhood bedroom, stuffed with clothes, my laptop, books, and a small bag of crystals.

I closed the door as I slumped heavily onto the sofa bed,

looking all around me in near disbelief at what can only be described as a shrine to a daughter. Lucky me. There were pictures of me ranging from newborn baby to only a few months ago. On my bedside table were copies of my first published yoga and nutrition books, plus a whole stack of brochures advertising all my past yoga retreats. What am I doing here? I thought to myself. I am thirty-eight years old, with no real passion for my work, no money behind me, no home, nothing to call my own, and now I am back living with my parents.

All my friends have already made it in the world, securely on the property ladder, mostly married with families, whereas I now find myself back in the role of daughter. By this stage in life, I should be the one mothering a child, not the other way around; surely I ought to be able to fend for myself? Ah, the voice of self-pity. But the truth was I was not able to fend for myself, as all that I had earned recently had gone into supporting Danny and I as we lived out the "house in the country" fantasy. I was broke, in more ways than one, and I sensed that mum and dad were only days away from broaching this particular subject. For now, it would have to wait.

A couple of quiet days passed as I settled into my once familiar territory. My parents lived in a detached two-bedroom bungalow on the outskirts of town, complete with their beloved caravan neatly parked on the front lawn. Mum and dad were so house proud of their little castle, in fact there was never a time when I would describe the house as "lived in." It was always perfectly clean and tidy, a theme that extended well into the two gardens. Because their house was not very spacious I would sit at the bottom of the garden whispering into my mobile. I had my own special seat, a beautiful painted white wrought iron two-seater that was perfectly suited for a Victorian garden.

I would often sneak the odd cigarette from out of the drinks cabinet, a place where the cigarettes were hiding just in case there was the highly unlikely chance that a friend of theirs might want one. I spent a lot of time out in the garden on the mobile with Chloe fretting about my situation, as she soothed my worries and fears that I might end up living with my parents forever. Chloe was my lifeline during those days, always reminding me that there was something inside of me waiting to be born, and that she was there for me in every moment.

Mum and dad kept their distance, as mum did all she could to empty the wardrobes and drawers of my old bedroom, enticing me to unpack my suitcase. But I could not. Or rather, I would not. I felt that if I really unpacked I would remain stuck there forever, so I firmly held onto the idea that if my suitcase was nearby, one day I would eventually leave. That suitcase represented my sanity and freedom, and I am not ashamed to say that I held onto it for dear life.

Every night I unfolded the sofa bed, and like the night before I climbed into the cold, empty barren chasm that awaited me. I wasn't used to the sofa bed, it felt uncomfortable. My only comfort was my two loyal cats that would sleep with me every night without fail. Phoenix, the boy, would sleep on top of my chest while Lilly, the girl, would snuggle between my two feet. Appointing themselves as my two guardians they watched over me from dusk to dawn.

Once the lights were out, I would start crying out with a blend of loneliness mixed with despair over the elusive answer to my prayers of, "How much longer until my Beloved arrives?" I would shove a pillow against my mouth as I allowed the deep sobs to be released, calling out for my Beloved to be with me, to make a sign that he was with me. Sure enough a wave of warmth would flood through me, giving me the much-needed fuel to continue on towards the freedom from my past.

But that was all my Beloved gave me. For some reason, I had to go through this ordeal seemingly unaided. While I could subtly sense him, it was not in the way that I had felt before; where his voice once was, only silence remained. He would send me some relief when I cried out, but in a much more 'hands-off' way. As for the reviving image of my Beloved's possible embodiment known as Sananda Gabriel, that too dissolved into the hellish depths that I was falling into.

Four months had passed since France, and I was well and truly too depressed to even care about making contact with Sananda, for now the Beloved on the inside was all that I needed. The idea of entering another relationship made me what to run to the bathroom to be sick; I was *so* not ready. I knew I was entering a dark night of the soul. Even the once golden lifeline that my Beloved would absolutely manifest within seven months began to diminish and mean nothing to me anymore. One hell of a healing crisis was coming on, and I was more than ready to enter into it with whatever gumption I had left. I was well within step two—embark on a self-healing journey (concerning past relationships and sexuality).

Mum and dad did not understand my depression, and every now and again from behind my "poor me" story, I would look out and see their concern as they watched their once radiant daughter diminish into a world where they could not reach her. On my days off from teaching I would spend all my time alone sitting in the conservatory with my two feline guardians often scribbling into my diary. If I wasn't writing, then I was sleeping. The days when I had to go to London to teach were difficult as it was my job description to bring about a sense of peace and oneness for all who attended class. Miraculously, I somehow always managed to pull it off, and it was during those times that I actually found I forgot all my troubles and woes. When I was teaching, something would come into me and temporarily transform all my human suffering, and in its place was a radiant being-ness that shone through my form. As soon as I finished teaching and boarded the train back to Newbury, it would all come rushing back again.

There was nothing I could do, as I knew I had to go through this alone. This was a crucial stage of the initiation of 'getting ready' for the Beloved to show up and enter my life in a very big way. I had to transform all of my past relationships, healing all and every disappointment that I had ever encountered. I had to be completely whole when I met him.

As the weeks passed a little bit of my usual life force returned, (a sign that I was coming out of this healing crisis). I guess it was simply a matter of time, rest, and meditation that caused the return of my buoyancy, which mum and dad took as their cue to begin our "family meetings." I just knew they would come in and try to "fix" everything! The subjects to be discussed were my financial situation, pension plan, and a way of meeting new friends. Dad thought it would be a wonderful idea if I came to church with him every Sunday to scout for prospective partners, as there was a group of people my own age he would love to introduce me to. Um, no thanks dad. Mum, on the other hand suggested that maybe an older man would be the wisest choice, preferably one with money, as basically, I had none, and by teaching yoga for a living, I was not likely to ever make any. How much more can one woman take?! This was brutal.

They had it all worked out. Mum took it upon herself to become my bank manager, consort advisor, and unforeseeable future planner. Dad nominated himself as staunch guardian of my entire well-being, whose skills specialized in the ruthless scrutiny of any and every male friend, whilst also being able to administer the mastery of dissecting any possible new romance with a member of the opposite sex within 48 hours max. I was too exhausted to argue, and handed over my entire life to these two people posing as my parents. I guess in many ways I found it supportive, as it was clear to me that up until this point, I had failed miserably. With a sense of surrender I decided to go with it all, not really knowing where it was leading.

As the weeks rolled into months, I began to mellow even more and at times, enjoyed being back at home hanging out with mum and dad. We all got on very well as each of us knew and played our role superbly. I was changing; even I could see and feel that. I was becoming softer, kinder, unconditionally loving, and tolerant. Nothing seemed to bother me anymore. Chloe kept her promise and made sure she sent life affirming text messages every day, as well as seeing me once a week when I was in London teaching yoga.

Unfortunately, the rest of the world wasn't as supportive. The news traveled fast that the once infamous yogini of the stars was now on her arse, living with her folks in the sleepy, backward Home Counties (the middle-class commuter belt that circles London), fifty miles outside the capital city. It became a bit of a joke that I happily entered into, using myself as an example that we never truly know what is around the next corner. I owned it all, and it felt both humbling and real. For so long I had been enjoying the supernova stardom of being a celebrity yoga teacher, it seemed only fair to experience something totally different. The lower I fell, the deeper my humility.

I spent every day in meditation to uproot deep-seated beliefs and patterns that were outdated and holding me back. I could now tangibly feel that something was beginning to lift. As autumn turned to winter, I began to notice beauty again as pure white snow fell over the softly undulating, rounded hills of England. Life was opening up, as I followed the distinct urge to start going out again to flex my social skills muscles, and to see how I got on with members of the opposite sex. There was one time in particular when I was having a drink with an old friend in London, who happened to be male, when he suggested that I needed to break the spell.

"What do you mean, break the spell?" I tipsily asked.

"Well, you are still under the spell of Danny. Until you kiss someone else, you will never be totally free from him," he replied with a mischievous glint in his eye.

"Are you suggesting that I kiss you now, here in this bar?" I joked back, not taking him seriously for a moment.

"If you had the balls you would, and of course it also depends how much you want to be free," he dared.

I stared at him in disbelief, and threw my head back laughing as I playfully slapped his knee. This was crazy; it wasn't as if I had spent the evening talking about Danny. I hadn't. Yes, we were speaking about that path of the Beloved, plus he knew all about my quest anyway. Who didn't? Even so, it felt so bloody good to be laughing again. I turned back to face him, doing my best to remain serious to see which card he was going to place on the table next.

"Well, what do you want? This is your moment to decide," he seductively teased as he took a slow sip of his drink, not taking his eyes off mine for a moment.

My God, he is serious! I looked around the Covent Garden Tapas bar to see if anyone noticed the ever-changing color of my face. I hadn't kissed anyone since Danny! It was the last few weeks before Christmas and the whole place was heaving with pre-theater merriment. The crowd was noisy and seasonally boisterous, but it was all in good spirits.

Back to the decision at hand (oh no, not those things again!), maybe he was right.

I took one steady look at him as the adrenaline pumped into my blood, and with that extra boost in my body I leaned over and gently kissed him on the mouth. I was about to pull back when he grabbed the back of my head and changed gears with the kiss. What had started off as a mildly ambitious new encounter with an old friend, turned into a passionate, rapturous embrace whilst sitting on bar stools in an over packed bar. As we kissed, I realized that the last time this happened I was twenty-three years old—full of bravado and brandy. Not too much unlike just now. After some time of examining each other's kissing skills, we naturally pulled apart and stared at one another for what seemed like a lifetime.

"There, that should do it!" he declared as we both burst into laughter, while a few people around us started clapping and cheering. Pretty soon, the whole bar had turned to see what all the fuss was about. We nodded and waved sheepishly, laughing, and enjoying the absurdity of it all. I felt a part of myself returning, the part that knew how to have fun and found happiness everywhere. Welcome back, S!

On the way home that night, I spent most of the journey frantically typing out my evening's adventures into a long-winded text to Chloe. She was astounded, as she knew only too well who my friend was. Oh it was marvelous, I felt like I was sixteen all over again, as I batted silly messages back and forth with my best friend. Yet even in my intoxicated haze my evening's escort genuinely touched me, as it was clear that he had no other agenda than to assist me in breaking the spell. I was so incredibly grateful for the wonderful circle of old friends around me. I felt blessed as I thanked God for my life and the way my parents were helping me through this challenging time. In that moment, I completely accepted where I was and surrendered to whatever was happening. With that appreciation I felt myself open up to what was next.

Chapter Eight

Inspiral Eye

Parents' Home, Newbury, Berkshire, England,
February 2009

ONTHS had now passed, as the winds of change gathered me up into her arms where it seemed, despite my earlier protests, that I was to permanently reside. It had been four months since I left Danny, and I had spent most of that time in hibernation at my parent's house. I sensed that the more I surrendered to this process and to embracing it, the more it would carry me to exactly where I needed to be.

And so, I lived under the banner of surrender, allowing life to naturally unfold, rather than pushing for things to happen before their time (which was what I was known for previously). I knew that surrender would be a key component when meeting and endeavoring to live with my Beloved. How else were two individuals going to become one? Every morning I awoke at 5am and tip-toed into the conservatory, so not to wake mum and dad, as I pushed myself through yet another sequence of yoga practices that promised to clear the past.

Afterwards I would wrap myself up in a warm blanket as I rested in corpse pose ready to receive the first rays of winter sun that danced upon my eyelids. Most mornings I would walk out into the garden allowing the barely warm sun to reflect over my face, before making my way to the kitchen to have breakfast with my parents. My life was simple. The only time I would leave my parents house was to cycle to the train station with my yoga mat over my shoulder as I boarded the train to London to teach my mid-weekly classes. Once I reached the Alchemy Yoga Studio and slipped my shoes off I would enter into a world where my problems dissolved and the greater part of me would take over.

Remember, Step Two: Prepare yourself.

During my days off I could be found swimming around head first in a stack of ancient books whose pages hinted of secret knowledge about Beloveds (sometimes known as Twin Flames/Souls). I spent every waking hour reading through the verses of exquisite love by Rumi and other Sufi poets, searching for any clues that they may have left behind on how to enter this world of the Beloved. When I had exhausted all those avenues I would turn to the Internet for a more modern day approach. Day in and day out I was building a picture, gathering the ingredients as I created a storyboard knowing that soon this sought after reality would become my own manifestation. In essence you could say I was staging a two-pronged attack. Number one: preparing myself by absorbing as much information and wisdom on previous Beloveds that I could find. And number two: delving deep into my own self-healing practices.

I grabbed all this newly discovered free time to literally resurrect myself. I introduced new ideas to widen my intellectual horizons by reading about the latest cutting edge discoveries in *New Scientist* magazine every week (a weekly journal for techie science heads), I also made sure that my body took on a whole new level of fitness so with an added zest I started going to the gym; trying out a different class every day. I changed my hair by opting for a lighter shade of blonde and going for an all out drastic restyle. I consciously decided to dress in a way that reflected the woman I was becoming. Choosing styles that oozed sensuality, rather than that of a blatant fashion victim (apart from when I was teaching yoga). I even changed my perfume from Envy by Gucci, to a more appropriate Angel by Thierry Mugler. Change was definitely in the air. I was literally remodeling myself, sculpting myself into the woman's shoes that I was destined to step into. I used every morsel of this time to remember; to get back in touch with the woman I actually was, or rather, was becoming.

I was spending as much time as I could alone to feel into the truest parts of myself that I had abandoned by being in relationship. I had always sensed that within me was a beautiful, wise, and elegant presence that was timeless and eternal. I was bored to tears with only being this woman every once and while. Now I was being asked (by myself) to fully become her, once and for all. It was a healing, truth-telling time, as I gently, yet ruthlessly saw the seemingly infinite ways I had compromised myself by falling into that feminine trap of serving her man. None of this could be blamed upon Danny as it was all my very own doing.

I discovered that I had some extremely outdated behavioral programs still running. Programs that most definitely belonged somewhere within the era of the second World War! What's a woman to do in this type of conundrum? Meditate. So, that's exactly what I did. Every day for forty consecutive days I would sit down for eleven minutes to practice a meditation that was designed to powerfully clear the past by releasing my old patterns of relating. See Meditation to clear the past (and dissolve any 'ghosts') in the Last Word section at the back of the book.

But there was something else that I added to the end of the practice.

At the end of the eleven minutes, I spent another eleven minutes in silent meditation. My intuition guided me to spend this time listening to the same piece of music every morning at a particular time. The music needed to somehow capture the feeling of when I finally got to see and touch my Beloved for the first time in the flesh. It had to be a highly intense piece where my emotions could reach a fever pitch of sensation. I knew I had to stimulate Shakti in this way every day to the point of goose bumps as a heavenly chill moved up my spine. This was an important piece of the puzzle, as it was this essential energy that would literally call in my Beloved.

Let's do the math. Eleven and eleven minutes (a super powerful number of manifestation) equals twenty-two. Twenty-two is the number of my birthday and it was also the date that I climbed the mountain. Not only that, but twenty-two is the most powerful number in esoteric circles, the number of Absolute Truth. Its qualities include a sense of honor, fulfilment, progress, elevation, and success achieved through the purification of profound energies. Yes, it was crystal clear that I had to dedicate twenty-two minutes a day to my Beloved. I would do this every morning in the conservatory upon waking, along with a new daily dance routine that I was learning from my contemporary dance classes at Pineapple, London's answer to Fame.

Step Three: Follow all impulses of Shakti.

A few weeks later, I began going out on some very casual and light-hearted dates with other men, purposely selecting them as ones who wouldn't fall into the category of my "usual type." I felt this was a wise decision, as my "usual type" was typically younger than me, highly creative, incredibly handsome in a hippy-Jesus sort of way, but totally broke, and generally had a "sell by" date that caused nothing but hardship all around. Once I switched on the signal (inwardly) that I was semi-available again, men from all walks of life began to crawl out of the woodwork. Because of all the yoga and meditation I was doing, I was coming across as being quite open and approachable. Like bees to a honey pot, they flocked in droves. Ah ha, all this healing is working—my radar was now super magnetic. All that was being asked for was to point it in the direction of my Beloved.

At first I found all this dating exciting and flattering as I got whisked from one private members bar to the other. Unexpected gifts and bouquets of roses would turn up the day after, along with a barrage of text messages that initially started off quite sweet until they ended up outrageously X-rated. I soon remembered dating meant mating, and then I kind of went off the idea pretty quickly. I was all up for 'breaking the spell with a kiss,' but having sex was totally out of the question. I was completely committed to healing all my sexual relationships, not adding more wood to the fire.

In fact, I found the whole dating game rather boring for many reasons, including that the depth of conversation wasn't there. After awhile of listening to their latest self-congratulatory achievements and the ways on how to get rich quick, I switched off. There was no passion or that certain "Je ne sais quoi," French for "I don't know what," on these dates. Certainly nothing like the exploits of the girls from *Sex in the City*. I knew within minutes that they were not my Beloved, so there was no point taking it further. Yes, it was fun and in many ways I was flattered by all the attention, but at the end of the day I knew I wasn't being true to myself. So I made it quite clear that I wasn't available for anything serious and that I was seeing other men, other than them. Ha! That wasn't a popular idea. One-by-one they fled in the opposite direction as soon as they knew they weren't number one. I quickly turned back to myself, back to my study of Beloveds and Sacred Union, and, of course, towards the more unconditional forms of love from Phoenix and Lilly, my beautiful cats.

Parent's House, Newbury, Berkshire, England,
February 22, 2009

It was a surprisingly warm Tuesday morning, as the typical English seasons were beginning their yearly cycle two months early. Papers, books, and paintings were strewn all over my bedroom. I was consumed with a vigor that was verging on madness. My days were spent getting my teeth into a rather psychedelic painting of Mary Magdalene while researching past historical Beloveds and the creation of Sacred Marriage between two souls, also known as Divine Union. I had been sailing dangerously close to becoming a complete hermit as I was totally consumed with my divine marriage studies and research. I was dancing with an uber obsession for Sacred Union and loving every minute of it. My only connection with the outside world was now via my Mac—constantly online, FaceBooking (one hit and you are instantly addicted!), emailing, chatting, instant messaging.

My painting was suddenly interrupted by the familiar bleep that an instant message had arrived for me on the cyber crack house that I call FaceBook. I rolled my eyes up, as the cyber seduction caught me once again. Without putting up a fight, I abandoned my work and reached over to turn the screen towards me.

"Thank you for befriending me."

I checked to see who the message was from, and nearly fainted on the spot. My heart leapt into my mouth. I had to pinch myself. How the hell did he find me on FaceBook? Hang on a second, was I seeing things? This was unbelievable, and reeked of a mystical illusion. I had been so engrossed with my painting and wrapped up in my imagination that this IM on FaceBook could well be a full-blown hallucination. How else could you explain this miraculous phenomenon? As SANANDA GABRIEL had just sent me an instant message, and we were not even FaceBook friends.

I felt as if I was traveling through a wormhole backwards as I tried to make heads or tails of the situation. My consciousness scanned the akashic records and all other universal scribes of action, word, and deed of the recent FaceBook action I had taken (you think I'm kidding, right? It's all true!). The ridiculously unexplainable truth is that I did not ask him to be my friend on FaceBook, as I didn't even know he was a member. So, who did? The Universe perhaps? I suppose we'll never know. But, in any event, he was online messaging me at this very moment!

I tentatively peeked to see which of my friends were also currently online on FaceBook and sure enough *he* was there. He really must have just sent that message. My blood pressure rose, along with the corners of my mouth as I grinned from ear to ear.

Could I be so bold to imagine that he may be waiting for an immediate reply? I typed out various smart and clever responses and deleted them all. This was crazy. I had to strike now while he was close by, hovering around in cyber space. "Ah, what shall I say? I have to appear sexy, intelligent, and fun all within a couple of sentences!" In the end, I went for the gold, and typed what was really on my mind in that moment.

"Hi, do you happen to know of anyone who teaches specifically about the path of the Beloved in sacred union, I am looking for an authentic teacher or author that really knows this subject," I typed.

I was hyper curious to receive his reaction. I knew that we somehow had a massive connection (hadn't everyone said he was the male me?!), but I was wondering, would he feel it too? Beloveds know who their other is deep within their soul. What often happens is that the first moment when they actually meet' and start interacting with each other in a human way, can often be a bit, how can I say—cumbersome. Suddenly you have no interpersonal skills whatsoever. All the many stylish and sophisticated ways of engaging with someone you are madly attracted to seem to fly aimlessly out the window. I knew deep down that the only way I would know for sure was to meet him face-to-face. Oh my, even that thought sent a bolt of lightning through my body that had enough voltage to light up the whole of London for the rest of the year.

Minutes passed as I fixated on the screen, almost burning a hole into the box window to see whether the little pencil would start moving indicating that he was writing a message back. I considered my question and wondered whether I had gone too far and had moved too quickly towards a highly intimate subject matter. Well, why not, I told myself. If that freaks him out, then so be it, I really have no time to lose on silly conversations. Somehow it felt right to ask him that question; it was as if he was the only one in the world who could give me an answer.

"That subject is for somewhere more private. You don't know who could be watching us."

"What? That's… interesting," I thought to myself. Either he is testing the waters to see whether there is an opportunity of a date on offer, or he is a complete conspiracy freak. Even if he was crazy, his last comment caused a stir as I looked around the room halfway expecting some man in black to be spying on me from the window. What *exactly* did he mean by that? More importantly why was I looking around the room? I smiled at the silliness of it all. My God, look at the effect he is having on me already!

We began to communicate via FaceBook IM and he went on to explain what I had already discovered; that there was no teacher, that it was a secret path, and the only way to discover the path of the Beloved was directly. In fact, the last time it was taught was with a few select initiates two thousand years ago. I knew he was referring to Jesus Christ and Mary Magdalene, Solomon and Sheba, and the Egyptian (and Atlantean) archetypes of Osiris and Isis. As we continued, I felt my heart burning with love, and when I closed my eyes I could feel that all I had ever longed for was now moving closer to me. All my life I had prayed for this conversation, another I could speak with about this, clearly and authentically. Now it was beginning to unfold. Only now did I understand that this subject is not one that can be studied or even taught. Only by meeting the Beloved could all this ever be known.

As we were speaking, I began to open up another window online so I could see his website, and perhaps move the conversation onto other engaging subjects. I noticed that he taught various forms of Tantra, Christ Consciousness, and Feminine Spirituality. He was clearly my type of guy, as these were exactly the same three subjects that got me out me of bed every morning. I continued to look around his site (why I never did it before, I'll never know!) noticing that he also taught ancient Egyptian wisdom, and was heavy into the use of sound and mantra. This was crazy! This was all the stuff I was into. It was uncanny, as well as slightly amusing.

I found myself feeling like he was perfect in every way—as though I had designed and created him myself. In that moment, I hurtled back to my early teenage years to a time in my bedroom when I sat with pen and paper and had done exactly that. For a moment I flushed with knowing, before I moved onto his events page, and was dumbstruck a second time, as throughout the year we were both heading to the same places and venues to teach. "Oh man this is crazy, we are like mirror images of each other," I whispered to myself not truly coming to grips with the reality that was presently unfolding.

I pulled back for a moment to center myself as I attempted to get a handle on what was happening. Okay, let's look at this straight. We have separately planned to travel across the world, visiting the exact same countries and holding retreats in the exact same venues. But for some weird reason like ships passing in the night, we always just miss each other by a slip of a few weeks. I breathed out a heavy groan, when I saw with my own two eyes how close I could have been to meeting him.

It was as if we were riding the same wave, but weren't coming together at any point along the way. I wondered whether Beloveds moved in the same concentric circles, orbiting one another from afar; just close enough to be able to feel one another's presence. Because let's face it, I had certainly felt his. I lingered on this thought for a minute longer until I felt the confirmation within my heart that this was often the case. Beloveds do in fact rotate around one another well in advance before their physical meeting. It is in their nature to do this, as they are two halves of the same soul.

Before returning back to the conversation I could not help noticing that he called himself, "a radical and revolutionary spiritual catalyst." It felt to me as if he transformed others through the process of rapid and unadulterated change. He felt exciting and pretty wild. Nice combo. I was extremely satisfied with my preliminary observations, and so moved on to the next stage. Photo's of Sananda. Swoon. "My god, he is so handsome," I sighed to myself. He did have that hippy-Jesus look I was normally drawn to, but this time he had a certain depth in his eyes that bewitched me suggesting a maturity of being that I longed for. His face enchanted me the first time I saw him on his website over four months ago, now when I saw him again I realized I was hopelessly captivated, utterly transfixed, and deliriously enraptured. I had it bad. From a website picture no less.

Thud! With a heavy heart I then realized I would not get to meet him in the near future, as he was based in Hawaii, (damn that rumor was true!) and seemingly traveled all over the world. I was based in England and was doing the exact same circuit, a couple of weeks after him. I worked it out in my head, and it was possible that I could meet up with him in Egypt in September of that year. But, that was over six months away!

"Well, perhaps we could see each other sooner than that?" he wrote back.

"How, I am right outside London and not going anywhere until I leave for France in March?" I replied.

I shall never forget the words that appeared next, "I am in London…"

What? But I thought you were in Hawaii? I inwardly screamed and *nearly* typed out.

I felt a wave of excitement as the miraculous dawned upon me. This was truly amazing, as the reason I had almost given up on him was because I thought he lived a million miles away. As excited as I was to meet him, in the back of my mind was the knowledge that we both had full schedules that panned out throughout the whole year. There seemed to be no space to be together. What with our combined travel itinerary's we would be lucky to spend a couple of days together throughout the course of a year!

But now, I was hearing something different. Now I was hearing that he was in London, and suddenly the idea of a few days together throughout the course of a year didn't seem too bad after all. I filled with a ravenous hope that I would get to see him sooner rather than later. Life can be so sweet, I had no idea this was going to happen when I woke up this morning. Even before any arrangement had been made I was repeating over and over, "My God, thank you."

Sure enough the words I longed to read appeared, "Would you like to meet up in the next couple of days?"

There was an explosion! It was my heart.

Yes, yes, yes, pounded throughout my entire body. I was completely overjoyed as we arranged to meet five days later at 4pm in a café called Inspiral, in London's infamous Camden Town. I was reeling with possibility and a sense of finally getting to meet him. Inside, I was tossing and turning with squirming butterflies and jitters. It was amazing; talk about being on cloud nine, it felt more like nine trillion.

Then, he dropped this bomb on me, "I have been feeling you in my consciousness for some time now. I have been aware of your hair and your body in my meditation."

He had been aware of my presence. This confirmed the orbiting theory, and now I knew why. For two weeks he had been staying in London, which was only forty miles from Newbury, and even less than that when I was teaching in the city. And my hair? Well, it's a wild mane of golden curls, a veritable fleece of knots and cascading ringlets that is often completely out of control. It is very noticeable, especially when I am sweaty, sleepy, or running around wild in nature. I can't imagine why my hair would show up in his meditations though! And my body... what was *that* about?

On my end, I had felt him forever. I had known of his existence since I was a child. I didn't know it was Sananda, this wondrous man messaging me. It was more the absolute knowledge that one day I would be graced to meet my Beloved. I had loved him forever as flesh on earth. And my prayer, over and over again was to simply meet him.

Even so, I couldn't fully bridge the gap that this Sananda was "The One," although my heart wished it to be so. I was experiencing a crazy cosmic tug of war. My mind stood firm in its belief of "no, it's too good to be true" and my heart swelled with passion as it declared "yes, it is him." So much for the power of meditation, eh? When you meet "The One," you fall to pieces. Within my progressive state of falling to pieces, I created a form of mental protection shielding my heart from being hurt. Because of this (and in an absolutely brilliant form of self-protection) I casually skipped over the piercingly intimate comment about my hair, and moved onto something else. How's that for embracing "The One?" I was clearly scared out of my mind.

After we closed our conversation, all I could do was fall back onto the floor and sigh deeply. I was astonished at how fast this was all happening. Somewhere in the recesses of my mind I heard a voice. "Check the date; look to see what day it is." I bolted upright. Its February 22, it's a Wednesday. Then, I got it. Like two atoms being smashed together within the Large Hadron Collider at warp speed—in came the epiphany. It is seven months *to the day* since I climbed the mountain in France! Oh, my dear god. On today of all days, he stands true to his word and makes contact with me.

Exactly like he promised he would.

My brain fired off a trillion neurons per second as I went mentally in search of the possible spectral reasons, ways, whys, and, hows this was happening. I collapsed onto my bed and began to drift in and out of times and places, as a swirl of images and voices enveloped me. This lasted a good hour or so, until I was able to slowly get up and get back to my painting. I reached for my mobile as I urgently scrolled down my list of numbers looking for Chloe's. I knew she was with new clients all day, so I sent her a clear and direct one liner. "I have met him. Call Me! X." I felt drunk and deliciously happy as I picked up my brush and added a new layer of sensuality to Magdalene's form upon the canvas. I had no idea what to do, what was going to happen, or how I would truly feel when I saw him. But it didn't matter. I was drunkenly surrendered, happily relaxed, contagiously merry, and thrilled to go with the flow.

A few hours later Chloe called as she ran down the street with one arm in her coat, rushing between appointments. It seems every time I meet her for lunch that's exactly how she leaves the office. Nine times out of ten, she never does quite manage to get the other arm through before she excitedly drops herself into the seat opposite me.

"Tell me everything in less than three minutes!" she cried.

So I told her all the details, all on one breath. FaceBook, Sananda, London, my blonde hair, possible men in black spying and Beloveds…

She was wild with excitement, as she bustled into people along Oxford Street. I could hear her apologizing every three seconds, which made me laugh and smile even more. Yeah, she was definitely doing the one-armed coat thing. Just before she hung up, she said those three little words, the ones you don't *really* want to hear, but the ones a best friend has to say anyway.

"Be careful, Bare."

I was not listening.

The next day I had a hair appointment, which was brilliantly timed as this meant I would get to see Sananda for the first time with absolutely fabulous hair. Just then, the same London number rang my Blackberry three separate times, as I was sitting in the salon. I am never a person to speak in public on the phone; it seems far too rude and ungraceful, especially with a ton of bleach on your hair wrapped up in foil. I was curious, though, as I didn't recognize the number. It felt important.

At last, a voicemail was left. Now speaking on the phone and retrieving messages are two different things (as everyone who knows mobile etiquette is aware) I grabbed the phone, dialed 123 and waited to hear who the message was from. I closed my eyes and sank deeper into the salon chair. I let out a murmur of delight as

Karen, my stylist, stopped what she was doing, turned to look at me and asked, "Did you just get some good news?"

Ohh… yes, I got some divinely good news. I pressed the number three on my phone so I could hear the message again and again. I was swimming with tantalizing thrills as I heard Sananda's voice speaking into my ear (he must have gotten my number off of FaceBook!), asking whether we could meet the very next day in the same place. He was on his way out, so was there a chance to meet sooner? I would have to confirm right away.

Dilemma, as I don't speak on my mobile in public, especially not to the love of my life for the very first time with a tinfoil helmet on my head. You never know, with his spiritual abilities, he may well be able to see me through the phone, and trust me—this look would not work for him. I still had three hours left at the salon, three hours that burned into my soul as my fingers caressed my mobile. Karen was curious as she began to fire a hundred questions per hour in my direction. I felt like I was sitting on a huge volcano that threatened to blow. I could barely hold it in a moment longer. I wanted to tell the whole world!

I did manage to hold back, making sure that these precious buds of possible love did not receive any unwanted attention from other people. When I was younger I read somewhere that the world's greatest lovers hid themselves away from the maddening crowds during the early days of their love affair. It kept their blessed love protected from other people's opinions and projections. It made sense to me then, as it does now. "Love blooms away from prying eyes," echo's the timeless poetic advice from Rumi. So I kept a tight lip, but gave some of what I was feeling away with a huge giggling smile as I stared into the mirror with wonder and disbelief. I felt alive.

I raced home and grabbed the landline as I dialed the number he left me. His mother picked up the phone. Bloody hell, I wasn't expecting that! Without hesitating I put on my most perfect and sweet sounding, well-educated English accent. Sananda had left for the day so I had missed him. I asked her to take a message should he return, as I would be at Inspiral at 4pm tomorrow (Friday). I would be there no matter what. Just in case he didn't get the message I flipped open FaceBook, and sure enough there was a message waiting for me. I replied straight back, with a 'Yes I will be there.'

As I sat nervously waiting at the Inspiral canal side café on Friday afternoon searching the face of everyone who entered the doors, I began to sense that Sananda wasn't going to show up. I knew it might be a bit touch and go, as I didn't confirm directly with him that I would be able to make our meeting earlier. It was so strange as usually I would have been annoyed, even though it must have been a genuine mistake that I sat alone. Something reassured me that all was in divine order.

I took the extended opportunity to soak in the café—I loved Inspiral. It was right across the road from Alchemy and was becoming quite hip as it was London's first raw food café and art gallery. It was a thriving hub of creativity; downstairs was the psychedelic art gallery while upstairs was the DJ decks that selected the exact right music for any mood. The clientele were mostly artsy muso types, with a few young European tourists desperately wanting to be part of the scene as they hung out drinking juices.

Just as I considered leaving the most bizarre sensation began to move within me. I felt that someone was close by; I felt like I had company. But I was alone on the café terrace. I checked to see, and yes, I was right, there was no one there. This was getting more and more curious. I walked over to the edge of the terrace as I peered down searching the length and breadth of the canal—no one there. The presence of Sananda moved in and was becoming almost overbearing. I swear, it felt like he was right beside me. I could feel him so strongly and smell him too. Every time I closed my eyes I could see his face gently smiling at me. He was trying to communicate with me. His presence was coming into my body like a swirling mist of delicious sensations.

He spoke to me, "I am sorry I am not with you, but I did not get the message in time. We will meet as arranged on Sunday." I was reassured. Suddenly all my nervousness depleted, leaving me feeling full of peace and gratitude that he existed, and soon, very soon we would finally meet. His presence stayed with me, as I asked, "Please do not go. Let us be together just a little longer." He smiled again, and I allowed this experience to reach back into the crevices of my mind to heal all those times I had ached for him. Whether it was in my mind, imagination, or consciousness I really do not know, but he sat there beside me as I felt him as present as any other flesh and blood person.

From Friday on, I spent the whole weekend teaching at Alchemy Yoga in Camden, which again was another interesting coincidence as I had booked it months earlier and thus in the same part of the world as Sananda without even knowing we would be brought together. Quite synchronistically, the workshop title was "Dissolving Past Relationships," and was an all out winner as it fully booked every time I taught it. There were twenty-two students (that number again!) and a mixture of mostly women with a handful of men thrown in for good measure. For two days I was completely absorbed as we opened chakra's, cleared them out, and totally erased all evidence of past partners via the practice of Kundalini Yoga. It was an electric weekend; everyone gave 100 percent in their efforts resulting in the studio becoming a cauldron of Shakti and joy. I worked everyone long and hard, and as Sunday arrived my students bathed in my extending field of happiness and joy as the countdown to 4pm began. You just know when you are on form, and I sure felt it.

After the yoga workshop, I hurriedly began to pack up to go to the changing rooms to get ready. However, the students who attended had other ideas. There was a queue of people loaded with questions and reports on their experiences. It is my natural way to hang around after class and spend intimate time with them, and they knew this, but today I had to go.

All I could do was announce that I was to meet the most important person in my life, and that I had to hurry out. Ah, big mistake! Instead of backing off, they swarmed in closer. Who, where, when, how, followed by endless smiles and hugs. Because of the contagiousness of it all, I could hardly blame them; a bubbling joy was filling the room. I just laughed, as more enticing excitement and anticipation filled the air.

Finally, I was able to pull myself free. Running through the raw food café of the yoga studio, I glanced at the clock: it was 3:45pm. I screwed up my face as I was now going to be late. I showered and changed at Olympic speed. The guys behind the counter wolf whistled as I walked through the yoga studio affirming that the crumpled satin and antique lace cream dress with alpaca crochet shawl from Stella McCartney was working in a big way. I winked back at them as I perched my cream tweed trilby hat to one side like a 1940's starlet and made my way towards Inspiral in what seemed like slow motion. It was only five minutes away, yet it felt as if I was walking through thick mud.

Come on, walk woman. You're already late!

Bleep, it was a message from Chloe, "Good Luck Bare, remember, be careful."

Ah, stop saying that I thought to myself, as I kissed the phone thanking her for remembering my big date.

Everything seemed surreal as I watched my hand reach out and open the door into the café. I slowly glanced around the ground floor, moving my eyes over faces, heights, weights, and genders. Because this was Inspiral, strategically positioned in the center of Camden Town, every representative of pop culture could be accounted for. This was the crème de le crème of London's rebels and postmodern cultural revolutionaries. Sitting side-by-side were anarchic punks, grisly Goths, heroin chic-ers, and hard-core ravers. But I wasn't looking for a person like that; I was looking for a dark-skinned, possibly Israeli looking man, with long, dark tousled hair.

Thumping ambient sounds drifted through the café seeking to distract me, but I was focused. Within half a second, I was drawn towards him like a heat seeking missile. I had found my target. All clocks across the planet stopped, birds stopped mid-flight, cars ground to a halt, and I caught my breath. Well, maybe not quite, but in my mind that is exactly what happened. His eyes instantly met mine, as we nodded our recognition. I had to propel myself forward, as my legs had turned to stone. I quickly remembered my most elegant, sensual walk as I beautifully approached his table and sat down. I put down my bag and adjusted my hair as I apologized for being late. I didn't even think to order anything. I just sat there and looked at him. We smiled at each other and at the same time said, "Hi."

As I got a closer look, I could see that he was in fact Indian and was undeniably handsome. Long, dark wavy hair flirted with his shoulders, as my eyes searched further across his face. There was no hint of his age, however at a guess he felt like he was in his forties. He seemed so mature, so settled in himself, so sure, strong, powerful yet so deeply loving. It was obvious I was with a man, when I have been so used to boys.

He gently took my hand and looked into my eyes. I looked back with not a hint of shyness. I became transfixed as I gazed deeper and deeper into those brown eyes that once looked at me from the safety of his website. His eyes burned their way into my entire lifetime, the more he looked, the more he saw. Time floated by, people came and went, the light of day moved into dusk. Hours passed. I received glimpses of endless emotions in his eyes; hope, sadness, passion, pain, love, recognition, and sorrow. Sometimes the force of love was so strong that I imagined myself reaching out with my hand to caress his cheek. We spoke together with our eyes and our hearts, as our fingers caressed and squeezed each other's hands.

Occasionally he would speak, and I would answer, usually with one word. Then, we'd return to gazing long and liquidly at one another. My heart was aflame, as I saw myself dancing around a fire deep within the desert. I saw our reunion in Palestine, in France, in Ireland. I witnessed our many lifetimes together end in agonizing pain as we became physically separated from one another. Finally, I saw the light of our one soul be pulled into two and catapulted into opposite directions within the dark void of space. With this image, a single lone tear fell from my eye.

He saw this, and for a moment he knew what I was seeing. His eyes winced and I swear he nodded as if to say, "Yes, I know." That was it, that was the final nail in the coffin of my resistance to thinking this was a casual meeting of two minds (or hearts, rather). This was a meeting of a lifetime. The café blurred into a collage of color and sound as we swam through endless scenes and memories together

In the midst of all this drunken bliss and revelation, I discovered that something else was present way beyond sexual attraction. If I could possibly describe it, I would say that all I wanted was to be held by him; I wanted to climb inside of him, to pull apart the two bodies that encased us. I wanted to smell him, listening to his breathing as I lay in his arms for the rest of my life. I trusted him. His eyes were gentle, yet also infused with a passionate fire. I knew in that moment that this man was wild, free, and uncompromising, and if I were to be at his side, I would be expected to be the same.

After an eon of gazing into each other's eyes and souls, from nowhere he asked me a question that brought me crashing back into the present day.

"Are you ready to be radical?"

With full authority and certainly I declared a wholehearted, "Yes."

He smiled, and went on to tell me that I needed to open my womb, work through the seven gates, and take in more black light. That I also had two jewels within my womb, that I was too nice and sweet, and needed to work with my shadow. Excuse me, what did you just say? I inwardly asked. Womb? How could he know such a thing? Black light, shadow, jewels, and seven gates? What on earth was he speaking about? With confidence I reassured him that I was more than well acquainted with my shadow, and that my womb was open and healthy. He laughed as he shook his head, "No, you need to discover more. You need to not be so nice!"

Interesting request. I was practically world-renowned for my niceness. I have never been asked not to be nice. Did he know what he was getting into? Beneath my "niceness" there was a wicked Irish temper, not only that but I had been famous in my previous romantic relationships for my Ice Queen tactics when the inevitable, "I have lost interest in you" phase set in. For now the comment regarding my womb got in first. I asked him how I could open my womb, as I had read that this was the way in for Sacred Union. I was all ears awaiting his wisdom, as well as a little cynical as how a man could tell a woman anything about her womb. He didn't even have one.

I asked about the seven gates, what was he referring to? He informed me that the seven gates were the clitoris, g-spot, cervix, and so on until you reach deep into the galactic center of the womb; the heart of a woman's creative potential and sexuality. He warned me that a woman needs a conscious man to open the fourth gate, and only by being in union together can they open gates four to seven. It is not a journey that can be taken alone, only ever in sacred union. He stated strongly that trust, consciousness, and love must be genuinely felt within both parties, otherwise the fourth gate would not open.

Whoa, maybe he does know his stuff. I was transfixed.

Hallelujah, I have found a person who knows about the techniques that I barely knew existed. I crossed my legs as I moved in with more questions. But now, he was having none of it and my words fell onto deaf ears. I was left hanging in silence.

Is he offering his services? Is there a hint of flirtation here? Is this a trick to seduce me? Is this a test to see where I'm at spiritually? I really couldn't tell what was at play. My mind skittered out of control, and again he laughed at the ridiculousness of it all. I too smiled, as if caught again by my obsessive thinking. I breathed in, settled again, and reveled in what could only be an ocean of recognition and familiarity. I didn't care whether he wanted me or not. I was utterly content to know him.

Dusk drifted into early evening, and in a rush of realism I glanced at the time. What? Two and a half hours had passed staring into each other's eyes, with merely a few minutes of talking. I needed to catch a train home. He noticed this, "Do you have to leave? I was hoping we could take this further."

Gulp. On your marks, get set, go! My mind picked up the previous pace of a million and one questions, excuses, reactions, the works. You name it, I thought it! No, no, I really do need to go, I told myself. Be strong, pick up your bag, and adjust your shawl. You madam, are leaving NOW!

Our meeting was so intense. I could only take him in bite size pieces at this stage. I swear to god, it felt as if I wouldn't be able to bare being with him for too long. It felt like we were creating a force field that was made of gigantic proportions whose energy promised to fry every brain cell in the process. It was electrifying and very disorientating. We stood to say goodbye to one another, and I nearly lost my balance. Oh my god, his embrace was to die for. This mammoth of a man reached out and took me in his arms. Delivering the chance to smell him, to rest against him, and to hold him. The warm nectar of trust and familiarity bathed and reassured me. My heart bubbled with an ancient, long lost love that was hinted at being reconciled. I knew him, I simply knew this man through and through. A wave of melancholic sadness squeezed my heart as I drank in his presence sensing the eons of time that we had been separated.

I winced at the idea that this might be the one and only time I get to hold him. I reluctantly remembered the supposed curse of the Beloveds, how they only ever get to spend a fraction of their existence together in physical form. How their reunion is short-lived, abruptly over by some unforeseen tragic ending. "Oh, stop being so dramatic and stay with the present moment!" I reminded myself.

He moved towards me. We gently kissed each other on the lips. It was a tender kiss; close enough for me to feel the warm exhale from his nostrils. The kiss hinted at going nowhere other than a kiss of tenderness and warmth. I was entranced, I was lost, and I was found all in one moment. I turned to walk away but first waved one more goodbye. It was also a good reminder of just how " nice" I was. God, what was I doing?!

Well, one thing I was doing was bursting at the seams with a bountiful radiance. I glided to Paddington station as if in a dream just in time to make the train. I grabbed a window seat and dropped into its velvety embrace. After a few deep breaths, I leaned against the window as I closed my eyes to reevaluate the day's events. He was still so evidently with me. There was no gap between us being together and this moment now. It was just as intense as it was in the café. It was unbelievable; my body was electrifyingly alive and pulsating. I was incredibly aware of warmth surging through my womb and a heart-like loop of energy. I could still feel Sananda, it was as if he was under my skin, breathing, and moving. I could still smell him and still taste those full lips and the brush of his goatee.

Oh, this is getting silly.

We had left physically, but our bodies had somehow remained joined. I began to go over his comments and wondered: what was he really suggesting? Yes, I was willing to be radical. I had waited for this chance to be challenged and stretched to the fullness of my potential. But a burning question remained.

Was he suggesting that he could take me through the fourth gate? How would he do this? Energetically, like some form of healing, or... was he suggesting that we physically make love? I didn't want to jump to any conclusions, as this was a spiritual man, who was known the world over for his teachings and books. There was no way he was hitting on me, right? Wrong! Inside I knew the truth. Yes, he was very much suggesting this. Only a blind fool could think otherwise. I laughed out loud, forgetting that I was still on the train. Oh my, this was too much!

As soon as I realized that the cards were well and truly on the table, my heart shield went up and clasped into place in an effort to protect me from being hurt. I tenderly acknowledged that I was afraid. I knew how deeply I could (could?) love him, and my God I was so going to put my heart on the line. The potential for getting hurt was colossal. This was going to be big, no huge, no infinite. I knew that I was going to fall in love in a way that even I couldn't imagine. As much as I wanted this, I still experienced fear. Although the protective heart shield was on, filtering out any potential for getting hurt, I knew that even the heart shield would soon have to go.

After contemplating this inevitability I discovered that I was more than willing; I was ready to do all that life asked of me. I needed to know about Sacred Union, the process of how two become one, I simply had to find out where all of this was leading to. I felt a swell of commitment and steadfastness. I was in! I sent Chloe a message that was jam packed with the whole evening's experience. She called me straight back, but because I was on the train I couldn't really speak. I answered her call explaining that I was on the train and could I call her...

"Time to get over your phone phobia Bare, this is really important," she demanded. Reluctantly I agreed that she could ask all the questions and I would give one-word answers. It was hilarious, and it went something like this:

"Was he sexy?" Err... yes.

"Do you fancy him?" Err... possibly (What a mammoth lie! But too late as that heart shield was in place.).

"Is he enlightened?" Not sure.

"Is he The One?" Yes.

"Are you seeing him again?" For sure.

"Have you arranged it?" No.

We hadn't formally arranged to meet again. There was no need, as wild horses couldn't stop us from seeing each other again. It was already firmly destined to happen, and through the feelings in my body I knew we had never actually left one another. After a two-hour journey on the train, I was lying in my sofa bed and settling down for sleep. Again that surge flowed through my body. The smell and the taste came to life again. In my half sleepy state I asked out loud, *"Are you still with me, Sananda?"*

An even stronger pulsation coursed through my body. Which was all the confirmation I needed. I knew that he was doing some kind of energetic lovemaking from a distance, disregarding all laws of nature, time, and space. I giggled to myself, although I had only just met him, it didn't surprise me one bit that this was happening, being the expert 'womb man' that he was. Speaking of which, the more I tuned into my womb, the larger it grew! It felt like it was becoming an inflatable balloon that was expanding by the second. While it might sound like a painful occurrence, it wasn't. In fact, it was unexpectedly pleasurable and incredibly grounding as all my thinking 'head' energy sunk like a stone to the center of my womb. I felt so lightheaded and empty-brained; it was brilliant to experience the ultimate spiritual goal of so-called enlightenment—no thoughts whatsoever. Ha! It was easy, just enter your womb space. Who knew?!

The expansion continued on much to my amazement (I had forgotten that wombs hold babies, and this was actually a piece of cake for my body), so within my surrendered state I released all barriers, allowing whatever was meant to be, to be. I felt him moving throughout my entire body, including my heart and brain as his presence expanded, filling me completely with his life force. He was inside of me; there was no denying this. I can't explain how or why, it was simply the truth.

Oh my love, my love, what is happening? I communicated to him.

I heard his voice reply, *We are still together my love; we have never left one another in all these eons of seemingly being apart. I have waited for you, and you have waited for me. I swore to you that I would be with you within seven months, and here I am.*

I was astonished again, as I was reminded that the prophecy was true.

In that moment Prudence's words rung in my ears:

"The legend continues that whoever walks up that mountain, reaches the top, and sincerely prays to find The One, will do so within one full year."

I searched my mind for further evidence during the fateful day that I climbed the mountain, and suddenly remembered the time when his presence warmed my right side as if he was walking right beside me.

"I will be with you within seven months. You have my word. To this I swear."

I turned back to present day.

Sananda darling, are you aware of how much I could love you should you permit me the chance? Is this where all of this is leading? I assure you it's huge; it's more than I could ever imagine it to be. Just say the word, and it shall begin. To end this life without loving you would be a life lost in vain.

Deep within my consciousness I heard the words:

"I invite you, come to me. I could say let it begin, but it has already..."

Chapter Nine

High Heels in Mud

Chloe's House, Muswell Hill, London, March 2009

F OR THE WHOLE WEEK we had been making love, not physically, but at a distance. I felt him almost every moment of the day, deliciously rising and falling within me and in the infinite depths of my soul. He was a constant presence, even though we only spoke once or twice on Skype (calls ranged from anywhere between one to three hours, giving us enough time to arrange our next meeting for the following Sunday, one week since we last saw each other). Time, space, and bodies were transcended and becoming a thing of the past as I merged with this man more and more. Just by thinking of him, resulted in him being there. I would talk with him, muse with him, laugh with him, play with him. Every night I would fall into his arms as he held me. It was incredible considering I was in Newbury and he was in London.

Chloe was beside herself with concern as I tried my hardest to explain all of this to her over the phone. She interrupted my cosmic story telling one night and asked me to carry on where I left off by staying over the next night when I was in London. She demanded that it was now time for a love conference call—she couldn't take any more of this via the phone waves. She was due to leave for New York for six weeks to piece together the final deal on some property in downtown Manhattan. She anxiously needed to see me before she left, even if it was just to make sure I was okay and relatively normal. As far as she was concerned, I had entered some kind of bewitching dream and was out of touch with reality.

I thought all of this was hilarious, and so when I arrived at her home the following evening, I decided to exaggerate it even more by rolling around on her baby blue sheepskin rug like some kind of fifties pin-up star. I teasingly played with my hair as I lifted up one shoulder making a sexy face, as I overemphasized the words "Isn't it great?" whenever she told me I had lost my mind. This drove her mad and drove me on, enjoying our little game of exasperated ecstasy. In the end she gave up, waving the white flag of surrender. "Okay, you win. What's he like?"

Like a ravenous beast, I turned to her with wild eyes and glistening teeth, filling her in on every little detail. Finally after two hours I allowed her to go to the bathroom for a break, before I began again. I told her all about our mysterious constant connection and how I felt him everywhere! I explained in great detail how this made me feel. Now that we were face-to-face, I delivered the complete lowdown of what it was like to meet him during our first date. I ended it all with the themes and topics of conversation we had already covered, even though we had only shared two telephone calls.

She listened in near disbelief at the sheer pace of it all. She couldn't fathom that we could move this quickly towards intimacy. She kept shaking her head in disapproval, sipping her wine—maybe it was more like gulping actually—whenever I told her how much I loved and trusted him. To Chloe, the speed of our reunion did not compute or make any sense whatsoever. This was alien territory for her as she was more accustomed to the, 'treating them mean, to keep them keen' type tactics. Eventually after a heated debate we had to agree to differ over our style of men and our relationships with them.

∞

Avebury Stone Circle, Wiltshire, England, March 2009

The following Sunday Sananda and I arranged to meet at one of England's largest, most ancient and impressive druidic stone circles, a place known as Avebury. I was eager to meet him outside of London, so that we could be in nature enjoying the sense of space and timelessness. From my parent's house Avebury took under an hour to drive to, which was no mean feat considering that the drive was incredibly beautiful. The winding roads of Wiltshire leading to Avebury were made famous by the yearly mysterious markings in the farmer's fields known throughout the world as crop circles. As the years progressed (and so did the frequency of them showing up), the term 'circles' didn't give these highly impressive, complex geometric designs the credit they deserved. They were absolutely astounding in presence and size.

Avebury was a tiny, mystical village nestled within the crop circle Mecca of Wiltshire and was on the map as the feminine stone circle of England, whereas Stonehenge was the masculine. Throughout history, Avebury had been used as a fertility and marriage sacred site; even to this day people flocked to this place to wed and conceive. And for some reason, we also felt drawn to choose this site for our second rendezvous. The meeting was to commence on Sunday at 1pm outside the gift shop in Avebury.

That morning, I woke up at 5am, did my early morning practice known as Sadhana (daily spiritual practice), which takes two and a half hours. I had now finished my previous forty-day practice, and marveled at its near miraculous results. Now I was working on opening up and clearing my communication skills (see Last Word for more info on how you can do this too!). Every morning, I sat religiously on my cream sheepskin and moved through this practice of yoga, chanting, and meditation. But on this particular morning it felt somewhat robotic and mechanical. I was ready to see Sananda, and even my practice felt like it was getting in the way.

I showered and rubbed almond oil onto my skin, and then bathed my face in ice-cold water to entice all the blood to the surface, which left me looking sensationally radiant with a bursting and rosy complexion. Because I am rather tiny in stature, (yet enormous in presence!) I selected marginally sensible high-heeled wedged leather boots to wear. I remembered how tall Sananda was, and so I wanted to appear less small as we walked around together. It was March, and damp and muddy underfoot. However, with years of experience under my belt I knew these boots wouldn't let me down even if we walked across the surrounding fields and barrows of the stone circle. I was practically a professional!

I chose an all-red outfit that comprised of a pair of skin-tight red jeans, with a simple red cotton t-shirt dress over the top. With my chocolate brown knee-length boots and caramel curls tumbling over my shoulders along with a fake red rose in my hair, I figured I had created just the right look. I wanted to knock him for six, and reveal my esoteric knowledge by wearing red, the powerful symbolic color of Mary Magdalene, Joan of Arc, and Shakti herself. I arrived well in advance, killing time by glancing around the village's one and only Celtic, pagan, and new age gift shop. This tumbling down, ye olde Tudor building stood the test of time. Although, you had to be the size of a hobbit to even get through the front door. Once inside, I was greeted with the familiar aroma of one-hundred and one different essential oils and incense sticks. Everywhere I looked there were pictures of last year's crop circles and their possible alien designers. Crystal's hung from every orifice, dream catchers dangled down from the rafters as an entourage of spiritual seekers clad in purple velvet and rainbow knit jumpers shuffled past, careful not to bump their heads.

I was so nervous and excited—all at the same time. My heart was thumping in my chest, causing my body temperature to rise. I groaned as I touched my cheeks with the back of my hand. "Oh no, I am blushing," I moaned, as I crouched down to look into the mirror expertly placed for expectant jewelry customers. The shop assistant raised one eyebrow, asking whether I was looking for something in particular. I beamed an infectious smile in her direction as I explained I was meeting a very special person. She beamed back. Oh heart, please calm down; I am sure everyone in the shop can hear you!

I continued to browse around slowing my breath down to settle my nerves, although I nearly passed out from breath retention instead. I had to laugh at my own hopeless attempts to appear sophisticated and together. I was a nervous wreck, and surprisingly enough, I didn't care. I was loving every moment of this delicious adventure.

It was 1:20pm now—where was he? ? Just as I was about to stroll around the village, he appeared from across the road. My stomach released a whole net of butterflies that skipped all over my body; tickling, and flickering. I smiled warmly at him as we walked towards each other.

I couldn't take my eyes off of him. Sananda was wearing a beautifully tailored, charcoal grey duffle coat, which was buttoned all the way to the top. He elegantly breathed into his cupped hands to warm them up. This man was delicious. His dark, tousled hair lifted with the wind as he walked, appearing for a moment like a dark Arabic King.

We embraced as my head rested upon his heart. I relaxed into him and all my tension and first-date nerves eased. Nothing needed to be said, except "Hi" as we walked towards the stones arm in arm. I was pleased at how tall I seemed beside him, smiling at my wise choice of footwear. Moments later I was cursing it.

We had walked into the Avebury field, which had been rained on the night before. This particular field is full of humps and dips, molehills, and mud. The moment I set foot on this terrain I was sliding and tumbling all over the place. I had to hold onto his arm for dear life as I could see that a complete three-hundred and sixty degree turn and roll was inevitable.

To distract him from my inability to walk like a normal person, I began to ask him about his life. Was he born a "special child" or did he become "enlightened" later in life, I innocently asked. God bless his patience, as I have no idea which was more ridiculous—my questions or my hopeless inability to walk unaided. He spoke little and often, although he seemed to enjoy my probing questions into his life's journey.

He confirmed that he was born fully aware of who he was and the reason he was here on Earth. I was impressed. It took me the best part of thirty-five years to figure that out for myself. He then went on to tell me that by the time he was four he had read the Bhagavad-Gita. Later when he was at boarding school he joyfully elaborated on how he ripped a Bible in half with a steel ruler when he was only eleven. Blimey, I guess he didn't think much about that book. In a more revered voice he spoke softly of his "Samadhi," his spiritual awakening of realizing God when he was only twenty-seven. Where else could we go after a conversation like this?

We continued on in silence, walking arm in arm around the stones as I attempted to process all he had shared. After a while he started to speak again about his teaching, his five books, and his lifetime goals, which were all destined to be fulfilled by 2012. He ended with the words "'I shall be done by that time too." That was a strange statement to make. I wonder what he meant by it? It was perfect that I was working on clear and open communication in my meditations, as a clear and direct question popped out of my mouth without my having the chance to think it through.

"What do you mean 'done' by 2012?" I probed.

He replied by telling me that by 2012, he would have fulfilled his destiny and that he would become a pure embodiment of love. Ah ha, you too, I thought. That was my spiritual goal also. I'm ashamed to say that I, too, had jumped on the spiritual bandwagon and nominated 2012 as my "Fully Awakened Day." The day that I would become completely enlightened, as I rose up in glorious streams of undulating light as a beauteous choir of angels sung of my magnificence. Wait—hang on—let's get back to reality. I decided to keep this little prize piece of information to myself, as it wasn't looking too likely in my current situation. I was parading around in wedge heels in the mud, after all. The angels and choir would have to wait.

We spent the afternoon talking and walking, simply and innocently. Neither wanting nor needing anything from each other. Earlier in the week we had agreed to spend the night together, to continue our journey. I was happy with this arrangement, as it felt right, and not contrived in any way. So we got our things and walked over to our chocolate box, picture perfect, traditionally English B&B cottage. To our utter astonishment the house was actually positioned inside the stone circle. It was incredible, the energy vortex of the stone circle would be pouring in through our bedroom! How often can you say that you slept inside an ancient Megalithic stone circle? We both looked at each other and raised one eyebrow. "Tonight should be interesting," I laughed.

We checked into our room; looking around at all the quaint little touches that made up the décor, like a white porcelain washing bowl next to a gorgeous Georgian jug painted in cobalt blue flowers, full of water should we wish to wash our hands. There were some strange family (possibly) portraits on the walls of polite young women from a couple hundred years ago sitting quietly, staring through us with Mona Lisa smiles while we put our overnight bags down. I jumped on the cast iron Victorian bed that was laden with copious amounts of white lace and a fake fur mink throw slung over the end of the bed.

After trying out a few bounces, I enthusiastically announced that it was great. He joined me on the bed as he propped himself up on one elbow. He reached for me and brought me closer. I became quiet as we looked into one another. This time I was a little braver, this time I did touch his face. I stroked the length of his hair and came to rest at his cheek, holding his face with my starving hand.

Our faces were slowly moving towards each other. He took the back of my head and gently guided my lips towards his. Our second tender kiss became deeper and stronger. Flickering flames of sexual energy began to ignite very gently, very beautifully warming my lower body as they rose up into my heart. Forget it; I was sexually attracted to him. He had now scored on all levels. I was super hooked on this man—it was official.

But, I was by no means able to sleep with him just yet. It was only the first week, it wasn't possible to move that fast, was it? I had never jumped into bed so quickly before and I wasn't about to start now. I made a promise to myself that I would remain intact. I had the will of an ox, so I knew I could handle the situation perfectly.

I allowed myself to relax and soften into the moment. The kiss was suffused with a quiet passion that didn't seem to threaten my stronghold. I noticed that I still didn't quite ignite into my full, fiery sexual nature that I had learned, developed, and crafted into a perfected fine art. I realized that this trait of mine would not be useful now. In the past I would have amped up and totally exaggerated my sexual prowess, thinking that was what all men wanted. But with Sananda I didn't feel compelled to go down that road as I knew I had to be purely myself; natural, open and 100 percent authentic. Anything that I had once relied upon would be ransacked. Already I was beginning to see what I had agreed to and was up against with Sananda was like no other man I had ever met.

After a bit of passionate kissing, we decided to go out for supper in the neighboring town of Marlborough. As the night unfolded I gleaned more information. He was thirty-four (shit, I was thirty-nine—I promised myself not to get involved with a younger guy ever again!), and was staying in London for a few more weeks before he traveled throughout Europe to teach some retreats. We also found out that we had many friends in common, and lo and behold, we were almost next-door neighbors when we both hung out in London's cool and trendy Blue Note in Hoxton Square back in 1996-97. I searched back into the storehouse of my mind. Had I seen him back then? I called up the faces of friends that we shared, and sure enough there was a slight resonance of him.

I also discovered that he lived like me. That he had no real home as such, often returning back to his mum's place in London for a few days before getting up to leave again. He doesn't live in Hawaii, he was only staying there for a couple of months as he finished writing his third book. It's no surprise really that our lives were so similar. I knew Beloveds are acclaimed to be polar opposites, but I realized now that was only in personality. In the essence of their being, they would be quite similar in lifestyle and preferences.

We raved about music, film, clubs, old friends, and the crazy outfits of our past lives in London's music and fashion scene. It was amazing to think that he was part of the Asian fusion scene that exploded in dance culture of London in the 90's. He was deejaying at the famous Blue Note club that was only five doors away from my fashion studio! It made me feel closer to him when I discovered this; narrowing the gap between highly spiritual teacher and funky human being. He was like the rest of us in many ways.

I started to tell him about all of the bands and celebrities I had dressed, and undressed (and by undressed, I mean styled). That was one of the greatest perks of being a fashion designer, you get to create and bring new life to all the most outrageous and flamboyant characters within your imagination. I told him how I once styled Bjork, The Prodigy, and many other one-hit wonder British bands. I spoke of the VIP parties and general mayhem that goes hand in hand with fashion, music, and drugs. I was really getting into the conversation, using my arms to create the stories when I noticed that he had stopped speaking and was just looking at me. I stopped speaking mid-sentence. He didn't care about all of this; this subject was not floating his boat at all. He wanted to know me now, not then, not fifteen years ago.

Our food arrived which broke the ice, as I knew I had begun to spout off about stuff that was completely out of place with a man like this. I felt silly, and slightly disappointed with myself. Again, this was a reminder that this was virgin territory for me (and us!), and to treat the beginnings of our relationship like a delicate precious bud. Not to pollute or poison it with the same old stuff from previous dating experiences.

After supper, we jumped into my red MG as we drove back to the B&B in silence, snatching glimpses of each other as we constantly kept turning our heads. Occasionally we would turn around at the same time and inevitably burst out laughing, even though I kept reminding him to keep his eyes on the road. No words were spoken, nor needed—as this expanding energy vibrated between us. We arrived at the guesthouse and grinned at each other as we made our way up to our room. I announced that I was going to run a bath, and beyond my own belief I invited him to join me! It felt like the most comfortable thing in the world to share a bath with him. It wasn't a sexual move, but rather the desire to be intimate and close.

Even so, I made it my business to get in that bath first, so I had the protected position to view his full nakedness where as he would only see my half. The bathroom was traditionally Victorian, complete with a stand-alone claw foot tub. It was decked out in all blue and white design, with an abundance of fresh flowers beside the sink. To help him (and let's be honest, me) out, I turned off the harsh lighting and lit a few select candles, which I positioned around the bath. I made sure the bathroom smelled heavenly as I climbed into the fragranced waters of spikenard and rose. (I had brought a few bottles of essential oils, knowing they would come in handy.) I called out that the bath was ready. Within moments he appeared at the doorway.

I didn't want to cause him any embarrassment, so I promised to look the other way as he got in. I don't know whether he was shy or not, I simply wanted to show that I respected him. I put my head into my hands, heard him undress, and drop his clothes to the floor. I heard his toes dip into the water as he climbed in to join me. One foot and then two, and then the full submersion, he was in.

I moved my head away from my hands and made sure I looked nowhere other than his face. Talk about concentration, I was so focused it hurt my eyes. Still, I would not look, well not yet, anyway. After a few minutes passed, it seemed okay to relax my vision a little. I managed to move on down to his mouth, throat, and then his chest. Whoa. Hold on a second. Let me linger here. What a magnificent chest; so broad, so full, with rich dark hair covering him. His shoulders were well formed, with strong arms that promised me the strength and the power to lift me up and move me into any position that he fancied. Yum! I continued to gaze on a little further down towards his belly, but that was it—no further.

Stop, back up to his face. NOW! All of this took place in a split second, giving me enough time to decide I loved his body and wanted to lose myself in it.

After finishing the bath, we moved back into the bedroom. Oh no, now what—what is the correct mode of operation here? Remember I have nothing to refer to, all my dating skills have evaporated and the thought of doing some kind of seduction number makes me want to crack up laughing. "This is ridiculous," I thought to myself. "I almost feel like a virgin. This is totally weird; it's as if all my past sexual experiences have vanished!" Then I remembered how my last forty-day meditation was to clear the past. "Oh my god, I knew the meditations were powerful, but this is crazy." I closed my eyes begging for more time before he entered the bedroom. I had to prepare! I silently asked myself, "Naked or knickers?" I selected knickers—red polka dots, frilly, and very cute if I do say so myself.

Again I made sure I claimed the bed position first, got in, and bundled under the duvet. Right before he arrived I placed a few drops of Holy Desire Essential Oil onto our pillows—a little something extra I had picked up a few weeks ago in Glastonbury. It was an oil that stimulated all the higher chakras setting the scene for a higher vibration of lovemaking. When I heard him coming, I changed position into something more natural and desirable. Now, I was ready!

Hang on before you jump to any conclusions… there are other ways of making love besides the obvious.

He dropped his towel as walked towards me smiling and climbed into bed in full nakedness. My heart leapt with anticipation. I pulled back the covers, inviting him in as I immediately poured myself into his arms, resting my head on his bed of yumminess, also known as his chest. A deep sigh left my body as yet another massive wave of tension dissolved. This was home. We belonged together in this entwined posture. This was how I would imagine us being together in my meditations and visions. Slowly, all thoughts and theory dissolved as we began to energetically merge together. The last thing I remember was communicating with him in a myriad of ways other than words.

My love, finally I find myself in your arms again. Please let this night last forever, I beg of you don't ask me to leave, not now.

I was so taken aback at how much I relaxed, almost falling asleep whilst resting on him. I wanted to stay in his arms forever. For the first time in my life I felt protected, safe, and loved. This massive man could hold me properly, just like I knew it would be. His giant arms wrapped around me, as he moved me deeper into him. I held on, wanting and getting more; more of his warmth, more of his presence, and more of his heart.

The flames of sex began to flicker and my mood changed, as I wanted his lips upon mine. We exploded into a passionate kiss as we grappled with each other's bodies, wanting, yearning for more. He grabbed my hair as he kissed my throat, I gasped as I pressed my breasts into him. I reached for his waist as I pulled him deeper towards me. We moved all over the bed in a heated frenzy that would occasionally subside, as we would stop mid-flow and immerse into each other's eyes. Then the inferno would begin again. This man reeked of passion, strength, and tenderness. Deep inside I heard the words of my feminine sexuality.

Please, yes I want you, my God, I want you. Do not stop ever.

Fill me, fulfill me as I move all of me towards you. Take me, move me, open me.

I was listening to my heart and soul yearning for union with this beauteous man. Truly longing like I had never ever experienced before. But I couldn't give it all away yet. If I did, I was afraid I would fall so deeply in love with him in a way that was irreversible. I knew I would never stop loving him and that once with him, no one would or could satisfy me again, ever. Yes, I would need a bit more time to acclimate to this intense connection.

I didn't even need to explain this to him; he must have sensed where I was happy to engage and where I was not. He did not push anything, not once. After hours of making love in new and varied ways without actually entering one another, we both fell back into bed as the night eventually claimed us. I settled into him as I rested my head on his chest and intertwined my legs around his. With every inhalation I could smell him; the scent of his skin and hair filled my nostrils and gently took me back to a place of deep comfort. It was the same kind of comfort that a child feels when being held closely by their mother, but more so.

As Beloveds (and for the future Beloveds out there) it was merely a hint of what was to come. This kind of ultimate union would one day become commonplace—being felt constantly during every waking (and sleeping) moment. For a brief second we touched a fraction of what it would be like when we eventually reunified, fully together as one being with two hearts and one soul. I felt as if nothing in the world could harm or touch me, for once I could rest like I had never experienced before. I plunged into a deep sleep as he lay silently meditating.

❧

The Morning After

A couple of hours later it was morning. During those twilight hours I drifted in and out of various memories, known and unknown. In the silence of the room that rested in the center of the Avebury stone circle, I could feel my head slowly rise and fall with his breath. Inwardly, I smiled as the memories from the day before crept back in. I drifted back to sleep, still aware of the stars above as yet another barrage of dreams filled my consciousness. I climbed higher and higher, out, into, and through the cosmos, taking my love with me, showering all of existence with joy and laughter. As I slept, I knew he was there with me, holding me closely throughout the whole night.

A beautiful dawn began to filter through the windows as the sounds of an English springtime permeated our dreams. Various animals and birds were waking up with calls of their celebration at the chance to live another day. I too began to wake up slowly, looking around the room for signs of where I was, who I was with, and how I felt. I shall never, ever, forget my first impression. I was still resting in his arms with my head upon his chest. I felt like I was home, in every sense of the word. I felt peaceful and so exquisitely relaxed. A gentle statement swam, nay escaped my mind;

This is your husband.

What? I jumped into the here and now moment. What and who just said that?!

He opened his eyes. "Good morning darling, did you sleep well?"

I stared at him like a rabbit in the headlights. Did he hear that thought? I looked at him, I mean really looked, as I asked myself: Is this really the face of my husband?

Yes.

Yikes! Another rush of adrenaline laced with love surged through my veins. My mind tried to put the pieces together. How is this even possible? He leaves London in a couple of weeks. He travels around the world and is based nowhere. I live here and have my whole life set up, how could we possibly be together? The voice of my heart soberly replied:

Trust the process. Trust all the way to the end of the road. Trust like you have never trusted before. Allow the love to come into you. This love will lead you into what you cannot yet imagine. Give yourself so completely to this journey. You have asked and you have been given. All you have done, all you have found was leading to this...

He interrupted my monkey mind as it conversed with my heart, reaching out to me and sinking his lips upon mine. I was entranced, yet still listening to my mind throwing up notes of caution and various other ways of avoiding the inevitable. I was beginning to pull back, as I knew I was falling into that great chasm that we all know ultimately as true love. I have loved many times before in my life, but this was something else. When I was in love before I was still in control of my life and myself. I knew if I fully surrendered to this tidal wave that was swelling, there would be no 'me' left to control. This was another hallmark of Beloveds; the complete longing to surrender into the other, with no desire left whatsoever of remaining as an individual. That is the end goal after all, to become one.

"Darling, why are you withholding from me?" he pulled his head away from mine and gazed into my eyes with this question that kept me spinning for a good answer.

Ignorance, a favorite tactic for the western mind, allows you to ignore or overlook what you know is the truth. I settled for this, siding with the old wives' tale: ignorance is bliss.

"What do you mean? I am not withholding anything from you," I quietly replied with the best-ever version of bewilderment upon my face.

"Are you afraid of falling deeply in love with me and me leaving you?" he quietly coaxed.

Bulls-eye! Perfectly aimed and superbly shot. I was stunned for a few minutes as my bewilderment broke down into vulnerability and my ignorance shattered into innocence. Minutes passed as I kept looking at him; shall I confess or hide the truth? And what's the dating etiquette on telling your Beloved on the second date that he is meant to be your husband? Someone needs to write a manual on this!

My heart won the battle; I inhaled as I allowed the most sincere and delicate "yes" to move up and out of my throat in the direction of my Beloved's face.

"I know darling, I can feel what is happening to you. It's beautiful and very touching," he gently replied.

I lingered for a while wondering whether he would join me on the ocean of love as the waves rose and fell within my chest. Would he possibly declare the same feeling? Silence. Nothing else came from his lips apart from endless kisses. But it didn't matter, as this chance to love without measure was more than enough to fill my life with purpose and meaning. The buoyancy and feeling of being out of control was nectar to my busy life and mind. I floated on these waves and allowed them to have their way with me, I was letting the barriers down and all withholding was withdrawn. I was open to love in a way I had never been before.

As we lay there, our emotional needs were filled to the brim, while our physical bodies were starving. We decided to get dressed and head downstairs for a much-needed feast. We entered the ultra-tiny dining room to find ourselves to be the only guests. Again the Victorian theme dominated the house. Quaint English crockery and floral lacy tablecloths hosted an array of eggs, croissants, and various preserves. Silver spoons dipped in honey slightly took the edge off the bitterness of the coffee that I was gulping down in the much-needed hope of some added gusto and grounding.

During breakfast we had endless fun with one another, laughing constantly at our stories and quirky characteristics. I was so thrilled when I realized that Sananda was the proud owner of a fantastic sense of humor. In all my years of hanging out in spiritual circles I must say, humor can be a little sparse, if not completely frowned upon. I was silently thanking my lucky stars that Sananda was not only different to anyone I had ever met, but uniquely infectious with his hilarity. As I was reflecting on all of this, I must have drifted off into a rose tinted soft focus trance and misheard his question. I buttered more toast and poured some tea as he looked at me and waited for an answer.

"Sorry darling, what did you say?"

"I asked what was the first thought you had this morning?"

Okay, um... I sidestepped the question, saying I couldn't remember. But my face told quite a different story.

"Come on," he teased. "Just tell me."

"No!" I exclaimed. "I will not tell you. It's private." I stood up and hid behind him, hoping he would avoid pressing me further. I wriggled around him, darting out of the way every time he turned to face me.

"Tell me," he demanded.

His power shuddered through me, bringing me to an absolute standstill. I knew in that moment to quit playing around. I was already well aware even in this short space of time that he would always insist on complete and utter transparency and honesty. It was obvious that he would never settle for any of my avoidance tactics or sidestepping. No, he was a full-on kind of guy, and to be honest I was inwardly cheering that at last I was with another who wanted the best, the most, and deepest experiences in life. On that morning it became clear that this relationship was going to be like nothing I had ever known before, and I honestly recognized that whatever I had learned in the past, I could now forget. Nothing could compare to this, nothing.

Silence. What shall I do? Should I tell him? Oh shit, what now? Should I, shall I, have I got the nerve? Oh God, let's do it. Yes, I am going to tell him. With total liberation I took a deep breath as I stepped away from behind him until I was back in full view.

I stared him straight in the eye as I spoke the truth without a trace of shyness or embarrassment, "When I woke up this morning, I had the strong feeling that you're to be my husband."

Despite my newfound confidence I was pretty certain that a statement like this on date number two had the potential to ruffle even the coolest cucumber. So I was prepared for the loaded gun to go off, or at least some tumbleweed to drift into the dining room. Nothing happened. Thump-bump, thump-bump was the sound of my pounding heart reverberating in my chest as I stood there and waited. He sat there staring at me for a pregnant, yet brief moment until he spoke:

"Well, that's because I am."

My eyes widened as my lower jaw slightly dropped. Next up was a wave of hysterical, nervous laughter, as my face burned with a mixture of happiness, gushing hormones, and shock. My hands leapt up to my mouth to try to quiet down the torrent of bemusement, as I constantly turned away and looked back again, letting out various noises that suggested my obvious losing of mind and composure. He laughed and laughed as he slapped the table, throwing back his head in a burst of spontaneous pleasure and happiness. What a moment; I had lost the plot and it looked like he had too! This was fantastic, I was so deliriously happy, yet in the quiet center of all this madness I realized that I was free to be myself with him. For the first time in my life.

We only had a small amount of time left, as he needed to get back to London to prepare for a retreat he was holding in Lyon, France the next day. It looked likely that we wouldn't get to see each other for some time now as in two weeks I would be in Egypt for a week-long yoga retreat. In between now and then I had a weekend workshop that I was running in Cologne, Germany called The Sacred Art of Manifestation (aptly named, don't you think?). Right about that time Sananda told me that he would be in Belgium spending some pre-arranged time with old friends. Therefore, we grasped the chance to be together as we bounded across the softly rolling meadows and barrows of Avebury, arm in arm as we wove our way in-between the stones. Turning left then right, interweaving our bodies like a serpent rising as we encircled this giant stone circle.

Suddenly, he turned deadly serious as he began to speak of how I was not fulfilling my purpose in life. He was certain that I had to break through the veils of illusion that I had created around myself. He challenged me to stop being a yoga teacher and to disassociate from the community that held me in that role. He said it was important that I bring in what yearns to move through me. We stopped walking, and to make a point he took both of my hands as he looked straight into my eyes, advising that I take these words very seriously and to consider my every action in order to make sure that I brought this about. It felt as if he was inviting me to let go of all that I had created for myself in the past and become what I was knowingly postponing. In essence he was taking me to the sheerest edge and whispering, "Jump."

I listened and took it all in, inwardly knowing that this was coming from the moment I met him. It was part of the reason why we came together. I knew that once we met, we would be stretched in ways we hadn't imagined. We would be on a fast track until we were ready to fully merge together and give back something victorious for all beings everywhere. I didn't know what that could be, yet. For years I *knew* that teaching yoga was becoming very limiting to me. There wasn't a day that passed without my knowledge that I had so much more to give. I longed to be able to teach and speak about the path of the Beloved with an infinite number of people. I wanted to leave the yoga world behind, but before that could happen I knew a massive step needed to be taken. How could I do this? How would I survive? My teaching was my life, and my means of income. I had been doing this for 12 years and was not qualified to do anything else apart from fashion design, and that was not an option. My mind began to reach for answers that were not there. I was afraid. Yet within that fear there was a freedom that beckoned.

We approached the car park and held each other one last time. I held onto this giant of a man. Oh God, let us be together again soon. He was about to begin a weekend retreat in France, teaching a *Shakti One* workshop, whereas I was destined to leave for Egypt in a few weeks for a ten-day yoga holiday that I was teaching. I held him close to me as I buried my head into my new favorite location in the world—his chest. His smell, his form, his voice, and his presence pressed themselves into my soul. I vowed to follow love all the way. I wanted to hold on for dear life. It seemed that my life as I once knew it was about to change radically. Eventually we let each other go. I walked over to my car in utter bliss taking a deep breath in as the morning sun warmed my face. What a day. What a life I was having!

Driving out of Avebury and past Silbury Hill—the man-made hill famous for being the embodiment of the Mother Earth when viewed from above—I began to evaluate our time together. In the privacy of my own thoughts, I realized that this man was pure fire, his character was similar to that of the galvanizing cannon ball in the game of tenpin bowling; you know the one that comes racing towards the skittles and sends them flying in numerous chaotic directions? Yes, this was an aspect of Sananda I admired and nearly loved; knowing that in the future it would become a double-edged sword. I knew it was going to be this ruthless method that enticed me to grow.

There was another aspect too that I was warming towards much faster than the cannon ball, and it was the part of him that was timeless, the part I had known forever. You see the cannon ball was his human flavor, the particular quality of his personality; yet what I saw and loved was what was behind that, and it was exquisite. As I continued to drive along the edges of the softly rounded, beautiful spring green meadows, a powerful voice spoke to me. I recognized immediately that this voice was the deeper, wiser counsel of my heart.

Beloved, listen to me and take in these words, and hold true to them when you need to. You have found The One, known as your Beloved that you have waited for. This is only the beginning and the path is already laid out before you. There is nothing that can go "wrong," between you if you persevere together. Times will be testing and you will feel like you cannot continue. But, you will. Follow me, follow your heart, follow love, and you will come to know who you are, and with that experience you will teach others how to follow the footsteps that you are creating.

Many people will want to walk this path, and you my love will be the one to show them. You cannot teach this, you can only speak of your experience and from this you shall light the world, as love will shine forth through you. People will see and feel this and trust in you and their ability to brave this journey. For so long now people have yearned to find their Beloved, and love with the freedom that this magnificent reunion deserves. To truly give themselves 100 percent, as they remember and acknowledge that their human life is so precious and over in such a short space of time. Both of you are treading the way for many millions to follow.

I am here in the cave of your heart always.

Waves of Shakti surged through my body, confirming that I had heard the truth. I gripped the steering wheel as silent tears poured down my cheeks, caused by the endless inner and outer waves of gratitude and beauty. I was awash with grace and humility as I felt into and imagined the words that my heart had prophesized. I drove back to mum and dad's house in a haze of euphoria. I was deliriously happy. I pulled up into the drive singing my heart out as Beyonce's "Halo" boomed through the car speakers; imagining that it was me singing to Sananda. Dad was in the front garden cleaning the caravan, looking up when he heard the raucous activity coming towards him.

"Dad, I'm so madly in love!" I declared as I stepped out of the car and hugged him.

"This is The One, I just know it," I said as I floated into the house on cloud nine.

"But you've only just met him…" I softly heard him reply.

CHAPTER TEN

SINAI DESERT: FORTY DAYS AND FORTY NIGHTS

Coral Coast, Dahab, Egypt, April 2009

THE STENCH of camels, calls to prayer at various times throughout the day, intense heat, and the mysterious beckoning of the Sinai Mountains surrounded me during my 10-day yoga holiday retreat in Dahab. I had been coming to Egypt's popular hippy trail hangout of Dahab for years and loved every aspect of it. Just an hour from the tourist capital Sharm El Sheikh, a heaving sprawl of hotels, clubs, and restaurants; Dahab was the cool bohemian place to be if you were into diving and yoga. Dahab was Egypt's flower power answer to Goa, or Thailand's tie-dyed Phuket. Only those with long hair and lean bodies that adhered to strict vegetarianism and who also happened to go by the name of Sky or Anastasia were magnetically drawn here (or were revered anyway!). Dahab is *the* original place where you can turn on, tune in, and drop out.

I was part of the yoga crew; running a yoga retreat called "A Journey through the Chakras" for a group of twelve women who varied in age as much as they varied in careers and hairstyles. They were all from England and a multi-talented flock of characters.

There was a woman from the BBC, a journalist, an exotic dancer, and a handful of single young mums. This melting pot of varied feminine souls were hanging out with me as I pushed, pulled, and twisted them back into peaceful radiant health on the edge of the Red Sea.

It was such a cushy deal being a yoga teacher on retreat. It was almost mid-day and I was laying on my sun lounger at the Eel Garden Café (*the* most hippy hangout in Dahab) with plans to get a tan, go for a swim, and then spend more time relaxing. The beauty of it was, I scheduled two classes a day (morning classes were between 7am-9am, while the evening ones were 6pm-8pm), and then the rest of the time was mine to do whatever I wanted. And all that I wanted at this particular time was to make mad, passionate love to Sananda. Since he couldn't be there, I opted for the next best thing, as X-rated poetry moistly dripped off the end of my pen as I imagined him lying with me. I was drunk with a passion that consumed my every waking hour. Every day I would pen another poem in a couple of minutes, furiously scribbling with such intensity that I would accidentally tear the page.

> *"Oh my Beloved, through my eyes*
> *I watch the savage wind*
> *Bend the palm trees and toss*
> *All that is not rooted up into*
> *The air, like play things.*
> *I too cry, "Take me, take me"*
> *All that dares to stand between us,*
> *take me and Love me too death*
> *Kill my resistance with*

One deep kiss that ends all
Other kisses
Slaughter my protective mind
With the deep penetrating
Fulfilled union, which ends all
Memories…
I am in line with the Cosmos
As I boil with impatience
I have restored my faith
And justified my love
My prostration delivers perfection
Pouring myself out into you
Invites the Universe
To pour itself
Out into me."

The heat was getting to me in a way that was bordering on concern for the safety of others around me. After writing yet another poetic epiphany, I swooned with a deep breath as if I had reached the summit of a mountain. Lifting my arms up and over my head, I stretched my body with a hint of sexual abandon… well maybe it wasn't merely a hint! A few tears fell as I felt the physical distance between Sananda and myself. I realized I was falling deeply in love with him. I wondered if that's why I had been having some dark dreams since arriving in Dahab—perhaps I was missing him too much. I shyly brushed my tears away, muttering something about being silly and getting a grip. I was poetry on two legs, knocking them out like ice creams to children at the beach. I simply could not stop myself.

All the sexual heat was getting to me in more ways than one. We unexpectedly consummated our Beloved union three weeks ago with a spontaneous night together when I returned to England after a weekend workshop in Germany. Sananda had recently returned from Belgium and was incredibly eager to see me before we went our separate ways again. Our first time making love was so incredibly passionate and urgent as we plunged into one another, confessing our eternal love for each other. It was on this night that he pledged his love to me by whispering the words, "Scarlett, I love you" into my ear as we lay together in the aftermath of our fulfilled longing.

The more we made love the more I noticed that the 'opening the seven gates' business was more in depth than I thought. I guess I had imagined that the openings would be consistently orgasmic and pleasurable. Mostly they were, but there were times when it felt like I was giving birth. Some of these openings were so intensely painful, both physically and emotionally. Old memories would well up, some my own, others that had to be from the collective feminine psyche. When this happened I experienced a lot of discomfort and irregularities within my cycle. To cut a long story short, I had begun to bleed the very first time we became intimate, and now three weeks later I still hadn't stopped.

I wasn't terribly hysterical about all of this. Fortunately, a few years ago, I read a book about Egyptian goddesses that stated quite clearly that if a woman bleeds when making love (and it was not her menstrual time) it was to be taken as a royal gift and sign that the woman had given something incredibly sacred to that man. Months later I read in another book that if you make love with your Beloved and bleed, it is known as the highest offering, like a second virginal phase.

Despite all this, please note that I encourage every individual to take full responsibility for their physical health; especially should you encounter a similar experience to mine. I did what I always do with my health—I took both traditional and alternative routes. My first port of call was naturally myself. Tuning in and checking with myself to confirm that all was well in spite of the continuous bleeding. I truly felt fit, healthy, and strong inside, but the bleeding didn't seem 100 percent natural. I was well aware that by making love with my Beloved, I would no doubt have some kind of internal reaction—but this was totally unexpected. Choosing to be safe rather than sorry I decided to make a doctor's appointment before I left from Egypt to find out what was happening and to see what, if anything could be done. So days before I left England I set aside time to have some tests done to ascertain what was happening.

Once I had explained everything to my doctor, she gave me a sorrowful stare as she suggested that I may be going through early menopause. Perhaps I would like a blood test to find out? Um, of course I would. Do it now! I nearly pushed her out of the way as I contemplated reaching for the syringe to perform the test myself. Menopause is not one of those things a vibrant, sexual woman takes lightly. I had to know what was going on!

Unfortunately, also, during the pap smear they spotted a polyp about the size of a marble attached to the side of my cervix. I was told not to worry and that in a few weeks time I could get it removed relatively quickly and easily. Apparently, polyps are quite commonplace and not harmful in any way. But, why was it created in the first place was my question?

When I searched within, it felt as I surrendered all my old ways of relating through my relationship with Sananda that the polyp acted like some kind of biological dustbin. As we learned to make love in a conscious and transparent way with the seven gates this polyp was able to collect all the inner garbage, patterns, and old fear responses. We had discussed this together, as obviously it was clear to him that I was having an unusual reaction to our lovemaking. He was so kind and open as we intimately shared our feelings and insights surrounding the situation. He was not too concerned, trusting that this bleeding was another confirming sign that things were shifting, and becoming healed and balanced within us both. We agreed that I was releasing past memories of having loveless sex, along with disappointments in relationships.

Through conscious lovemaking, we vulnerably opened to one another, truly meeting as one Soul as we merged together, leaving nothing for ourselves. When not squirming in discomfort, our lovemaking was out of this world—literally. We seemed to instinctively surrender to the urges of our souls to fuse together seamlessly. In the depths of my feminine wisdom, I was confident that my bodily intelligence knew what it was doing, and in that I was reassured. I still felt it would be responsible to check things out just in case. One's health is not something to mess with.

Fortunately, I had received the blood test results from that appointment as I was waited in the departures lounge of Gatwick Airport to come to Dahab. My lovely mum text messaged me with the results that had arrived in the post that morning.

Results of blood test: You are not menopausal. Love mum x

(Isn't this the text every red-blooded woman hopes to receive?!)

Thank God that was a close call.

Now, lounging in Dahab in between yoga classes, I was still awaiting the results of the smear test, although I had been told it may take six weeks. At this point, I couldn't worry about it just yet. I was, however, curious to know what it all meant—the voracious sexual appetite for Sananda, the out of this world lovemaking, bleeding, and now a polyp. I hoped that this time in Dahab would allow me to go deeper within to ascertain what was brewing inside of me.

On the fourth day of our yoga retreat, I anticipated having some time to do exactly that. As we all sat together for breakfast after the 7am yoga class, an air of excitement filled the group. We were going to be taken as far as the taxis could travel to rendezvous with the Bedouin tribal people who actually *lived* smack bang in the middle of nowhere who would meet us with their camels to guide us into the vastness of the Sinai Desert. I was bombarded with 101 questions about sleeping, toilets, what to wear, and the consistent confirmation that we would all have enough water.

At 10am our mini-buses were waiting for us outside the hotel. We crammed in and waited for last minute loo checks. I made sure I was at the back with my sunglasses on, iPod earphones in, and a clear "do not disturb" energy all around me. I needed some space to myself, as I was preparing for something big. Intuitively, I had decided to draw a circle in the sand and I was going to sit in my circle for a 12-hour period, totally alone and far from the group camp. Sure, it was a long way from styling celebs and leading the rich and famous through various yoga poses, but this was how I lived my life now—I had to follow my intuition.

It was like an initiation, a challenge to overcome my fear of being completely alone as I faced the unknown. I knew this would be the key for me to meet my greatest darkness. If I was going to do this Beloved thing (which I was), I knew I had to fully release this fear of being alone. I had to know that I wouldn't bolt in the face of fear, I had to know that I could really face anything in life, and welcome its presence. To be the manifestation of love one can't allow fear to dominate any part of their life. Fear would arise, that's only natural, but it couldn't control you, it couldn't dim the light of love.

The *idea* of sitting in the desert alone made me go cold, so I knew it was something I had to overcome as part of my mission. What we fear most, we must examine. As I played this all out for myself on the mini bus, I was beginning to get a sense of exactly what might be lying in wait for me. Oh God, maybe it's not such a good idea after all?? I closed my eyes as I drifted into the soundtrack of *Lord of the Rings*, when I suddenly remembered that I had foolishly announced that I was taking on this daring stunt on FaceBook. My eyes sprung open as I came to a start. I couldn't decide what could be worse: publicly telling the world that I didn't have the guts to go through with it, or scaring myself to death and possibly never being the same or rather sane, again. The truth of the matter was that a torrid flow of fear was rushing in thick and fast, and it was only 10:30 in the morning!

The engine of the 12-seater mini-bus burst into life alongside a barrage of cheers. As we escaped the tourist confines of Dahab, we drove silently into the vast stretches of the orange-lilac mountains of Sinai, passing through various checkpoints where Egyptian security guards with machine guns and sultry eyes checked our passports and contents. There was a hushed silence as we all politely handed over our passports. Yet as soon as we got past the guards, the tension lifted as the women burst into a chaotic fusion of laughter, fun, and excitement. This was going to be a brand new experience for all of them, and after hyping it up the way I did earlier, they were on the edge of their seats with white-knuckled anticipation.

The Sinai Peninsula has a history as long and colorful as the Earth herself. It was here that Moses allegedly led his people out of Egypt when they were without a country to settle, where Christ spent 40 days in the wilderness being tempted and tested before starting his greatest mission, as well as being the homeland of Lilith, a Hebrew Goddess that incarnated as the first woman before Eve. According to legend, Lilith chose to leave Adam in the Garden of Eden for being too full of himself. For years, I had been taking women to the Sinai, telling them about the story of Lilith and how this place was a soft, yet ruthless sanctuary for womankind to heal their broken hearts and feminine betrayals.

With the initial high energy of the kick-off of our trip beginning to fade, the group one-by-one fell silent as we continued to twist and turn our way through the various colored canyons. It was as if we were the paintbrush, adding another lavish layer of lavender to the mountains and cliff faces as we drove by. The light was incredible, casting huge elongated shadows throughout the canyons and valleys. I was content to lean against the window of the mini-bus, watching how its dark twin-like silhouette glided alongside us. We seemed to pour through the desert, as we left the constant hubbub of normal daily life behind us. I could feel the women letting go, loosening up as they began to experience the freedom and spaciousness that was on offer here. They drank it in and adapted pretty quickly, by either falling asleep or staring out of the window transfixed.

We stopped at the halfway point and exchanged our mini-bus for camels. This was more like it. Now we were really in the desert. Conversations changed from the mundane to the profound. I decided to walk my camel at the back making sure everyone was comfortable as I again took advantage of some solo time to absorb the atmosphere and silence. As we softly crunched our way over the sand dunes, each member of the group took turns to walk with me. We spoke of the more meaningful aspects of life, love, and how to live in truth and, of course, what all that personally meant to us. They started to see how they too had been stifling the flow of love, holding onto their broken hearts in protection, hoping that they wouldn't get hurt again. As we continued to share, they realized that they had to let go of the past and open up once again to love.

Endless smiles beamed across their faces as they felt the freedom return, demonstrating the truth of their discovery. As the camels carried us further into the purifying landscape of this barren void, all conversations fell silent and were instead traded in for contemplation. Abdul, our Egyptian guide, always stood close by. He was never far from my side, as over the week we had begun to talk about our ways of life and exchanged stories about how our own experiences had made us who we were. He was young, in his early twenties, yet he had the maturity of someone in his forties. He was a very philosophical thinker and hungered for these types of conversations. Not only that, but he was a great help to the group. He was strong and reliable; a man you could trust.

We were making our way to a Bedouin settlement, where some tea would be waiting for us. Abdul and I walked together as I told him my plans for the night. I told him that I needed him to keep the group safe and comfortable as I was going to sleep somewhere else, out of sight and earshot. He seemed worried, as he had never heard of such a request before. I settled his mind, telling him that together we would select the spot, so he knew where I was.

He asked me why I was doing such a crazy thing. I explained that it was something I had to do, that I had to face this fear inside of me. The idea of sitting in the middle of the desert all night alone by myself terrified me. It was like a fear of the unknown or the unseen. I explained that my life was in complete service to love, and that on this night I would be given the chance to invite love to withstand the terror and dissolve the fear of being totally alone, forever. I went on to tell him that I had met a very special man, that he was in fact my, "Beloved," and that I instinctively knew I had to enter this relationship free from fear. He was mesmerized by what I was saying and begged me to carry on.

Happy to do so, I spoke from my years of study and inner contemplations, clearly explaining that when we meet "The One," it is only a matter of time before all our deepest fears and inadequacies rise to the surface. It is one of the purposes of the Beloved to trigger those hidden, most secretive forms of resistance, so that the couple can open the way for the most powerful love to flow through them. A love that still to this day, most human beings are not aware of. The silence deepened as he reflected on what I was saying.

"But, what if they do enter the relationship with fear?" he slowly whispered.

"Then that fear could potentially be used against them, as an attempt to destroy their love. You see, this love that I am speaking about will eventually wipe out any part of them that holds onto any concept that the person involved is separate or individual.

When Beloveds meet, there is a chance for those two people to dissolve all that they once knew themselves to be and become the living embodiment of love. They will become wild and free from all fear, reborn as an untamable celebration of love."

He was speechless.

There was just one more thing I had to explain. That the fear inside was alive, and it would do everything within its power to sabotage this reunion with love. Fear is the opposite of love, and when humans feel strong waves of fear they are capable of *anything*. And so, if the person in question was not aware of what was happening, that they were meeting their Beloved, then the opportunity being offered to the two of them could diminish and end until they were again ready. Because of the sheer amount of power involved with the meeting of these two beings, the breaking apart process could be quite possibly life-threatening, and without a doubt insanely destructive.

A Beloved is often everything you "think" you are not. But that is not completely the truth. All it means is that you most likely experienced different types of lessons and insights that sculpted the particular essence and flavor of your character. At first sight, Sananda could be seen as a man dedicated to power and truth (consciousness), whereas I could be perceived as being full of love and kindness. At first it can be (and was) like a Clash of the Titans, until finally there is surrender on both sides to release their ideas of individuality and independence, and return back once again to the reunion of their one Soul. I went on to reassure Abdul by saying that Beloveds do not meet unless there is a high chance that they will overcome these challenges. I reminded him that there is an intelligence in their destined meeting, and that God rarely makes mistakes, it's only us humans that can do that.

His face darkened as he sensed the truth of what I was saying, and then reached for my hand. "You are an amazing woman, Scarlett. I have never met anyone like you before from the west. You have a big heart and you are strong like a warrior. But I must tell you, I am afraid for you."

I did not ask why, as it did not matter to me. He turned his head away as he gazed out over the vast stretches of untouched sand and sky, but not before I noticed that he was softly crying, no doubt touched by these words. As we continued to silently walk together, I shaded my eyes with my hand as I squinted into the distance up ahead. It looked as we were nearly at the Bedouin village. Through the heat haze I caught a glimpse of a smattering of ramshackles, makeshift huts and shelters, as goats, chickens, donkeys, and camels wandered around in complete freedom. The closer I got, the more I could see, as I noticed that the Bedouin tents used heavy hessian blankets as roofs, with various forms of fencing ingeniously created from anything they could find. I marveled when I saw the local children playing joyfully with the animals, using sticks and rubbish as toys.

The group heaved and groaned their way off the camels, complaining of tight hips and aching butts. I laughed to myself when I noticed that they were walking with bandy bowlegs towards the settlement as they climbed into one of the huts, where straw matting was put down for us to sit. There was no furniture whatsoever, so we all sat on the floor cross-legged (thank goodness we were yoginis). In the corner was a fire, where the women were making tea while smoking under their veils. We couldn't see the women's faces as they were covered head to toe in black burkas. Yet

I could see their tattooed hands, as they moved quickly and efficiently over the fire washing cups, making tea, and rolling cigarettes.

The western women were shy and uncomfortable as they found themselves in this most unusual situation. Flies were everywhere, landing on their faces and arms. They got busy swatting them and waving their arms all over the place. I smiled, as I had seen this oh so many times before over the ten years that I have been bringing groups to Dahab.

A little girl with a terribly runny nose brought our tea to us on a silver tray in tiny glass tumblers alongside the swarm of flies. I could see the women each going for the glass with the least amount of flies, as they looked around for my go-ahead as to whether they should drink it or not. It was a tense moment, as the Bedouin women could sense the growing unease. I grabbed my glass, drank the whole lot, remarked how great it was, and looked around to see whether there was any more in the pot. This cheered the Bedouin who were only too happy to please, and instantly the tension lifted.

I sat for a while observing the situation. The group had gone back to chitchatting, rather than engaging in the present situation. I noticed how the yoga group all sat together, checking their phones, wiping the rim of the tea tumblers with their wet wipes, and shifting uncomfortably when the children would ask whether they wanted to buy some necklaces that they had made.

The Bedouin women squatted around the fire with none of the things this modern world could offer. They washed their tea glasses in a bowl of water, baked bread on an upside down wok, and tended to their children and husbands. Life was simple.

I saw the difference of our lives, as well as the physical distance, as we Westerners sat in one corner and the Bedouin in the other. There was much to be learned by both. I wondered what could bring us together. I speculated that perhaps it was Beloved love that could unite different races, genders, and generations of people. This had been my greatest prayer to bring about a global reunion—to bring an end to all the ways that we had divided ourselves through skin, country, religion, and status. My heart felt heavy, wishing we could all sit together and be present with one another in this once in a lifetime experience.

Abdul and I decided to sneak off and have a bit of space, once all the retreat participants had their tea and were beginning to relax and check out the camp. I took one last glance to make sure that they would all be okay, noticing that they were busy examining the hand-crafted jewelry and various shapes and sizes of camel toys that the children were proudly selling. We walked for a while in silence, drinking in the glory of the place. He could tell that I was moved when we were having tea, and from our earlier conversation could no doubt sense that I had a lot on my mind. He shyly asked whether I would like a cigarette. I guess he thought because I was a yogini the answer would be an all out no. Usually it would have been, but with tonight looming up ahead, I thought twice.

"I would love one Abdul, thank you," I replied.

We lit up our cigarettes like school kids, creeping around the back of the corrugated iron shed where the goats were kept. I had never enjoyed a cigarette as much as this one. Standing there smoking had a Hollywood moment about it, as we inhaled long and deep, and exhaled with a slight moan. We didn't speak, as we didn't need to. We were spellbound by the desert, powerfully lost in our thoughts. Besides, Abdul and I were soul friends, I could feel it.

I was grateful to have him around on my upcoming night alone in the desert.

Once finished with our delightful cigarettes and mutual respect for one another, I sat down on an upside down milk crate as the children set up shop, placing all their handmade jewelry on the sand in front of me. Abdul walked back to the camp to rally the women, making sure we hadn't left anything behind. As everyone began to set off, I walked back into the camp to say my goodbyes to the Bedouin women. The oldest one, who seemed like the grandmother, beckoned me to come over to her. She placed a necklace in my hands and closed my fingers over the top. "For you," she said. She then pointed at her eyes and then at mine, as she traced a finger down my cheek.

"I see you," she said. More tears welled up, and before I knew what I was doing, we had embraced. All the children flocked to where we stood, jaws hanging open with eyes as wide as saucers. This was obviously a one off.

I wanted to give that woman all that I had, which was actually nothing. But she needed nothing. She was giving to me. She had nothing, yet what she did have, she gave to me as a gift. I looked down at the necklace, which looked like a shark's tooth on a beaded necklace. There were two initials scribed onto the tooth: SS.

Scarlett and Sananda...

This synchronicity was yet another huge sign from the Universe confirming the importance of Sananda and I's love. It felt like a show of support from the Universe as my destined night loomed closer. I was greatly appreciative for the kindness and the support. It set the perfect stage for my upcoming night in the desert. I said my goodbyes and headed in the direction of the camels. The sky yawned open, as my mind stumbled to make sense of it all.

All I could do was walk in silence towards our shelter for the night. After an hour or so, we reached our isolated destination. There was no one around us, except for Abdul and thirteen camels as guardians. Four wooden poles held up a heavy brown and grey blanket. Outside was a fire pit, with a roaring fire already on the go. Abdul was going great guns with preparations for our supper. The group was selecting their beds for the night, which was quite simply a mattress with as many blankets as needed. They were all going to sleep together, lined up like a girls dormitory. It was wonderful to see them playing and laughing together, as they joked at the bathroom facilities and lack of privacy.

I looked around at our location to gauge where I would be heading. I glanced all around waiting for a signal to tell me where to go. As you can imagine the desert pretty much looks the same wherever you turn, so a clear landmark was not going to be the deciding factor. All I could do was close my eyes and sense the direction to aim for, using my feelings as a guide. After a while I knew exactly where to go. It wasn't that far from the group—only a ten-minute walk—but far enough to be completely out of sight and earshot.

Abdul saw me looking. "Are you sure you still want to do this, Scarlett?"

I nodded back at him. "Yep, there's no stopping this now," I replied. I was determined to see this through.

Besides, I had put it on FaceBook—there was no way I could get out of it now. My subconscious mind must have ensured that I set myself up so that there was no means of escape! We huddled around the fire for extra warmth as the sun dropped from the sky.

Despite the grueling cold desert temperatures at night, the fire and our blankets kept us as warm as toast. It was now my cue to leave. With only three days left in the retreat, tonight was the ideal time to meet my fears head on and still have a few days left to recover from it all. As the group was settling into their beds, chatting and laughing, I pulled Abdul to one side.

"It's time to go," I softly murmured to him. "Keep an eye on the group; I will be right around the side of the mountain. I have everything I need. I'll see you in the morning. I'll be fine, don't worry."

"Sure thing, Scarlett," he reached into his pocket. "Here, these are for you, I think you'll need them."

He pushed a couple of candles and a lighter into my hand. I squeezed his hand and smiled.

I grabbed my rucksack and headed off into the night, as I took a deep breath, and whispered the words, "Now, it begins…"

❧

I found my place immediately, its hallmarks being the absolute center point of a wide-open canyon. I deliberately chose a spot that gave me the feeling of a 360-degree circle of exposure, a place where I was not hidden or shielded by anything, only pure naked vulnerability. I guess you could say I am one of those characters who never does anything by halves; if I am to take on a crazy stunt, I make sure I do it properly. I searched around for something to draw my circle and found a nearby parched twig that was ideal. After a few deep breaths and psyching myself up, I slowly and deliberately carved out my circle, making sure it was large enough for me to lie down in if I wanted to sleep. Once that was completed,

I marked out the four directions and wrote the initials of various guardians in each direction. JC for Jesus Christ at my right (masculine), MM for Mary Magdalene at my left (feminine), AM for Archangel Michael in front (guiding force) and SG for Sananda Gabriel at my back (protection and guardian). There was now nothing else left to do but step inside, sit down, and wait.

I made a comfortable lump with one blanket to sit on cross-legged and then wrapped the other one all around me and over the top of my head. I lit one small table candle and pushed it into the sand in front of me, thanking Abdul as I did so. I narrowed my eyes as I looked around the desert, noticing the strange ghostly silhouettes of the ominous mountains and their elongated shadows being cast by the moonlight. I shuddered as I saw how the gentle breeze would lift up and twirl around the odd empty plastic water bottle that had been carelessly tossed away by other Bedouin travelers.

As I sat there, my hearing became even more sensitive as I began to detect noises from all over the desert floor. I could not hear the group, so it was not them, but I could hear something. I strained to listen, but the sounds quickly disappeared and all that was left was the raspy heaviness of my quickened breath. Upon hearing this, I froze in shock as it scared the life out of me to hear my own abnormal, thundering animal-like panting set against the roaring silence of the vast open spaces of the Sinai desert. I longed for Chloe—she would have a splendid joke for me right now. But I knew she would never be one to take on such a ridiculous scenario. Suddenly, I couldn't remember why I needed to do this.

I took a long, slow breath, settling myself down again, this time closing my eyes to meditate. Big mistake! In the darkness I immediately came face-to-face with a tormenting evil apparition that I recognized from a series of recent nightmares that began on my first night at the hotel in Dahab. These dreams plagued me, tormenting me with ideas that Sananda was not all that he seemed. This creature would laugh at me, suggesting that Sananda had cheated on me recently and that he was keeping it secret. Horrible visuals filled my mind of Sananda with another woman.

I pushed the dreams aside as a tormenting test, and thought nothing more of it. I knew I would have to face it again, and fearfully dreaded that it would be during this fateful night. It looks as though my intuition was right, as the visual haunted me yet again. It wasn't so much that the face that appeared in my dreams and in this visual was so terrifying; it was more the energy, the feel of this being. It was completely loveless, cold, sadistic, and completely focused on me. I remembered my dream; how it manipulated me, pulled me towards it by sheer magnetic force. No matter how hard I fought, I could not control its power over me. It would throw me around the room, picking me up by the throat and hurling me against a wall where I would crack open my face and become filled with hate, as every part of me was consumed with vengeance. This was full on shadow work—something I had never ever experienced before.

Slowly over the course of the dream, what started off as a cosmic battle of dark and light, ended with me seething in blood lust, as he enticed me on to try and kill him. There was no more dark and light as I gave in to the animal-like urges, and became lost in the delusion of darkness. In my blindness I had joined forces with him. His laughter would show me that he had won and with that the dream would end.

Now I understood what was happening, those dreams were all part of this build-up. No matter what happened tonight, I must not react the way I did in my dreams. I must conquer the fear, and not get drawn away from love. This was going to be the ultimate challenge for me. It was perfect, as I knew this would prepare me for being in relationship with my Beloved. If I conquered this fear there could be nothing on earth that could make me bail if things got rocky between us. Once one battles the fear within (the greatest of all), there is no more fear—only love.

After a few hours of sitting there, observing all the futile attempts of my own mind to create endless fearful situations, a heavy blanket of tiredness got the better of me. I curled up into a fetus position, making sure that I was still within my circle, and drifted off into sleep. I woke up in the middle of my dream, observing myself in the circle surrounded by the darkness of the desert. I sensed this unearthly dread as a tall, dark, liquid-like being spun, darted, and circled all around me. He did not move like a human, more like a jerky, rapid, chaotic form of madness. He was trying every way of getting into the circle, looking for a weak point, or break in my line. I knelt beside my body, frantically trying to awaken myself to the danger that was present. Every time my hand went to touch my face or shoulder to make contact, it would vaporize, rendering all my efforts futile. Behind me, I could hear the twisted, lunatic laugh of what could only be described as the fear of all fears.

In my dream I called forth the four guardians I had set up to protect my circle for immediate help and protection, but no one arrived. I called again and again against the backdrop of this demonic hysteria. I was alone with this heinous chaos, which somehow knew my every weakness and would prey upon me, until I found the way to end this, once and for all. I screamed at myself to wake up, as I constantly hit my face over and over to wake up.

Then, I did finally wake up from the consistent banging of my head against the sandy floor of the desert. Strange, as I was sure I fell asleep using the blanket as a pillow. Then an almighty surge of fear flooded through my body, clawing at my heart, as I realized that I was being dragged out of the circle by one of my feet. I could feel a hand around my ankle yanking me backwards, one tug after the other. My eyes sprung open, as I watched my hands slide along the sand. My God, I was actually moving! This was not a dream, this was happening right here, right now!

My survival instincts came to a start and without even seeing who or what it was, I kicked with all my might against the thing that was dragging me. With a blood-curdling shriek, I yelled out, "Get away from me!" as I made contact with the intruder. It immediately let go, sending my leg crashing to the floor. I scrambled up onto my knees, like a hunted animal, wildly turning my head in every direction to see if anyone was around.

The desert was empty.

In the moonlight I looked at my ankle, rubbing away the pain. My heart was pounding, as my shaking hands fumbled for my Blackberry. Shit! I had no reception and couldn't call Sananda. I kept looking all around me, feverishly turning left and right, jumping at every sound and movement of wind in the desert. With erratic fingers I typed out a near illiterate email to Sananda, asking that if he got this message in time, to help me if he could. Luckily there was an intermittent signal. Yes, it got sent. Thank God! I laughed out loud nervously, as I marveled that in the middle of the

Sinai desert I could speak to him at all.

A few moments later, his reply came back. He too had sensed what was going on and knew that I was calling for him. This dark magician had showed up in his meditation and warned him not to help me, because I no longer loved him. He did not believe it and was standing firm, but was feeling shaken by the ferocity of the messages and impulses coming to him, thousands of miles away in London. He went on to share that he also felt...

Then the message was cut, as only half was delivered.

Sananda, please, if you can hear me call me now. I whispered again and again fervently.

My phone rang. I snatched the handset from underneath the blanket. With eyes wide, my heart melted when I saw it was him. All of a sudden, nothing mattered anymore if I could speak with him, if only for a few minutes. This connection would give me the courage to face this situation for an entire lifetime if I had to.

"Darling, don't be afraid. I know you can do this. I am here with you. This is all a test. To become love, one has to meet the presence and embodiment of all that is not love first. This is what we, as Beloveds, must face. It is part of our destiny, and..." the phone cut out.

"Hello, hello, hello!" I screamed into the desert. No answer from man or beast. I was alone. Again.

I checked the time; it was 3am and bloody cold. I wrapped myself up one more time, checking the circle, making sure it was intact, which it was. I must have slipped away into the awaiting arms of sleep, as the same thing happened again.

I woke up just outside the circle watching myself sleeping on the inside.

I could hear ghastly groans echoing around me, interspersed with screams of pain and torture, bellowing through the canyon; women's voices were coming from every direction, and still I slept on, even though the sound felt as if it would burst my ear drums. Then, from the shadows, came the twisted, mutilated forms of three women crawling their way towards me. With bedraggled hair and lesions on their skin, they inched their way to my circle. With long talon like fingernails, they attempted to reach me inside the circle, but were instantly repulsed and burnt by the surrounding force field. They spat at my sleeping form, wailing as they withered away. All I could do was watch and pray that I would awaken, as more and more dark entities appeared at the circle, frantically looking for a way through the circle.

The next thing I remember was waking up inside the circle, as the dawn's rays penetrated my eyelids. At last, it was morning. I rubbed the sleep from my eyes as I lifted my body up into a sitting position. I reached for my Blackberry, hoping there would be a signal, but there was still no reception. I stretched my hardened body, rubbing my neck and shoulders as I inspected the circle. All of a sudden the ordeal of last night came rushing back to me. I lunged to the bottom of the circle to see if there were any footprints, or signs of struggle. There was nothing!

I looked to the left of the circle to try to find the evidence of the three women, and the writhing nature of their movements. Again, only clear, flat sand. I stood up, walking around outside the circle, checking for the initials that I had carved in the sand the night before. They were all there, still strongly marked out, except for SG. Sananda was missing! His initials had completely disappeared. I looked everywhere for evidence that something or someone had trampled on them, or maybe it was the wind that had covered them up. But no, the sand was completely flat and undisturbed. If was as it they were never there.

I was completely taken back. What? How did… how could that happen? I pushed my fevered thoughts aside, packing my things up to make my way back to the camp. I had been right. This night had been a true meeting of my fears—was it real? Or was it a lucid dream that engaged all my senses? For now I did not know, and had to trust that all was unfolding in divine order—whether or not it made any "sense." Right before I left, I decided to take a photo of the circle where I slept as evidence that it actually happened, making sure I captured the three initials *and* the one blank space, where SG once was.

I walked around the corner, and immediately saw a concerned Abdul standing wide legged as he searched all around in the direction that I had wandered off in from the night before. The moment he saw me, he waved both arms as if guiding in a plane for landing. Boy, was I glad to see him! As soon as I reached the camp, I greeted the women by excusing myself for getting up early, confessing to some morning yoga. Another white lie. Still, I rather they thought I was hooked on yoga, than really know what I was up to.

The mood at the camp was jubilant as the women congratulated themselves for braving the elements, and waking up in one piece. Ha, if only they knew, I thought to myself as I smiled. Everyone was ravenous and eager to feast, including myself. As we sat down together in a circle around the fire that Abdul had tended to all night, we laughed and joked over our appearances. I think I stood out the most as my hair was all over the place and I was covered in sand from head to toe. But I did not care—I was alive, and had survived my own worst nightmare.

I felt so wonderful, so free, and victorious. This freedom was quickly overcome by a ravenous craving for food. I joined the other women for breakfast, scoffing down one mouthful after the other of falafel, cheese, bread, yogurt, and coffee. In between mouthfuls, I checked my Crackberry to discover a whole barrage of email messages stacked up, one after the other. They were all from Sananda, poetic messages of concern, love, and understanding of the situation. He knew, because I had told him in previous emails, that this ordeal was something I had to do alone. I told him he would not be able to protect me in anyway, that I had to face this myself. This was hard for him, as he was sworn to be my protector, but he acquiesced, albeit somewhat reluctantly. This was why his initials were nowhere to be found. And why I didn't feel the presence of my other guardians; to do the job properly I had to be utterly alone for when the darkness arrived.

As the Sufis say, "The flight to God is the journey of the alone to the alone." This was a test I had to go through so I could enter the next stage of the journey with my Beloved. Now, I was ready for anything, or so I thought. After breakfast, Abdul signaled me for another around-the-back-of-the-tent secret meeting. As if on cue, the moment I joined him, two cigarettes were waiting in his hand.

With a hushed voice he asked, "How was it, last night I mean?"

"Piece of cake," I replied, as I breathed out a waft of smoke.

Chapter Eleven

Giving It All Up

Dahab, Egypt, April 2009

I T WAS MY LAST DAY in Dahab before I flew back to England. The yoga group left two days ago, giving me some precious time to integrate all that had happened in the desert. I felt incredibly courageous, which sent me promptly to the nearest Internet café to announce my victory on FaceBook. Although I felt on top of the world, there was still one uneasy feeling that lingered.

It was one I couldn't shake from my mind—Sananda and the mysterious other woman. Yes, I knew it was a dream and was part of my test to enter into the path of the Beloved, but still something didn't feel right. I had to put it aside, for now. Whether it was true or not was a different matter. One thing I knew for sure is that if it was true, there was no way it could stay hidden for much longer. There can be no secrets between Beloveds. I felt like I wanted to be back home in England to address such a possibility. Plus I was also battling with my own sense of denial, I really didn't want to believe it was true; surely it was my own overactive imagination? It had to be, didn't it? Denial won hands down as I turned my focus on bigger matters at hand—like the direction of my life.

I decided to spend my last day seriously contemplating some huge changes that were well past their due date. Sananda had advised me to cut all ties with the yoga world. To stop teaching, to cancel all my workshops, and to drop the 'yoga name' Siri Datta, (a name that had been given to me by Yogi Bhajan, the last living master of Kundalini Yoga); in a nutshell he was inviting me to disentangle myself from the past thirteen years of my life. This idea filled me with a wild, oceanic excitement that beckoned me towards it shores, as well as a colossal sense of the unknown. It felt like I was standing on the parapet, the jumping off point of a high flying aircraft, as I lined up my life to take that particular initiation that all spiritual movements speak about—'the leap of faith.' As I took another step closer to the edge, I knew I was nearing the time when I would have to live with my choice of actions.

I had known for a couple of years that I wanted to move on from teaching yoga, that there was something much deeper inside that needed to be expressed, free from any form of practice or set of rules. Don't get me wrong, I loved teaching yoga, but there was so much more I longed to do, and yoga was only a part of it. I had gone through the motions of leaving the yoga scene twice before, but just as I was breaking free I would get cold feet and go back to what I knew and what felt safe. This time, however, I knew that would not happen, this time I knew it would be for good.

Sananda, unfortunately, was not the most patient of people. Every time we talked, whether it was in person or on Skype; this was our number one topic of conversation. He didn't seem to understand that I was beginning to edge close to throwing away the majority of my life, not to mention doing some crazy stunts like sitting in the middle of the desert facing my darkness. Surely it was obvious that I was moving as fast as I could. He wanted so much from me, so soon.

In my most frustrated moments with him, I questioned whether I was a 'project' of his, rather than his flesh and blood woman. At times it looked and felt as if he was carving me, chipping off bits, rubbing away the irritants with sandpaper with not a care in the world that it hurt like hell. For some reason it looked like it was me that had to move forward first leading the way for the succession of changes. Ladies first and all of that. But I instinctively knew, he would be asked to do the same in the near future. It is the way of the Beloveds—we both had serious work to do with each other.

Thank God I had some time to myself here in Egypt. I felt I could at last settle into myself and take a much needed break away from the intensity, the wild pace of change that wrapped me up into its vortex the moment I laid eyes on Sananda. I decided that the last couple of days in Dahab would be devoted to returning back to England with not only an answer, but an action plan that would ignite the process of 'giving it all up' at a pace that I could handle and with a sense of integrity for all the people that would be affected by these changes.

For days I considered, contemplated, and calibrated how I felt about making all these suggested changes. I looked back over all the obstacles that had arose since meeting Sananda and what I was learning by overcoming the challenges. I continued to deeply feel into myself to see whether I wanted to go down this path that was opening up. The truth was, I did. I was ready to do this; it felt genuine within me. I knew there was so much more that was being asked other than giving up yoga, that part was merely stage one. Honestly, I didn't know how many stages there actually were. So, I decided to journal to see what I could possibly be missing in all of this.

Was I willing to face the challenges as they naturally arose?

Yes.

Was I willing to see this process through and not stop halfway?

Yes.

Was this truly what I wanted, and not something I was doing to please Sananda?

Yes.

Was I aware that as soon as I stopped teaching yoga I would have no income?

Yes.

What was I going to do about that?

I do not know.

Can you see another way of earning money?

No.

So, what's going to happen to you?

I do not know. But I have to do it regardless.

That's pretty much how it always panned out. Every time I reached the end of the sequence I would shake my own head in utter disbelief that I was actually going through with all of this. Voluntarily walking into unemployment with no foreseeable income, and giving everything away, for no real reason, apart from because it felt like the right thing to do? It was so crazy, it was almost suicidal.

All that I had ever created, the sound and dependable reputation that I had steadily worked towards, was about to slip to the ground, like a silk dress you gently step out of at the end of a wonderful evening. And hey, I liked that silk dress, thank you very much. But I had been wearing it a long, long time. I sensed there would be a more befitting dress with my name on it out there somewhere. Leaving yoga and starting fresh (at what I did not know) felt marvelous. Like tasting complete freedom. The freedom to not know and to not plan. But, not to question all the accompanying feelings—that was a real challenge.

It was all this and more that I continued to ponder on the morning I was due to leave behind the sweltering heat and imposing forces of Dahab. I decided to get up and make one last pilgrimage to the waters of the Red Sea, to marvel as to why the Red Sea is named such a thing. *FYI*—The name stems from the fact that at sunrise the water turns a bright and glistening blood red, giving the appearance of watery blood. Ingenious creation.

The Red Sea ended up being the perfect spot to plan my next steps. As I looked out over the sea, the only sounds I was aware of were the gentle lapping of the waves, the odd dog barking, and my pen scribbling in my journal. I came up with a game plan, a course of action, and a timeline for all of the changes to take place. By the end of the scribbling frenzy, I felt aligned, on target, and on purpose. I would leave yoga behind.

Gazing out across the Red Sea, I began to let my mind drift over the years of research I had spent looking for sacred practices that previous Beloveds had embarked on together. I knew these practices were a science *and* an art that was once known by a few select initiates who perhaps taught and maybe helped guide some Beloveds in the past. But, I could not live with the idea that all this knowledge died with the death of those Beloveds. That newly incarnated Beloveds would have to feel for themselves the best ways of coming back together without any help or guidance whatsoever.

No, I knew different. There were ways, and there were practices—and they were very potent ones at that too!

I would not stop until I found out what they were.

With added vigor, I began to piece various sources of information that I had gathered over the years. I noted the power of seeding (planting powerful intentions or grounding new cycles) that happens within a full lunar cycle. I remembered how Romeo and Juliet and countless other great lovers would stay away from all other people, keeping their love safe and away from prying eyes. Treasuring their sanctity as they hid their love away in the early days so that it would become strong and rooted, untainted by rumors and other peoples opinion. Lastly I recalled a practice from the ancient Orient when Beloveds would spend days on end in the bedroom, making love, staying naked, eating in the bridal chamber, and in fact refusing to do anything else other than love one another in some strange and varied ways.

Something was beginning to stir within. There was a swirl of inner activity that confirmed that knowledge was being pieced together, and where there were once gaps, now there was completion. Now I understood within the entirety of my being that this guidance and teaching that I had spent nearly every waking moment looking for could only ever be given like this. Bits and pieces at a time. There is no flesh and blood teacher, no complete school of knowledge and there are no books. There never has been. It would merely work as it had with me this entire time—as an individual grows, stepping more fully into their authenticity, pearls of wisdom are given to guide the way.

I was radiating like a rose in bloom, because I was going back to England with a game plan. I would teach and write about this great work of the Beloveds. I was also returning back to my "One" with a sacred task for us to perform in research for the direction I was now taking with my life. I could feel a sense of destiny weaving itself throughout my fabric of my life, and once clarified all I could think about was returning back to England with the good news.

I couldn't wait to announce to Sananda that I was ready to embark on an unknown journey with him into what is known as the Sacred Union with the Beloved. This is a deeply intimate twenty-eight day retreat where the two Beloveds retire away from the world to enjoy one another's company with no distractions from the outside world or from other people. This complete full lunar cycle would begin on the New Moon and would be the initial key that unlocks the potential for them to truly become intimate. This enables them to build the trusted bonds desperately required to gently unleash, one step at a time, the power and love that has been locked away within their Beloved blueprint. Beloveds must be able to make it through the twenty-eight days without any 'outside world' disturbances, arguments, or injury. This twenty-eight day cycle kick starts the delicate and often turbulent process of merging back together.

Right before I left the hotel and took a taxi to the airport, I sent Sananda an email asking him to meet me later that night in London. I could not wait a moment longer. I had to see him as soon as possible and declare my choice of action. He replied right back, asking for a time and a place; confirming that he would be there. We decided to meet at 2am on one of the side roads off the Hanger Lane gyratory system, one of greater London's busiest roundabouts, home of the legendary North/South circular roads that lead to many of the capitals landmarks, Wembley Stadium being one of them. Seemed like a good idea at the time, as it was close to where he was staying. What a crazy place to meet and what an even crazier time, I thought, even though it was my idea. With its fast and chaotic nature, yet weirdly organized traffic light system that resulted in little to no fatalities, I later realized that Hanger Lane was a sign of what was to come for Sananda and I.

Several hours later, I cruised into London listening to the rhythmic beats of Natasha Atlas, a CD I had picked up in Egypt. She had created a fusion of Arabic vocal sounds with a dance inspired, slightly hip-hop backdrop. It worked. The deep and dirty swagger of the music aroused my sexuality and her piercing, haunting cries echoed back to the days when I would dance for Sananda in the midst of the desert in my dreams. By the time I pulled up on the side road right off the main roundabout and parked the car to meet Sananda, I was like a volcano waiting to erupt.

He was standing underneath a lamppost, wrapping his coat close to him to keep the wind and rain out. His appearance moved me. I became filled with even more desire to touch and kiss him, and the overwhelming desire to love him, forever, always, without fail, to never stop, to never give up, to constantly be with him, until the end of time. I loved him so, so much. It ached to love him this way, at times like these if felt as if my heart was not big or wide enough to allow this amount of love to pass through it.

As I walked towards him, shadowed by the night, my steps muffled by the traffic, I was able to approach him without his knowing. I drank in his silhouette, his long knee-length flannel coat against his dark jeans and trainers. I on the other hand was head to toe in my chocolate brown Prana yoga pants and matching vest (forgot it was freezing in England), accessorized with a few select pieces of elaborate Egyptian jewelry here and there. I fantasized over his dark tousled hair, watching as if hypnotized, how it helplessly became lifted by the wind and then in a moment, surrendered past his shoulders. I studied his profile in detail, tracing the shape of his nose and his upper lip, knowing in moments that my lips would be upon his, tasting this decadent man, showing him how much I missed and craved him.

"Sananda," I whispered as I walked up behind him, wrapping my arms around his waist, kissing his shoulders over the top of his coat as I inhaled the smell of his hair.

"Scarlett," he breathed as he turned to face me. "My love, come to me."

We merged and poured ourselves into one another. Nothing on earth could have got in the way of our embrace, like two magnets we were magnificently and irrevocably drawn together, and stayed that way for at least a half an hour. Holding, stroking, crying, laughing, kissing, touching, and gazing deeply into each other's eyes, and what lies behind the eye, the true depths of our one, shared Soul. We did not care about the rain, or the wind, or the time. We loved each other, and nothing else mattered in the world apart from this tender heartfelt moment of reunion.

I have no idea how we got back to where Sananda's was staying with his mother, but we found ourselves there nonetheless. A small back bedroom housed us for the night, as Sananda lit some candles and drew me close to him on his single bed (?!). I smiled as it reminded me of my own set up with my parents. We spent the most divine night together, hardly sleeping, too alive to sleep, too hungry for one another's face to close our eyes, and far too breathless to rest. With urgency we made love, eager to please, and desperate to enter into one another on our journey of ever deepening intimacy, vulnerability and love. Hours passed as we once again merged together, becoming one with all of life everywhere.

Again, I experienced a deep sensation of ancient, heavy doors being pushed open after eons of being firmly held shut as we made love. We were entering the seven gates, the energetic gateways that lead to the powerful presence of the womb—the doorway to the divine feminine. I was opening, we were opening and together we held each other through the process. Moments before we drifted off I whispered to him about our soon to be up and coming twenty-eight day retreat into Sacred Union. Only the squeeze of his hand confirmed to me that he ached for this as much as I did.

A few hours of blissful sleep later, I tiptoed downstairs to make a cup of tea, trying my best not to spill my excitement and wake up the whole house. His mother's kitchen was spotlessly clean with not a thing out of place. Ah, I would have to be careful here not to disrupt the perfection. Finally I found two cups, some teabags, and worked out how to switch on the kettle. As I waited for it to boil, I decided to have a little look around the place. I discovered photos of Sananda, copies of his books, and items of his clothing that she had washed and neatly folded. This is beyond belief, he really is the same version of me, as my living situation totally mirrored his.

After making tea, I softly climbed the stairs to discover Sananda sitting upright in bed with a warm smile welcoming me back to bed. This was another aspect of Sananda I so greatly appreciated, that no matter what time it was in the morning, he was always ready to receive me in a joyful mood. I jumped onto the bed in glee (putting our tea down first) as I eagerly told him about my decision to detach from all my worldly responsibilities and to commit to the process of diminishing my high-profile life. I assured him that I was now ready to move into a space of complete freedom, to re-create and choose a new expression of this self that was longing to be born.

He was overjoyed, but not really surprised, because he knew that I would always choose this. I was made of the same gumption, the same 'all or nothing' spirit of adventure, and the *very same* passion and spirit that drove us *both* on. It always had been, and it always will be. Slowly, day after day, we were beginning to realize that the essences of our beings were not only very similar, they were in fact symmetrical, complete, and precise mirror images of themselves. It was only our outward personalities, due to our polar opposite experiences that we encountered in our lives prior to our meeting that appeared different.

The purely romantic notion of being a Soul Mate was long gone like an enchanting fairytale, whereas now, the big guns of realization were beginning to dawn upon us as we conversed. The favorite topic of conversation (apart from my leaving the yoga world) was the daily unfolding circumstances that confirmed that we were without a doubt Beloveds. We knew it all along, but we had a lot of fun discovering the many ways that life validated this for us. Whether it was when we were sharing the same dream, or hearing each other telepathically, thinking the same things at the same time, or simply realizing how we orbited each other in the build up to our eventual meeting—it all pointed to the same truth— we were destined to be together.

The more we merged, the more we longed for each other. We were both growing tired and restless of all these snatched m of time, meeting each other in between flights as we landed and took off from countries as frequently as we came and went from each other's lives. It had been two months too long and we both wanted, or rather needed, to create a place of our own, where we lived together to experience some private time and space together. More importantly, we needed to have a spacious bed that was ours from the start, with no ghosts or memories from previous encounters, and of course a bedroom that was out of earshot of parental ears. We also needed to feel a sense of commitment, a symbol or action that marked our dedication to our blessed reunion. With all this coming and going, we wanted something that was still and unmoving. Then, it came to me.

I had an idea, a wild, crazy, mad idea.

"Sananda, let's get a tattoo done, something that symbolizes the seal of our love, a commitment to our journey, and each other," I suggested with spontaneous bravado.

He loved the idea, and jumped at the chance. "Let's do it today, I have the whole day to play with before I need to be at the airport."

And it just kept rolling, as fabulous idea number two came in.

"How do you fancy meeting Chloe during her lunch hour, she is on Oxford Street all day and it's just around the corner?" I asked.

"Go ahead and text her to find out whether she is free," he replied.

She texted back, that yes she was free. And free to meet Sananda. So it was decided, that after we had our tattoos done we were to take that destined step and actually bring Sananda and Chloe together in one place. I was so relieved that they could finally meet each other, yet also a little anxious as I had a feeling that things could turn slightly askew, depending on what mood they were both in. I filled Chloe in by telling her that I would call her later that evening with the lowdown on Egypt, and that this afternoon's meeting was to introduce the "The One" love of my life to the other.

We quickly dressed and jumped aboard the tube into London's Soho Town. I knew where to take us, as I had a tattoo already and trusted the shop immensely. It was called Into You, a fabulous little parlor in the heart of London's gay community. On the tube, we scribbled away at possible ideas and shapes. Until we found it. It was an Aramaic symbol that we both loved, and knew to be as the Seal of the Immaculate Heart, the epiphany of God's love in human form. Yes this was the one, and we both decided to have it tattooed right across our hearts, in the center of our chests. We both felt strongly that it had to be positioned over our heart center as a 'seal' of the Beloved. For me it was the ultimate step of my full commitment towards this process, and a declaration to the Universe that I was one hundred percent dedicated. Underneath our seal we also decided we would also scribe the name of each other into our flesh. Clearly, neither of us ever do things in halves—we were going all the way!

Our two artists, both Italian and dashingly gay took wonderful care of us. We were having the work done together in the same room, which was lucky as usually you have a private booth to yourselves. After a couple of hours of intense, stinging, and bloody pain for me, and hilariously ticklish sensations for Sananda we walked out of the Soho tattoo parlor like two punk teenagers, arm-in-arm as we giggled at everything—no doubt due to the naturally created endorphins from the experience. We were now on our way to the tiny little bijou organic raw food café called Mildred's where

Chloe was waiting for us. We tumbled through the front door like two wild stallions, guns blazing, and announcing our arrival by the sheer volume of our laughter and merriment. We were high on life, massively in love, and totally pumped full of copious amounts of serotonin from the permanent art emblazoned across our chests.

Chloe waved us over to where she was sitting, as we weaved in and out of other raw foodies happily demolishing their lunches. I nervously introduced them with both sets of fingers crossed behind my back. Chloe coolly greeted him with a look that said, "You're going to have to work hard to get me to believe that you are as amazing as Scarlett makes you out to be." In turn, Sananda greeted her with a conscious distance. His look was altogether different. Immediately he knew what she was thinking, so in response he opted for a discerning detachment to see how things unfolded. He already made no bones to me about the fact that Chloe and her lifestyle did not impress him. He openly declared to me on several occasions that she needed some serious healing because he could sense that fear was motivating her in all aspects of her life. It's easy to see—given all of that—why I was not in a rush to get them together.

Unfortunately, it did not look like love at first sight for these two kids. We all sat together and ordered lunch, as I did my very best to keep the conversation going in futile attempts to weave them together. Pulling up my t-shirt I discreetly revealed to Chloe my fresh tattoo, as she 'oohed' and 'ahhed' over its position, asking whether or not it hurt. Nothing fazed her anymore; she was immune to all my impromptu ways. After half an hour of lightly chatting together, I realized that the weaving was not going to happen, not today anyway.

It felt as if Chloe did not trust Sananda, imagining that he was too good to be true. She never believed all the lip service that men give when they first met a woman; she was far too wise for those games. But what she didn't realize was that Sananda and I were not in that game; we were not like the type of people she rubbed shoulders with. I had told her this in the past, but she chose not to listen, merely waving her hand in my face. My reality was not part of her reality any more.

She wanted to get to the truth of the matter—was this man good enough for her friend? Until she found out, she would keep him at arm's length. Remember the cannon ball theory? Well, Sananda could sense all this going on and began to get itchy and impatient with the whole game. I am sure he was looking at her in such a way that he was contemplating an all out strike. I ducked for cover as I knew what could come next...

But you know what? He had a little poke, a tiny prod here and there by mentioning various tactics that she hid beneath, but in the end he decided to just go quiet and allow whatever was meant to be, to be. I felt her prickle as she iced over at the sheer nerve of it! Oh man, this was going from bad to worse. I remembered the key word surrender and immediately melted as it reminded me to "trust the process." We continued to talk about our tattoos and various other lighthearted subjects, steering clear of any further topics of intimacy. After an hour Chloe had to return back to work, and as always she left her award-winning trademark on both of our cheeks, a pale pink glossy kiss mark and a waft of her perfume.

I looked at Sananda, as I said, "Well, that was my best friend."

He did not reply, but instead beamed at me in such a way that his eyes glazed over as he slowly leaned over and kissed me on my slightly less glossy mouth. After a few sacred hours of being together like so many times before, inevitably it was time to go our separate ways once again. This time it was Sananda who was leaving for France, while I was making my way back to my parents to begin the process of letting everything in my life go. I drove him to the airport, dropped him outside, and continued on.

I prayed for an answer, a way of being together in a more concrete way, to actually have the chance of a *normal* life together, and the time to really get to know one another. I felt the heavy weight of sadness approach me as I saw the last vestiges of Heathrow Airport fade out of sight in my rearview mirror. I began to cry from a sense of helplessness and the feeling of being unable to offer my heart a sanctuary. Still I continued on, as I touched the cotton dressing that covered my tattoo and smiled.

As soon as I got back to my parents and unpacked from the trip to Egypt, I settled down to the more important matters at hand. First things first, I needed to call Chloe and tell her my decision at a time when it was just us. I had a feeling she would not be entirely supportive at first, but she would come around.

"Hi Chloe, it's me again," I gushed down the phone towards her. When I love someone the whole world knows about it. This time we caught up properly as we talked nonstop about the yoga holiday, Dahab, deserts, Bedouin, Abdul, food, and Arabic fashion while I caught up on her latest dates, dresses, and drinking disasters. I deliberated whether I should tell her about my circle in the desert thing, and felt it better to not mention, not over the phone anyway as that topic would take up far too much time. Leaving the best until last, I asked her. "Well, what do you think of Sananda?"

One sentence said it all. "He is absolutely perfect for you, I can see why you are together," came her cool reply.

She wasn't sold on him. Not yet anyway.

"Actually Chloe, I called you for two reasons. One was to say, 'It's me again!' and the second reason was to tell you that... um... I have decided to stop teaching yoga, and that I am ending this type of lifestyle completely. There is more inside of me Chloe, and by staying with what I know, I will never have the chance to find out what that is. I have to do this, I have to enter this period of quiet inner reflection and then, over time I shall rebirth back into life with the real expression of what I have to share."

There was a long silence, a really long silence.

"I can't believe you are saying this Scarlett. You have worked so hard to reach where you are now. You are known throughout the whole world, and you are going to give that up? If you do this, you will have to start again with a brand new identity... people are so fickle, they will forget you once you disappear," she warned.

"I know Chloe, but I simply can't carry on. I know it's a lie. I have to do this, I know it through and through!" I confirmed back to her.

She sighed on the other end of the line, knowing that my mind was made up. We have been together in this place before, me complaining about having cold feet, and her warning me not to be so impulsive, to hang in there and see if I felt the same in six months.

"What are you going to live on? Where are you going to live? Your parents won't allow you to not work."

There was a moment's silence, before she played her trump card. A trump card any best friend would play, but not until the eleventh hour, of course.

"Does this decision have anything to do with Sananda?" she quietly asked with an air of suspicion.

"Yes it does," I announced, having no urge to hide my Beloved. "He knows that I am not content and is encouraging me to take the necessary action to break away so that I am free to choose a new path in life. How many times have I got this close in the past, to only turn back carrying on in hope that things would change?' I gently raised my voice, making sure she could feel my passion and resolve.

She sighed again.

"Whatever Scarlett, it's your life. But it doesn't feel good; it's too hasty for my liking. But hey, I am not you, and let's face it I have been doing my job for nearly twenty years, and I'm not about to change now. We are different people, you and I. So go on, go for it! I'll be behind you every step of the way," she promised.

"Chloe, it means so much to know that you are supporting me. It's going to be a tough time. I can feel it already. I sense there will be many people who won't understand. I can feel it coming already, the rumors and gossip, but it's too late to change the winds of destiny; the process has already begun," I foretold.

"Be careful Bare, watch your step. Try not to step on any extra toes, keep a low profile, and leave as elegantly as possible," she advised. Strangely enough, I had once imagined that working within the spiritual field would mean leaving behind the competitive, dishonest world of non-spiritual organizations. But no! It was still going on, and I had been on the receiving a few times too many. Even Chloe was amazed at the stories I shared with her. It was definitely time for me to make my exit from the yoga world.

"You have my word Barb. Elegant is my middle name," I

teased. "So come on Barb, what did you think of him?" I coyly asked.

"He is perfect for you, just your cup of tea. I am happy for you Scarlett, you of all people deserve to find The One, it's all you have ever spoken about since the moment I met you. That is precisely the reason why I came to France, to support you as you reeled him in," she laughed. "One thing darling, don't allow him to squash your spirit, you're too special to let that happen sweetie. Promise me?" she pressed.

"I promise you, but I have a funny feeling he's going to try. But it's okay Barb, I know the difference between my natural spirit and egoic tendencies. I assure you my spirit is eternally untouchable, however he can do what he likes to my ego. Its two-way traffic Barb. When Beloveds come together they wield the sword of change in both their hands. I know what I am doing. Have faith in me," I declared.

"I do, that's what is so amazing about all of this. I completely have faith in you. You always do come out shining whatever you turn your attention to. I have always said you are one lucky lady," she declared

Later that afternoon, I created and delicately crafted my emails that were destined to be sent to the entire yoga world announcing my retirement. I made sure I gave all the studios and establishments one month's notice, and that in some cases I would find the most appropriate replacement. I did all I could to ease out of my situation as gracefully as possible. When I eventually got around to pressing that 'send' button my heart was pounding, and my fingers were trembling. I had given myself a countdown before pressing the button, coaching myself out loud the moment I felt any doubts creep in. Within a couple of hours, my whole life was beginning to unpeel and un-stick from what I thought was once solid and real.

In one afternoon I "let go of" my:

- Yoga Career
- Yoga Teacher Training
- Yoga Writing (for books, magazines, and newspapers)
- Yoga Radio Show
- Yoga Classes, Workshops, and Retreats
- Yoga Name (and all associations to the lineage that I studied under)
- And "picked up" a rockin' Be 'love'd tattoo.

Seems like a fair trade, right?

I stretched back in the bamboo armchair that sat in my parent's conservatory, interlacing my hands as I cradled the back of my head, turning my attention to the glow of the setting sun. Mum and dad were so supportive of me as they knew how much I wanted to move onto bigger and better things. I had poured my heart out to them many times about my desire to be a teacher/speaker of love and write inspiring books on the subject. Having their support with Sananda's meant everything. Eventually Chloe would come around as well, or at least I hoped so.

I have done it, I thought to myself. I have finally taken those steps that I had dreamt about years ago. Now my real choice was being made. I closed my eyes and sighed to myself as I became aware of this sacred, precious moment, the moment when I chose my truth. I felt such a sense of freedom and excitement that a slight smile formed over my lips. I stayed like that for minutes, maybe even half an hour, bathing in the warmth of the late evening sunset, gently rocking back and forth until I realized that the initial buzz had worn off. The instant that the 'high' dissolved was the very same moment when a sobering reality hit me right between the eyes, like a runaway freight train. Pow!

"How are you going to survive? What are you going to do?"

Basic stuff really. Unfortunately, questions that I did not have the answers too. I looked at one of my cats for an answer. Nope, none there either. His only response was to jump onto my lap, eventually settle down, and begin purring. Good enough for me, I suppose. I closed my eyes again, and placed one hand over my heart as I sensed the space in my chest, and felt into the cavernous nature of my heart. How does my heart feel in response to these decisions?

My heart was buoyant and full. There was no fear or trepidation whatsoever; in fact there was an upsurge of happiness at the potential of a fantastic adventure on the near horizon. Case closed, court (mind) dismissed. According to the evidence of my heart, all is well. From this moment on, every step, choice, word, and response shall come from this place. I shall navigate through these tenuous waters with only my heart as the map, mast, and compass. This life now belongs to love. All that shall ever come from me, will be love, only ever love. The telephone rang; I leapt from my bamboo armchair almost launching the cat into the nether regions of outer space as I reached for the phone, knowing it was going to be Sananda.

It was.

Connection again. Divine timing.

"Darling, I have been thinking about some things since arriving here in France. I have been out for supper with the organizers of the retreat and have been quite touched by the light and beauty of this place. Scarlett, I really want to live with you sweetheart, I can't bear this being apart from you any longer," he mercifully expressed.

Naturally I swooned, as they were the words I longed to hear.

"My love, I am so ready. My answer is yes—let's do it. There is something though that I need to tell you. Today I put the wheels in motion. I have told all my yoga associations that I am leaving in one month. I have done it Sananda, I am leaving! I have ended everything in honor of becoming who I truly am and all that I long to share."

I whispered, "However, it puts me in a different financial position. I would say that I have enough savings to last about three months without working or earning in anyway. As much as I long to live with you, I don't see how I will be able to afford to," I sighed.

"Darling, don't be ridiculous. I am going to pay for everything and support you through this process. Did you not know that, love? I am here for you in every way," he declared.

Well, well, well. To be honest, I could not believe my ears. I never in a million years imagined that he would support me. It was not an experience I had ever come across before in life. I came from a family where if you wanted money you had to earn it. Money was never given in our family, unless of course there was an extreme 'leg hanging off' emergency or the odd car parking fine charge that quadrupled over time (due to a sea of constant address changes over the years—yes, that would be me!).

So here I was. Receiving the news that he would take care of me, not only was he my Beloved, he was now offering to take complete financial care of me while I went through the trials and birth pains of creating a new life. Was I hearing things? Was this for real?

"Darling are you there? What do you say? Shall we move to

France in June? In the next two months?" He repeated.

I realized I had switched off as I contemplated my dream coming true. Living in France was my ultimate wish. A wish I had not yet expressed to him. How this man seemed to know me through and through—another marker of the Beloved! His final words instantly brought me back into the present moment.

"Yes darling, yes. I would love to. Oh my God, that is fantastic, I love France. Do you think we could we move to the southwest corner, on the border of Spain close to Carcassonne?" I begged.

"Of course, you choose the place and we'll take it. I shall leave it up to you to find our first home together. All I ask is that it's in nature, isolated, spacious, and beautiful," he stated.

"Sure I will be able to find something, I know the area well," I promised.

We hung up. I leaned back into the chair once more, this time to gaze up into the vastness of space. The night sky had swallowed up the luminescent trails of light and subtle nuances of the dissolving and diminishing sun. Before me the eternal darkness of the universe pressed itself around the darkened half of the planet. I blew out the candles that attempted to hold back the impending blackness and entered into its void, into the unknown, and into the unformed.

I came to understand that something else was manifesting around me. I could now see that I was preparing to leave my parents house, the country I grew up in, my surrounding friends and family, and take a leap of faith to move in with Sananda after being together for only three months, at a time when I had nothing to offer. Only myself, and I was not sure how stable even that would be as this process continued. Still those thoughts of Sananda with another woman continued to come up every now and again. I knew that I would have to raise the subject, because if I didn't they would continue to plague me and possibly lead to some kind of withdrawing on my part.

No, I knew that I would have to do something radically different and that was to be vulnerable, nakedly honest, and reveal my own insecurities. Yuck—that felt very uncomfortable. This was totally new territory. But I knew it was the truth. I was not in charge anymore, love was. Would love be embarrassed about being vulnerable? Of course not, and therefore neither would I. I was no longer in control, so I had let go of the reins of my life and enter into the free fall.

When love beckons to you, follow him,
Though his ways are hard and steep.
And when his wings enfold you yield to him,
Though the sword hidden among his pinions
May wound you.
And when he speaks to you believe in him,
Though his voice may shatter your dreams
As the north wind lays waste the garden.
For even as love crowns you
So shall he crucify you.
Even as he is for your growth
So is he for your pruning.
Even as he ascends to your height and caresses
Your tenderest branches that quiver in the sun,
So shall he descend to your roots and
Shake them in their clinging to the earth.

—KAHLIL GIBRAN, *THE PROPHET*

Chapter Twelve

Betrayal: the Fight for Love

Parents' Home, England, Beginning of April
(Easter Weekend), 2009

THE EASTER WEEKEND was turning into a rollercoaster of raw creativity and endless insight. With mum and dad away for the weekend, I had the house to myself and all the time in the world to explore my new passion—love. After Sananda's reassurance that he would support me as I left the yoga world behind and entered into the exploration of finding my path, I dove into my research like some mad scientist. All around me were papers, notes, images, and symbols alongside earmarked books and sacred texts. I was furiously scribbling notes on endless pieces of paper that I cast aside all over my bed, as my obsession bordered on genius.

I was now certain that the moment Sananda and I had our tattoos inscribed into our flesh we had set in motion an irreversible chain of events. Ever since that day in Soho, I had become obsessed and consumed with the presence of the Beloved. I was seeing its symbolism everywhere—within art, culture, society and poetry— sensing that a higher intelligence was guiding us to a time and place where we could all love each other without the fear of ever being hurt, rejected, or abandoned.

I was calling my mild dose of madness: 'falling *madly* in love.' To do so, I needed to remain centered, so I purposely disconnected myself from the outside world, ignoring all telephone calls (apart from Sananda's) and emails. Only Chloe, who was used to this behavioral trait of mine, could forgive and understand that every now and again I would be offline and unobtainable. We had a solid agreement that guaranteed her a full report complete with dramatic and passionate storytelling once I had discovered the answers I was searching for. I decided I was now a self-declared "Lover" who could easily sit alongside Rumi, one of the greatest Sufi poets of all time. I imagined us working together as we bent over our shared desk with a feathered quill in our hands, rustling up another batch of breathlessly exquisite poetry on sheets of local papyrus.

I had become a self-confessed expert on love, and my conclusion at this point was that love was totally out of control, always has been, always will be. Kneeling on the bed with my glasses perched on the end of my nose, hair cascading in all directions I zoomed in with my head down, searching for the clue and the thread that would lead to the eureka moment! I fumbled through papers and notes researching to see whether there was a pattern, a certain sequence that played out once Beloveds met. Something magnificent was orchestrating all the events and circumstances that Sananda and I had to pass through in order to play out every form of resistance between us. It wasn't random, it was all divine—I was certain of it.

Upon even closer inspection, I started to find strong associations between the Beloved and the mysterious labyrinth (there were 22 pathways, 11 turns on the path into the center, and 11 to get back out again) and a 5-pointed star (5 is the number and symbol of the Divine feminine, and perhaps more?). Then there was the Tibetan Tantra; full of daka's and their dakini's in rapturous love making positions, along with the ancient Indian temples that were (and still to this day) elaborately carved in ecstatic Tantrika's in explicit sexual union. As far as I could see there was plenty of growing evidence that previous Beloveds had left clues behind, messages contained within art and symbolism, as well as the strikingly obvious alchemical texts embedded within ancient poetry, like this piece taken from the Song of Solomon, written by King Solomon: "My beloved spoke, and said unto me, rise up, my love, my fair one, and come away with me." Ah yes, its enticing deliciousness was everywhere. All of this deliciousness had me so absorbed that I could not stop for anything as meaningless as eating, sleeping, or peeing; it was clear to me that I had found my ultimate body of work, my life's work perhaps. And there was no doubt about it; the numbers 22 and 5 had something to do with it.

As the sun began setting on one of the most exhilarating Easter Sunday's of my life, suddenly a flash of wisdom revealed itself to me. I looked at the main ways in which people withdraw from love. I looked back over my life and examined the 'big hurts' that I had encountered, remembering their wounds, and shuddering at the thought of having to live through them again. I listed all the ways that people can experience hurt when in an intimate loving relationship; the list grew and grew as I reencountered my own pain and imagined others. Reviewing my list, I immediately spotted how I had used different words to describe the same emotional response. So with a fine toothcomb I dissected each word until I was satisfied that each individual word represented a unique and individual emotional response. From a list of over thirty descriptive words only five remained. I reached for a new sheet of paper, which I titled, "The Wounds to Love" and in huge letters, boldly marked them out.

Betrayal.

Denial.

Judgment.

Separation.

Abandonment.

I collapsed back onto my bed from exhaustion after finally discovering what I knew to be true. There was indeed a path of initiation, a pre-arranged sequence of events that needed to be experienced and overcome in order for the two lovers to truly become one. I felt that this sequence was organic and would be different for each Beloved couple knowing that the sequence was not fixed in any way. I also knew that because we are all different some wounds would hardly cause a stir, while others would create a tsunami.

Waves of wisdom responded within, while feelings and sensations acknowledged that this was indeed the path for Beloved's and some deeply committed Soul Mates. All must embark upon this journey if they want to experience becoming one. This journey would fully unite them to open all the doors of the potential they carried within. It was this kernel of truth that could lead to a potential worldwide transformation. Can you imagine a world where these wounds were obsolete? It would be an emblazoned example of love in action on Earth. And guess whose job it would be to be the forerunning pioneers of this transformation? That's right; the Beloveds. I closed my eyes as I released a huge sigh of relief. Images, words, and faces flew across my mind like migrating birds, as I heard the familiar voice of my heart.

You have made a wondrous discovery. You have unveiled the five wounds to love. It is one of your soul purpose's to discover their antidotes. The healing balm shall be known by living through the experience of the wound. However, beware their power, these wounds are often ferociously guarded by powerful emotional energy, and can be infused with the temptation of momentary blindness and ignorance. Some of the wounds will be more aggressive than others, and it will be different for all people. Stay true to love at all costs… I cannot overemphasize the importance of what you are about to do. Now that you know this, it is only a matter of time before you will encounter the first one.

All five must be experienced, in order to burn free from their hold. This is the way of love, and all who are on this path must face these rites of passage. This is the test of your commitment. To stay true to love, even when your human heart experiences being hurt in a way like never before.

I gulped as I listened, feeling the enormity of what I was moving towards. My stomach began to churn uncomfortably with the unexpected news that I would have to go through these wounds once again, this time consciously choosing to experience the pain, refraining from the hard-wired, ingrained urge to run away or numb it all out. Just then my mobile rang, and brought my attention crashing back to present time. It was 1am, who could be calling me?

"Hi darling, it's me. I was feeling you and felt the need to call." As always, Sananda's precise timing was immaculate. He was currently still in France nearing the end of his teaching retreat on the feminine mysteries. He had been away for over a week now and I was missing him terribly. Fortunately, his phone calls were regular, reviving, and always timely. However, it would still be some time before we actually got to see one another again in the flesh, as our pre-arranged travel plans continued to drag us in separate directions all over Europe.

Hearing his voice, though, brought happiness to my heart. I was almost beside myself with joy and excitement to share with him what had been discovered during the day. Sananda never carries a mobile (he doesn't like to be bothered by people), so I would often have to sit on breaking news until the time came when he was able to Skype me. And now the time was here. After an hour of excitedly explaining everything to him, while pacing back and forth waving papers in my hand to emphasize my points, I finally ceased talking. I glued my ear to the receiver, awaiting his response. Jubilation exploded throughout my bedroom as I heard his infectious laughter, as he joined in with my wild joy of stumbling upon a fascinating discovery. Whatever would we do with the wounds to love now that they had been uncovered? We threw our combined insights together and decided the best thing would be to allow our ideas to breathe, to see what would naturally arise next.

Our excitable dialogue began to naturally dissolve into sighs and kisses over the phone; sharing how much we were missing each other, wishing we could be in bed with one another holding our bodies close together. Swooning, I sunk back onto the bed as I closed my eyes to imagine Sananda and I intertwined in a lovers embrace in front of a roaring log fire as we writhed around in our bare-naked flesh over giant sheepskins rugs. Not a bad fantasy for a mad scientist, eh? Just as I was beginning to enjoy our newly developed skill of making love at a distance (a method similar to a guided, visual meditation, which works incredibly well if you have a highly developed imagination—with us both adding in details as we led the way), a most unusual and shocking thing happened.

In my vision, I sensed someone walk in on our lovemaking and stand above us. In my dream, I opened my eyes and saw another woman who I did not recognize by face, but in the depths of my being knew was Catherine, the friend that Sananda had stayed with while he was in Belgium for the weekend last month. I just knew it was her, I could feel it. All of a sudden everything began to make sense. The energy of the vision was *exactly* like the time when I had recurring nightmares in the desert, not to mention the full on lucid dream when I sat in my circle all night. Oh yes, this was precisely what my shadowy black magician was trying to show me; images that I had refused to truly acknowledge, imagining that they were some kind of purposeful interference that was based on fear.

I now realized that my shadow was in fact trying to help me, showing me a glimpse of another reality that was already happening in Sananda's world. (The shadow gets so much bad press, but in truth—it's all about love—it is always trying to help guide us to our highest purpose.) My stomach ached with sickness as I immediately pressed the 'eject' button to abruptly end our long-distance lovemaking in less than a split second.

A crawling, sickening feeling began to seep through my veins. I had thought about this Catherine ever since Sananda told me he had to unexpectedly cut short his weekend. He never gave too many details on why, only to say that it was not right for him to stay there any longer, and so he had decided to leave the next morning. His early departure was already too late for me; my heckles were up and the alarm bells were sounding in the basement of my belly.

But I ignored the signals, the dreams, and the constant inner nudging that warned of foul play—well, the best I could anyway. I opted for the spiritual route, telling myself that Sananda was a 'spiritual' man and could not possibly be tempted by the flesh and that these feelings of mine were a form of insecurity and should not be confessed. My brilliant mind asserted that Sananda may not think I was up to the mark in terms of true enlightenment if I suggested that he had cheated on me. Even so, no matter how hard I tried to transcend, ignore, laugh at, or psychobabble myself with uplifting affirmations, every time that weekend sprung to mind, my claws came out.

It was beginning to happen again now, armed with the feeling that Catherine was attempting to haunt us after appearing in my vision. My throat tightened and burned at the thought of speaking out about what I was feeling, yet I knew I had run out of choices. I knew once the dreams refused to go away that I had to bring it up. Spiritual or not this was a conversation we had to have. I did not have to wait too much longer "to see what would naturally arise next," as here I stood, face-to-face with the validating fear that Sananda had quite possibly betrayed me.

"Darling, what is it? I sense you withdrawing from me," Sananda's voice interrupted my building sense of dread.

At first I brushed it off, with a, "Nothing sweetheart, I'm just tired that's all," while inside me the big guns of an almighty showdown were moving into position.

With a dry mouth and churning stomach, I began to hear the soft voice of my heart speaking gently with soothing, reassuring words, arousing the courage to continue on. Slowly together, step-by-step we began to tread through the quagmire of snares and traps that potentially awaited us:

Breathe sweetheart, breathe. Just be brave and open. Reveal this to him. You can walk through this wound and receive its healing. It may take some time, but it is here for you.

I searched high and low for the courage to speak with vulnerability of how this fear was arising in me. It would have been too easy to flare up and accuse him in anger and jealously, threatening to make him pay for his mistake. But I knew this was not what was being asked of me. I did my utmost to remain open to the truth, holding the door open for Sananda should he declare his innocence, showing me that these feelings may be simply my own insecurities.

The power of my certainty, however, was beginning to cloud my loving feelings for him. I was forewarned about the powerful energetic guardians that protected these wounds. If touched, these wounds could unleash copious amounts of energy ranging from anger to utter despair. From where I was standing it looked as if betrayal was a highly personal one for me. I had been no stranger to it, although typically on the other side of the fence. I debated where and how to begin this question that burned at my throat, when suddenly I heard my own numb words speak into the receiver.

"Sananda, what actually happened between you and Catherine in Belgium?"

Silence.

That silence told me everything I needed to know. And yet somehow I needed the full truth from him to move forward.

"Please Sananda, tell me the truth," I pleaded, feeling powerless. His previous story reeked of a lie. I could no longer hold it in. I stayed on the line listening for some kind of answer, awaiting my fate, as if somebody else had the power to change my life forever.

"Why are you asking me this now?"

Oh God, it's true, it did happen. My heart began to thump furiously against my ribs as nausea moved up from my stomach and clenched my throat.

"Sananda, please tell me," I spoke from a cold and empty space. My entire body was covered in chills as I watched the trust between us dissolve.

I had to do something quick; I sensed I was beginning to lose myself in the arousal of all of the old emotions of betrayal. These were powerful energies (hadn't I just uncovered this knowledge?!) and this time I had to do something different. I began to pray.

Oh God, please be here with me now. In this moment let me stand for love, don't desert me now into this darkness that threatens to consume me.

Still I waited.

"Sananda, please! Speak to me," I demanded one more time.

"Yes, I did sleep with her."

The room began to spin. The five wounds, the excitement, the thrill of discovery, the promised happiness, blood, hands, and nails twisted and turned into a macabre of chaos. What seemed like an eternity abruptly ended as an internal inferno coursed through my body, heart, and mind. I paced and circled around my room like a caged animal (with a phone to my ear), swearing and cursing at Sananda and myself for the deceit of it all.

I remembered how only four weeks ago I was in Cologne, Germany facilitating "The Sacred Art of Manifestation" yoga workshop when this happened. I had gushed like some infatuated teenager with my close yogi friends of the news that I had found great love. I recalled how we all celebrated together, clinking glasses to toast our union, and how our story of love breathed new life into their diminishing dreams of meeting their Beloveds or Soul Mates. While we danced and sang into the night, completely drenched with happiness, my Beloved lay in the arms of another.

As we celebrated. He cheated.

I felt as though my faith in him had been murdered. My spirit decided to take this great leap of faith and give everything to this man, and now, here I was—betrayed. I was bewildered and stunned by this news. I didn't know which way to turn. While I was telling everyone how great he was, that he was this incredible spiritual person, he was falling into the most clichéd statistic about men. And I thought he was beyond these types of things.

My eyes dropped to my bed. The Five Wounds to Love stood out like a neon beacon. Now I knew why five had jumped out as an important number for this fated journey—it stood for the five wounds.

And here was my first one.

Betrayal.

It all came rushing in, as the fullness of this wound was revealed to me. Betrayal shows up in the stomach or third chakra. It is a dreaded feeling that twists and turns in your stomach, giving rise to nausea that suffocates and stifles your breath. Even the suspicion of betrayal has the power to trigger these feelings within the body and mind, causing one to react in a multitude of feelings from rage and revenge, to hopeless despair, hate, or depression. Betrayal is usually a two-fold wound. First is the act, words, or thoughts that take place behind another's back. Second is the concealment, and the purposeful ways to cover up the action.

It was clear that I had to act fast, before I became blinded by resentment, and the endless ways I could make him pay. My prayer was answered in the nick of time as my heart said:

Breathe, sweetheart, breathe. I am with you, see it all, feel it all, love cannot be harmed. You too have the power and strength to overcome this. Embrace this, your heart is deep enough to consume all this hurt and heal it completely.

I took a long, deep breath as I calmed down. The pacing began to slow enough for me to contemplate sitting on the edge of the bed so I could think clearly. I closed my eyes and entered the place within me that was not touched by the course of events that had just unfolded. The more I deepened into that place, the more I realized that love was encouraging me to go beyond the usual scenario's where I would have bolted in the past, hurling a string of abuse in my wake. I remembered back to the voice of my heart:

All five must be experienced, in order to burn free from their hold. This is the way of love, and all who are on this path must face these rites of passage. This is the test of your commitment. To stay true to love, even when your human heart experiences being hurt in a way like never before.

I hung my head in sorrow and regret. I had lived under the constant fear that a lover would one day betray me. This had resulted in my never actually allowing myself to… trust. I came to a start with that last revelation. Trust. That was the antidote to Betrayal! But now what? How am I supposed to trust in this moment? Trust in what exactly? My heart spoke:

Trust in this process. Trust that there is a hugely valid reason why this is happening. To trust that within Sananda's actions there is a key for your own healing.

How on earth am I supposed to do that, now that he's proven he is completely untrustworthy?

My Love, you are being asked to trust this moment, trust that this is happening to you, for you, for a very good reason. Trust that you have to face this situation, for your own reasons and breakthrough. Can you do that? Can you trust that?

Yes. Yes, I can. I am willing to go through this, this time.

Remember the times that you have played the other role in this situation. You have never known betrayal, only ever the betrayer. Who more loving is there to teach you this lesson, than your Beloved Sananda?

Sananda was quiet and present on the end of the phone as I went through this agonizing process. Whenever he did speak it was to profusely apologize, I could hear the tears in his eyes as he begged for me to stay present and calm. He explained that this was all his own doing, that he was scared about the way he felt about me. He knew that this relationship was going to be huge, and as a knee-jerk reaction bolted against what he loved the most—his Beloved. He betrayed Love. Again my head dropped in regret, as I cried in sorrow for finally being able to experience betrayal. Like a yo-yo I would drop into feeling the agony and the hurt, to then catapult myself out and into believing that all this was wrong, that Sananda was a womanizer and should be dropped like a hot brick.

This constant change of positions caused me much confusion and anxiety. I could not decide whether I was coming or going—and all in a span of 10 minutes. I felt as if I was losing trust in myself, Sananda, and the process of uniting with my Beloved. I was grasping around for something, anything that felt real and dependable, something I could hold onto for support and steadiness. I found nothing. All I could do was surrender and continue on.

Despite struggling with whether I had any trust left in Sananda, he was remarkably calm and steady in himself. He was willing to walk with me every step of the way, as I took him through my painful process. There was so much shouting and interruption going on initially that we decided we would deal with this process one person at a time. I wanted to go first, to flesh out my part and uncover what I needed to learn. And so, he guided me back to the places within that housed with all the betrayals I had made in the past towards others and myself. I remembered my own path of destruction caused by my dishonesty and lies. Tears of regret slid down my face, as I confessed my own betrayals and prayed for forgiveness. I always knew betrayal would find me. It had my name on its 'wish' list, and there would be no escape. I too had been unfaithful to partners; in fact there was not one I had remained loyal to. I had chosen to do the dirty, rather than face the hopelessness of a dying relationship. I saw their broken hearts, the burning tears, the uncontrollable anger, and their searing pain.

So yes, I knew betrayal would find me, and in some way I was relieved. Acknowledging my past was the first part of healing the wound of betrayal. The other part concerned the healing between Sananda and me in this present day. As I sat upright on my bed, I consciously began to envision the possible images of Sananda and Catherine. My inner guidance advised that this process would rapidly heal our traumatic moment. It spoke of how many avoid the truth after an affair by burying the details and refusing to speak about what actually happened. My guidance admonished me that not walking through this visualization would lead to a whole host of resentments that would grow and fester diminishing our love over time. It urged me to swiftly move into this next phase—striking while the iron was hot!

While Sananda was heavy in heart and spirit, he agreed to walk through this with me for full healing. I sat in my internal cinema of sexual deceit and saw the entire scene. I asked questions of Sananda to confirm whether what I was seeing was the truth. I witnessed the kiss, the nakedness, the bodies, the intimacy, the desire, and lust that were consuming both Catherine and Sananda. I was there in that room, face to face with my worst nightmare.

I held my breath, as I knew one more image needed to be witnessed.

With a full heart I asked the image to come to me. I saw Sananda's heaving body on top of Catherine's. I looked closer to see how he held and guided himself in as he entered his woman. My last visual was of both their heads rolling back with ecstasy and sexual pleasure, as their bodies plunged into the depths of one another. I stood to the side of them frozen with pain and disbelief. I searched for Sananda's eyes, as if trying to find a way to reach him, as only his Beloved could. I wanted to pry his attention away from the other woman, to come back to me for a moment, to think about me if only just once.

He felt me, as his head turned to glance into the empty space that was drenched in my essence. For a couple of seconds we saw each other, and all protection and weaponry that I could have wielded against him, dropped to the floor. I opened my hands in surrender, and my heart pleaded with him, as the only word that could be formed was:

"Why?"

The scene closed and dissolved, the emotional charge drained away, and I was left suspended, in a void-like place, neither here nor there. I was left dangling, like a hangman swaying in the dark night wind. My body was lifeless, yet my spirit was agonizingly still alive. It knew I had to walk through this fire. Most of the time it's the 'avoidance' of fear that is more painful that the fear itself. Once we face something completely, leaving no detail out, we realize that it wasn't as big as we made it out to be. Somehow, I still had to get to that point. My mind began rattling off a litany of positive affirmations saying I could do this. I was telling myself it was all okay, that we had only been together for three weeks at the time. That it was the early days and these things happen. On and on and on, I kept counseling myself, trying to become the perfect spiritual example of enlightenment. Finally, my mind gave up; and my heart spoke:

Breathe Scarlett, breathe. This is one of the great tests of the path of the Beloveds. This is where you could (and typically would) bolt and throw it all away by convincing yourself that this is 'wrong' and that you would be weak to forgive him. This is the voice of the mind, and its myriad ways of avoiding the heart, avoiding love. You knew that this would have to be faced. It was only a matter of time…

I felt the certainty of what was being said, despite the battle in my mind over doing it all "right." Suddenly, I could breathe a bit more. Once the visualization process was complete, it was now Sananda's turn to contribute to the healing. I heard him sigh deeply as he carefully chose his words, knowing that this would be a delicate process. He began by saying how regretful he was, humbly acknowledging that he had made a huge mistake. He explained that Catherine was a final last minute fling. That it meant nothing to him, it was some impulse that got the better of him, and that afterwards his heart felt heavy and untrue. He was aware that the moment he truly committed to me, would be the same moment he endeavored to keep our relationship free from infidelity. He admitted that he was afraid of the enormity of our relationship, and that this fear resulted in the betrayal.

Now I understood why he returned from Belgium so sure of our love and eager to move on into a more committed phase. He too had passed over an obstacle. While I was not too pleased with his methods, there can be no denying it, I had to face the receiving end of this wound that I had so often dished out. Another hour slowly passed by the time I whispered to Sananda that I was exhausted, and that we could speak again tomorrow. We ended our conversation with a deeper and more intimate understanding of one another and what it means to be human, whilst yearning for divinity.

We also knew that a powerful healing had taken place, despite feeling like we had done ten rounds with the world's heavyweight boxing champion. We were battered and bruised, but we were together. We had spoken the truth, confessed, revealed, shared, and forgiven each other. I couldn't believe it. If someone had told me a few months ago that I would forgive a man for cheating on me—I would have told them they were insane. But, that is what love was asking me to do. As much as I had to forgive Sananda for his cheating, I had to forgive myself first for my past betrayals.

And now, there was nothing but time to process all of this. Our snatched chances to be together would not be for a while now as we were still destined to be separated by land and water. Sananda was scheduled to fly to Ireland after France, and I would remain in England. It looked as if it would be three weeks before we saw each other again. Yet in hindsight, this was a good thing, as extra time apart would provide a chance for the dust to settle.

I cleared all the papers and books from my bed and gently climbed in, moving slowly and tenderly. I needed to talk to Chloe, but she was away on holiday in Bali. This was her first holiday in a long while and I refused to burden her with this. Plus, I didn't feel like getting an ear full from her I groaned as I imagined all the things she would say about Sananda cheating on me. I couldn't decide what hurt most, my bruised pride or longing to be comforted (even if by a friend that would no doubt admonish me!).

My body was still full of adrenaline and the remaining pulses of fear and hurt. I lay on my back and closed my eyes, as I fell back and into my awaiting heart. I could hardly remember where the bedside light was, knocking over crystals and essential oils as my hand fumbled for the switch. I fell into the sheets asking to be swallowed up by the night. We had just conquered (or attempted to) our first hell.

To my surprise, a radiance of unspeakable love began to fill the room, meandering its way into my agonizing heart and parched throat. Its warm delicate fingers searched all around to rekindle all the lost and afraid parts of me back together again, to wrap me once more in wholeness. By dropping more and more into my heart all pain and anguish drained from within me. I steered this love into my mind, to coat and saturate all the images that I had encountered that evening. The once torturous visualization scenes became insignificant characters from a film, nothing mattered anymore as I loosened my attention from Sananda. "He is only human after all," were the last words I heard before I reached out to roll over and into this divine essence that constantly pulled at my heart to keep surrendering to love, to life.

As love reassured and rested within me, I was able to look a little deeper into other reasons why this was happening. I guided my attention into the time I spent in Cologne that weekend. I realized it was not all entirely one-sided. There was a particularly tense moment when I too questioned my loyalty to Sananda, and almost forgot our love. There was a certain friend who was part of the group living in Cologne that bowled me over with his hysterical antics and fantastic sense of humor. At times, I found myself looking at him in a different way, as if entranced and enraptured by his light. In that reflection, I was able to understand Sananda a little more. Immediately I felt the warm embrace of compassion for him as I acknowledged the near lethal power of seduction.

We had been faced with a crossroads that presented us with a temptation, a test to see which way we would go. A purposeful obstacle was placed in our path (wrapped in quite intriguing packages), as life carried on all around us, observing how we would respond to certain stimulus. Would we waiver or would we take refuge in our love? Although it was in the early days, already the Universe was engineering challenges and circumstances that were designed to ignite change and lead to tremendous growth for our union as Beloveds. It was clear to me that these often harrowing experiences would one day be used to greatly support the enormity and colossal power of our meeting on Earth.

As soon as we got through this, I knew we would be used in some mammoth way to teach others to do the same. Or I sure as hell hoped so; as this was more painful than I ever imagined the path to the Beloved to be!

☙

Endless messages from Sananda appeared immediately on FaceBook, the very next day. I wasn't quite ready to respond, as I knew I had to give myself the space to recuperate from the almighty blow to my heart. After a shock like that, you can become quite fragile and humble. Thank God for online communication and the ability to send messages from the heart the moment they arise. Slowly but surely I began to feel myself reaching out to him again in a new way. My love had a particular quality of softness that was not there before. Love was beginning to flow again through the cosmos and along the telephone lines and keypads. We began to make plans to spend more time together in the coming month of May and somehow merge our schedules together, however impossible it seemed.

I was still in England, going through the process of serving my final month of yoga classes, while Sananda was across the water in Ireland running a *Power of Shakti* retreat; touring local sacred sites, igniting participant's Shakti, and connecting it with the powerful goddess energies of ancient Ireland.

I missed him terribly, and knew that the final healing of this episode would not arrive until we were physically together again. We needed to rest in each other's arms, to sleep together, to speak together, and reassure one another that everything was okay. Every night since Sananda had left for Ireland my dreams were plagued by demons coming to destroy our love. Doubt, jealously, and insecurity haunted me as I began to distrust him, doubting his integrity.

I wrestled with finding a good enough reason to not call the whole thing off. If I did, I wouldn't have to go through this massive change that was looming; I could use his past as an excuse to back out. Even so, I decided not to tell anyone, as I sensed that they would tell me to leave him. I would have told me to leave him! But I knew in my heart and soul that this was the process of the healing the wounds—I simply had to stay on track. My mind worked diligently to play tricks, asking questions that undermined our relationship: Can I trust him? Is he speaking the truth? My God, I wouldn't even trust *me* if I were to look back at my own past. Thankfully, my heart would come to the rescue with one-liners that silenced the mind, for a little while anyway:

People can change, especially those with a hunger and the heart to face anything. Love has the power to face and be with everything.

Every morning I would take the lingering aftertaste from these nightmares into my early morning yoga practice and, sure enough, hours later it passed; that is until the sun went down and it began all over again. I truly felt like I was involved in a battle for my soul, like the cosmic battle between love and fear that plays out brilliantly in the epic tale of *Lord of the Rings*. There were days I imagined that I was Frodo Baggins, heavy and exhausted from carrying the weight of the ring to Mount Doom. I was tortured daily by waves of temptation to become seduced by the powers of my mind and join forces with fear and distrust. To turn this all around I imagined a different scenario. Only in this version of the movie, I was more like Arwen Evenstar than Frodo Baggins. If anyone could make the battle of my soul look good, it was me. Or at least I was going to do my best to try!

A couple of days later I was on the train to teach yoga to the up-and-coming muso crowd of London's Camden Town. It seemed to me they were all fixated on becoming another Amy Winehouse or Russell Brand. Every single one of them was stick thin, wore heavy black eye make-up, and had a swagger in their hips. It didn't bother me one bit, though, as I was in a fantastic mood after receiving yet another love letter from Sananda via email speaking of our renewed trust in one another. I could feel the jubilation and confidence in his words, declaring that we could conquer anything that could ever stand in our way now that we had faced the first wound together. These messages uplifted and encouraged me, confirming that we had indeed accomplished a great thing. Slowly, but surely I could feel my love beginning to return.

Smiling to myself as I sat on the train, I slipped on my headphones and slid into a soundscape of passion, ecstasy, and rhythmic incantations that fired my imagination. I was inwardly dancing at a wild night in Ibiza whilst sitting next to some man squeezed into his suit as he worked on figures, chatting loudly on his mobile. The music continued to move me, as I listened to *The Best of Balearic Trance Tunes*, a classic anathematic album of the big tunes from last summer. This music caused me to imagine the sexy dance I would perform for Sananda at some point in our eventual future. I smiled again, sensing that Sananda and I were getting back on track.

My mobile began to pulse; an anonymous caller was waiting for me to pick up. But you know the rules; it was a public space, so I flicked the person into the waiting room to leave a message. No message, another try. Flick into the waiting room they go. Third time, a lucky charm? Nope, public space equals no speaking, sorry. At last a message was left. I was more than a little miffed as I was forced to leave my dancing sunrise on Ibiza. I apologized to the suit as I fingered in 123 to hear the message.

It was Sananda! He was about to go into Newgrange, Ireland's main sacred site and wanted to connect with me first. I noticed his slight irritation that I was ignoring him and sending him to my voicemail. My heart squeezed a little as I made a note to tell him the next time we spoke about my rule of not speaking on the phone in public spaces. Guess I would have to wait until Skype and his schedule allowed him to reach out again.

Later that afternoon he called. This time I was in the yoga studio, being silly and mischievous with my friend Darren. We were in hysterics over some story he was telling me; I answered the phone full of laughter whilst still commenting back to Darren. When I realized it was Sananda, I let out a swoop of cheer. This was the signal that Darren was waiting for, as he moved his face close to mine, almost nose to nose as he repeatedly mouthed.

"Is it him?" "Is it Him?"

I shielded the mouthpiece as I nodded wildly and demanded that he shut up. This was like a red flag to a bull, as he lit up and took our wonderful infectious laughter and buoyancy to the next level. I must have sounded so immature and ridiculous, as I attempted to explain where I was and who I was with, as Sananda knew Darren and his reputation for drama and antics. Darren is an exceptionally gifted energy healer as well as being an incredibly sought after camp as Christmas, male model. He was brimming with fashionista confidence, outrageousness, and a presence that demanded that everyone take notice.

Sananda and I spoke a little, but we were not in the same place energetically. He was coming out of a sacred site, full of tranquil peace and oneness, whereas I was in the thick of central London with a mad, fabulously gay, and flamboyant model/off the planet cosmic New Age healer. I could sense something move across my heart, like a cloud appearing on the horizon suggesting a storm up ahead. I shivered inside, as my subconscious mind intuited that something was indeed brewing. Sananda said it was not the time to talk and he would call me later when I was alone.

It was on my mind all day. Shit! I remembered ignoring his call. I went over and over in my mind checking to see whether he knew Darren was gay, because if he didn't it could look suspicious to someone who didn't know our dynamic. Sananda wasn't usually jealous, but after our recent soiree with betrayal, I didn't want any further confusion.

Eventually, as the day passed I came to grips with my mind. I laughed as I reminded myself that this was not the past—it was *now*. I do not know what he wants to talk about, nor will I ever, so until we speak, there is nothing to do about it. In my reclaimed mind, I walked into the chamber of fear and doubt with my luminescent staff of love and power, and I plunged it deep into the ground. With the ferocity of a mighty Queen, I heralded, "My life stands for love!" Period. How do you like them apples?

Later that night, once I returned back home, the phone rang. It was Sananda.

"Hi darling, it's me. I have something I would like to speak to you about." He began to clear his throat to select the correct tone of voice. And if that didn't kick my woman's intuition into high gear—I don't know what would. Intuition is a wonderful gift, as well as a tracking device to warn of danger ahead. My intuition was now on red alert. I braced myself.

"I have been feeling you for the last couple of days and I don't feel like we should continue our relationship as it is."

I immediately went to my heart. What was with this guy?!

Swallow, breathe, and gather yourself together. There is no need to cry, just clearly and steadily ask why. You can do this.

With all the maturity and unwavering courage I could lay my hands on, I quietly, yet demurely asked, "Why?"

He cleared his throat again, "Well I have been feeling that the nature of our relationship is not as man and woman, but more as teacher and student. I have been looking into the nature of your consciousness and to be honest, I need to be with a woman of higher consciousness, someone nearer to my frequency. Someone who can hold and receive me. It is here in this space that I feel there is a gap."

Denial: The second wound to love.

Denial occurs when you shut out the truth, sometimes even when you know better. It is located in the throat, or fifth chakra. To refuse to admit, recognize, or deal with an aspect of your life that blatantly exists, and is shown to you in many ways, is denial. Our first denial is always one of love. This leads to a betrayal of love, by escaping and running away from the issue and into the mind with its web of excuses, judgments, reasons, and rebuttals. In other words, denial is a big, fat defense mechanism. The only way out is to confess, honestly and openly. Full disclosure is the key.

Before I had a chance to file a complaint that all this was going too fast, I prepared myself for what was about to come next. He certainly knew where to aim as I had been quietly nursing an insecurity that I was indeed less spiritually developed than him. Yet despite the discomfort of a revealed hurt, there was an enormous part of me that recognized that there were other areas where I brilliantly shone with ease, whereas he was still struggling and fumbling in the dark for the light switch.

Like understanding why were together in the first place.

He went on to explain that he had been at various sacred sites in Ireland, and that on one of the mountains he received a message from Maeve, an Irish Goddess, warning him of this impeding issue. I must give credit where credit is due—and full credit with lights on to Sananda for the most unbelievable reason to dump someone. I almost laughed out loud; perhaps I did as I was swirling in and out of realities, one moment I was Scarlett, the next a Shakti warrior maiden looking to find and behead the particular Irish Goddess that Sananda had been chatting with. I listened to what sounded like the most serious case of horseshit.

I was almost eating the phone as he continued deeper into his reasoning, logic, and clarification. I decided to join Sananda on the spiritual bandwagon as I told him that no matter what, I would continue to love him, be it as teacher, friend, or one-time lover. I was as smooth as butter. But inside?

I was torn apart.

My Beloved that I knew was so close, yet so far and moving further still. What can I do? His mind is made up and it is so unfair that he made the decision without me. Could I pull something out of the bag and save this? Shakti however, laughed at the ridiculousness of it all.

"Where are your balls gal?" she teased me. "Can't you see that this is a get out clause, he is afraid of what we may do to him, once we get our hands on him." With that she threw her head back laughing as she danced with the wind, her anklets chiming against her soft and sensual murmurs of pleasure. "Wow, what a lady…" I mused to myself, as I watched her writhe and weave through the landscape.

Sananda's voice shattered the vision.

He asked how I was feeling. I explained that I was okay, that things hadn't gone too far for me to fall deeply in love (complete and utter lie), that in time I would be able to find peace with this decision, but if he could give me some time to get over it, I would be fine in a couple of days.

First, let me explain the true meaning of FINE:

F – Fucked up

I – Insecure

N – Neurotic

E – Emotional

So, yes I was well and truly fine, as I denied my feelings for him, denied speaking out to confront and pull apart what he was saying. It was the wound of denial we were clearly facing—why not join in on the party? My mind assured me that "spiritual" people don't have reactions to anything in life, they do not suffer from the plight of strong emotions; real spiritual people glide through life, detached and free from all suffering. So I was pretending to be that. What crap was *I* thinking?

By the time we got off the phone it was a little after midnight. I felt heavy, robotic, and very, very cold. I was the Titanic, sunken, and grounded to a halt on the first day of setting sail. It is utterly amazing how only a few hours ago I was so high, so full and rich with life and now, a dark lump of flesh and bones with no soul. My dad heard me moping around and came to see what was up. I told him, and burst into tears. He took me in his arms and told me to be strong, that in a couple of days things may change. He went on to explain about men and women, as I switched off and glanced into empty space, making noises of agreement in all the right places.

I climbed into bed and prayed to be taken, but this time I meant it. Get me off planet Earth now; it is cruel and full of horrible hurtful humans! Yeah, I'm really good at the drama when life hits me between the eyes. I fell asleep whispering in prayer to be taken away from all this pain. I longed for a release out of the suffering and back to the place where all this human emotion was meaningless. Within the dark ripples of my heart, I heard the words that miraculously touched a place that was still listening:

Be patient, have courage to take this denial of your love and transform it for you both. You have within you the power to transform all that is not love into beauty. He has given you his expression, take his words, take them in deep, feel the pain, feel the hurt, and transform it with the power of your feelings for him. This is a test. He is testing you to see the depths of your heart, and testing the sturdiness of your vessel.

My Love, you are in for a rough ride across love's terrain, you need to get ready and steady for this journey. You have prayed for the Beloved and the majesty of Sacred Union. This initiation is not for the faint of heart, only the fullness. You will have to find within you the strength that you did not know you had. You will need to burn within a baptism of fire until all that is not love transforms into love. You both will. But you have chosen to do this first, to lead the way so to speak.

Rest now, but it does not end here. This is only the very beginning.

The light of the sunrise danced upon my eyelids until I gave in and opened them. For a moment there was stillness and a glimmer of peace. Then it began, the wave of picking up where I left off last night. I couldn't move; I didn't have the inspiration to do yoga or meditate. I just lay there, going over and over what he had said. I had no idea how he reached his conclusion. I couldn't get how he changed his mind so quickly, without me even being there.

I dragged myself out of bed trying to refuse the lure of depression and worthlessness, marching myself into town for a once-reliable means of relief—retail therapy. Only now it seemed more like a pointless exercise. As I walked into the once welcoming doors of TK Maxx, deeper layers of awareness brought about by meditation began to ask self-inquiring questions. As you can imagine, one does not expect to be prodded and poked by their inner guru when situated in the woman's department of reduced designer dresses.

'Who are you buying clothes for? Yourself? What Self?'

'Errmmm...Pass.'

'For Another?'

'No definitely not!'

'Then who or why are you doing this for? What is the purpose of your actions?'

To that there is no answer, well no answer that would silently satisfy my newly expanded consciousness. Once tried and tested methods had now become worn out. Useless attempts to 'buy' some momentary happiness only brought an even greater ache to my heart. But still, that dress over there would look great with my...

I continued to browse, mulling over the real meaning of denial, and what the possible antidote could be. Suddenly, in between kaftans and evening wear I got it. It was embrace. The opposite of denial was embrace! I became consumed and intoxicated with a fantasy of sending Sananda a message on FaceBook, (one of our 'alternative' ways of communicating with each other) telling him exactly what I thought of his actions last night. I imagined myself to be the divine feminine power of Shakti, the most idealized version of myself (BTW—all women should have a vision of the highest version of herself. Trust me, channeling her comes in handy for situations such as this!).

. I then typed the words that needed to be spoken, words of power and dignity. I wasn't being rude, confrontational, or attacking. I was strong, radiant, and coming from a higher perspective. Embracing the moment, taking the bull by the horns. Mmm… I liked that! Put that in your peace pipe and smoke it, Sananda Gabriel! Questioning my consciousness, are you? Well, question this!

This fantasy and possible dress rehearsal in my mind filled me with a love that refused to be denied. I was on fire again. My love sprung to life, not caring whether he responded or not; I simply knew I had to do it. I had to send this message in honor and devotion of love, for love must express itself clearly. It was the truth and I knew it through and through. Forget the dress, I have far more important issues on my mind.

I have never done this before, fought for love, that is. My pride would always get in the way and block its actions. I could never allow myself to be seen as hurt, weak, or needing somebody. I would not give anyone the satisfaction that they could possibly hurt or wound me in any way. From this denial of love, I could never love fully. I was defended and protected, and would always walk away first if the slightest possible hint of hurt was lurking around the corner. It was a crazy game that became second nature.

But here's the thing, the avoidance of hurt becomes the avoidance of love. So in my meditation that morning I delved into the hurt, and waded around looking for what was underneath it all. To my surprise I discovered feelings of 'unworthiness' hinting that they were in agreement with Sananda's earlier character assessment (!) Even before I knew Sananda, I had observed this pattern in myself and vowed to no longer be addicted to this pointless strategy. Hurt is hurt; anyone would think it's the end of the world. And to the ends of the world I was willing to go.

With no further ado, I dropped into all the emotions of "not being enough" as I literally cried myself dry. A few hours later, once I was done—I felt ready to embrace my next step on this wild adventure.

I began the message of all messages as I wrote privately to Sananda on FaceBook. I once again slipped into my role as Shakti— inviting this majestic, sensual woman to speak. His denial did not weaken me, nor did I doubt myself in anyway. I stood before him unmoving, embracing the situation as I expressed who I knew myself to be. Whether he got it or not, was not my concern.

FaceBook Message
Scarlett O'Shea
12 March 2009 at 11:35

Remember that I am Irish, my love. And more importantly I am alive and kicking, unlike certain other Irish deities I could mention!

Are you open enough to allow that you could have been misguided Sananda? Or played with? I know that the "gap in consciousness" that you perceive is your own illusion.

My frequency, my octave, my vibration is.... Measurable?

That is purely your mind talking to me, and such a masculine mind too...

My consciousness could never be measured, as I contract and expand eternally.

You have overlooked this woman's essence. It is not to match you, but to harmonize with you, taking us both to the next level.

Every fiber of my being knows I could "hold and receive" you. Every moment of my existence knows that I will bring you gifts and experiences that will magnify you ten-fold.

I believe "here is" the space that is closer to the truth.

Stay safe with your "goddesses," imagined and real...fluffing around on the fence, keeping you safe from love. Whilst all the time you shall remain wanting to love and be loved.

I burned with love as I wrote the truth of my feelings, not backing down in anyway. That I *am* the woman he has searched for, that I stand before him declaring myself as She. I ended the lengthy epiphany with the words:

"Know that when you face me, YOU die... and only WE shall live."

Scarlett

I signed off with a powerful sentence that seemed to rise up from the depths of my Being. As I typed the words, my heart began to pound with the power of my own conviction, in reward of this act my heavenly hosts cheered and threw rose petals at my feet. I was in the full authority of my soul and everything in my world was right again. My favorite quote rose up in my heart like a phoenix bringing confirmation upon its wings.

"I am not afraid... I was born to do it. I would rather die than do something against God's Will." Joan of Arc

He replied half an hour later, with two simple words "Prove it." He then went on to say that when I go to Australia later in the year I would meet my equal. Way to let the air out of my sails Mr. Fancypants. Pllleeeassse.

I replied, "Irrelevant information."

What a load of bollocks I thought, as I slammed the top of my Mac down into sleep mode. I was fuming with that last outrageous message. If he had been within striking distance, he would have received a mouthful of purely undiluted spiritually incorrect anger, actually it was not anger, but rather frustrated exasperation. Upon deeper reflection, I felt an aching sadness. A sadness that tore at my open heart, a heart that was watching her target move out of the way, as he suggested an alternative bulls eye.

I needed to get some space, I had to get outside and take in some fresh air. I jumped on my bike, plugged in my iPod, and headed for the hills as I huffed and puffed out all my resentments and another barrage of dashed hopes. By the time I got home there was another message waiting.

Sananda Gabriel
12 March 2009 at 15:57

Scarlett, you are right in many ways... and I have been waiting for someone to somehow speak Truth with the passion I can feel.

I like it when you freely and fully express without hiding or evading… I like it when you express your heart and your feelings to me.

Would be nice to speak about this…xS

I smiled, our love was being resurrected and more importantly, winning.

A couple of hours passed when the phone rang. I knew it would be him, in fact I pretty much knew everything that was going on these days. My intuition had gone through the roof since healing many of my old patterns of relating and classically avoiding pain.

"Hi darling, I just re-read your message. I am intrigued and moved by your words. You have stirred something within me, and it feels good."

I replied, "I have only spoken the truth, and there is no way that I am going to accept anything less. I am the one that you speak of. I know this. Now it's up to you to decide whether you know this."

He confessed that he too woke up with a heavy heart with the knowledge that he had possibly moved away from the woman who would love him the most in his life. I inwardly smiled. He said things didn't feel right, that he felt he had made a possible wrong choice. He realized that he had acted out of fear, and was denying himself the chance to *really* love and be loved. Rather than embracing the situation, he was resisting it. I was beginning to smile broader still as his openness confirmed that I had taken the right course of action.

Denial and Embrace. I punched the air around me, turning

around and around while still on the phone. I tickled to wake the cats, to tell them the good news. They stretched, yawned, turned around, and went straight back to sleep in the sun. I had fought for love! By my embrace, passion, and commitment I had turned the tide, as he now asked for my forgiveness and the chance to continue onwards, together. In this moment I was Rocky Balboa at the top of the steps... and the world.

We knew we had opened Pandora's Box; that we had invited the fullness of love to grace our shores by moving forward through both betrayal and denial. We stood together not only because we wished for some amazing relationship, but because we were offering ourselves as pioneers of love. Because we knew we were Beloveds, we knew we were destined to be together so we could branch out into unchartered territory and report back to others who wanted love more than anything. Our conversation unfolded as we explored our experiences. We laughed and played with each other across the Irish Sea. We had overcome our second obstacle, and it felt so damn good.

The Privileged Lovers

They are the chosen ones, who have surrendered.

Once they were particles of light, now they are the radiant sun.

They have left behind the world of deceitful games.

They are the privileged lovers who create a new world

with their eyes of fiery passion.

—RUMI

Chapter Thirteen

Reconciliation

L.A. Fitness, England, end of April 2009

THREE WEEKS had passed since Sananda and I worked through our first two wounds to love—betrayal and denial. I had just finished my high endurance cycling class, and raced to my locker to get changed. Almost breaking the door down, I flung myself into the women's changing rooms at the local gym. Ahhh! I glanced in the mirror at a frightful spectacle staring straight back at me. My hair was soaking wet and plastered to my head, and my face resembled a beetroot. No worries, a cold shower will sort that out. Besides, I was way too excited to care, as in twenty minutes time I would be in the arms of my Beloved.

Laughing to myself at the absurdity of my mounting excitement, I tiptoed, so not to slip in my wraparound towel, armed with the latest Mango Delirium sensual shower gel, towards the showers. A fleeting glance at the clock reflected that I had fifteen minutes left to get ready for Sananda, who was meeting me outside. This was the first time we would see each other in three weeks!

I showered at lightning speed and quickly squeezed into my white denim flared jeans, slipped on my "You are Soul" (read it how you will) cotton t-shirt with gold wings printed on the back. I tussled with my hair, checked my visage, threw all my sodden gym clothes into my rucksack, and glided through the gym leaving a trail of Gardenia behind me. The guys stood behind the reception desk watching me, mouths agape, as if catching flies. "Yep, desired effect!" I mused to myself as I pushed open the door, adjusted my eyes to the springtime sun, slipped on my DKNY sunglasses and waited on the steps of LA Fitness. The LA Fitness used to be the old cinema in Newbury, which was the town I grew up in. Now it was enjoying all the attention of being a state of the art mega gym that was all lights and pumping music. I remembered how I used to stand on these very steps waiting to get into the Saturday morning cinema, loaded with popcorn, sweets, and my best friend when I was ten years old. Now look at me, approaching forty, yet feeling sixteen as I waited for the love of my life to finally arrive.

Fortunately, he was late. Thank god. I could now take some time to relax, breathe, and get it together.

The cold air blasted me; it was the middle of spring, yet the wind still carried a chill. I wrapped my cream flannel blazer around me as I smiled into its collar. It was a sensational day; the light was clear and golden, and there was a particular quality of magic in the air. It was one of those days where everything just felt "right." I had waves of anticipation flowing through me everyday confirming that it was only a matter of time before I underwent some massive transformational change. I simply had this knowingness (strong intuitive feeling) that something huge was about to happen. And I sure hoped so, since I was leaving the yoga world behind and ready for my next assignment from the Universe.

Suddenly, from around the corner, Sananda materialized in the swirling cloud of dust and sunlight before my very eyes. My knees weakened as my belly somersaulted in approval. He was dressed in dark chocolate jeans and a black knee length embroidered kurta. He looked so incredibly handsome and exotic like an extravagant Indian Prince, and by the time my eyes took in his approaching form I was completely paralysed by shyness as I blushed and looked down at my feet. I did not know whether to look up, wave and smile, or to wait until he was in earshot and say "Hi." Butterflies danced in my stomach. I grew warm all over with excitement. Question: Why does a thirty-nine year old woman, who has had her very fair share of the opposite sex (if I do say so myself), blush and become painfully shy when she sees her Beloved walk out of a car park? Ridiculous, yet so what I had been wanting—my whole life.

As he continued to approach, I began to contemplate how I was going to embrace him without dislocating my neck. Compared to me, Sananda was incredibly tall. I was about the same height as one of my favorite Australian performers, Kylie Minogue, and had to seriously create a strategy on how to go about embracing him. Do I put my arms under or over his? Or, maybe one under, one over? Is there any way I can prevent myself from snapping my neck when I look up at him? Perhaps if I hold my head on the side I could look up, but on a slant?

These truly were the questions going through my mind as he reached out for me, and silenced my mental debate with one enormous kiss that lasted and lasted. Now remember what I said about Newbury? Small town mentality accompanied by small mind emotionality. Well, imagine this if you will. Two adults; one Indian, dark, and gorgeous, the other Irish, golden, and glowing, kissing outside the local gym at lunchtime on a Tuesday. He bent me back, as my neck braced itself—and phew, made it—as he then pulled me towards him. His arm encircled the small of my back as the other hand reached for my hair, sweeping his fingers through my mane as he played with my curls.

It was twenty minutes later (I swear!) before we came up for air, twisting and turning on the steps of LA Fitness. All the while, cars honked, guys shouted, and girls whistled out catcalls. This middle class town of Middle England was becoming privy to the boundless freedom of love—where two people were openly demonstrating their love for each other, with no shame, no boundaries, and no compromise whatsoever. He stroked my face with such tenderness and love, that I almost choked up with emotion. I could see that he was trying to say something, but couldn't figure out where to begin. Eventually the words that I longed to hear in person were spoken.

"My Beloved, I have been feeling so heavy and sick inside since we walked through the wounds of both betrayal and denial. Now that we are here face to face, I have to ask for your forgiveness. I have been a complete fool, can you forgive me?"

He took my hands and placed them in front of his heart. Any protection I had around my heart melted instantly. I could see that he was searching my eyes for true and complete forgiveness from the past, and he found it everywhere. He let go of my hands and reached for my face as he kissed me again on the mouth, breathing out a humble, heartfelt, "Thank you, my love." Our eyes clasped as every stroke of his fingers through my hair revealed sounds as beautiful as any angelic harp. I trembled under the velocity of this love that I was feeling for him; it was enormous and growing by the second.

When we did eventually break free we laughed non-stop. It was incredible how our loving embrace and full-on kissing (bordering on making out!) was immediately impacting the lives of others. All around us people smiled and stared, cheering us on. As far as I was concerned our love was to be given and shared with the whole of life. Take that Newbury!

It would be my turn to share with Sananda, as I planned to take him to the ancient Roman city of Bath to celebrate our reunion. Bath was only an hour's drive from Newbury, so it would be a quick trip there. I was totally gobsmacked when he told me he had never been. It was one of England's most beautiful cities, nourished by natural hot springs that the Celts and Romans once enjoyed over two thousand years ago. Not to mention the once home of Jane Austen, an English novelist famed for her great romantic works. Bath was the ideal place for Beloveds. We had decided to go to the city's thermal spa, where we planned to luxuriate and relax in the warm healing mineral waters, and then have a delicious organic lunch somewhere near the Abbey.

Arm in arm we walked (almost floating really) back to where he parked his car. As we left Newbury and headed towards Bath, I noticed the same magical buoyancy I had experienced on the steps of the gym. The magic space of love was permeating every orifice. We kept looking at each other in fits of giggles as we were actually beginning to glow, and so was the inside of the car. Something big was happening, and it felt delicious. We spent the whole journey turning to look at one another, just to feast our eyes on one another's face one more time.

An hour later, we got what we came for, as we melted into the warm mineral-rich waters of England's original and only natural thermal spring. After winning a millennium award grant of eight million pounds, the city of Bath put all that money to good use. The spa was incredible, a work of artistic flair and modern aesthetics. I remember reading that the waters of Bath fell as rain around 10,000 years ago and then sank to a depth of about three kilometers. It was here where the water was heated by high temperature rocks before rising back up through one of the three hot springs in the center of the city.

The healing fluidity of Aqua Sulis (the name of the Roman Goddess that resides over all natural springs) seeped into our heavy bodies and effulgent hearts. We floated, steamed, sweated, yelped at the cold-water jets, and sunk deeper into the wondrous experience. We floated and stretched one another as if doing Watsu, played sea horses, and made rafts with all the bright blue floating sausages. There were also times when we were very still and silent, truly appreciating being in the simple presence of one another.

By the time we left, it felt as if we were ten kilo's heavier. Laughing like teenagers we agreed in unison that this feeling was similar to being heavily sedated. In a good way, of course. Like men on the moon, we space walked towards The Madhatter Café in the center of Bath, holding hands and smiling endlessly at each other. We did our best to be mindful of approaching lampposts and the odd hole in the pavement, in addition to all the small designer dogs so typical of Bath.

We sat down underneath an enormous willow tree in a beautiful Georgian Square, complete with pigeons, prams, and pigtails. The busy hustle and bustle of aristocracy was happening all around us. Open top sports Jaguar's, thirsty Range Rovers, well-spoken English accents, and the occasional over-the-top flamboyant thespian would glide past our table. Very Los Angeles, in a quiet British sort of way. Despite all the potential distractions, we only had eyes for each other.

The waiter interrupted our dewy love moment as he awkwardly took our order for two lattes and a scrumptious raw salad. As soon as he left it was back to the fits of laughter brought on from our spa experience. It was hilarious; we looked like two red juicy tomatoes that were glowing larger by the minute. Then, I noticed that Sananda seemed uncomfortable in his seat; he constantly kept rearranging himself and clearing his throat, which made me laugh even more. What on earth was happening to him? He took a massive deep breath as he reached over and took both my hands, whispering, "Scarlett, there is something I have been meaning to ask you for a while now."

I gulped. Didn't I say I had a feeling that something monumental was about to happen?

"Darling, I can hardly hold back a moment longer. Today is clearly the day, considering the amount of laughter and love we have been sharing. Scarlett, my Beloved, will you marry me?" he asked.

Tears welled up in my eyes, as the words echoed all around me. *Will you marry me?*

I looked him deep in the eyes, and saw that he was squinting as if bracing himself for the answer. I observed his delicate vulnerability and tender anticipation, as his eyes darted back and forth searching for my response, squeezing my hands as if prompting me for the answer.

I felt a rush of excitement, then a deep tidal wave of love as I realized the enormity of what he was saying. I closed my eyes as I imagined the numerous times he had asked me this very question in our past life encounters together. I drank in the moment; appreciating the split second before one chapter ended and another one began in the story of our lives together. I carefully eyed the glass of a married life together...

My eyes flickered as some doubts lurched at my stomach. Was I really ready to do this? It had been only three months since we met each other. Do I really want to marry this man? Will life always continue at this break neck speed with him? Do I have the capacity to keep up?

I knew these were my egoic personality thoughts that panicked at the idea of losing my so-called freedom, in addition to being slightly concerned about the high velocity of our past interactions. Two wounds in one month? That seemed like some kind of world record. Our endless up and down emotional roller coaster had become commonplace. What would I be getting myself into?

Even though I could hear my mind pleading for more time to consider the offer, my heart and soul got in first. Hadn't I promised myself that on the journey of the Beloved I would say "Yes!" no matter what? I trusted in the heat of the moment, and I sure as hell trusted in love. For me this was the only way to make such a decision. In one sure movement, I slowly lifted my eyes to gaze into the face of the man that I would soon spend the rest of my life with.

"Yes, my Love. The answer is yes, I would love to marry you," I whispered to him, as I squeezed his hands in mine, witnessing how his dark chocolate eyes slowly filled up with tears of gratitude and unspeakable joy.

This moment was etched into my soul. According to various schools of esoteric thought, when we die each and every one of us has a three-minute playback of our lifetime. I knew for certain, that

I was recording this scene for the final opening and closing premiere of *The Movie of Me.*

Again, the same waiter walked in on our love fest carrying a tray full of delights. He had to place our food and drinks in-between our clasped hands, as we couldn't let go. Lunch came and went in a haze. I had strangely lost my appetite, but dug in anyway—I would need my strength for the road ahead. All of our senses were switched on to the maximum levels as our exuberance overflowed into the cobbled side streets that encircled the café. I suddenly remembered that nearby was the old residence of the legendary author, Jane Austen. I imagined her at the window looking down on us as she smiled, knowing all too well the power of love.

Oh yes she knew about love; just ask Mr Darcy.

"Come on darling, let's go and tell the world the good news!" Sananda cried, as he stood up from the table, reaching for my hand to join him. I was swimming in happiness as I typed out a bubbling text message of our engagement to all our friends and family. I knew better than to text Chloe, she rightfully required a phone call, with plenty of time to share and discuss. Every time we got a reply, we would cheer together as we felt our friends one-by-one joining in the cyber space merriment!

We immediately decided that we would go to Glastonbury to get our rings individually made by a wonderful friend I knew who worked with the most exquisite gemstones. Together, we agreed that on the inside would be the inscription:

"Love one other as I have loved you."

I read somewhere that this was Christ's last commandment to his disciples. And this was the richness Sananda and I wanted to embrace in our love. I looked at Sananda and realized yet again that I had found another willing to live this life as the extension of love. I respected and honoured Sananda so deeply, and the more I understood him, the deeper my respect. It was an extraordinary process, as the love between Beloveds covers all roles in life ranging from divine, brother/sister, best friend, humanitarian, erotic, passion and courageous love, and so many more shades in-between. We were simply at the beginning of this incredible Beloved love.

Just then, a truly outrageous idea popped into my mind. "Sananda, let's go and tell my parents, they are just down the road in Newbury, let's do it in person and get yours to meet us there too! Let's do it *now*," I teasingly suggested.

My eyes were wild with spontaneity hoping he would feel my enthusiasm and say yes.

"You're on!" he declared.

We nearly ran back to the car as we jumped in and revved the engine to life, preparing to move out into life. What a crazy moment, driving back to Newbury to announce to my unbeknownst parents that we were going to get married as soon as we could. Now this was going to be *really* interesting! I smiled to myself as I could begin to sense Sananda's trepidation now that the initial adrenaline was beginning to wear off. He kept looking sideways at me, not saying anything in particular, just checking that I was still with him. I reassuringly squeezed his thigh as I nodded a silent 'yes' to inspire him and to reaffirm my support in this monumental episode that was unfolding before our very eyes. This was the first time that Sananda would meet my parents, so I made sure he knew I was fully present with him.

I was about to lead Sananda into the parental lair, after all—the dark, dusty, and damp underworld of lie detector tests that link up to the world's criminal records bureau and most eligible bachelor archives. My parents were professionals; since my returning home they had virtually become highly trained interrogators. The time had arrived for my Beloved Sananda to step into their world in a big way. We pulled up into the driveway of my parent's house, switched the engine off, pulled up the handbrake, and paused— nervously looking at one another. Sananda's parents had already arrived from London; their car sat parked in the drive. Instantly, he put my mind at ease by affirming that he was ready, and was feeling absolutely fine about all of it. Remember that word—*fine*? Well, that's not exactly the word I wanted to hear. As we got out of the car I reached over and grabbed my pretend popcorn; announcing that this was about to be the best show ever! (Hey, sometimes a woman has to use her imagination to get through these types of life scenarios.)

And so, we were off! Sananda playfully smacked my bottom as I led the way.

Mum answered the door in one of her floral Sunday dresses, with a near matching apron around her waist, complete with tea towel already in hand as she welcomed us in. Luckily I pre-warned her of our arrival by sending her a text well in advance. Magically mid-afternoon tea was being prepared and already some initial offerings had made it to the table. We were ushered into the kitchen, as mum hugged Sananda and introduced him to the cats. I noticed that Mr. and Mrs. Gabriel were in the garden walking around hand-in-hand as they enjoyed the flowers and shrubs that mum constantly preens and tends to.

Dad did his bit, which is to come into the kitchen about ten minutes later, making sure that the possible newcomer to the family had ample time to sweat a little bit more. I knew this tactic so well; dad imagined that if he purposely delayed the meeting, he would create a lavish 'grand entrance' intended to build mystery and intrigue with lashings of good ole fashioned dread.

But this time his supreme plan wasn't working.

By the time dad did make his entrance, I believe I saw fear in *his* eyes as he slowly looked up to take in the whole of Sananda's. My Beloved towered over dad, and I giggled as I watched him bend to administer the famous masculine "back slap" after they shook hands and exchanged formalities. After they were introduced, I swear to God I saw dad shrink back a bit to reconsider his game plan.

Dad did not even attempt his usual one hundred and one rapid-fire questions routine towards the possible new man in his daughter's life. In fact he was very quiet, reasonably polite and incredibly reserved. Sananda did what he did best and took charge of the situation, gelling immediately with mum, who seemed to instantly adore him. I helped mum bring the 'high tea' out to the patio table, while Sananda went over to greet his parents. Because it was a reasonably warm afternoon mum decided to have tea on the lawn. Bless her heart she had made copious rounds of eggs and cress sandwiches, some ham and mustard, and a delicious homemade vegetarian quiche. With whatever minuscule amount of table space that was left, she proudly wedged in a plate of dainty fairy cakes. I smiled to myself as I arranged everything accordingly to satisfy her Virgo tendencies as I announced that tea was ready to be served. I shyly walked over and affectionately hugged Sananda's folks. Even though I had already met them a couple of times before in London, I still was a little bashful when I saw them again, especially as I knew what was coming next.

I could hardly eat, although Sananda was tucking in rather well, much to mum's absolute delight. Both sets of parents were talking and sharing past stories about their little 'angels' and the naughty things they used to get into. I was told (again) how Sananda had tossed a Bible around his religious education classroom; whereas my folks informed us of the time when I was fourteen and shaved off most of my hair, dying what little I had left pillar-box red.

Once the parents had simmered down a bit, Sananda turned to me and openly asked, "Are you ready?"

"Yes," I confirmed as I reached for his hand. Both sets of bewildered parents looked around at each other, not knowing what was going on. I did not say a word, although I am certain my face said it all.

"We have an announcement that we would like to make, and you are the first people to hear our good news," Sananda spoke with dignity and elegance without moving his eyes from mine.

I took a quick glance around the table to see what was happening, (crikey it was spectacular, they were all well and truly captivated!) upon which I quickly resumed my gaze with my future husband.

"Anaiya and I are getting married," declared Sananda. Turning to face my dad, he softened his voice as he asked for his permission to marry his daughter. "Patrick, I would like to ask for your blessing. May I please have your daughter's hand in marriage?"

Dad was surprised to say the least. I am sure I could hear the bass rhythm of David Bowie's *Under Pressure* being carried by the wind as it swirled around the garden, thumping particularly close to his ears.

Dad looked to my mother who sweetly smiled back at him, whilst telepathically urging him to, 'Hurry up and put the poor boy out of his misery.' Dad looked at me, with all my eager anticipation and bursting happiness, as I waited for his reply.

Dad found his center, cleared his throat, and stood up. With both hands firmly placed on the patio table, he spoke the words that we all longed to hear.

"Yes, Sananda, you have my blessing!"

Five, four, three, two, one…

I waited for the bomb to drop, the rabbit to jump out of the hat, and the flock of doves to be released from underneath the polka dot hankie. This was sheer Hollywood, or even Bollywood… or maybe both? I do not know who spoke first, as it all seemed to happen at once. A sensational melodrama took to the stage, as everyone began talking over the top of one another, begging to be heard and answered first:

"When, where, how many, what theme, what style, who is marrying you, in a church, in a temple, who is bridesmaid, who is best man?"

We answered them in turn—well the best we could, as we didn't technically have all the answers. It was a spur of the moment kind of thing, but they didn't seem to understand that. They wanted fine, precise details and planning. We were not at all on the same page with them. Finally, silence. In quiet contemplation, they processed the information and filed their answers into their appropriate boxes. We relaxed a little as we smiled at one another, loosening the grip slightly between our hands. All of a sudden, out of the blue they were off again with another round of questions:

"We think this is too soon, how do you know, are you really ready, do you truly love each other, are you totally sure, have you thought about it, where will you live, are you planning children?"

We did our very best to answer every question with as much clarity and consideration as possible, but I could see and feel that Sananda was getting impatient with the whole scenario. 'He's going to blow,' I thought to myself. I knew how much Sananda disliked being told what to do, and could feel him heating up over the endless litany of questions, that to him seemed irrational and had nothing to do with the present moment. Sure enough, I was right. He stood away from the table and sliced through all questions with one almighty sentence that ended the entire conversation.

"That is enough! This marriage is between Scarlett and myself. As soon as we have something to tell you, we will. In the meantime do not interfere."

Well, that certainly sorted out the wood from the trees.

"Would anyone like more tea?" mum asked.

"Good idea," said dad as he walked into the kitchen to get his camera.

I took this moment as my cue to call Chloe; now I had to face my best friend, who was already mildly uneasy and at best outright disproving. I retreated to the bottom of the garden where we used to have our old heart-to-heart conversations, and pressed 'Yoga Barb' on my mobile.

"Hi Chloe, it's me Scarlett, I have some news to tell you!" I prepared myself by pacing around the lawn, with one hand on my hip to settle my excitable nerves.

"There is a possibility that you are going to tell me one of two things," she coolly replied. "That you are either pregnant or getting married." I swear to God she sounded like Morpheus from *The Matrix*, all matter-of-fact and detached.

"It's the second one," I blurted.

I waited.

"Oh my God, really? That's amazing Scarlett! I am so happy for you. When are you getting married?" she asked.

"We don't know yet, but when we do you will be the first to know. All I know is that it's going to be sometime this year," I promised. I explained that we were in the middle of a family party and I would fill her in on all the details later.

As I hung up, I sat for a while on the garden bench, glancing over towards Sananda who was cracking open a bottle of champagne. It was a moment to cherish, one of those blink-of-an-eye realizations when you observe that you're growing up, that life is changing all around you and by its very nature, dragging you with it. I have always been child-like, never really imagining that marriage and mortgages would be for me. Now, it was like all of that was changing. In this moment of profound reflection, I knew that if I had my Beloved at my side I would and could sail through all rites of passage. Again that feeling was a graceful result of merging with the Beloved—there is no fear, anywhere, anymore. As much as I tried to hold onto it, this sense of utter fearlessness would sweep right through me, wriggling free of my grasp. I smiled to myself, knowing it would continue to return until we embodied it—fully.

Surrender to truth as it is presented
Accept yourself as a child
Allow yourself to be carried on this stream
Become naked, vulnerable
Knowing you are safe from harm tonight

Allow the cold walls of mind to melt
Thawed by the embrace of loves quiet gaze
Allow the Beloved to coax you
Away from all that is rigid
Into the gentling, the humbling
Softening what tears you in two

No more icy division
As love rents asunder
All the layers that are not you
Into golden streams of naked harmony
Weaving you back into loves quiet gaze …

—SANANDA GABRIEL

CHAPTER FOURTEEN

NEWS FROM THE DOCTOR

Parents' home, England, May 2009

ARE KRISHNA, Hare Krishna, Krishna, Krishna Hare Hare," fills the bedroom as I dance around singing my heart out as an exquisite, overflowing joyful spirit of happiness floats through my parent's home. My parents have now run out of excuses when their friends call, armed with the irresistible urge to wish me good luck in my forthcoming marriage. The once normal household that hoped to appear 'middle class' on Craven Road had transcended into a hippy hangout, complete with the kissing and embracing of unsuspecting strangers at the front door. Thanks to my parents, I had set up a one-woman ashram (I was guru as well as guest!), where every person who stepped foot through the front door became adorned with the aroma of Nag Champa and the penetrating voice of the latest YouTube guru. This was just as well, as I had now completely left the yoga world and had plenty of free time to play the love guru.

I began to notice that mum had taken on rhythmic swaying of divine bliss as she washed up at the kitchen sink, gazing out into the garden. Dad was also touched by the recent trend within the house, mysteriously appearing at my bedroom door listening to the latest Gangaji Satsang. He would stand there nodding in agreement, and then get all choked up when she spoke about the nature of love. He could now understand why this rapturous wave of infectious freedom and love had captivated me, and by its nature threatens to devour everything within my sight. The path of the Beloved was well and truly alive within our residence; even mum and dad were beginning to look at each other in a different way, a way that whispered of rekindled love and passion.

Despite my escalating euphoria and the delirious smile permanently etched upon my face since Sananda's proposal, I was doing my best to sensibly pack for a ten-day retreat in Peru. It was Sananda's *Shakti Two Retreat: Embodying Higher Frequencies*. Personally I didn't want to embody any higher frequencies, fearing that I would spontaneously combust if I harnessed any more energy or dramas. But there was no way I was going to miss out on ten-day's with Sananda (this would be the longest time we had ever spent together in one go), especially since he asked me to co-teach with him. I was so overjoyed when he asked, and honored to be teaching alongside such a renowned spiritual leader.

Now, days before we were set to leave, I was beginning to have second thoughts. It was first-show nerves, mixed in with a little shyness about joining an already formed group. There was going be around thirty-five people on this touring retreat through the Andean landscapes, and they all knew one another from previous gatherings with Sananda. This was a hardcore crowd of serious followers, and I was curious to see how they would accept me. Not only that, Sananda was going to be introducing me in the very first meeting as his Beloved, and I had a funny feeling there might be a number of women who fancied the idea for themselves.

My heart interrupted the mounting concerns filling my head.

Just breathe. Love has the power to face anything.

I immediately decided that this is the mantra I will take with me to Peru. The culminating dread vanished into thin air as I focused on something far more immediate—flinging my most unattractive, highly sensible walking shoes in my case over the top of my cerise pink Japanese silk kimono and beaded slippers (for the times when we would be at the hotel). Despite the need for yogic comfort, I still wanted to look my best for when Sananda and I were alone together. I smiled down proudly at my suitcase. It was a suitcase whose contents could unabashedly parade down the catwalks of Paris. There was DKNY, Mathew Williamson, and a few pieces from the latest spring/summer Chloe collection.

I was interrupted suddenly by the telephone ringing louder than ever before, almost begging for my attention. For some unexplainable reason, the heightened sound of the ring made my stomach turn. I closed the top of my suitcase, glancing into the mirror above my sofa bed, and saw the reflection of an ashen white face. Something was about to happen; my soul could feel it.

I heard mum answer the phone and speak with the person on the other end.

"Yes, she is here. What's the matter, can you tell me?" I could hear the fear and worry in her voice.

"Okay, I'll just get her." She walked into my bedroom cupping the receiver in one hand whilst the other one clutched her throat. She too had a deathly pale pallor, with a look of concern that only a mother has for her child.

"Darling, it's the nurse on the phone. She has the results from your pap test. She needs to speak to you directly."

My heart was beating fast, as dryness filled my mouth and throat. I moved the suitcase out of the way and sat down on the sofa bed. Mum sat next to me. I took the phone and spoke into the receiver to face whatever was on the other end of the line.

"Is this Scarlett O'Shea?" I recognized the voice immediately.

"Yes, it is," I replied, inwardly bracing myself for what was coming next.

"This is the nurse from Newbury Surgery. We have just received the results back from your latest pap smear. I am sorry to tell you that it's positive. You have grade four cancer cells, and we will have to move you forward to receive a colposcopy as soon as you can."

My mind searched for understanding and meaning in my own language. Her medical descriptions didn't make sense. *Please just speak English! Do I have cancer? Am I going to die? And if so, when?* I screamed inside. In a moment I went from preparing for Peru to what could be my worst nightmare.

The nurse began to more clearly explain the situation. I had cancerous cells, and I was being urgently advised to seek treatment known as a colposcopy to remove the section of my cervix that was showing strong signs of developing cancer. Usually patients with this condition are discovered at stage two or even three. But this was stage four. Stage five would have meant immediate surgery to cut away all suspected organs and tissues to avoid the cancer spreading further.

On and on my mind was churning. When I came back to the present moment, she was asking whether she could arrange an appointment in the next couple of weeks with the local hospital to have a biopsy. Ironically, or synchronistically depending on how one looks at life, I was set to be at Reading Hospital the next day to have the polyp removed. I asked whether they could take another look then and there. She replied no, as this was an entirely different procedure within a different department.

I now had two strange abnormalities to contend with. Ever since meeting Sananda, something unusual was happening in my reproductive organs. I sensed that it was a result of lovingly and consciously opening up the seven gates. This was the first time that I had ever experienced making love with a man in this way, as it was so heartfelt and healing. I trusted him to explore and touch those places inside that were strictly off limits. Places that were loaded with emotions and almost primordial cries. I remembered how he forewarned me in the earlier days that opening the seven gates was a huge inner undertaking, as women had slowly drifted away from their wombs, residing instead in their heads. Abandoning their natural centre, they have lost contact with their true, rich and wild innate nature. Once they begun the journey home, there was a chance that some women would struggle to let go of control and linear (logical) thinking, as they returned once again to the creative urges of spontaneity and intuition. I was convinced that my gynecological problems were a direct result of this journey. A journey that only my Beloved could awaken and support me through. Whichever way I looked at it, one thing was sure, something was brewing and I could not ignore it a moment longer.

I considered what she was proposing, but it was out of the question. I couldn't go in for surgery; in ten days I would be on a plane to Peru and would be gone for two weeks. I went on to tell her that when I returned I would leave England in a matter of days to move to France.

"This really isn't a good idea Scarlett. You need to have a biopsy as soon as possible to ascertain how far it has spread," she warned.

No matter how hard I looked at it, there didn't seem to be a way out. We thrashed it out back and forth, with me spelling out my situation in black and white, while she insisted on the urgency of treatment with my local hospital. It wasn't getting us anywhere, so I asked her for a third option. She replied straight away that there wasn't one. Sigh. Medicine. I couldn't believe what she was telling me. I was thirty-nine years old, had been doing yoga for fifteen years, ate a healthy diet, exercised every day, and made sure I did regular, yearly detoxes. What was happening, and why was it happening now? Despite the temptation to spin off into total angst, I took a long, slow breath and became aware of another energy, (other than fear) that was powerfully present. I realized that while I was marginally afraid, I was not *totally* afraid. In the midst of this drama was the quiet ground of being, or knowing if you like, which whispered:

Keep going. Continue with your plans, this trip will be part of the healing journey. You need the extra time to heal this yourself. The answer is not to cut out part of your cervix, but to continue to trust the process that you're already in.

Yes, I could have cancelled my trip to Peru, and delayed my move to France. I could have gone into hospital within a couple of weeks, moved quickly without any real clear thought, handed myself over into the hands of the doctors, like I would have done so many times in the past. But this time I said no. And said "yes" to following love and the path of the Beloved to heal myself. With that, I calmly told the nurse that I had a third option. I would need to transfer my patient notes over to a doctor in France, and the moment I arrived I would check myself for another test to uncover what the latest developments were. I asked her advice on the steps I would need to take in order to make this possible.

I was amazed at how calm and clear I was feeling, and obviously becoming. I was taking charge of my life and steering it in ways that reassured me, not merely following other people's advice without first checking in with myself. We continued to talk it out as the budding of a plan took form. I was going to be transferred over to the Carcassonne Hospital in France. I was given the details of a doctor in Couiza, the nearest town where we would soon be living. I was advised to check in with this doctor the very day of arrival, explain the situation, and hand over the faxed notes that she was about to send me. She would highlight the importance of this case and urge the doctor to arrange priority treatment in Carcassonne.

I was choosing to heal myself, to uproot those cancerous cells and discover what had led to this disturbance within my cervix in the first place. I knew there was a reason, whether it was some unexpressed emotion, some painful memory, some hardened idea that had contaminated these cells and caused them to disease. I could hear the nurse's admiration as she wished me luck in my future. Her sincerity caused me to tear up. We both hadn't expected such a heartfelt connection, but it happened anyway. And this is how life unfolds when you follow your own guidance. When you say "yes" to the Path of Love and to yourself.

I put the phone down and discovered a bewildered mum sitting quietly next to me as tears threatened to fall. Out of instinct I moved in towards mum's waiting embrace. Mum instinctively began to rub my back and smooth my hair. It felt so good to have her with me, to allow and receive this once upon a time comfort that dissolves the moment you become an adult. I was afraid and overcome. I had taken such good care of myself over the years. I really didn't think this could happen to me. Yet the reality was—why not me? It happens every day, and I was not immune.

"Don't worry darling, I am sure you will be okay. These things happen…" She whispered.

She then proceeded to reel off a list of women that I knew who also had problems in this area. But, at that point, I had stopped listening. I was inwardly gathering the strength and resolve to begin this journey that had in actuality already begun. One thing in particular encouraged me; the constant bleeding (that had begun when Sananda and I started making love) had stopped. For about two weeks now everything seemed to return back to normal—even when we made love there was no longer any discomfort or bleeding.

Something transformative was going on inside of me, and I was sure I was only aware of a fraction of it. There seemed to be a massive opening and awakening within my entire reproductive system and womb. I knew that all this disease was the result of twenty odd years worth of unexpressed and suppressed emotional build-up. I could feel the layers of regret and self-betrayal resulting in this internal disturbance. For years I had experienced loveless sex, but never admitted it to myself; only now the truth of these feelings were starting to show and finally become healed the more I opened to Sananda and to love. I was sure this was another verifying sign of the Beloved at work as I remembered its true meaning—Be 'love'd—and realized all the times that I wasn't. In my heart I knew that Sananda was the only one I was prepared to let in at such a deep level.

Mum and I stayed holding one another as we took turns wiping each other's tears away. I was so grateful for my mother's love in that moment. She had seen me through it all. And truly, who would have thought, even 6 months earlier as I taught yoga, hobnobbed with New Agers in London, and traveled to my heart's content that I would be facing all of this? With this news, I was being asked to transform even more profoundly! I knew what I had to do. I would heal whatever my body was showing me. I knew my Beloved, Sananda, was coming in at this time in my life so I could do this very thing. I was certain of it.

The phone rang again and we jumped out of our skin in surprise. It was Sananda. I reached for the phone as my heart yearned to connect with his. I told him all that had happened this morning and the crying began all over again. He said he felt me reach out to him while he was meditating that morning and knew I needed him. I breathed a huge sigh of relief, as I then knew he was with me no matter what. We had arranged to see each other the next day as I was due to go to the hospital to have the polyp removed. Because of the turn of events, he was jumping in the car right away and would be with me in a couple of hours.

I whimpered a thank you and put down the receiver.

I walked out barefoot into the garden and picked a spot to lay down on the grass with my hands over my womb. I was listening as the birds sang their joyous songs feeling the caress of the breeze against my skin as the sun warmed my face. Even with my worry and upset, life continued all around me. I continued to immerse myself with the sounds of nature, allowing myself to drop into my womb space, where all the answers were lying to be discovered. Once all my bodily functions had slowed down, I drifted off listlessly for what seemed like hours, to awake to the doorbell chiming. Sananda was here! His strong, handsome and steady form filled the garden as he slowly strode over towards me. He lifted me up and into his arms as he quietly held me close. I was all cried out.

"Thank you so much for coming, it means the world to me that you are here with me now," I confessed.

"My love, how could I not be with you when you need me the most? You are the most important person in my life, you are my priority, and when you need me I will always be there," he proclaimed.

That sentence rocked my world. Could I really trust in what he was saying? I wanted to, but if I trusted him and he let me down again, I would be heartbroken. I knew that these voices were the faint echoes of distrust after the incident with Catherine. I knew the only way to settle and heal these voices was to go forward and prove to myself that Sananda was indeed trustworthy. I had to trust myself first, before I could trust Sananda. Trusting myself meant moving forward in following my guidance to heal through love. Trust and consciousness are the two key elements of the path of the Beloved, without these—things get very messy.

I decided that I would rather trust with an open heart, than deny this possibility of unconditional support because of the fear of losing him based on reminders from the past. I would rather be hurt a million, trillion times in the name of love, rather than avoid a broken heart. What craziness! Yet I knew that almost all of us live this way. But what if we didn't? What if we chose love, no matter what? I decided to do exactly that, come what may. After all, what did I now have to lose? It was looking likely that I was developing cancer; and with that potential stark reality I decided with whatever power I had left, I would choose life, choose love, and choose yes!

I was now saying my yes, even louder than before.

Sananda and I sat together for the whole afternoon drawing up a plan to heal the pre-cancerous cervix. He explained to me about an ancient Tibetan form of bodywork called Pulsing, and how this method would saturate my womb with life force and blood that would be full of vitality and cleansing properties. I reminded him about the importance of a raw food diet, complete with daily vegetable juices (which he agreed to do with me!), and also that I would meditate daily on each of the seven gates as I journeyed through my womb, reclaiming my sacred space, using consciousness to scan and reconnect everything back to my loving heart. He also promised to do his own form of hands-on healing and that together we were about to embark on a powerful healing journey to make sure that I came out of this process one hundred percent cured.

Trust in love, proceed in consciousness. That would be my prescription.

❧

Reading Hospital, England, The next day, May 2009

The following morning we set off for Reading Hospital, which was only half an hour from my parent's house; and strangely enough the hospital I was born in. I wondered whether I would get another lease on life as we weaved our way through the various corridors of the new maternity building looking for the elusive gynecology department. We found it, and were shown to the waiting room. I was anxious, and yet also strangely relieved that this day had finally come. I was prepared for the surgery. I was ready for the polyp to be removed from the outside wall of my cervix. Sananda had reassured me that everything would be fine, frequently laughing at my worries in a kind and gentle way, thoroughly convinced that all was well despite my protests to the contrary. He was with me every step of the way, announcing he would love to be with me as I went into the room with the doctor. This came as a huge surprise, along with an uneasiness of being so naked and revealed in front of him. Making love is one thing, having your legs up and open in stirrups in the cold harsh reality of fluorescent lighting is quite another!

Again, that same choice. Fear or Love? I immediately squeezed his hand with a resounding, "Yes darling, I would love you to be there."

"Scarlett O'Shea, would you come this way please," a beautiful, gregarious black

African woman called out my name. The doctor reminded me of Whoopi Goldberg, complete with dreadlocks, a mischievous grin, and a warm, easy nature. She beamed at me across the corridor, beckoning us to follow her into a small consulting room. Sananda and I sneakily smiled at each other. "Wow, she is lovely," I mouthed to Sananda. He nodded, as if he knew all along that it could only ever be this way—with me being perfectly supported by the perfect people.

She explained the procedure in detail; she would take a quick look inside to locate the polyp and then insert an ultra-sound probe to check the womb and ovaries. I undressed and climbed aboard the bed, inserted my feet into the stirrups, laid back, and awaited the return of the doctor and Sananda. I sheepishly smiled at Sananda to ease the edge of my nerves in this fully exposed, nothing left to the imagination reclining position. Sananda reached for my hand, holding it closely in his, his fingers occasionally squeezing mine, reassuring and comforting. He stayed like this the whole time, making sure I was comfortable and that I could feel him. The doctor commented on how refreshing it was that my partner was with me, saying that, in the twenty-odd years she had been working in this hospital, the only other time a man was present was as a translator. I smiled, knowing that as Beloveds were now being brought together in a greater way, she would start seeing a lot more support from partners.

The doctor gently attempted to locate the polyp. After a few minutes, she said she could not find it. She was going to try again, this time by inserting a device and then use a spotlight to have a closer look. She looked puzzled. I looked nervous.

So we tried again. She looked high and low, and again announced that my cervix did not have a polyp attached to it. It was gone! She explained how this can naturally happen, that a polyp can disappear all by itself. I turned to Sananda with absolute delight in my eyes. He warmly looked down at me, holding my hand with both of his.

The doctor continued to go ahead with the ultrasound scan, and have a look over the womb and the rest of my reproductive organs to check for any other abnormalities. I told her about the pap smear results I received the day before and asked whether she could look into that area with the probe. She shook her head even before I finished my sentence. Apparently the probe wouldn't be able to spot any unusual cellular activity; the probe could only detect growths, cysts or dark patches, indicating the possibility of any abnormal activity. She did however promise to have a good look around my cervix to see whether anything else could be found. But again, she reconfirmed that I must continue with the suggested procedure of a biopsy with a different department as soon as I could.

She inserted the probe and turned the TV screen around to face me so we could both see what was going on. It was incredible—I could see everything on the small TV screen. She pushed right up against the walls of my womb, and looked inside. I winced as she moved over to each ovary, checking the entire length of the fallopian tubes for any blockages.

We then went to the tip of the cervix where the abnormality was detected. I squeezed Sananda's hand, as his thumb brushed over the top of mine. "Keep looking at the screen," he told me. So I did; I looked everywhere, asking the doctor to stop at certain places, asking whether she could see anything I couldn't. It all seemed clear. She took the probe out and left me to get dressed. We all sat together as she finished off my notes. No polyp, normal scan, no abnormality detected. Case closed, witness dismissed.

One down, one more to go! As soon as we reached the great outdoors I called mum and dad to announce the good news. They were thrilled as they both cheered down the end of the phone as we walked towards the car. Sananda hugged and spun me around in the car park, repeating the words, "You see, you see, you see! You can do it!" And in that moment, it certainly did look that way.

I realized that as I healed all the remnants of my old relationships, as I continued to trust in the way of love, and by letting go of the tendency to react in fear, the polyp had dissolved and transformed. I knew intuitively that the polyp created its own eco-system, that it was created as an act of bodily intelligence as it worked to recycle and transform the polluted cells, the layers of protection and the numerous patterns of resistance. When the healing work was done, the cells returned back to my reproductive system and the polyp dissolved, leaving no trace of its existence anywhere.

It was a causal effect of consistently not being in authentic relationships. The moment I began to make love with Sananda, my Beloved, my cells recognized the presence of tremendous trust (which is an aspect of love) and consciousness (awareness) for the very first time. Inwardly I experienced a total relaxation that allowed him into me at the greatest levels both physically and emotionally. In a word I completely trusted him, and as the saying goes 'gave myself to him completely.' This sense of trust can only ever be experienced with the Beloved, and is the key that opened up the diseased and contracted cells that needed healing. Again, this was the work of the Beloved, like the wounds, it was only with Sananda that I could experience this. It just wouldn't have happened with anyone else. Now that this piece was complete, I was clear and ready for the next stage of co-teaching with Sananda as we ventured through Peru.

⚭

Parents House, Newbury, England, May 2009

Days later Sananda was in Mexico where he was hanging out for a week before I joined him in Peru. It was during that time while we were in different parts of the world that I witnessed firsthand how my healing had clearly taken place not only within me, but us both.

With Sananda gone, I had a moment to breathe and reflect on the path of the Beloved happening between us. So after another long, eventful night of otherworldly dreams and interplanetary conversations, I awoke with a huge wave of understanding. It was on this particular morning, (just three days after Sananda left) that I recalled how the Beloved has the key 'element' to a tremendous physical healing of the other.

It worked a bit like homeopathy, working within the law of similarity, or in other words, like attracts like. The sheer presence of the Beloved (because he/she is shares your soul, and has accumulated polar opposite experiences), can cause a powerful physical reaction, possibly accelerating a once dormant, yet impending health issue. Because they carry the healing nectar, the antidote if you like, from their opposing experiences in life, it can kick you off into a massive healing crisis. I could feel the waves of truth flowing through me—I had hit the nail on the head! Not only do they carry the trigger, but the antidote itself. Whether they know this or not, is a different matter. My insights continued; the trigger is the antidote itself—by triggering the healing in the other, they would be released from carrying this minute amount of the toxin (just like homeopathy), and will go on to experience a profound shift of wellness and jubilation, as their task will be done. And all of this before 10am. What a morning I was having!

Wide-awake and giddy with insight, I gently rolled out of the sofa bed, trying my hardest to avoid disturbing the sleeping forms of my cats. I snuck into the conservatory and sat down on my sheepskin to begin my morning practice of yoga. For some reason my conscience was nudging me to check my emails before I began, as something important was waiting for me!

My Gmail account opened up to reveal the most exquisite email from Sananda. I had to re-read it a couple of times, as a) it was profoundly loving and beautiful, b) a confirming sign that the more we journeyed together, the closer and more intimate we became and c) this was *the* living proof that something massive had shifted in him, confirming my earlier contemplations.

As I healed, he healed,

As he healed, I healed.

My Dearest Scarlett,

This is probably the most important letter I have ever written.

I see my whole life with you. It is unfolding as we live and breathe, as the past uncurls and the future unfolds. I see the rest of my life with you, and then afterwards as we shed our human forms. An infinite lifetime containing all other lifetimes, resulting in the culmination of all lifetimes.

A lifetime of Play, of Passion, of Love, of doing and being that which has never been done before on this Earth, a path carved out by our brothers and sisters which today, tomorrow, the next days and years ahead can finally be fulfilled through us.

A lifetime of loving, of supporting each other, and the serving of all beings. A lifetime spent playing in the infinite where all is laid to rest in the eternal bosom of our love anchored through our bodies, our hearts, and through our home.

My home lies within you. The seal of my tattoo is pulsing and tingling as I write this to you.

You are my Beloved, and I have prayed today that all of our love descends into us both. Our vessels, our love, our holy desire, our wisdom, and our power will help us to hold this Flame on Earth as it is Heaven.

Earth is Heaven… this is the Lord's Prayer of the Beloved. This is what we are living and unfolding into!

This is not just about you and me; that which is far greater is unfolding through us. As we give everything, all gets given through us.

Our upcoming marriage is the herald for this. Our Seals of Immaculate Love, the Seal of the Full Embodying of Love, is how we navigate in nobility, and in totality.

We are so Blessed… so blessed darling. What we are living is the stuff of dreams, of stardust, of the deepest hearts desires of humanity, the deepest longing of every man and woman and we have it! My God! We are living humanities dream of Union, of Love, for them, through us! Do you know what that means? We have been given the greatest opportunity of all time …let's fully seize it together.

Your Beloved,

Sananda

With the receiving of this email, many pieces of the puzzle precisely fitted into their rightful place. Sananda was also confirming what I already knew to be true—I would no longer meet any more Soul Mates. I knew that it was only the Beloved that could satisfy the incredible longing I had to find and merge with 'the other' who shared my soul. Soul Mates were those 'coated' with the light of your soul, while a Beloved stands with you at the source of that light. This was Sananda for me. It's one of those realizations that cannot be spoken or written, only the one who experiences this, knows. The full weight of this realization was beginning to integrate within me and with it came a love that washed clean every memory of life without him. He now he felt the same way about me.

I gracefully closed the lid of my Mac screen, as I jubilantly turned to face the rising sun through the sparkling windows of my parent's conservatory. I felt victorious and so full of life, so full of yes! In this moment, there was only one thing that was missing from this near paradisiacal dewy morning. So with a deep breath, straight spine, and eyes closed at the third-eye point, I began.

"Hare Krishna, Hare Krishna, Krishna, Krishna Hare Hare..."

Tired of Speaking Sweetly

Love wants to reach out and man handle us,
break all our teacup talk of God
If you have the courage to give the Beloved his choice,
Some nights he would just drag you around the room by your
    hair,
Ripping from your grip all of your toys that bring you no joy

Love sometimes gets tired of speaking sweetly
and wants to rip to shreds all your erroneous notions of truth
that make you fight with yourself, dear one, and others
causing the world to weep on one too many fine days

God wants to man handle us,
and lock us in a tiny room with himself
and practice his drop kick

The Beloved sometimes wants to do us a great favor
and hold us upside down, and shake the non-sense out
But when we hear he is in such a playful mood
almost everyone I know high tails it out of town...

—HAFIZ

Chapter Fifteen

Peru: The Island of the Sun and Moon

On the road to Lake Titicaca, Peru/Bolivia border,
May 2009

THE OLD SEVENTIES STYLE retro bus swung off the road, kicking up a cloud of dusty gravel as it swerved to an abrupt halt in what looked and smelled like the back end of nowhere! The entire bus load of passengers that made up our retreat group lunged forward, not before first being pinned like a bunch of dissected frogs to the back of their chairs by the sheer power of g-force. Half our group was asleep in various sprawled positions all over the seats, as the six-hour drive to Lake Titicaca knocked us out. As you can imagine the last thing we expected was the sudden decision by the driver to try out an old Evel Knievel stunt with us all onboard. This shocking scenario had everyone sitting bolt upright in their seats like hyper alert meerkat's, looking left and right with bright wide eyes, spying the terrain for signs of imminent danger.

The sweet Peruvian driver turned around in his driver's seat and launched into a full display of apologies complete with arm and theatrical facial expressions. I was laughing with him, as I too shared his nervousness, in fact I would have laughed with anything remotely vulnerable or sincerely human at the time. Turns out, I was both co-teacher and student on this tour, as Sananda had assigned me to uncover and work with my shadow today. And let's just say this; it wasn't very pretty.

"I am so sorry, so sorry, brakes not very good, so sorry!" he repeated in his broken English. There was a massive sigh of relief as we all collectively climbed back down from the bus. He explained we had now reached our destination and gave us the directions on how to find the passport control office at the border. I spun around doing my own meerkat impression, as I mouthed the words "What border?" to various people behind me.

No one looked, let alone answered as they were all glued to the driver and his parting instructions. My God, I had no idea we were changing countries! I stepped off the coach with my trusty passport in hand into an ocean of different colored parka jackets and brightly woven Peruvian blankets. I found myself wandering around in a daze when I remembered that in order to get an answer you first need to ask the question. I slowly meandered over to ask someone from the group to find out what was happening. I was told, with an "I can't believe you didn't know" expression from one of the women that we were at the border of Peru and Bolivia, and we now needed to go through passport control and change our currency.

How much more surreal can life get? Just as I was moving further into the internal healing process, I now found myself forced to readjust back into "normal" life, deal with officialdom, change languages, countries, and money all the time having no idea where Bolivia actually is on the planet. Not to mention that my Beloved Sananda was emotionally a trillion light years away from our love.

It made me feel so very alone, afraid, and exhausted.

We had been arguing all night over totally mindless and insignificant matters that seemed to grow large and fearsome as the night wore on. We were feeling jealous and threatened by potential lovers that we could have gotten together with before we met (people that both of us knew… ick… dicey territory!). Now in the cold, hard light of day, I could see that we allowed our argument to escalate way beyond what was necessary. We were paying the price with an icy currency that left frostbite in its wake, causing our hearts to chill and harden. No matter how heavy my heart was if I wanted to stay with our group somehow, just somehow, I had to swiftly get my organized head on, and get on with the imminent job at hand of crossing one of the world's most sensitive borders.

I linked arms with a member of the group, Rebecca. She was a pillar of strength and support (literally) as she physically held me up as we walked across the official line that separated Peru from Bolivia. I was exhausted from the trip, emotionally strained from arguing all night, and to top it off feeling so incredibly vulnerable that any gesture of human kindness threatened to start off a flood of tears that would never stop. She reminded me that as women, our capacity to love is our greatest gift. But first I needed to love myself right now, and rest. She placed her hand over my heart and advised that I take it easy as she could see everything that was going on between Sananda and I.

"Be strong, as it's that strength and power that lights you up from inside. Remember, that is what attracted him to you in the first place. Don't give up your spirit, baby."

A rush of ecstatic Shakti flowed through my body, as all my

hairs prickled up. I was alive again. I thanked Rebecca for reminding me of who I truly am. I walked away to take some deep breaths to center myself before joining the queue for the passport control office. As I wandered off, I felt the familiar sensation of 'something happening' inside, when suddenly a vision—an entourage of heavenly warrior queens appeared in front of me. First to greet me was Joan of Arc on horseback with a banner in hand smiling down on me. She nodded her approval as she reached down to touch my shoulder. Next up, was Boudicca (queen of a great British tribe in 60 A.D.), complete with her battle cats, who handed over the leashes of her feline friends, promising me their guardianship. Cleopatra and Helen of Troy stepped forward to reveal their supportive presence as various other Ladies of Light fell in line behind these powerful queens. They all represented the face of feminine power that fought with dignity and honor for what they knew was right in this world. Their presence confirmed that I was indeed made of the same qualities, that I was part of this lineage of female icons. Whilst their joy and celebration declared that I was welcome to draw upon their strength, I was able to see that I was made of mightier stuff. I took a breath of courage and support as I regained my composure and commitment to continue onward for the honor of our love.

After border control, we got back on the bus, to be told that a short twenty-minute drive was the only thing standing between lunch and ourselves. "Hurray!" was the response from the hungry meerkats, as they all sat up again. Encouraged and feeling inspired again, I decided to use this precious time to do the job Sananda had been urging me to do all day: discover the pillar of my shadow. This process was taken from his resource of teachings, based on one of his best-selling books, *The Nine Eyes of Light.* The shadow is the energy you feel when you inwardly hear all sorts of judgments and criticisms about yourself or others. It's the darker aspects of ourselves, usually the parts we try very hard to hide, suppress, or deny.

We all have a shadow, and its nature can also be known in those times of wild anger, jealousy, or spitefulness. It's those recognizable times when we remark, "I have no idea what came over me!" or "That's just not like me to behave that way!" Bingo, that's the shadow. Now it was my turn to take a closer look to see what its game was.

Making sure that I found an empty seat at the back of the bus, I closed my eyes as I drifted in and out of my past along with landscapes that were alien to me, yet also strangely familiar. I began to see how I had this strong sense of self-preservation and that I would jump ship at the idea of losing my freedom. I noticed that I was always in the driver's seat when it came to my intimate relationships, and would cringe and squirm if anyone attempted to tell me what to do regarding my choices or direction in life. There was no choice but to admit it. I was a control freak. Ah ha! I had found the core of my shadow.

The bus continued to speed and rattle along the road as I let the naming of my shadow sink in. Opening up my notepad I shakily drew a circle which I named CONTROL and then drew lines off the circle into the other areas of my life: work, relationships (friends and family), home, sexuality and partner. I looked at all these areas of my life and then wrote down the ways in which I attempted to control them.

This is what I wrote:

The Pillar of my Shadow

- Work – I *had* to be successful, purposeful, gifted, *had* to "teach" something, *had* to give to people, and no one or anything could get in the way of this.
- Friends and Family Relationships – I had to be independent, alone, no ties or responsibilities, I valued my own space and time to work fiercely.
- Home – My living environment had to be tidy, organized, a sanctuary, quiet and peaceful. I did not like too many people around as I felt it interrupted my private time.
- Sexuality – I would not give myself completely or open up. I protected my freedom and my power. I was driving, guiding, and dictating when, where, and how I would become sexually intimate with another. I was fearful of being "taken."
- Partner – I would protect myself from being hurt, used, taken for granted, rejected, and abandoned. I did this by keeping an escape route available and always ajar. In any moment I could pack and leave for good.

When looking at my list you may ask what the problem was, that many may also live this way. The issue was the powerful and immovable quality of the "had-to's" threaded throughout the sentences. This meant I experienced huge amounts of discomfort if these needs were not met. What a breakthrough! I had always thought I was an independent "free spirit." Family and friends had been telling me this for years, which received no dispute on my end as I secretly liked this description of my character. It brought up images of roaming gypsies and traveling hippies, being free to do what "I" wanted to do in any moment.

Upon closer inspection, I could see quite clearly what this idea was actually built on. Here I was, face-to-face with this "free" spirit that was based upon the foundation of fear of not being in control. It's amazing, as one of the tendencies I used to find distasteful in others were those I labeled as "control freaks." Their consistent controlling of others or holding on tightly when in the face of change upset me the most. Ha! Fantastic, what a paradox, what a truth. I was doing the very thing that got my knickers in a twist in relation to others.

So, what do you do in those moments when you see yourself clearly, and it's not pretty? The First Step: is to a) forgive yourself (embrace all your controlling ways into your heart, and love them as a mother would a child—we are all still learning) and b) truly appreciate the discovery of such a truthful insight. Second Step: find the antidote. So I turned the page and titled it:

Become Powerless:

- Have no structure
- Have no "work"
- Have no name for yourself (no reputation based on being/doing great)
- Have no home
- Have no money
- Have no old friends for now
- Have no connection that feeds your idea of being "great"
- Have no spiritual practice

- Have no form of past
- Have no old ways of being
- Have nothing!

When I completed the exercise I sat back in the seat listening to the words of my divine guidance:

My love, the truth is that you are not in control, you never have been. This small, minute sense of control that you 'think' you have enjoyed is actually your own self-imposed control to stop yourself living more fully in love. To be with your Beloved, you will both be asked to let go of any control, to allow the wild nature of this love its full domain. True freedom, is total surrender. Once you let go, then you shall become the living heart that is constantly welcoming everything home.

When you meet the pain of being human, you have to be willing to stop telling the story about the pain. Release and drop into the pure experience of what you have been avoiding or rejected. Nothing can happen without this willingness to innocently withdraw and fall into your direct experience of what you have been avoiding.

I wasn't sure how long I would need to implement these changes for, but I knew I could relax with the confidence that my guidance would show me the way. And for the first time in a long while, even as we bumped along, I relaxed and let go. Finally, sleep welcomed me into her arms.

"Okay, we're here, its lunchtime!" were the words tugging at my consciousness to return back to the bus, and reluctantly back into my hungry body.

During lunch Sananda and I sat together in total silence. A

fortress was being built, a place where no hope lived. He was still holding on to last night's argument, and refusing to back down and make amends. He was angry, while I was sad. Sad that we couldn't seem to move forward, hurt that he was still angry with me, and surprised that this was even happening at all. He looked like he was firmly rooted in his position to be angry over a squabble regarding friendships with past lovers. Yep, he was holding strong.

To some, this may seem like an ideal state; detached, a strong sense of self, unmovable, and impenetrable. In the eyes of love, this is a poison; it's the venom that intravenously drips into the heart, which flows into the blood that feeds the body. Within a matter of minutes the body hardens, as bitterness sweeps through the fortress, chilling its walls. The presence of love is banished to sit patiently outside the walls and is neither felt nor acknowledged. Yet, still she waits, forever standing true and strong in her essence.

I looked around noticing that everyone else was chatting away with anticipation as we ventured ever closer to Lake Titicaca. Confident that we wouldn't be interrupted, I reached for his hand under the tablecloth. He did not move, his eyes were fixed into the distance as he pursed his lips together to reinforce his righteous detachment. I gently reassured him that we could get through this and that I was able and ready to move forward. He continued to stare ahead unflinching, as he flatly told me he needed to feel something from me to prove what I was saying was true.

I sat there wondering for some time about his request. How can you actually prove such a thing without being given the chance by the natural passing of time? I knew that life would conjure up the opportunity for me to prove my words, but I had no idea when. In the meantime, here was Sananda, asking me to prove it right here, right now at this very lunchtime in a Bolivian cafe. How do you prove love? How do you prove commitment? How do you prove trust when sitting in a cafe? There was only one answer. Words. Words could speak of it, but never prove it. Only life could prove it. But he wants something now, so all I could do was speak.

Why, I didn't realize that he was deeply entrenched in a 'wound' I shall never know. All I know is he would say "jump!" and I would say "How high?" Even though we were holding hands, his hand was as limp as a lettuce left out in the sun. I sat opposite him, looking for a sign that he wasn't serious. This was a game, right? Or was it another one of those, "do you really love me" tests? Oh, but I knew what it was. He was forcing me to go deeper. Even in this seemingly silly situation, a part of me recognized that this was an important place I needed to go with myself. A place I had never gone before. I was no spring chick anymore, I was a responsible woman whose fortieth birthday was only months away. I was at a stage in my life where I was willing to delve into myself.

So, without further character analysis regarding Sananda and his alien ways of doing things, I breathed in the almighty presence of love as I declared my allegiance to him. I imagined the story of when Jesus Christ spoke on The Mount of Olives, and gave The Lord's Prayer. That original, untouched version, where every word found their way into the core of the listener's hearts and rested there. I imagined what it would feel like to be in the presence of one who was intrinsically united with the source of pure love.

There, it was felt. The surge of love came alive and from that aliveness, from the depths of my heart, I stood up from the table and spoke of my resolute strength and courage, and then on bended knee, with one hand over my heart I offered my humble readiness to become mature. I stayed there for a moment crying softly as I felt the absolute truth of what I was saying. This was a very raw and real moment. With sheer knightly valor, I stood again as I assured him that I did have the robust ability to not go into my shadow and its old pattern of running away. No matter what he said or did, I would remain in love and be willing to continue on.

After my delivery, I sat back into my chair looking for some, in fact any kind of response from Sananda. But he still just continued to gaze past me, remaining isolated, unreachable, and distrusting. After a good ten minutes he slowly shifted his gaze from the horizon to stare me dead in the eye. I let out a slight murmur of disbelief, when I saw that his eyes were cold, dark, empty, and devoid of all love!

Time passed as I searched his face for some flicker of friendship, some glimmer of recognition that I was his wife-to-be, or some hint that I was his Beloved, surely he remembered his playmate? But I found nothing. I silently begged him to trust in me, and give me a chance. After what felt like an eternity, there was a breakthrough as he squeezed my hand as if to indicate that he understood and accepted my words. From the depths of my belly I let out a deep exhale as I warmly smiled at him, and squeezed back whispering a "thank you."

Moments later our order came, and all my manners flew out the window. A plateful of tuna salad arrived, along with an order of French fries and guacamole. With a hunched back, high flying elbows, and agreeable grunts between mouthfuls I tucked in as if I had not seen food for months. I momentarily looked up long enough to see that the whole group relaxed and eased up with us. I knew that although they had not heard the argument, it was wise to assume that they did indeed feel what was happening between us. They were highly intuitive beings.

The glowing faces of the group beamed with relieved smiles, knowing all too well what it feels like to be on the end of Sananda's surgical instrument of egoic dissection. This was one of his rigorous teaching trademarks, the ability to turn someone inside out in a matter of seconds, slicing ruthlessly at their ego, and its attempts to justify itself. The problem was that I was rather good at that game too—hence the almighty argument the night before. I relaxed again, allowing myself to become more present and available for everyone.

Phew, another obstacle cleared and dealt with.

After lunch we headed for the boats that would take us to the Islands of the Sun and Moon that floated in the middle of Lake Titicaca. The Isla Del Sol or Island of the Sun is the revered birthplace of the Incas, the place where their god Viracocha created the sun and the Inca civilization. The sister island to Isla Del Sol and its female counterpart is Isla de la Luna, or Island of the Moon. After god Viracocha created the sun it is believed that he went to Isla de la Luna and created the moon.

The whole group was buzzing with excitement and giddy as schoolgirls, as we all contemplated the great adventure that lay ahead of us. The last couple of days of the retreat were going to be the most important, the most crucial; for it was on these islands that our greatest work was to be done. We were told by Sananda that we were now ready to come together and work as a collective force, as our shadows were finally clear enough. We were all open to be able to give to the whole planet, and this was the greatest work a human being could ever do in a lifetime. Oh yes, I was up for it! I gushed with admiration as he shared this news with all of us.

Just as I was boarding the boat to take us to the Island of the Sun, Sananda pulled me to one side and instructed me to receive three drops of a liquid crystal to amplify any further shadowy elements that may still be lurking within. He told me I was still not clear of my shadow and that I was now in jeopardy of holding the group back from their greatest work. He warned me that somehow I had to quickly sort it out. If I did not, I would not be included. Ouch, that hurt! It was a blow way below the belt. While Sananda was a Shadow Master and had detailed experience working with the shadow, I knew he was not perfect, nor his shadow completely clear. I couldn't understand why he was singling me out now.

"What is he talking about?" Was my immediate question. "Why is he saying this to me?" I continued to ponder over these questions as I reflected on what I could have possibly said or done to give him the idea that I created a monster within myself. Something strange was going on; it seemed as if Sananda had nominated himself as my teacher. I had to address this issue very quickly and stamp out any notions he may have of fulfilling this role. It was not an option. I had a teacher and as every woman knows, you cannot love and become intimate with your teacher— the dynamics won't work. It's messy, not to mention a pain in the arse. I wasn't having any of that.

Wrapped in sadness and aloneness, somehow I managed to get my things together and find a place to sit on the floor of the boat as it began its journey to the islands. This situation was really getting out of hand. I had so much to contend with that I didn't notice that Sananda was suddenly at my side asking me a question.

"What are you doing?"

I stared at him blankly as I was also asking myself the same question. Luckily some reasonable answer surfaced. "I'm sitting on the boat," I replied.

This pissed him right off. It wasn't meant to, (or was it?) I was just worn out.

"I mean, what are you doing about your shadow?" he hissed at me.

He spoke so loudly that all the others in the boat noticed. Heads went down, voices became hushed, as they moved away to give us our space.

I felt broken with all of this shadow work and confused about Sananda's true role in it. "I don't know, but I will find out," I whispered.

"Tell me, how are you going to do this? You don't have a clue; you think yoga will sort this out? Go into some little meditation, pray to God, and run away into your little world? That will never do it. I want to know how you are going to sort your shadow out?" He bellowed at me.

Tears began to fall. "Sananda, please stop."

"You are pathetic," he tutted as he turned on his heels and walked away.

My constant change between feeling empowered and then victimized (or light and dark) were the classic signs that I was moving through some heavy issues as my shadow was triggered. Although Sananda was known for this type of teaching method, I knew that his own personal anger was being mixed into the procedure. Note to self: shadow work gets sticky when your Beloved is a shadow teacher.

His anger was no doubt linked to me administering the same

process on him, highlighting his own traits and tendencies that were calling out to be released and surrendered (behind closed doors, though). For us, this was the early stages of our work together as Beloveds. For some reason, clearly decided upon before we met in person, we had decided we would work intensely with the light and dark aspects of our being, making sure that all shadow elements were seen and exposed quickly. Because we were made of powerful stuff, we had the capacity to withstand the on-going, grueling nature of this process. As far as I was concerned, we had two options; either we do it brilliantly well or not at all. There was no way I was going to take all that flack when I could clearly see area's within Sananda's life that were being overlooked, or maybe not even realized in some circumstances.

Shortly after Sananda finished off his latest round on me, my ego picked up exactly where he had left off:

Excuse me, what is going on young lady? Are you going to let him walk all over you? What has happened to your spirit, your dignity, have you no respect for yourself? My God are you turning into a doormat? Are you are just going to lie down and allow him to wipe his shoes across your heart and trample over your love? Why are you doing this? Why do you subject yourself to such humiliation?

Being human can be seen as one huge joke. Just as one tyrant storms off in the outer world, the inner dictator begins on you too. But there was a reason, and a very good one. As I reflected inwardly I noticed that I had a rather sizable complex concerning authority figures and confrontations. Whenever I would encounter either of them I would become subservient and apologetic, or fire up into a wild storm and take things too far. I knew I had to encounter a male authority figure and master the art of being detached.

Boy, was Sananda playing that role superbly! He was pressing every button imaginable. However, I was observing the entire situation from a detached perspective as this breakthrough made me realize that I was handling the situation better than I ever had before. While I bounced back and forth between being triggered and seeing my dark elements roar up before me, I was observing them more clearly and able to get back to the light sooner than in times past. It was slow and painful, but I was making progress.

Again my ego went up to bat. I could literally see her contemplating what I should say to him when he came around next, her hands on her hips and toes tapping the floor as she cocked her head to one side. After a while longer she decided to play ball, for as much as the ego may kick and scream against my conscious choices and actions, it had no choice but to go through the eye of the needle up ahead. Soul was in the driver's seat, heart was on the pedal, spirit was changing gears, and ego was the passenger! *"There's nowhere to run to baby, there's nowhere to hide,"* crooned the dulcet tones of Martha Reeves and The Vandellas as the song played in my head.

I sincerely wished to know what I was truly made of, so since Sananda was not around and I could be left in peace (the other students chose not to sit next to me as they knew I had to do this all on my own) I resumed the practice of working with my shadow. I sat there with a heavy heart as I searched the archives for murderous thoughts and evil intentions. Although I found nothing, I was aware of feeling a sense of regret that I was possibly holding the group back and worse still, jeopardizing the mission. The pit of despair opened up once again, as the momentary solid footing I thought was now reliable and trustworthy, crumbled underfoot.

I silently continued the search for truth as I sat on the floor of the boat, hugging my knees to my chest rocking back and forth. In the depths of my soul I knew that all of this was happening as it was meant to, that despite Sananda's pushing personal triggers in me, he was being purposeful and using tactics to help me breakthrough to my most authentic self. Thank God I heard that whisper, if not I may have traded it all in and headed back to London!

Insights from some of the more ugly parts of my nature bubbled up to the surface to be seen and liberated. A few hidden agendas, masks, lies, and egotistical strategies came and reintroduced themselves to me. But this was all basic stuff; things that I had been aware of for years all based on normal human and animal survival patterns. At the end of the day we are all part animal; and I guess those traits do not go away, it's a case of whether you respond or not. I simply did not get what he was saying, I knew myself through and through, and I was beginning to think he had made a mistake, or worse still... that he could be making it all up. It was entirely possible he would be capable of such a thing. I had now seen him in action with the people on the retreat and he was... umm... vicious at times, pummeling their ego's into a paste and coasting through their ideas and beliefs with a sledge hammer. Not entirely the best course of action for when you're falling in love and wanting to experience trust and intimacy.

I was also contending with healing the cancerous cells that were a new addition to my daily internal concerns. Yes, I was in a very strange situation, one I had never encountered before in my whole life. Despite the chaos, and all the turmoil that was going on, I persisted. I knew he was my Beloved, and I knew and recognized that all that was happening was pain. A place within me knew he had exposed the painful light of truth. I could intensely feel it. His tactics may not have inspired, but I was journeying to a new place within. And isn't that what I had wanted? Isn't that why I climbed that mountain and called for my one and only?

I could see he was a fantastic teacher; it was evident he could take people to some very deep and profound places. His presence was colossal, and his students would love and trust him until the end of time. Sananda was not like other spiritual teachers, as he worked with the light and dark aspects of human nature. One of his main gripes within the spiritual community was that they only ever worked with the light, and he felt this concept and method was doomed to fail. So I knew what he was up to on some levels and at a distance admired his work profoundly. But when you're in the thick of it like I was, admiration tends to dry up, and off you slide, down that slippery slope known as the 'rabbit hole.'

And there were perks to this work (or at least I was hanging on to any that manifested!). Walking past a mirror only hours before in the café bathroom, I had the confirming sign that all this work was worth its weight in gold in more ways than one. As I gazed into my own reflection, a vision stared back that caused me to stumble backwards, as a second glimpse longed to be taken. My god, I looked so young! In fact I looked about twelve years old. My skin was luminescent, the crow's feet around my eyes had altogether disappeared and pouring through my eyes was this sparkling light that reminded me of pure innocence. I made a mental note to keep going. Perhaps I had discovered the fountain of youth...

As I continued to sit huddled on the floor for the remainder of the journey to the Island of the Sun, I occasionally opened my eyes searching for a glimpse of land to indicate we had arrived. After spending the past few days in Machu Picchu, it was so refreshing and cleansing to reach the higher altitudes of the Island of the Sun, an island that is part of a small cluster in the middle of Lake Titicaca, the highest lake in the world above sea level. A couple of members of our group jumped into the lake in wild celebration with all their clothes on. I smiled and cheered, wishing I could have done the same. But I was feeling so tender, naked, and alone. If I had jumped in I feared I might have swam in the opposite direction away from where I was supposed to be going.

This depression did not last long as the sheer beauty of the island was calling out to be seen and felt. This tiny island in the middle of Lake Titicaca was like a moist green emerald glinting in the sapphire blue pool of a lofty, thinly aired paradise. I was overjoyed as I basked in the realization that this island was untouched by the modern world. It was isolated, simple, and basic. As we walked to our rooms for the night we passed the locals homes and makeshift villages. These people bubbled over with a happiness that was so hopelessly infectious and full. How I wished I could be one of them living here! All of this neo-spiritual, navel gazing was starting to look more like some kind of narcissist, self-flagellating personal ritual.

And with that I could see it all, the western virus. Wanting, needing, more, better, faster, bigger, consuming everything, sex, drugs, and rock and roll. More punishment for my past, more pain for my sins, I need to be told more times that I am right, or wrong. On and on and on the whining goes. What I should have got, who I should be with, how it should be different. "Should" is a word that *should* be cast out of our language, never to return again. Why is it so difficult to be absolutely and utterly content with it all?

I stopped and smiled at the local Bolivians, shaking their hands and touching their arms, as we attempted to speak to one another as they stood in the doorways of their huts. But, we understood perfectly. I was welcome to their island, and they in turn, received from me a deep thanks for their hospitality. I continued to walk along the winding track that promised our food and shelter for the next two evenings. After the better part of an hour I arrived, as I looked around for Sananda, since we were supposed to be sharing a room together. I found him sitting alone on a picnic table overlooking the lake. I gulped, as his countenance resembled a dark and foreboding potential thunderstorm. I hesitated for a moment, wondering whether I should go over, when I heard the voice of my heart:

Okay, let's do it! Walk over to him and be that unspeakable love that you have just shared with the locals. Broadcast to him the beauty and rapture of this island; embody the fullness of your journey, as you stand before him naked in only your love.

I sat next to him and asked how he was doing.

Blimey, his force field was up and growling at me. It was so bloody strong and cold. I swear to god, NASA or any of the world's armed forces would pay good money for that quality of defensive protection. I was sure that this particular force field could be the one and only chance to save humanity from the highly prophesized (and marketable) doomsday of 2012, when a gigantic comet is due to hit planet earth. Seriously, it was that intense. Not surprisingly, I was certain Sananda was not in any mood to save the world, just yet.

He continued to gaze across the lake as he coldly asked, "Do you know what it takes to become a woman?"

I decided to gaze out towards the lake as well, climbing and crawling around my inner library for some divine answer. Nothing came to me except for more and more empty silence.

"Do you even know how to be a woman?' he glared at my ear. I wasn't looking; the water had my full attention, as I knew what was behind his face. I could hear it within his voice; he was mocking me again.

"Can't you ever answer? Have you nothing to say? You don't even have the depth to answer, do you? Do you even know how to give to a man?" he tormented.

"I have decided that I don't want to marry you Scarlett, because I wish to be with a woman, and you obviously are not and have never proved yourself to be one. You can't even answer me, and I am bored with waiting for you." There he had said it. Finally, he revealed the full inner torment and hostility of *his* abandonment. When one abandons first, it is because, at their core (and whether they recognize it or not), they are terrified of being abandoned themselves.

Abandonment: The fifth wound to love.

Abandonment is that secret feeling that surges through your veins charged with emotion, which screams "victim!" It is located in the first chakra, at the base of the spine. Abandonment is self-sabotage, self-pity, and has narcissistic tendencies that are cruel and punishing. To avoid abandonment the person will inflict their projections on the other. The situation appeared that Sananda was abandoning me, the truth was he had abandoned love and his Beloved way before his recent words.

Abandonment is the voice of the shadow speaking and moving its way into your thoughts, speaking to your already low self-esteem of the reasons why you do not belong, why you are not good enough, and that you have nothing of value to say or give. It tells you that you are uninvited, you have not been chosen; you are the black sheep cast out.

Was I going to listen to all his accusations of me? Was this really my wound? It didn't feel like it was. But, to hell with it. Some powerful energy was at play here and I had to find the true antidote.

As I searched my heart I gazed out over the lake recognizing that I was on the razor's edge. I have never experienced hurt like it before. I did not realize humans could say such wicked and cruel words to one another. I was under the impression that if you had something hurtful to say, you did your best to soften the blow, not amp up the power and deliver it harder and faster. I felt completely gutted, trodden on, wretched, and disposable.

I stood there for a while in shock. It must have been shock, as I had no thoughts whatsoever and it certainly did not feel like enlightenment. I finally discovered the ability to move, as I slowly walked around in circles for a bit, contemplating my next action. It would have been easy to walk off completely heartbroken and traumatized, or to tell him what an arrogant pig he is, reminding him that he had failed and lost the one and only time of being with his Beloved. But that was not what was being asked of me. I was on the path of Love, love wouldn't do that (would it?). Maybe love of myself would of walked away…But I decided to stay and see this battle through to the other side.

Now, in this new stage of life I had to reach down deep towards a response that was made of mightier stuff. I remembered from my notes that the healing balm of abandonment was reunion. By the looks of Sananda, he was not ready for that, therefore it was up to me to reunify myself. That was it. To confirm this truth, I heard the voice of my inner guidance as it spoke out.

Accept your fate and die, or resurrect yourself and live brighter than you have ever known. The healing balm of abandonment is reunion, draw yourself together and push through for the healing of your Beloved. Trust in love, proceed in consciousness.

I stood up in front of him slowly drawing all my strength and loving power from the lake as I spoke out loud in full reunification. "You are so disillusioned Sananda, blinded by your own intelligent mind. Within three months I will be a woman in every sense of the word. I am in the middle of an essential process, which we both agreed upon back in England. It's your choice whether you have the patience and commitment to see this through with me, as you once promised. I have full faith in myself to come through this. With or without you I will do it."

"You'll never do it in three months, it's going to take you until you are forty-two to complete this," he stated slyly.

I was being led into a debate of the mind, and I was aware of it. 'Proceed in consciousness' echoed within me, reminding me caution was needed as I carefully chose my response. The power to stand by what I knew to be true won the roll of the dice. I knew, felt intuitively that I was exactly where I was meant to be on my path. In three months I sensed I would have overcome some of the biggest obstacles of my life. Obstacles that had kept me from love, from light, from my truest self. With or without Sananda I would do it. Take that Mr. Gabriel!

The once passive lake turned into an oceanic whirlpool, with a few undulating sea serpents thrown in for good measure.

"Watch this space and you will see it beginning to happen

before your eyes within three weeks. I am very grateful for all you have already moved me through. But I will do this, and do not ever underestimate me again!" I pressed both hands on the table in front of him, as I lined up my face towards his to find his attention. I could feel the electricity crackling out of my eyes as they burnt into his, holding his gaze.

"The power of my Soul to transform and re-create is inextinguishable," I hissed, "You have no idea who you are dealing with," I said, as I slowly walked over to get the key to our room.

Without any threats, no cruel words, or using any ammunition from his past as a way to hurt him—I had done it! I had confronted an angry male, kept my cool, directly corrected him, and held onto my dignity. "That's not bad," I thought to myself. "It only took about 40 years to learn!"

My great and mighty warrior queens from times past inspired me, as I envisioned Joan of Arc lifting up her sword to catch the light of the sun; Magdalene raising the Holy Dove up unto the heavens while Isis placed the final piece of Osiris back together on the capstone of the Great Pyramid. It was a triumphant moment, full of victory and resurrection in the celestial realms, whereas back down on earth I slowly unlocked the door to our retreat room. I undressed and climbed into the shower to discover that the water was not working.

Unbelievable! I had to laugh, as there was nothing else left inside of me to do. I went back to basics and filled the sink with ice-cold water from our drinking bottles and had a strip wash. It felt so good, despite being so raw and simple. Oh, to feel human and receive the cleansing from this liquid life. We usually take it for granted that water shall appear at the turn of a tap. With that, as I splashed ice cold water all over my skin and yelped, laughed, and screamed.

Nothing mattered anymore, I felt wonderfully alive as I stripped off in that bathroom on every level, naked, pure, and alone. Yet the room was filled with my Soul, my expression, and my cheerfulness. I felt so supported, and I knew this support would never die. I declared that I was willing to have my heart broken a million times in this Pilgrimage of Love. Why stop now; it's only the early days really?! I had faced some of my biggest personal conflicts in the past several months. Somehow, in every moment (and sometimes at the 11th hour as just moments before with Sananda), I found the strength to choose love and self-empowerment. I could not lose when it came to love, because this love was always within me. I felt pure joy. Then, I heard the door of the room squeak open and groan to a close.

"Darling, what are you doing in there?" he spoke outside the bathroom door knocking gently. I screamed with playfulness as I splashed water against the door, hoping he would somehow get wet.

Hang on a second...

Wait—darling? Did he just call me darling?

I roared with laughter as I realized he was out the other end of his dark, cold cruel tunnel. I opened the door and flung my arms around him in exquisite reunion. He had tested, prodded, and poked and love came through. He had his answer in my defiance, the defiance of love, and he had seen the power of love flowing through me. That was what he wanted to see, but my God, what a way to go about it!

He did not need to apologize because he did nothing "wrong."

This was how he was *truly* feeling inside. We can not deny our feelings to one another, all we need to do is 'own' them. Ideally, we would not project them onto another. We have to acknowledge our own feelings, as we find a way of being able to cry as we move through them responsibly. But at the beginning, projection will most likely happen—until we learn otherwise.

Again, whether he knew it or not he had set the stage for a perfect performance. I could not compare my relationship with Sananda to anything I had ever encountered before in my past. This was the Beloved, a reunion that will take all and anything that is necessary to free and liberate both beings from the snare and entrapments of fear. As far as I was concerned, we were facilitating an amazing array of experiences for each other that were designed to cut one another loose from our egos and from false beliefs that kept us trapped. Sananda was undergoing his own experience with our Beloved connection (and you can wait for him to write his book to learn more about that!), navigating the twists and turns and triggers it brought up for him. For my part, I worked to stay focused on what I knew to be true: Sananda was my Beloved and being with him meant looking at myself in a very real way, and doing some tough internal work.

The rest of the trip unfolded beautifully and harmoniously as we came together for the finale of the trip, resulting in a panoply of varied experiences for the whole group. We had three days left until the retreat ended. It was a delicious time, one where Sananda and I joyfully shared our purpose with the group, and joined together to be used for something greater. We facilitated a powerful ceremony that awakened and opened up the feminine energies of the Island of the Moon, to then be dispersed throughout the entire planet. The clouds parted as a ray of sunlight drenched us, plunging us in a shaft of pink and gold light. We all looked up towards the sky laughing with wonder and awe, feeling the companionship and love that united us. It was an experience that will remain forever etched upon my soul.

After the retreat ended, Sananda and I spent a couple of well-earned restful days alone on the Peruvian shore of Lake Titicaca. Every moment was spent in bed; making love, sleeping, or eating. In fact, we only got up once to go outside for a walk. All too soon it was time to fly back to London. Once again I would go one way and Sananda would go another.

CHAPTER SIXTEEN

TWENTY-EIGHT DAYS IN FRANCE

Parents' Home, England, June 2009

OH MY GOD, they've accepted our offer!" I joyfully cried on the phone to a bemused Sananda. I felt him searching his mind for what I was talking about. Click. Finally, I felt him get it.

"Fantastic darling! I knew they would. So when do we leave?" he gushed.

"We can move in on the June 29th, that's in about two week's time!" I replied.

I had just received the call from the homeowners in France. I had spent the best part of two weeks tracking them down, as I had my eye on this particular house for more than ten years. I had discovered the home during my travels to the Languedoc area teaching yoga retreats. I would occasionally drive by this home, wistfully dreaming of one day living there. When Sananda said I could pick anywhere for us to live in France, I knew this was just the spot. I immediately put the word out to friends in the area that we were looking to move to France, and this house was mentioned as a possibility. I found out that the homeowners lived in America for half the year, and the other half on the Balearic Islands.

After emailing them almost every day, they finally replied. They told me they were more than happy to rent out their home for six months to Sananda and I, while they were working in the States. They had received recommendations from their friends that we were indeed a reliable and trustworthy couple (!?). I was thrilled after speaking with Sananda, feeling his infectious joy in response to the news; it was obvious he was over the moon with this latest development in the next chapter in our lives together. His star sign was Cancer, renowned for being the 'homemaker' of the astrological signs. I knew that finding a home was a big deal for Sananda, one that would bring him tremendous pleasure.

I also released a huge sigh of relief, feeling for the first time that I now had a safe and secure place to begin my healing journey. I had pushed aside my health dilemma, not knowing where I would be living and how it would be done—until this moment. Now I knew. I could feel the sanctuary that was being offered in this beautiful old French house nestled into the foothills of The Pyrenees. Sensing the invitation of rest and rehabilitation that was by now so desperately being called for, I skipped with joy into the kitchen to announce the delightful news to mum and dad.

They were moderately pleased. Excited that I would at last be living in France (one of my dreams) as I had been teaching there for years, yet concerned that it was too soon to be jumping into living with Sananda, especially in a place that was so isolated and out of their reach. 'Exactly,' I mused to myself. I was ready to jump into this next phase of my life—to fulfill some of the dreams I had carried with me for years. Now I would live in France and with my Beloved, no less!

Using my Capricorn horns, I ploughed through all their fear-based nostalgia, tossing aside all negative remarks until I eventually caught sight of their sincere joy and happiness. We stood there laughing when I became humbled at what I was seeing. I noticed how they glanced at each other when a private and tender moment of acknowledgment arose between them. Together they shared the pain of a future separation from their 'little girl' (nearly 40) who was about to leave the nest again, and for some bizarre reason she was going on an even more unexpected adventure.

For a moment I stepped into my parents shoes. Their daughter had met this wild man of spirituality, and chose to give up her life to discover her real gift to the world, had just received news that she had a serious health issue, was now about to move to another country to live in complete isolation, and hopefully receive the medical treatment to save her life… and she doesn't even speak the language. Ah, yes, I understand. I looked at them with endless compassion.

"Mum, Dad it's going to be okay. It's only for six months, and I assure you my first job will be to register with the nearest hospital. I promise you both that it is my intention to heal this problem, and I will do so with my own approach to wellness, and with the expertise of the medical system. I will go for my tests and monitor the situation responsibly," I reassured them.

In that one moment of true recognition and the chance for everyone to be heard, mum and dad leapt up with creative impulse. They got my suitcases down from the loft; at the same time handing over a pen and paper, urging me to write a list of everything I needed for France. One down, one more to go—Chloe. Being my best friend she knew every single one of my dreams (moving to

France), she also knew my tendencies (impulsive) and she could also read me like a book (moving to another country). I knew it wouldn't be too much of a shock to her system when I eventually got around to 'officially' telling her.

Eventually I tracked her down on one of her two mobiles. She was in Harvey Nichols, in Knightsbridge, ordering a 'feather topper,' an additional lightweight duvet that goes over the mattress making your bed feel as though you're sleeping on a nest of feathers.

Once she knew it was me, she momentarily sidestepped her shopping mission to give me her full attention. I knew I had to speak fast as Chloe warned me that she was now in an environment that had the power to totally possess her. Oh no! I realized where she was, a warning that could only mean one thing—she was in the lingerie section. I told her to pay attention, as I had something important to tell her. I gently told her I was moving to France with Sananda, to the part of the country she knew I loved. I reassured her that it was only for six months as we were trying it out first, and that I would be back in the UK a couple of times during that period. We were still so undecided about where we would eventually end up on a more permanent basis. Given this, we felt it best to try out a few locations first before finally buying a place together.

I knew I had called when she was at her most willing to listen. Because of her location, she was being really cool about it, bursting with energy as she wished me luck, making me promise we would have a girl's weekend to ourselves soon. I could tell she was itching to get off the phone and continue her shopping for the ultimate nest of feathers, so with a huge smile I told her how much I loved her, and that I would send her a message the moment I got to France with my new address.

❦

Rennes Les Bains, France, 29th June 2009

Since leaving England, we drove for two days through France, following the exact route of my fated journey to the mountain that I made under a year ago. And now, one year later, my Beloved is by my side! We carefully inched our way around bends and bushes, as our sleek black convertible BMW Z4 purred along the narrow tree-shaded tracks up towards Hameau de Montferrand, the tiny little hamlet perched on the side of Peche Cardou where we would live. The Hamlet was shrouded in myth and legend, part of the infamous natural mountainous Pentagram of Rennes Le Chateau. According to informed speculation, and in no particular order, Mary Magdalene was buried here in an ancient underground Temple of Isis that was waiting to be uncovered, amidst a whole host of other Knights Templar treasures and pagan mysteries.

This pocket of southern France, which was close to the border of Spain, was widely known as the Languedoc and was celebrated as the legendary Cathar Country. It was an ancient land formed by Spain and France that was shrouded in magic and intrigue since the 12th century, and was one of the many reasons why I loved this place. I always knew one day I would live here, but I never imagined in a million years I would return with my soon-to-be husband on my arm.

Rennes Les Chateau was France's answer to Mount Shasta in Northern America, a melting pot of cosmic happenings, UFO sightings, ancient tombs (supposedly stuffed with treasure and world-altering wisdom) and hordes of traveling spiritual teachers and their followers. We would fit in perfectly.

We pulled up outside the tiny hamlet of five houses and thoroughly beamed with delight; holding hands and squeezing each other with rapturous anticipation and giddy abandon. All around us chickens, cats, and dogs walked over to meet us. This was pure rustic living, French style. The air was clean although heavily perfumed with the aroma of gardenia and jasmine. Flowers were in abundance in this area. Our house was a newly renovated old barn equipped with views that took our breath away. We were like little children, as we let ourselves into our new home. Peering into cupboards, popping heads around corners, we slowly walked throughout all of its rooms; gasping at our view across the whole pentagram into the earth, trees, and surrounding castles and monuments.

We unpacked all our things from the car, and rearranged the house to suit our aesthetic preferences. Sananda stayed at home 'clearing the space' with a rainbow assortment of sprays, mantras, and crystals, while I went to the nearest organic supermarket to stock our cupboards, for our upcoming 28-day sacred union retreat.

Weeks before moving to France, I had been meditating on ways in which Sananda and I could really ground and deepen our love. Just like the five wounds, I knew there were other paths of initiation that would ignite more profound ways of relating together and perhaps awaken once dormant memories and qualities. I was convinced that an extended period of time spent in the 'lovemaking' aftermath could be the key to this discovery. I had a strong intuitive feeling that this period was to be for 28-days, a full lunar cycle. Once we got settled we planned to talk more about what it would entail, as it was something I had been guided to create for us.

By the time I returned to the house it had been transformed

into a heavenly temple, complete with the intoxicating aroma's of frankincense and rose that diffused throughout the whole house. Indian throws and Balinese fabrics dripped over once neutral sofas and soothing dulcet sounds pervaded deep into the depths of the house and my heart. Nothing could be more complete, more perfect. This was our home.

I dropped my shopping bags and ran towards Sananda, thanking him for making everything so perfect and wonderful. I wrapped my arms around him, crying in joy for the chance to experience such contentment and fulfillment in this simple invitation to live together. I did not need or want anything anymore; I had everything I had ever needed. I realized now that all I ever wanted was to find him; to love this man, for better or for worse, in sickness and in health, until death us did not part. We knew death was merely the gateway to our full absolute reunion, the time when we would do away with our bodies and merge delectably back into one. This is true for all Beloveds.

I couldn't believe my life! Here I was in France, the most enchanted area of the entire land, with my Beloved who was a gregarious ball of energy. Larger than life itself, he lit up my days and nights, and blew my mind all at the same time. He was a stream of flowing consciousness and intelligence; fast, pressing, and ruthlessly direct. You always knew where you stood when Sananda was around. He was a knowing lover; and knew when I was hiding sexually, holding backing or withdrawing altogether. There was nothing I could not reveal to him; every face of mine was pleasing for him, even the most ugly and cruel. He was my best friend, the one and only human being I had ever been so close to.

I shared everything with him, my simple everyday happiness

and the way my child-like imagination would turn every inanimate object into a unique character. Not forgetting the other bizarre habit of giving all members of the animal kingdom a personality and voice, which often led to a spontaneous play or comedy sketch. I told him all my womanly secrets and how I, as a member of that gender, would think, feel, and respond. I showed him the sacred art of divine feminine dancing. In those early nights, I would dance for him as an expression of my feelings. Choosing his favorite soundtracks, I would dress up so he wouldn't necessarily recognize me and then dance to the fullness of my heart. I danced as if I was alone and had the space to myself; using the floor as a canvas to paint my picture. I closed my eyes and allowed the journey to take me. He would sit there, totally mesmerized and unable to say a thing. Yet, I could see the appreciation pouring through his eyes.

Other nights we would take part in the new nightly activity we warmly named 'star watch.' This involved both of us wrapping up in warm dressing gowns, and laying back on sun loungers, gazing up into the heavens. For hours we would dreamily discuss the nature of the Universe, our place in it, and where we felt it was all heading. Sometimes we would talk into the night debating the concepts of love and truth, which could lead to heated exchanges, as we were both so passionate regarding our discoveries and what we knew to be true. It was a joy-filled time. We both knew coming to France was the best choice for our relationship.

I also fulfilled the promise I had made to my doctor, and registered myself at the nearest hospital and went under the wing of the local doctor there. I made sure I had everything around that I needed to heal my body: raw foods, vegetable juices, hot natural springs, and a local sauna. I was now ready to embark on this healing journey at a physical level. I had six weeks before I was due at Carcassonne Hospital, where I would be checked again, and possibly booked in for the colposcopy, with that in mind it was my sole intention that by the time the appointment arrived I would be clear of any signs of disease Last, but by no means least, my daily prayers were full of gratitude for the life I had already lived, and the grace that was evident on a daily basis.

One afternoon, after spending the day in the natural hot springs of Rennes-Les-Bains, we were walking home through the forest of Montferrand, and began discussing the exact time we should begin our 'Sacred Union' 28-day retreat into the deeper chambers of our love. We both felt we were ready to begin soon, and absolutely agreed that our home was the most perfect place for this holy reunion. We knew it was essential to stay within the bridal chamber for the full cycle of the moon in the environment of trust and consciousness, allowing nothing to come between us. The purpose was to stay within that field of absolute love, so that as two we could become one, and from that oneness be given the mysteries of union. And from this field of love, we would not experience the urge to argue or any impulse to hurt one another— we would be the presence of love at all times. This would be a true test of our love, one we felt we must encounter.

Although all these ideas were relatively new to me, I was more than willing to follow my guidance. My meditations were so clear. Back in the archives of my being, I remembered everything, every detail, every moment, and every experience; it was as if we had done all this before in some previous incarnation. It seemed to be the most natural thing in the world, to fully give myself to this process. I had no qualms about losing my individual identity, and becoming 'one being' with another was something I always knew I would do. It made perfect sense when I envisioned us becoming one, and then sharing that oneness with the whole world.

Like the wounds of love, I was more than certain that the twenty-eight day retreat was yet another essential step on the path for all Beloveds. Since there was no readily available or reliable wellspring of clear and factual information on Beloveds anywhere in the world, we were left to feel for ourselves the steps that needed to be taken. It became my intention that I would leave behind a map and pathway for others to follow, so that people after us would have a smoother journey.

Using ourselves as the catalyst to ignite others onto The Path of Love, presenting ourselves as the evidence, as the living face of love; I set out to prove that this quality of love was real. That everyone had the opportunity to discover this for themselves. I knew this love was the greatest power on earth and I knew those in love would and could have the willingness to face everything, if they had the gumption to say 'yes' to love in every way. I had always sensed some kind of radical revolution coming to light; it was only a matter of time, and by what we were doing, the speed in which others would embark upon this sacred journey would be accelerated as well. I knew we were shaping the way for others to discover their Beloved.

We both decided that July twenty-second was to be the day of our sacred wedding, for not only was it Magdalene's Day (one year to the day when I climbed Mont de Coeur), but it was also the time of a powerful Capricorn/Cancer (both our star signs) lunar eclipse and a total eclipse of the Sun. What other signs did we possibly need? It was divinely set to be our day—we both felt it!

On the morning on the twenty-second, I awoke feeling a mixture of somberness and dignity. Somber, because I could sense the weight of what we were about to do. Of course it was romantic and would involve days and nights in bed, making love, and refusing to leave the house. An ideal time one would imagine, yet I knew the enormity of what we were beginning. From an outsiders perspective we were two highly individualized and independent people who were about to begin a powerful alchemical process to unite and merge on all levels. You see, that is a trait of Beloveds; they are born with this deep knowing that there is another half of them somewhere else, and that this lifetime is to search for that other. There is this constant knowing and feeling, which cannot be ignored; it is with you in every moment of all moments in your life. Like your breath, it becomes part of you, constantly and regularly walking alongside you.

After years of searching and discovering that the Beloved has not yet shown up, a hardening can often take place resulting in an acute individualization being born. These people become highly independent with perfected individualization, and that was what had happened to us. I knew it was going to take some doing to reprogram all those patterns and ideas that told us we were individual, and baulked at the idea of becoming one. Yet within our soulful realms we were of course already one, and we knew it. But our human addiction to a separate self was deeply engrained and entrenched.

I already knew this was not going to be a constantly blissful experience, as is usually described in various 'romanticized' scared union texts. Maybe it was two thousand years ago, but with western thinking and the 'more, better, faster' attitude to life, this was going to be a very different story. It saddened me so deeply to acknowledge the rivers and mountains we were destined to overcome together. I could feel the majesty of our love within our souls for each other; it was infinite, it was divine, and it was beyond whatever I could have imagined it to be. We were that effervescent other, who now understood that the elusive longing was finally over. For some unknowable reason, 'the other' was now embodied, and not only that, we were looking right at each other every single day. So, why oh why, did we waste so much time squabbling?

It broke my heart every time we clashed, as I knew it was a waste of energy, a waste of precious time and in the end delaying the inevitable. I understood we had to break down the patterns within us that clung onto our old ways of being, but I just knew there was a more graceful way of going about it. For some time now we had encountered the velocity of darkness and resistance to our love within us both in Peru, and a few other times in England. We met our own adversaries, and had sized him/her up at a relative distance, but now that distance was about to close, now the real work was about to begin.

My sense of dignity described my attitude to the task at hand. Again, just like the wound of Betrayal, I knew I had to walk through this gateway. I knew, through and through, that I had to face all that was not love in us both. Not only did I know, I wanted to, I had to close the gap as soon as possible, so we could return back to our true state, and begin to live on earth that way, combining our gifts and doubling our resources, to share with all life everywhere. I would do anything that was asked to end the ways and reasons we resisted each other. This was my Beloved, the other half of my soul, how could I ever turn my back on him? How could

I spend my whole life praying to meet him, to pack it all in when he arrives because it felt like too much work?

No, never would I do such a thing, although I would be a liar if I did not mention that the thought crossed my mind, many, many times. But, it was never meant to be a reality. I sensed Sananda had another set of lessons quite different from mine. And with both of us working together we could conquer the insufferable years of pain and agony we had spent in separation from one another in the many lifetimes before.

It was as if we had to first heal the colossal heartache that we both felt in the times we were denied life together, as usually only one other is embodied at a time, while the other one acts more like a guide or protecting force. As with all couples, heartaches of the past had been carried into the present. It really did feel like we were pioneers, as this type of work was not for the fainthearted. It was for the ones who had no choice; they were created for this journey, already branded by the Beloved and happy, oh so happy to leap into the fire together. I imagined being asked whether I would do it again. I knew I would always reply in precisely the same way. Yes! And that's exactly why I felt somberness and dignity. There was much to unfold and I knew it would not be easy. But that would not detract from my willingness to jump into the fire with my other by my side!

The day began with the familiar meowing at the terrace door from the neighbor's cats wanting to come in for some cuddles and play. I pulled back the shutters and allowed the magnificence of the view to drench our bedroom. I still couldn't fully grasp that we lived here—our place was like a dream. We could hear the thermal waters of Rennes Les Bains trickling through the streets of the village down below. Sananda was busy stroking the cats while I padded upstairs to the kitchen to make us some tea. As I opened all the windows of the house to allow the penetrative heat from the sun to warm up the inside of the barn, a huge, warm smile graced my lips as I hugged myself in the sunlight. I had waited for this day for so long. Although anxious, I was also ready and capable.

The whole day passed in a surreal haze, as if we had walked these very same pathways, oh so many times before. We had chosen to do our ceremony to begin the twenty-eight day sacred union inside a legendary, prehistoric subterranean cave, complete with stalactites and stalagmites, and a supposed dragon. However, this 'legendary' cave was not on the local map, and as I mentioned earlier it was not only underground, but also smack bang in the middle of nowhere. Luckily I had ignored the impulse to wear strappy sandals and had instead opted for sensible hiking shoes. Although I did hold on tight to the impulse to wear a rather fetching bright red prana yoga outfit, with a shocking purple beaded shawl. I felt this was not only a response to our important day, but a rather handy beacon if we got lost on the endless stretches of French outback. I am a Capricorn after all—looking good and being sensible is practically hardwired into our DNA.

After a few hours of walking around, looking here and there, I started to feel uneasy, and yet at the same time knew that even this 'lostness' was a test of our companionship. I began to pray for assistance, and lo and behold, a local man showed up who also happened to know the way. We were going to make it to the cave after all. By the time we finally uncovered its whereabouts it was six in the evening.

The cave was well worth all the sweat and effort of finding it.

Dusty and disheveled, we crouched down to enter the space for our sacred union ceremony. As we crawled through the hole, the cavern opened up into a huge kaleidoscope of light and color. Sure enough, every sense revealed it was a magical 'otherworldly' domed cathedral of spectral light, a gateway in-between worlds and a known meeting place of the seen and unseen realms. We sat down on a blanket underneath a shaft of light, which glittered with particles of dust that poured into the cave from the setting sun. Like eloping lovers we took each other's hands and tenderly kissed them, as we looked deep into each other's eyes. For days we had been playing around with our words and vows, feeling what we wanted to say to one another. We were not following a particular ritual; we were being guided by the longing within our hearts and surrendered fully to its voice.

Sananda went first as he whispered words of love and vows of loyalty that were only to be shared between our ears and hearts. I spoke out loud of my eternal love for Sananda, and declared my cherished vows of everlasting union. The cave was shimmering with majestic effulgence; the result of the immense power behind our words and promises. Both our bodies shook with sincerity and heated up with passion, causing beads of perspiration to gently roll into the tears that were silently falling.

In this moment I realized that since my birth, I had slowly become aware of my need to be with him—reunited really—with my Beloved. This is one truth that needs to be shared. The impulse of creation comes in two's. I could feel the millennia of time that passed since now and then, and yet... so easy to see the beginning again. I searched for him when I was animal, mineral, organic, and inorganic. When I was machine, re-produced, cloned, separated from Soul, and cast into the neither regions of all of life everywhere. Nothing, no thing would, could, ever wipe the impulse of my desire to find him. And nothing ever will. God him/herself cannot destroy this. I shall live in the lifeless void for eternity if I have to, knowing that my love for him is alive.

I can now see the capacity and capability of this love, and understand, with a compassionate human heart, that I was afraid to fully embody and bring forth this love for him in this lifetime. That is why I know I am Love, as I literally feel the fibers being woven to include more of itself everywhere. I am the finger's that weave creation; I am the one expansion, forging the propulsion on. As are you. Beloveds cannot deny one another; they are set to meet from the very beginning. We all have a Beloved and it is up to us to decide if this will be the lifetime to join together. Nothing can tear apart the Beloveds, but themselves.

In this joining together, we must realize, we cannot 'manage' it; we cannot be in control of how much we love our other. And anything less than our entirety darkens our individual soul, as well as our combined soul.

I looked down at my ring, then up into Sananda's eyes, looking at him through the glittering dust motes, wondering how the hell I was going to do this. How would I show up as love in every moment for my Beloved? How would I spend twenty-eight days face to face with him, healing all that must be healed within us both? In the same breath, I also knew that if there ever was one who could help me with this almighty task, it could only ever be the one I was looking at in this moment.

We walked out of that cave markedly different than the two people that walked in. Something had changed; there was a more mature resonance between us. Something had anchored itself; a cog in the wheel of life had turned. Hand in hand, we turned to walk into the sunset, back towards the parked car that was over half an hour away. We walked in silence, drinking in the charge of the atmosphere, leaving a trail of ferocious love in our path.

From within the cave, we felt a primordial energy stirring, arising and swirling; watching us leave. It carefully observed the one unified shadowy form walking away from the cave, knowing it was us that called 'it' forth. Deeply conscious eyes witnessed us as we became smaller and smaller, until unrecognizable, and then vanished altogether.

Now it begins.

The cave was empty again.

We were now on a new cycle, a new chapter was opening up and all we had to do was wait and see what showed up next...

We spent the first week in rapturous love and glorious gratification of one another, sharing within the boundless exquisite nature that surrounded us. The days passed by in a stream of happiness and tentative intimacy, learning about each other, watching our ways and responses, and deliciously enjoying every moment. All of our lovemaking was in honor of my healing and the further opening of my womb, with Sananda serving this beautifully and powerfully. The more we made love the more I felt the cancerous cells being healed. Even so, in the darkest parts of the night I would awaken with the knowledge that there was something in the way. I had made the connection that problems in relationships often tie in with problems in reproductive health. While I could not quite put my finger on it, there was something blocking us from fully connecting beyond where we were.

One day, soon after that realization, it became perfectly clear what that 'something' was. It was on this particular day when I witnessed another side of Sananda. There was an aspect of him that arose that had no patience, no compassion, or any understanding of human error. Once vexed he become like a swarm of wasps, looking for flesh, and looking to sting. In one moment he morphed from the Sananda I knew, loved, and trusted into what felt like a robot, devoid of all and any emotion, with a mad glint in his eye that seemed to enjoy the insanity of it all. I had gotten glimpses of this in Peru, but this took those experiences to a whole other level.

I was totally beside myself, not knowing which way to turn or how to react. The one thing that was crystal clear was whatever I said (and no matter what it was) was more fuel to his already white fire. It was as if I alone was his nemesis; that what he so loved in me was also the same thing he despised. He wanted more from me, more connection than I felt I was able to give. Because he was my Beloved, he was hungry for a depth that was deeper than I had ever known. He needed to feel my soul at all times, which is typical of a Beloved connection. But, I was not fully equipped for this! I just didn't know how to show up for him in this way and it was making us both a bit crazed.

I was shaken and scared by what I saw and knew, known so well from 'the times' before in previous lifetimes. With clear seeing eyes and a steady heart I knew what was at play here, I had met this energy in my dreams, in the desert, and now coming through my

Beloved. It was the dreadful dark fear that would arise whenever I dreamt of this black magician from my childhood nightmares, the ones I would have when in the middle of a fever and from my time in the Sinai desert. It was the energy of my shadow. When I saw the film *Nightmare on Elm Street*, I shuddered uncomfortably as this was the closest I had ever seen in real life to the frightening figure I would regularly do battle with. This fear was chaos itself. But I did not know what to do about it. The tall dark masculine figure in my dreams would always hunt me down, tracking my every movement, hurtling down corridors, backing me into corners, pressing itself up against my face. It overwhelmed me, causing me to run, to back track, to escape the intense scrutiny. It was the epitome of the hunt, the chase, and the entrapment. Why was the energy of my shadow coming through Sananda? I could see that the connection, the link that bridged Sananda to this energy was exactly what he was doing in my waking world. Of course—I got it! The Beloved has the power to transmute and heal the other one's shadow by becoming and embodying the other's entire shadow self. Great! This sounded like fun. Not. I soon became aware that these dreams were a premonition of what I would have to encounter once I met my Beloved. Whether the two people involved know they were healing the others shadow—I have no idea! But I did know that Sananda could so easily be transformative chaos—my very shadow. That energy would overwhelm me, making me want to… run… cry… fight.

Despite this chaos that he sometimes swirled around himself in a maelstrom, the deepest currents of my love were untouched and undisturbed, untroubled by such drama and antics. It's very simple, I loved him, and nothing would ever change that, no matter what aspects of his (or my shadow) character were on show. There was no way I was going to abandon him. It was not an option, only in this place of trust and openness could Sananda safely reveal the parts within him that cried out for a loving touch. From this still and unmoving place arose the knowing that this too would pass, and of course, that it was precisely here in these moments that the healing balm of love was greatly needed.

Quietly sitting in stillness was the wealth of wisdom that arose from the voice of my heart. Its presence reminded me that I needed to reach in and administer its message to the parts of me that were questioning the process.

Before you can become love, you first have to experience that which appears to not be love. By facing what it is not and by loving it, you will transform its masquerade and reveal its true nature. Love brings up the dross of all that is not love within you seeing all those parts that you assigned your 'sole' identity. But, nothing can stand against the truth of your Soul love, as love is the only power in existence. Look around and see for yourself, what other power is there, truly?

I knew these were words of truth, but what I failed to see was *how* I could transmute this wall of resistance within myself. I had contracted so much during these times of conflict. I really couldn't tell anymore what was going on, was it my shadow, his shadow, maybe there was only one, being Beloveds and everything? I had run out of answers. I knew I had to do something to turn all this around, as my health was being gambled away with every choice and action. It was hard to actually determine whether all this heaviness was a result of the healing of my reproductive system, or perhaps making things worse.

Our days darkened, and shortened. My natural buoyancy and happiness diminished and whatever trickles of life force I had left, I kept for myself and the ongoing journey to heal my cervix. It was a crazy time, when all my ideas of the Beloved flew out the window on the wings of a nightingale—the most beautiful love bird that ever existed. I had carried some seriously high expectations that my Beloved would be gentle, mellow, and peaceful. As it turns out for me, I was experiencing a slightly different outcome.

Every couple of days, Sananda and I would engage in another shadowy explosion. I could see he was asking for something from me; he had even shared at the beginning of our relationship that he needed to feel a certain aspect of love from me, an experience that he had always yearned for, always remembered, but didn't know what it was. I withdrew into myself, carrying with me a sense of hopeless failure and futility. I could see that Sananda needed something from me, something only a woman, the feminine could give him, but I was mystified and so very confused. It was not as if I knew what it was and purposely kept it from him; I did not know, I had no reference point to the elusive treasure he was seeking. I kept choosing to take everything he was saying and doing personally, allowing my own wounds and feelings of hurt to blind me. I was unable to help him, completely lost and handicapped from giving him what he needed the most.

Love.

The very same thing I was telling myself I also needed.

Checkmate.

Feeling exhausted and starved of love and kindness, I became a flicker of the once radiant light I was. Every now and again beauty would pierce through my polarized perception, and for a moment

I would drink at the well of love, only then to dive back into the drama that awaited me.

You may well be asking why—why did I do such a thing?

Because I knew I had to. I had made the conscious decision (at some point before I incarnated into this life) to face all that was not love, and then *love*. In truth, there is nothing that is *not* love. But I was well and truly entrenched in duality, like we all are: good/bad, right/wrong, open/closed. I had to ultimately step beyond these dualities and become all-encompassing love. It is the path of the Beloved, one I had embraced with open arms and had to see through even in dark times.

One night we had a particularly intense battle when Sananda felt that yet again I wasn't there for him, or that I couldn't receive him in a way that fulfilled him. I reacted in exasperated frustration—annoyed that he always wanted more, more than I thought I could give, and disheartened that he couldn't feel the truth of my devotion towards him. After a ridiculous showdown that lasted for hours, I climbed into the softness of our bed, making sure it was long before Sananda retired.

With hands over my womb and heart I allowed myself to sink into the folds of awaiting arms of the ones who had walked this path before me. I surrendered into vast and strangely close energies that urged me on. Was all this the result of healing my womb? Or the backlash from entering into Sacred Union? Or maybe it was something I disturbed in the desert, or maybe in the cave? Maybe it was some of those things, but it was much closer than that, hidden in plain sight; which, as we all know, is one of the very best places to hide things. We were facing the eons of suffering we had experienced together and separately from our past incarnations of resisting love and the path of sorrow and death. We were walking down a never-ending path of the Beloved.

As I relaxed ever deeper into our bed, I softened with tenderness as I felt a wave of compassion for us both on this arduous and often harrowing journey that we were committed to. For a moment I stepped into his shoes to experience and understand his side of the story, and felt the cruel separation that he was in. I shivered with coldness as I scanned through his eyes; aghast at how empty his stone prison was, filled only with calamity and chaos. At the same time, I dimly recognized this too was happening within me, on some level. I too was cut off, isolated, numbed, but where and how I knew not.

Separation: The fourth wound of Love.

Separation is a powerful shift of our energy when we choose to detach and stop feeling, and is located in the crown, or seventh chakra (our connection to love, god, source). Separation is one of the greatest methods of protection, as it means we do not get hurt. We create a box within ourselves, a place where we can view the world and others from a safe distance without feeling. Separation cuts off love in all ways—both in the giving and receiving. As soon you protect yourself from anything, then you are entering fear.

As soon as one enters separation, others around you will feel a prickly sensation in your auric field that fiercely bellows "Back Off." With most people, the natural response is to do the same, and it is here that many can enter a power struggle of who can cause the most harm, by various ways of being cruel and unkind to the other.

For Beloveds this is the most deadly of all wounds, as it is the most challenging to overcome. When you are in separation, its feels powerful and righteous, as you sit upon your icy high and mighty throne. The idea of becoming loving and warm repels you—which is completely at odds with creating a conscious relationship. In my experience, it is only time that can thaw the icy divide, or to harness the tremendous internal power to return to love no matter how many excuses and reasons your mind suggests in order for you to stick to your guns.

This was the wound that struck at our hearts with a bludgeon. For many, many lifetimes we had been separated and now that we had found each other, along came the insidious fear that we could lose each other again. What a paradox! There was no way that I was going to let separation win! With this precious understanding I immediately climbed out of bed and went to where Sananda was sitting. Welcoming him into my arms I invited him back into bed to where the velvet black darkness was waiting, ready to wipe clean and dissolve all hostilities and resentments between us. It was not the answer, but it was a step in the right direction. We fell asleep in silence, holding onto each other for dear life, praying for a new day when all the chaos inside of us would end.

The following morning I had an appointment at Carcassonne General Hospital to undergo a procedure known as a Colposcopy. I only knew the basic procedure: a slice of my cervix was to be removed and examined under a high intensity microscope to find out exactly what was happening with the stage four cancerous cells that had initially been discovered. Sananda made sure he drove me there and back, constantly reassuring me that this was 'our' journey and 'our' healing that we were completing together. I could feel his sincerity and the weight of him beside me, but truly I would have preferred a different way of going about learning these lessons. Sitting in the car watching the fields of sunflowers rush past while listening to the powerfully moving soundtrack of *Gladiator*, I felt hot, sorrowful tears begin to well up. I began to wonder why I was feeling so much like Maximus, as though I too had lost everything and had nothing more to live for, other than to put right what had gone so horrifically wrong.

By the time we reached the hospital parking lot, I was a bubbling mess. I confess that I had allowed my mind to relish and delight in the joys of feeling like a victim. I was shocked to realize that I was projecting a harsh and cold future, and could see no other way out. I felt so alone, and no matter how many times Sananda drifted into my consciousness and told me I was not going through this by myself, I still could not feel him. I did not feel him, because I did not fully trust him. On and on I let my mind spin. By the time I arrived, I was vulnerable and feeling painfully alone. Something else was there too; I was facing life in the raw, no fancy frills or bows were on show just one version of stark reality: you come into life alone and you die alone. Even Sananda could not penetrate the darkness I had allowed myself in. I had gone well past healthy into my sense of separation. The wound was alive and kicking within me now.

The hospital, unfortunately, did not inspire any positive turnarounds in my thoughts. It was cold, machine-like, and empty of all human consideration and care. Sananda and I waited outside the room where the doctor of the day would perform the procedure. I was provided an interesting perspective, as we were sitting in the maternity ward, watching young mothers come and go, some heavily pregnant, others in the beginning stages. It was a heartbreaking experience with joy and sorrow simultaneously intermixed. Joyful because of the shared celebration of their wondrous, unfolding journey, followed by sorrowful regret that something was happening inside of me that was causing so much abnormality. I felt absolutely helpless to the whole process. My faith and belief was at an all-time ridiculous low.

"Scarlett O'Shea, si'l vous plait," came a voice that belonged to a welcoming and open face.

That must be the doctor; I thought as I got up and walked into his treatment room. I was instantly put at ease as his English was clear, and he was kind and gentle. Sananda sat close holding my hand as the doctor explained everything he was going to do. He let me know that in about one weeks time I would have the results from the procedure, and then we would know whether my cervix needed to be removed or not. I felt so reassured with everything the doctor was telling me, that I relaxed. He was clearly an angel, as I now felt ready to let go and simply allow the doctor to do what he had to do.

With this relaxation, I was then able to surrender all my fears surrounding Sananda. My resistance to his insecurity, his chaos, his outbursts created resistance in my body. When I could allow my body and the medical procedure to unfold naturally, then I could let go of trying or wanting Sananda to be different. I could allow what was happening to happen and still love fully. I looked towards him, smiling and softening as I squeezed his hand. I was grateful he was with me yet again, as I ventured into unknown medical territory.

I undressed and climbed onto a chair that stood alone in the center of a huge empty room. This contraption reminded me of some kind of Victorian instrument of torture or perhaps some weird kinky apparatus used for sexual games. Chloe probably had a catalogue filled with these types of chairs somewhere! I had never seen anything like it before, and it certainly was not what I was accustomed to in England. After figuring out what parts of my body went where, I called both Sananda and the doctor back in to begin.

"Déjà vu... Been here before," I murmured to myself.

Sananda stood beside me, holding my hand and shoulder as I turned to face him, holding his gaze as the doctor prepared himself to take a slice of my cervix. I was nervous, not because of the possible pain that could result in the procedure, but more from the fear that one day soon my whole womb would have to be removed. From all my yogic and feminine wisdom studies, and internal contemplations, I knew the womb as the 'seat' of feminine power as well as her rich source of essence. To have it removed felt like a mini-death.

I looked up into Sananda's eyes as I ventured into this fear, using my eyes as a way of communicating to him how I was feeling. It was such an intense moment loaded with an entourage of emotions ranging from guilt, shame and regret, and sadness that threatened to never end; feeling as if I could cry forever. I inwardly wailed at the idea of losing that which I had only just rediscovered. All of this work to heal my sexual past, and clear my womb of past memories and lovers, to momentarily enjoy the boundless energy and delight of a cleansed past, to then have the well-spring of my femininity removed? This seemed like far too much to handle.

I silently cried with Sananda, hand-in-hand with only our eyes being used, both of us feeling and sharing with one another for all the times in my past when I had sex when I did not want to, all the times I knew the man did not love me, but gave myself to him anyway. I cried for using sex as a way of resolving problems, I cried for losing my virginity as a way to keep my boyfriend at the time, and then I began to cry on behalf of every woman I knew. I cried for Chloe, my mum, my aunties, my students, my friends, and on and on and on…

It was not physically painful. But in truth the blade from the scalpel cut into something else, something deeper which was far more tender than mere flesh—my soul. My wounds were unwinding and with this slice much within me was being healed. Sitting in the car only an hour before I never could have contemplated this type of unfolding. There is truly a lesson in every moment and in every moment we are being called to love more fully. Such a gift my cervix was giving me! Even though I was keeping all this commotion quiet, the poor doctor was so concerned he was hurting me, he kept asking whether I was okay or not. I smiled at him and assured him I was fine and asked him to keep going. He seemed settled with my answer as he carried on. Sananda looked into my eyes, placed his hand over my heart and softly whispered "Forgive yourself love, forgive yourself." I closed my eyes as I dropped down into an awaiting vision:

Love, a blade stuck into my heart, spilling the droplets of many lifetimes all over my bridal gown… These droplets were a testament that I had loved, and will love again.

In that precious moment with Sananda I turned inward and with the love of a mother I picked up those cherished pieces of myself and brought them close to my pounding heart. Like drops of ice, memories frozen in time, I gently warmed them inside my heart forgiving the past over and over again—freeing myself from the bonds of regret.

I Am and I Am Not

I'm drenched in the flood, which has yet to come
I'm tied up in the prison, which has yet to exist

Not having played the game of chess
I'm already the checkmate

Not having tasted a single cup of your wine
I'm already drunk

Not having entered the battlefield
I'm already wounded and slain

I no longer know the difference
between image and reality

Like the shadow
I am
And
I am not.

—RUMI

Chapter Seventeen

Odyssean

Montserrat, Spain, August 2009

If you are irritated by every rub, how will you become polished?

—Rumi

THE ODYSSEY continued for us both as we ventured into places and spaces together that were once hidden and guarded until trust and intimacy revealed them to us. Moments and days of incredible love, followed by periods of darkness and fear, led us with heavy hearts to make the decision that after three weeks we needed to postpone our twenty-eight day initiation. We were desperate for rest, and deprived of fun and laughter, agreeing together (for the first time in weeks) that we would begin again when the time felt right. All this inner work was leaving us exhausted and was taking a toll on our bodies.

We took some time to get out and about during our respite, to journey farther south into the ancient land of Occitania, dropping in on Girona, Barcelona, and finally onto the Benedictine Monastery of Montserrat, the residence of one of the Black Madonna's, a spontaneous manifestation of the Divine Mother.

Every moment was a pleasure to experience, as Sananda and I relaxed and began to enjoy life again. All the darkness that had been swirling around us began to retreat and eventually diminish back into the shadows from where they came. We knew we had not healed the split between us, that this time was simply a time for sanctuary before we regained our strength and ventured once again into the wounds of love.

We were in the right place at Montserrat, built on a rugged mountain overlooking Barcelona in the far distance; she is one of the greatest sanctuaries of this time. The energy of the place is tremendous, and pilgrims far and wide travel to drink from this well of peace, which flourishes and replenishes all who climb her steps. During the three days we spent in Montserrat, I kept finding myself drawn to a small cave that clung to the steep cliffs of the monastery. I later discovered that this place was called the Santa Cova (holy cave) and it was here the Black Madonna was discovered in 50AD. I knew I had to go there, and Sananda and I needed to go together.

Taking a precarious path eventually led us to two exquisite, ornately carved wooden doors built into the cliff. Together we pushed open the heavy doors to reveal the most breathtaking beautiful chapel, a refuge I can only describe as being the unforgettable presence of the eternal love of the Divine Mother. We were both so touched and moved that tears of tender humility began to swell in our eyes. We knew we had found a very special place as we slowly walked to the altar to pray together hand-in-hand on the pews. I was finding it hard to breathe as the 'weight' of this love pressed into my chest, whispering to my soul. I listened to a softly spoken voice, one I felt I had never heard before. I continued to listen quietly receiving the information, when I suddenly became aware that these words belonged to the voice of the Divine Mother:

My Pilgrim, rest in me now and lay down your heavy hearts. Take from me what you need, knowing you are received. I urge to you, continue on with your pilgrimage, you must find within the strength to begin again with your Beloved. You must be 'together' by the time you arrive in Egypt. Go forward and begin again...

By the time I finished praying it was clear to both of us what we had to do. We looked at each other in the tiny chapel and nodded in agreement at our task. We knew this twenty-eight day cycle had to be completed by the time we went to Egypt for our next ten-day retreat in September, as it was imperative that we were 'together'— without arguments—in total union during that time. Even though it had only been a week since we ended our first attempt at the twenty-eight days of sacred union—we had to get back to it immediately. It was now the first week in August, so we had to work fast!

By the time we arrived home in France, we looked at the calendar, tallied up the astronomical events and decided that the tenth of August would be the ideal starting date, making sure we completed the lunar cycle two days before we left for Egypt. To crystallize our heartfelt intentions we made a plan to drive to Lucca, in Tuscany, northern Italy to stand at the foot of the Volto Santo inside the San Martino church and recommit to our initiation once more. There were days when I questioned whether I would be able to make all the trips we were planning, as there was always in the back of my mind a sense of building unease as I still had not heard back from the doctor with the results of my test.

However, my physical energy was great in every way. There was no depreciation in my energy levels and I was not in pain. I just wanted to know what was going on! I would daily close my eyes in meditation to inwardly look and feel how I was doing. It looked as if everything was healing nicely; there was no discomfort, no dark areas, and no emotion or sensation that indicated any form of anguish. Everything felt good and well. And I had to trust that. If I knew anything it was that I knew myself better than anyone else. I had to believe all was well inside and out.

It was the fear of not knowing officially from the doctors that continued to eat away at me, despite the reassurances I felt energetically. I was not getting any clear answers from the hospital even though I called every couple of days. They kept saying that the results were still not in. It was now two weeks since my last appointment when the doctor said that the results would be back in five days. I chose not share this inner turmoil with Sananda, as these human issues did not make any sense to him, for he knew there was nothing to be worried about; it was healed. I wish I could have stayed in that frame of mind the entire time, but instead and I floated between trusting and worry.

I chose not to share these feelings with mum or Chloe either. I wanted to shield mum from any further worry. I kept her informed, but was sure to leave any real emotion to a minimum. With Chloe, she had been through a similar situation and constantly reassured me not to worry. She too carried the eternal faith that I would be able to heal this the natural way. Besides, my only forms of communication during these days were via email, as there was no telephone at the house. To call mobiles was horrendously expensive and often intermittent; resulting in feeling it was nearly impossible to share with the outside world. I was alone on this one in all ways!

As much as I tried to transcend the fears in my mind, there was always a part of me that wanted to curl up and be held as I shared my human frailties, and the fear of dying way before I was ready. I was living day-to-day, feeling absolutely grateful for every moment I shared with Sananda and alone. My meditations and prayers were saturated with gratitude for my charmed life and all the moments of grace I had experienced. I recognized how important it was for me to fully love and live in every moment. My path was confirmed—the way of the Beloved was the way of my soul. Learning to love Sananda and work though the wounds was also showing me how to step more completely into being an expression of love in all I did.

And it was with this love that we journeyed to the charming walled city of Lucca to see the Volto Santo; just days after our return from Montserrat. There was much to see and do in this part of the world! Various legends have blossomed around the Volto Santo (holy face), given its uncertain origin. According to the most credited one, represented also throughout a cycle of frescoes inside San Frediano's church, the crucifix was sculpted in Jerusalem by one of Jesus' disciples known as Nicodemus. He, guided by an angel, started the depiction on a piece of Lebanese citrus wood, but when he arrived at the delineation of the face, he was seized by the fear of not portraying it faithfully. Thus upon awaking after a long dream, he saw the face was already delicately sculpted, and the work of art miraculously complete. We were excited for this reason and many others to make this journey to Lucca.

❧

The Italian Alps, August 6th, 2009

We took the well-known route made famous by *The Italian Job* that casually cruises along the French Riviera, through the Italian Alps to then finally drop down into the pearl of Tuscany, Lucca herself. We were so excited to take this drive—it was a chance to get out in our sexy, black convertible. With the roof down and sound up, we were having a blast. Every moment of the journey was spectacular; the scenery, the music—which varied from hard-core trance to exquisite film soundtracks to bhakti mantras and Indian ragas. As was typical for us, there were times when our varied and stimulating conversations often got the better of us, resulting in one of us having to turn the volume down in order to emphasise our points. Oh, and the first class gourmet delights of Italian food and wine! Unbelievable. No wonder Elizabeth Gilbert gained extra weight as she traveled through Italy in *Eat Pray Love*. My jeans were confirming I had done the very same, but I was far too in love to care.

Our days in Lucca were a godsend, nestled in the luscious natural beauty of cypress trees and Tuscan vineyards. We leisurely walked around the walled city, rented bikes, laughed at each other's jokes and made love within the walls of the stunning fortress we stayed at. We felt safe to love and rest within one another. As the first rays of light began to filter through the wooden shutters of the old medieval guesthouse we were staying in, I opened my eyes and lazily sounded my morning mewl, letting Sananda know I was officially awake. We laid in each other's arms, snuggling deeper to discover the perfect fit between our bodies, soaking in this exquisite, peaceful time together.

The nearest church announced the time (6am!) by sounding six resonant rings, clearly reminding us we were in Italy—and that it was the start of our twenty-eight day cycle, once again. I beamed at Sananda as I lay on his chest, knowing today was going to be a day to remember, an opening into a world I had always remembered and dreamed of. A world full of love, forgiveness, acceptance, and the ease of being that included everyone and all life everywhere. Some would call it a utopia; I called it only a matter of time. On the path of the Beloved, we were destined to be here.

We pulled our rings out of their safe velvet boxes to begin our recommitment to the twenty-eight day cycle. We knew the rings carried the energies we ignited during the previous twenty-eight day journey, so we were very respectful when we wore them. These rings were not a piece of jewelry that went well with certain colors. They were instruments of quantum science, engineering a myriad of experiences that were destined to effect and shape us. Made by a close friend, the rings consisted of gold to represent the masculine, silver for the feminine, and a gigantic star sapphire to represent the royal path of Sacred Union. This time when we placed the rings on each other's fingers, I felt the warm rush of an expanding happiness that made me laugh out loud as I reached for Sananda to steady myself at the unexpected, yet welcomed arrival of uncontrollable jubilance. This day felt like it was the first herald of spring, and all was right in my world once again.

It was also in that moment when I felt an obvious change in my health. I knew without any doubt now that I had healed my cervix, and when the results did come back they would confirm my healing. This flush of realization purged through my body, and all fear and bitterness that once was, was washed away by the grace of love. I felt so alive and at the same time could feel how this aliveness unfurled and opened to include everyone.

All too soon, after four days in the enchanted land of Lucca, it was time to leave and head back towards our home in France. Once back, Sananda's assistant Maria would come to visit for a while, before all three of us traveled to Egypt for the retreat. We decided to be a little more lenient with the 'rules' of the twenty-eight day cycle; well we had to really, as Maria's stay with us was planned months ago. Because she was travelling from the States, we all decided it would be fun for Maria to stay with us in France for a few days before we headed off to Egypt together. Maria had been Sananda's assistant for a couple of years, and I had met her while I was in Peru. We did not really get a chance to connect at any deep level during that time, as I was, mmm… how shall I put it? All over the place at the time. Such is a life of healing and dealing, eh?!

Maria was an older lady, maybe in her late fifties, who reminded me of a typical Mother Superior, or head matron. She was a blonde, well-rounded American, who traveled back and forth from Hawaii to California teaching Sananda's work in all the various cities along the way. Our first meeting was pleasant enough, but let's just say we were not long-lost friends. What did matter, however, was that Maria was absolutely devoted to Sananda, and in her devotion she took her role very seriously, and did her job superbly.

I felt it was not going to be an easy ride to connect with her, as I was the 'new kid on the block,' and sadly we had some of our own womanly conditions to contend with. After all, she had been the 'main woman' in his life for years now; how was she going to take, and hopefully, accept me? By the sounds of all the rumors and gossip that were being shared with me, there was some work to be done. This was going to take a skilled and discerning human relations masterpiece to ensure that our time together was smooth and progressive, as all three of us had to learn to come together as the retreat in Egypt was only weeks away. To top it off, we were in the midst of another twenty-eight day cycle. It would appear that Sananda and I thoroughly loved a challenge, wouldn't it?

We had been home a couple of days when I sensed another storm brewing. Like before, it would swirl around for days in my mind before fully launching its attack. Sananda would say something that I perceived as controlling or interfering with my individuality and I would instinctively withdraw, which, of course, aggravated Sananda. This was a pattern that was calling for healing, yet its impulse was so strong I would forget and fall for its fearful implications all over again. It would begin as the avoidance of having any bodily contact with Sananda. Naturally this included making love, but there was an added layer because I did not want to touch him at all. I did not wish to sit next to him, to even hold his hand while walking together, or look at him for too long. I was feeling really trapped in this sur-reality I was creating. A "reality" where Sananda apparently had the upper hand over everything I did, said, thought, or expressed.

In this madness it seemed as if everything was used against me; I could not simply be without him questioning what I was doing or thinking. And so the war would begin again with Option A, where he would come forward and want to know what I was feeling, and when I was brave enough to answer, it would usually lead to a row, as my answer would wind him up. So Option B, would take the form of me withdrawing, which would drive him even more crazy, feeling as if he was being ignored and disregarded. I was still in the process of figuring out Option C when Maria arrived.

Sananda went to meet her at Carcassonne airport, while I made up her room making sure fresh flowers and presents greeted her when she walked in. The moment they arrived, she took one look at me and knew I was at my wits end. She quickly grabbed my hand and insisted I help her unpack so that we had some private time to ourselves. I hugged her and burst out crying. She may have reminded me of a Mother Superior in the past, but in this moment she was every inch a woman, and it was all I could do but fall into her arms begging to understand what was happening.

"Keep going sweetie, just keep going," she whispered.

"Maria, what is going on? I have no idea what is happening. Did he put you through this too?" my eyes were pleading for some answers from her, and for once there seemed to be some light at the end of the tunnel that suggested she might actually have some concrete answers.

She pulled away holding me at arm's length as she answered with neither a yes nor a no. We just stared at one another, and by her non-committal answer I gauged that the answer was a yes, she had encountered a very similar process with Sananda. I was beginning to put the pieces together. Sananda had a history of testing the people in his life with chaos to ensure he was safe to love and trust them fully. He was in his own battle with love, as I was. And no wonder—we were Beloveds! Of course the battle to love fully would be in both of us, yet manifesting in different ways. Maria's visit was already helping me, and she had only just arrived.

I walked barefoot back into the house as I helped her carry in the rest of her bags. Maria brought a burst of life into the house, her enormous laughter filling the walls. I could see just how much Sananda enjoyed being with her. It looked as if Maria was going to be our saving grace, maybe she could even help us get through the obstacles that were building up all around us in this twenty-eight day cycle. However, within a day that idea crumbled and turned to ashes in my open hands.

Sananda decided it was time to invite Maria into our ongoing feud one afternoon while we were sitting around the house. He announced I was ignoring him and not listening to a word he was saying. To be honest it may have seemed that way to Sananda, but from where I was sitting I was simply avoiding another argument. Maria lifted up her head from the book she was reading, promptly closed it, placing it on the table in front of her, as she raised a questioning eyebrow in my direction. I laughed out loud at the ridiculousness of the brewing situation.

You've got to be joking! I thought to myself. She is looking at me as if I am some alien specimen under a Petri dish. What is Sananda up to now? I braced myself for what was about to come. And by golly come, it did!

"Why do you ignore him, Scarlett?" Maria opened up the debate, and naively I answered thinking this was going to be conscious and fair communication.

After an hour of thrashing it out, back and forth, like we were in some kind of Supreme Court (guess who was on the witness stand), I reached the conclusion that these people were actually serious. They were relentless, as they played tag team with their endless questions and accusations, which were pointed in my general direction. They were certain they had me all figured out—all the reasons I couldn't open to love the way Sananda needed me to, insinuating that I was closing myself off willingly. It was all so preposterous, I had to get up a few times and check that I was in the right room, as I was sure we were devoted to being loving people, who spoke from the heart, and whose purpose was to bring each other back into love. It was as if we were on different planets, speaking completely foreign languages to one another. After a while of realizing there were going to be no winners in this game, I let go of any impulse to speak and relaxed my body, letting them continue pointing out all my faults, flaws, traits, and problems.

Far away in the distance I began to feel the rumble of thunder that sent shivers down my spine. This sound was not normal or recognizable in any way; it was as if the booming drone was reverberating from the bowels of the earth herself. I could sense its hungry growls rising up through the foundations of the house and then vibrate up and into my body. I looked at them both to see if they could feel it too, but they didn't seem to notice. I got up and looked outside expecting to see dark black storm clouds, but to my utter dismay, it was a normal sunny afternoon, without a cloud in the sky.

I closed my eyes and could immediately see the storm. There! Then in that moment I was transported back in time.

Judgment: The third wound to Love.

Judgment arises form reason, logic, wounding, projection, self-criticism, belief, and assumed moral and emotional superiority over another. It is a veritable mélange of pride, anger, wounding, and punishment mixing together to create judgment over another, and therefore yourself. Judgment is always taken from a lofty, hierarchical and separated position and resides in between the brows on the face or sixth chakra, otherwise known as the third-eye. It is the wound that fills and swims throughout the head, whether judging or being judged. It sits within the mind and projects out into the face of another.

When being judged, it is the shadow within the corridors of the mind that picks up the energy of your persecutor and later when you are alone, starts to replay the tape. The voice of judgment takes the negativity it has received, turns it inward, and projects it back towards you. The wounds of judgment can then tease and belittle you, or wind you up with plans of revenge that eats at your self-esteem.

The wound of judgment was now presenting itself to me. All of a sudden everything around me changed. I could see both of them still heated with their opinions, as they leaned towards me, hands and elbows on the table, fingers pointing as they swelled with power, but there was no noise. It was as if the mute button had been turned on. I could see their mouths moving and the odd bit of spittle spray from their lips, but no sound. They became wax-like caricatures of themselves; morphing and twisting into grotesque and bizarre tripped-out Alice in Wonderland creatures. I watched from afar as I was gently transported into this silent, comfortable world. The only sound was of my breathing and the regular liquid squelch of my eyelids blinking.

This was incredible. My brain waves had slowed right down to a theta state, like I was in a dream, or inside an anti-gravity machine. It was as if I had taken a tranquilizer, which was mixed in with a little laughing gas. It was fantastic! I was clearly having some kind of heightened altered experience. I tried to speak to them but could not, only the first syllable of the words could sound. I tried to use my hands to explain what has happening, but they too were unable to form any gestures that were recognizable. The more I attempted to be part of their world, the more hilarious it became for me. I really need to highlight the absolute ease of being I was feeling. It was as if I was not part of the human drama anymore. Everything, including myself, was revealed to be beautiful and resting within perfect balance and harmony.

This was weird, but for some reason it did not register as problematic to me. I imagined if I had been wired up to a life support machine, the blip that was once my beating heart would now show only a flat line. I was outta there, gone, floored, deconstructed, no mind, zero point, also known in the New Age trade as "completely free!" There was nothing else to do in that moment, but to deliciously roll back in exquisite slow motion onto my sheepskin rug and rest.

Going, going, gone...

I seem to remember Sananda trying to get me up as he steered me downstairs towards the bedroom. I have no idea how much time had passed, nor did I care. I realized I still could not hear him, but attempted to communicate anyway, as I wanted him to know I was okay and cool with everything. This place was heaven, there was no pain, no pleasure, no right, no wrong, no kindness, no cruelty, and best of all it was silent and peaceful.

For three days I stayed in bed, sleeping for hours on end, occasionally getting up to step outside for a while to feel the sun on my skin and then retire to bed once more. I would dream of past lives, known and unknown, waking suddenly with wide eyes, convinced my brain was on fire. I could feel Sananda next to me at night, but it was as if I would have to transcend space and time to reach him, and well, to be honest in that moment I had other things to attend to. I drifted in and out of lifetimes, never really knowing whether I was still asleep or awake. I would get up and walk to the bathroom, not really convinced I was peeing in the toilet, but doing it anyway.

I was in the middle of a huge breakthrough. My mind had stopped, and I was enjoying the break. The constant struggle and frenetic pace of all these changes had finally caught up with me. My health issues, arguments with Sananda, moving houses, changing my name, ending my career, healing this, healing that, finally resulted in a massive, final stopping.

On the third day I awoke and knew it was over. I slowly climbed out of bed checking my legs to determine whether I was functioning properly and yes, all seemed in good working order. I stretched my body, bending to each side and then finally all the way over as I looked in the mirror, marveling at how much weight I had lost. I touched and smoothed over my hips and stroked my flat stomach as I glanced at myself from different angles, bringing a graceful Mona Lisa smile to my lips.

I spun around eyeing my boots as I prepared to go AWOL from this joint. With boots in tow, I promptly walked upstairs and opened the door like a bear in heat, spying a surprised Sananda and Maria. I announced I was going down into the village to have a feast, and not only that, I was going to walk downhill in my pajamas! I soon realized I could hear again, as all of a sudden I received their unison of protests relaying in various harmonics that I should not walk, as I was too weak. Instead, they would drive me.

"Get outta town," I thought to myself. "What is this, *One Flew Over The Cuckoo's Nest?*"

Oh wow, a thought! I had never known until now how loud

thoughts actually are. After spending three days in a complete meltdown, it's quite an ordeal to re-enter what's known as normal life Everything appears to be so colorful, vivid and larger than life. Noises seem to become amplified, which reminded me of the time I went to the Glastonbury Festival and begged everyone for some earplugs in the hopeless attempt to get some sleep. But now, I had my sleep and was enjoying this ecstatic return to life.

"I'm back!" I mused to myself. "Wow, another thought."

"What a bonus, it looks as if I still have my sense of humor," I inwardly cheered.

I was too busy dancing around the kitchen, wiggling my hips as I opened every cupboard door to see what I could eat. I was far too busy announcing how fantastic I felt to notice that they were putting on their boots and coats, and heading for the car. But true to my word, I stuck to the pajamas, as I sat in the back of the car grinning like a Cheshire cat.

Is this what it's like to be mad? I wondered to myself.

And the day came when the risk to remain tight in a bud was more painful than the risk it took to blossom.

—ANAIS NIN

Chapter Eighteen

The Keys of Egypt

Cairo, Egypt, September 2009

M Y DANCE with madness and its subsequent breakthrough led perfectly to Sananda and I's next adventure—Egypt. While we didn't complete the 28-day cycle as effortlessly as we had desired, we had come through the fire. And from that experience I felt transformed into a completely new woman. A woman who could walk, speak, and act on the path of the Beloved.

In this newness, I was beginning to understand the essence of being a woman and the divine feminine. A woman's essence is protected, for good reason, by a series of concentric walls, like a labyrinth. To move inwardly, from one wall to the next, requires that anyone interacting with the feminine intensify their devotion, and as it is done, a reward of grace is bestowed. This is not, however, something that can be negotiated verbally with a woman. She doesn't even know consciously how to open these walls herself.

In short, there is nothing a woman can "'do," to open these walls, it is instead something effortlessly given as a natural flow when the environment is safe and loving. It is through the keys of veneration that these walls magically and invisibly open, as all a woman truly longs for is to give herself to her Beloved, forever.

Somewhere around the second wall from the center of a woman's essence, she casts the veils of her personality aside and shows she is both a human being and also a portal into something much greater. She shows wrath that is not hers, but all women's. She shows universal patience. She shows her wisdom. Then, at the very center, in the innermost temple itself, all the layers of her Beloved's devotion are flooded with reward at once. The Beloved discovers that the very essence of the feminine transcends romance and all human ideas around love, and yet is undeniably and profoundly sacred all the same. There, Beloveds meet in the cave of the heart, the most unspeakable, barely sustainable flow of humility and grace, which exiles every notion of separation forever.

These were the delicate buds of understanding that were gently coming to my attention as my journey with Sananda continued. This was what he was speaking about, writing about, and this was what he wanted to live by so deeply. I sighed with compassion for us both, as I realized this was never going to be given through force or demand. The more he used his incantations on me, the more I retreated into my inner temple. I wish for both of us I could have 'controlled' this impulse to withdraw and pull over the veil of illusion, but it was divinely hardwired into my feminine essence. I needed to feel safe and loved before I could fully share myself with him. It was part of the path of the Beloved—trust and consciousness.

There are some laws in the Universe that can never change.

With this understanding came a relaxation that opened to the courage and resolve to continue on with the pilgrimage. I also knew

I had to dissolve the accumulated stash of negatives memories I had collected over the recent months with Sananda. I could no longer see him as an instigator of my withdrawal; love would not allow for that. I had to throw away any ideas I had formed around him, as I could not love an idea. I had to choose to see him with fresh eyes, true eyes, and then in that instance I would be able to love free from the past, with no expectations. I vowed to hold in my mind what was true about him—his heroic nature, kingly heart, and wise counsel. I needed to clear away any impressions I may have made about him being a spoiled brat or angry little boy (my previous opinions of him during our heated exchanges).

It is possible to do this; it *just* takes wild amounts of discipline, as the ego is always ready to flag up copious amounts of seemingly justified past experiences, which is incredibly seductive. If we latch onto the past, we will end up in a vicious circle, going round and round the same old stuff. If you break free from the 'opinion' you may have already formed, and burn the entire library of 'painful' experiences you have already shared with the person/place or circumstance, then you will be free to experience something fresh. With the light of awareness and a true, unwavering commitment to love, one can become victorious and sail through the constructs of ego to the immense freedom to love, in a way we know is possible and yearn for.

The wheels skidded on the tarmac runway, jolting me from my thoughts. "Good Evening Ladies and Gentlemen, we have now arrived in Cairo where the temperature is a warm 95 degrees Fahrenheit." I rubbed my eyes and tousled my hair, as I gently kissed Sananda on the cheek, whispering our arrival. I would often look at him in these moments in between sleep and wakefulness and catch the light of his beauty and his true essence. Believe me; I drank it all in, as this nectar took care of all the times when I questioned my own sanity.

We were in Cairo for another one of our ten-day retreats with a group of people from all corners of the world. This retreat was a continuation from the one in Peru, and our next step into more advanced shadow work. I guessed that it was for this reason that Sananda was pushing me so hard over the last couple of days in France—to overcome the tendency of running away when it all got to be too much. A few times I would consider and occasionally threaten to leave France and return back to England, primarily during our more heated exchanges. But we both knew I wouldn't, as it would only be a matter of time before I returned to pick up exactly where we had left off. This was my Beloved, and no matter what, I would make sure we cleared and healed our supposed differences together.

As the plane taxied to its designated place for disembarking, I had an overwhelming sense this retreat was going to be huge, and that Sananda was planning some almighty crescendo to take place at the end of the ten days. This excited and unnerved me all at the same time, as I knew he had no limits. I giggled to myself as I realized that it was for this precise reason why I loved and admired him so much. This was going to fun, I could feel it. This time, unlike Peru, the idea of meeting everyone on the retreat was filled with bursting excitement. Maria and I had settled any differences, and I finally felt comfortable being part of the group and Sananda's world.

We were staying at The Mena House, a palatial hotel in the shadow of the great pyramids right in the middle of ancient Cairo.

Located in forty acres of jasmine-scented gardens, this wondrous venue has played host to kings and emperors, heads of state, and celebrities. Its royal history is reflected in its luxurious interiors embellished with exquisite antiques, handcrafted furniture, and rich textiles. As we drove towards it, I suddenly caught sight of the pyramids through the windscreen of our taxi. I caught my breath as I squeezed Sananda's hand. Something ancient and buried moved around inside me, causing a certain degree of discomfort. What seemed to be past life memories bubbled up to the surface, as faces appeared, the familiar aroma of oils and ointments wafted to my nose, and a stab of intense pain drove through my heart. My hand went up to soothe the blow, as Sananda looked at me with wide eyes.

"What's happening?" he asked as he turned his full attention to me.

I could not reply immediately as I was lost for words. After a while, I was able to catch my breath to reassure him that it was a torrent of strong memories and emotions. And with that I was sucked back in. The pyramids and I locked on to one another like the red darting eye of Sauron in *Lord of the Rings*. Fixating on each other, we zoomed in from a variety of different angles. Like infatuated lovers, who had been separated for over seven thousand years, the moment we saw one another was the precise moment we remembered. In that instance I felt as if the whole of Cairo reverberated and reformed in the explosive aftermath of our powerful rendezvous.

I closed my eyes to center myself, only to be immediately pulled back into a vision that opened up inside the same pyramid that was having this powerful effect on me. To my utter astonishment I *heard* a wild inhale of sound through the stone walls, a startled breath that was once spent, and tenacious in its knowing. Something was stirring, what was once sleeping was now very much awake inside of me. Flashing eyes heavily made up with sparkles of reflective light threaded through eyebrows focused upon mine. I shifted uncomfortably in response to her penetrating gaze. Who is this *she* that I sense? I inwardly looked deeper and felt the unmistakable presence of a Queen. It was Isis herself.

"You have returned! What kept you away for so long? I always knew you would come. Step into me, I await you in the depths of the hidden chamber..."

I was thrust back into the here and now, to open my eyes into a spew of activity and commotion. Sananda was still holding onto my hand as he shouted at the taxi driver (who was on his mobile) to watch where he was going, as he narrowly escaped crashing into the back of another car. As we hurtled down the sprawling main streets of Cairo I realized I could actually hear the sound of the pyramids inside of me, the pulsing rhythmic drone was their own heartbeat, and dance of life. All three of them had a different sound and form of communication. But it was the Queens Pyramid, the one in the center, now known as Khafre, which claimed all of my attention. She was alive and was calling me towards her. This was technically my first time in Cairo, but it was now unquestionably clear that I had been here many times before in past lifetimes.

It is important to note here, that these kinds of psycho-spiritual experiences were not commonplace in my day-to-day life. Yes, I confess I had a healthy imagination, buckets of creativity, and also had my fair share of dramatic flair and pizzazz, but I knew when I was imagining something, and when I was not. This was not my imagination; this pyramid was pushing itself into my awareness, whereas imagination is the other way around. When I imagine I only see my image generation, and here there was the highly attuned ingredients of sound, vibration, and smell.

We pulled up outside the Mena House and stepped out into the warm, sticky climate, and soiled air filled with fumes of overpopulation and petrol. In the background was the familiar sound of the call to prayer and the endless honks and toots of the city traffic. I went to the back of the car to get my suitcase and there she was, lit up like a beacon whispering of her longing to reconnect. I took a deep breath, wiping away the beads of perspiration from my forehead, as I pulled my adjustable handle and wheeled my suitcase into the foyer, glancing over my shoulder one more time, for a last glimpse.

This was crazy, how can a pyramid get me so hot and bothered? The actual shape of the structure aroused me, and had I not been here with Sananda and Maria I would have run across the road, abandoning my belongings at the front desk and running into her as I tore all my clothes off. Although, I'm not entirely sure that would have gone over too well in a place like Cairo. Of course, these are merely my private thoughts. We can keep this just between us, right? I had to find a way to calm myself down.

Half an hour later I found my answer. Sananda and I were in our room, unpacking and taking turns to shower as we washed away all the in-flight grime and smog after being packed into a flying sardine tin for six hours. We emerged from the bathroom in our matching his and hers fluffy white dressing gowns, and one-size-fits-all white matching slippers. As if entranced, both of us hypnotically glided onto the outside terrace, pulled up a chair, sat down, and in unison placed our crossed feet on the railings. We leaned back into our chairs as we interlaced our fingers and cupped the backs of our heads, easing out the tension in our backs and shoulders.

We each entered deep contemplation as we gazed straight ahead at the Giza Plateau. We had arrived. We were here, and we were ready for something big. You could feel it sizzling in the air, something was alive and making itself known to us. I leaned back on my chair, rolling up and onto the two back legs. I could almost hear the ticking clock and simmering primordial gurgles of something stirring in the underworld, rising and swirling up to the surface and any minute now it...

"Scarlett, you have been born for this moment..." Sananda's voice startled me, causing me to lose my balance as I instinctively thrust myself forward onto the chair's legs.

"Jesus, Sananda, you totally scared me. What did you just say?" I narrowed my eyes as I pulled the oversized collar of my dressing gown closer towards me.

He took a long, slow inhale on his cigarette as his eyes dug into the night sky, unmoving, unblinking.

"Everything has been leading to this moment. Our reason for meeting, the meaning of your birth, it all leads to this point," he replied in a long and drawn out, smoky exhale.

I must be honest and confess I felt a galactic amount of responsibility descend upon my shoulders. And in the very same breath, I could admit that I always knew it was there. It was more like his words targeted the whereabouts of this extra weight I had been carrying around. I knew exactly what he was speaking of, but it was only now that I felt it, deep in the pit of my stomach.

"You have something huge to do here, Scarlett. It is going to require your greatest surrender and every last drop of trust to complete your work. You are going to be tested in a way you have never experienced before. We both will." He continued to stare into a place way beyond the visible world.

When you get to know Sananda as well as I do, you soon come to realize he is capable of absolutely anything you can care to imagine. So when he uttered those words with the shadow of the pyramids in the background, for one very intense moment, I considered that he might be suggesting some sort of live sacrifice. As I looked over at him innocently, I silently pleaded for more clarity into the precise terms and conditions of my surrendered role. Yikes! Could this be another of his famous tests?

I had to laugh to myself, as questioning the outcome is not entirely the true art of surrender. Surrender is to not know, but rather to embrace and become willing to face anything. That was and is my mantra, my slogan, my flag. So, as the Universe would have it, here was my chance.

I hoped he would elaborate further, but he did not. Although he did say he knew what my role was, but he could not tell me now, as I still was not ready. That set me off. Not ready?! What is this crazy notion he has about me not being ready? And he is? When is he really going to get it? I am his Beloved, we are the same, neither one of us is better, more, less, or not ready. We are in each moment the same, the same, *the same!*

Did I voice this? No. Did I stand up and justify myself? No. Why? Because I had this pervading idea, that all too soon, in the natural passage of time, he would realize this without me having to get my rod of power out and start brandishing it in his face. At the end of the day, despite all that was said between us and all the experiences which *seemed* to contradict what I knew to be true, I held this deep knowing that love would eventually permeate his being and he would see me fully for who I truly am. And as I was to find out, vice versa!

That was the tone upon which Egypt opened herself up to us. I never said a word to Sananda or anyone else about my connection with the pyramid. I was ready to see what would unfold on my own. As the days passed, the people who booked the retreat began to gather, until all too soon the whole group had arrived and the evening supper was awaiting us. The time had come.

Over the next nine days we flew to Aswan, drifted along the Nile for three days and three nights dropping in on Philae, Dendera, Abydos, and Luxor, bussed our way to the step pyramid of Djoser known as Saqqara, and then finally returned to the hotel filled with stories, experiences, and meaningful friendships. Also during that time the ancient legends of Egypt revealed themselves to me; through dreams, meditations, and inner reflections. I was told about the time of the original split that occurred between the masculine and the feminine in Egypt five thousand years ago. As soon as I contemplated the story for myself, I discovered there was an echo, a residue of pain of separation within me.

So many times before in the past, I would begin to feel the movement of the wound of the masculine and feminine when in an intimate relationship with a man. I did not understand why it would happen, and why it so often tainted and polluted the flow of love between us. It would always play out in the same way and once it began it was only a matter of time before the relationship would end with me leaving rather than hanging around for my fears to manifest. In all honesty, I didn't trust the masculine in the past.

Whenever I felt his natural urge to expand, change, or pioneer, it would feel like a threat that left me suspicious. It could be something as small as him wanting to go away for the weekend with some friends by himself, or something much bigger like going away to India for a twelve-week yoga course at an ashram in the middle of the jungle without me. It would then only be a matter of hours before I became emotionally cold and withdrawn. That was how I once became known as the "Ice Queen." The fear of not being invited (or included) was so deep; it lay hidden under layers of protection and smoking mirrors. But it was in the intense fires of Egypt that I decided to dive down and heal the crevasse that over time had become commonplace that fearing the masculine was normal.

With this new knowledge, I was thrown into the same compulsion that had possessed me when stumbling upon new information before. Like the time during Easter when I had discovered the five wounds to love, every waking hour, every space in our teaching program, every ounce of free time was devoted to understanding and capturing all that was coming to light. I was often seen scribbling into my diary as if the end of the world was nigh. In my diary, I wrote out my understanding regarding the truth of the masculine and feminine, and their original separation, which still to this day is widespread across the planet. It is what I call The Great Undoing.

The Great Undoing

Once upon a time, in the archives of human experience, there was once a great tragedy that still to this day strikes at the hearts of all human beings.

This heartache comes from the memory of a time when there was a distortion upon the Earth, when the masculine and feminine went into great separation and turned their backs on one another. The masculine held the deep desire to expand, and the feminine felt this as a rejection, even as abandonment in some way. She felt she was not enough for the masculine, and began to doubt the truth of herself, feeling she could not hold love, and that somehow the love she held was not enough.

She did not realize she could grow in support of the masculine that her own masculine essence could open and expand likewise within her own being. Instead, she felt this as a memory of wounding, being left behind and dishonored by the masculine; that the masculine did not appreciate or value the love she held, but rather wished to grow, expand, and leave her behind.

The masculine, in response to this, began to feel that somehow the feminine could not support the masculine or handle his power even though he needed her. He felt his expansion and the birthing of his brilliance could not be held by her, and he felt this in some way as a separation from love. He began to hold the idea that in order to grow, somehow he had to be alone, in his cave, to work things out, to get close to the divine. She did not know that it was her choice to open the masculine deeply as they journeyed into expansion; that this was not abandonment, but rather a journey they could share together.

After some time, the masculine realized he had left something out within his existence. He could recognize that some element was missing, and in its place was emptiness. But he had this notion that if the masculine united and opened with the feminine, he would be consumed, controlled, domesticated, and lost in the material world, and would not be free. He did not realize that the feminine could share with him the gentle ease of being, and the myriads of ways in which he could experience the endless freedom of love, which would lead him to discover the true essence of the feminine. She was the gateway to the great mystery of love, and could, through grace, open the way for the masculine to experience unspeakable union with God in a rapturous and ecstatic way.

And, not surprisingly, this was the biggie that Sananda and I were dealing with on a weekly basis, within ourselves and between us. You too can no doubt feel the weight of the situation, which we human beings have to face and heal if we are to truly love, free from old wounds. The real truth is beyond these ideas of masculine/feminine, the love we experience and feel is discovered far before we even become aware of our gender definition. And what we love in another is also genderless. I knew this, and so my mission (masculine) was to surrender (feminine) to this, to hold true and see through the thoughts and feelings that suggested otherwise. It was during those times that if Sananda suggested I go for a walk with him for a mile, and in that time he insulted, hurt, poked, or provoked me, I would ask if we could make it two miles. I was so ready to heal this, so prepared to keep seeing where and how that hurt would arise, and to then apply the healing nectar of the loving light of consciousness to its core.

Being in Egypt was the best place on the planet to set this masculine and feminine laced intention because everything is amplified more greatly here, especially along the Nile and within the Giza plateau. It was all in divine order. So, I was working externally with this concept (my relationship with Sananda), as I was also busying away on the inside. I increased my awareness of my own internal dynamic, feeling into my inner masculine (drive and ambition) and feminine (nurturing and intuitive). I stayed vigilant to the two flows of energy, making sure they were balanced. I took these ideas into my teaching, often guiding the group into the extremes of their own gender polarity, so when it was time for relaxation they would exhaustedly drop into balance and harmony. It was blissful to share these techniques with retreat participants, right as I was learning them.

As we neared the end of the retreat, Sananda whisked Maria and me to the cocktail bar for a private conversation to discuss how the retreat would wrap up. The bar was a thriving melting pot of human flavors where Americans mixed with Sudanese, who mingled with Arabs, who rubbed shoulders with Australians. We finally found a table located between an Asian businessman and a Kiwi model, and huddled together for a hushed conversation.

"I now see what we have to do to complete this retreat," Sananda said, looking at both of us as he placed his hands on the table, fingers spread and steady. He continued to tell us that he had arranged some private time in the pyramids, and that we would be going into *the Queen's Pyramid* later this afternoon and tomorrow for the finale. I grew with excitement as I stared at him with wide eyes, hanging on his every word. The Queen's Pyramid...

It was only a few mornings prior when I awoke from yet another dream of being inside the pyramid. Sananda told me I was talking in my sleep most of the night and that he was getting concerned as my body was roasting hot. This was new for us, as we usually dream the same dreams, most Beloveds do. It was quite normal for us to share our dreams in the middle of the night or the next morning, confirming yet again we were both in the same dream. But this time it was different. So over breakfast that morning, I shared with him my reaction when I first arrived in Cairo, along with the dreams and visions I had been having. I explained that the reason why I didn't tell him straight away was because I wanted to see how all of these phenomena would unfold. He held my gaze as he listened to every word, and when I had finished he simply smiled. Now, he was setting the stage for something far greater than I had imagined.

"Scarlett, you are now ready to fulfil your purpose. Because of your open heart and willingness to follow wherever it may lead, you are to be used in the closing ceremony."

He then proceeded to tell Maria what she would be doing, but I switched off as my attention was being drawn yet again to the Queen's Pyramid, which I could see through the window.

Sananda quietly drew my attention back, "Scarlett, tomorrow you will be asked to climb inside the Queen's Sarcophagus and lay there while we do our ceremony. You will serve as a gateway, a bridge between worlds that will bring about a massive harmonization here on Earth. Once we are inside, for two hours all power will leave the pyramid, casting us into the greatest darkness imaginable, where we will chant and pray to move beyond all our deepest fears, to be taken into the heart of love."

He continued to explain that he would engineer a certain scenario to trigger off the groups fears, in a really big way. It would be my role to gather and draw in all the fears deep into my heart, and transform that fear into love. I was to step into the shoes of the Divine Feminine, and compassionately embrace the entire group from the confines of the sarcophagus. I would energetically link to the ancestral line of Isis (this was her pyramid after all), and transmute all their suffering, as this was exactly what I had been doing all summer with him.

My jaw slowly dropped as I stared at him. I could hardly believe my ears. Which wasn't entirely a surprise, as the pounding of my heart was deafening in my eardrums. It was like standing next to the PA system at a Prodigy gig—all baselines and fireworks. My mouth went dry, as I found it difficult to swallow the news of my awaiting mission.

I was a bubbling, gurgling mixture of surprise, bewilderment, fear, and excitement. Now I knew why the Queen's pyramid was eyeing me, she knew I was coming. In fact, she had been waiting all this time for another to climb inside her tomb. Then, all of me grew quiet; soberly contemplating what all this meant as I came to terms with the huge responsibility that went hand-in-hand with this act of surrender.

I am going to lie in the Queen's Sarcophagus. I am going to lie in her supposed tomb, my body shall lie in the exact place where hers did. On my god, with that last thought I felt like I was going to faint. What does all this mean? 'Could I have been Isis in another lifetime? Was I one of the one hundred and forty-four High Priestesses? My brain groaned with the endless possibilities. I could spend another lifetime trying to work that one out.

Instead, I dropped my incessant questions like a hot brick, and sunk down deep into the brewing sensations within my body. I closed my eyes and was again taken into the chamber where Isis was standing, waiting for me. I watched how my body superimposed over the top of hers, I saw both of us suspended, divided only by time, until the eons between us began to dissolve. I observed how both our bodies gently, tentatively became surrendered to the inevitable pull of magnetism that brought us back together, until we were the same woman, the one and only woman within all women. I shuddered with this feeling and tremors of anticipation flushed through me, carving open greater depths in my heart, that in turn prised open even deeper remembrances in my soul.

I always knew that I would do something like this in my life. I knew that one day I would be called to stand in for something larger than myself in service to others. My path of the Beloved was leading me to this exact place. I knew I was capable of not only facing, but also overcoming a seemingly huge fear by giving of myself completely. In a way I was more than willing to bring an end to the forgetting of love, and in its place bring to life the quality of forgiving by saying "yes!" to love.

Opening my eyes I noticed that Sananda and Maria had left the bar. They were used to me periodically dropping into spiritual visions by now. Sitting alone I shifted around in my chair as I shook my head trying to make sense of it all. Rummaging in my bag I reached for my diary and grabbed a pen from off the bar. I wrote as much as I could remember from this last vision.

I relaxed as I uncovered another piece of my path of the Beloved.

Tomorrow could not come soon enough.

❧

I stood at the entrance to the Queens Pyramid, gazing down into the long dark passageway that led to the inner chamber. It was 5pm, and the desert sun was creeping towards the horizon. The last of the tourists were being ushered away as preparations for our group to take the stairway down and into the pyramid were being made. A gust of cool, charged air bellowed up along the shaft causing me to take a few steps back to steady myself. A smile formed on my lips as I knew this was her way of greeting us, letting us know that she was down there, waiting.

I inhaled the scent of her, an aroma hinting at birth, life, death, and rebirth. Thousands upon thousands of years of creation were soaked into these walls. I was ready to descend, walking down the steps one at a time into the murky darkness, leading the way, as Sananda for the very first time, stepped in behind me. I felt like a Queen, and became suffused with a feminine essence, majesty, elegance, and compassion. I felt Isis's energy in every way—tonight would be transformative for all involved, including myself and Sananda. We all dropped naturally into silence, and the strangely amplified sound of my own raw, heated breath quickened the deeper we went. My hand reached for the stair rail the moment we plunged into darkness, to act as my guide now that my eyes were obsolete. There was only a dim light at the end of the tunnel indicating where the chamber began and the stairs ended.

The air in the pyramid changed, it became heavier, thicker, so much so that I had to almost drink in the oxygen to breathe. Step-by-step, delving deeper into the bowels of the earth, it became hotter, closer, so that beads of sweat pushed through my brow, moistening my skin. Deep breaths, animal breaths, ancient breaths, voices, half-formed words swirled around me. Up ahead I could sense the end of the shaft, as we neared the chamber, where the sarcophagus was laying open towards the far side of the wall. As promised there was a dim glow lighting the chamber, revealing its shape and size. I walked in and stopped.

There was the stone sarcophagus, with its lid pulled halfway across the opening. It looked every inch a gateway, a doorway into the underworld. Heavy, time worn, dark grey black stone was what created this tomb, this mausoleum, this burial chamber, this grave. The place where soon I was going to lay. Thank God it was empty!

The power of the sarcophagus was enormous; its sheer, immense magnetic pull dragged me towards it like an iron filing. I was entranced; I was already gone from this world. I could see the group but could not hear them, and all my other senses were fading fast. I had to get in, I had to...

I stepped inside; bending my knees as I finally released my grip from the walls of the chamber, and lay down into the velvet darkness and cool, smooth ancient stone. As I relaxed, breathing to calm my jangled nerves and mounting fears, I began to let go as Sananda had instructed me, surrendering to a wave of combustive explosions within every cell of my body. Waves of light, tunnels, worm holes, openings, closings, in, through, and over I traveled at the speed of light, sound? I didn't know. High octave sounds and frequencies gnawed away at any resistance, transforming, recreating, and melding human with Divine. I felt myself being taken down, way beyond, into a place where I suddenly halted to a standstill. After some time, if such a thing existed, I lay there suspended in space and time, and was then guided with immaculate precision, gently wafting like a feather, to glide from side to side, towards the pulsing source of creation herself.

From the deep recesses of my memory, a faint wisp of knowing swam into my awareness that somewhere up above me Sananda was orchestrating the group through their deepest fears. It was the last and only connection I made, before I surrendered that final thread of my humanity, plunging into the deep void of unborn love. I truly wish I could create the words that could possibly hint, or at least point the way towards the beauty, and heavenly embrace of that place. All I can say is that I tasted God, I ventured into heaven, I found paradise, and I became lost in nirvana as I entered the higher meditations of Samadhi. For just under two hours we all stayed in the darkness, deep inside the pyramid, while the whole of the Giza plateau emptied with the setting sun. There was no other soul around, only our group.

"Scarlett, Scarlett, come back, please…"

I returned to the darkness as I felt Sananda's hand nudging my stomach as I lay in the sarcophagus. He was standing over the opening to the chamber, and I still could not see him, but knew he was close. Somehow I managed to move one of my arms as I reached over and laid my hand over the top of his to let him know I was with him. I slowly opened my eyes and saw nothing, but felt everything.

Every sense was heightened, as slowly an incredible wave of joy washed through me. My first thought was, "My Beloved, where is he?" Oh how I needed him, how I ached for his kiss. I felt so much more of myself, and longed to share that with him. I felt that a deeper part of me was finally ready to meet with him. He helped me climb out of the sarcophagus, where I came to rest for a while sitting on the ledge, staring into the room which was still in darkness. I could hear him breathing and could feel the heat of his body, and the sweat all over his skin

From out of the darkness the power was switched back on and suddenly the whole chamber was visible again. An ocean of beaming, radiant faces surrounded me, as I too lit up from inside and gushed with euphoria. There was an upheaval of cheer and celebration, as everyone embraced and danced their joy. It was the signal to leave. We had done what we set out to do. It seemed as though everyone was saying "yes" to love. I took one last final glance around the chamber gathering up the last of my belongings and making sure no one left anything behind.

To my utter surprise, there was a bright red juicy apple sitting on top of the sarcophagus lid, right smack bang in the middle, obvious, impossible to miss, and somehow highly significant. I walked over to where it sat, and just stared in disbelief. How did that get here? I would have noticed it when we first arrived. Even if I didn't, Sananda surely would have. I picked it up and examined it, turning it over and over again in amazement. I took it with me, stuffing it in my pocket as I turned and walked out, bowing before the sarcophagus in humble gratitude for the experience.

"Sananda, look, I found an apple on top of the sarcophagus, did you see it when we first walked in?" I asked.

'No! There was nothing there at all, I checked. That was what I was doing before you got in, making sure that the sarcophagus was empty in case any tourists dropped some rubbish," he exclaimed, looking at the apple in amazement.

He took it from me, as he looked skyward up towards the top of the pyramid. I saw tears brimming in his eyes.

"What is it, Sananda?" I asked.

"An apple is the sign of creation, like in the Garden of Eden. Eve ate from the apple alone, and so began her great adventure, but she was alone. We have been given an apple, a symbol that represents starting again. This is a new era, Scarlett, the chance to choose again," he whispered, as he attempted to speak in-between choked breaths and words.

He looked at me in awe, as his words finally registered inside of me. We threw our arms around one another, crying with amazement and soulful humility.

"Let's bite from it together, so we can join and create a new adventure together. Forget the old stories of separation. Now, we can make it, together, as one!" he jubilantly declared.

Together, we both held the apple between our mouths, cheeks puffed and red, and in unison we bit into it at the same time, spraying ourselves with the juice from this heavenly fruit. Laughing and dancing in front of the pyramids, we knew that our prayer to create a newly evolved and loving cycle for humanity was answered. Now, we would go on to do the work we truly came here to do.

Chapter Nineteen

Wounds to Love

Back home in France, October 2009

THERE ARE SOME things in life that come along and change everything forever in one sweeping moment, and that was exactly what happened in Egypt. I felt as though I had crash-landed back to Earth with a bit of a bump, and despite feeling dazed and confused I brushed myself off realizing I was back home in France. In some ways it was difficult to return back to the sleepy pace of rustic Rennes Les Bains, after the action-packed adventure through ancient Egypt. But nevertheless, that was what we did, re-entering our days of walking through the evergreen forests of Hameau de Montferrand, trundling towards the local village, gasping in joy as we swam in ice-cold rushing rivers, and ooh-ing with pleasure as we plunged into the steaming hot natural thermal pools.

We were beginning to prepare for a brand new retreat we had formulated together, that would be held in the heartland of our local pentagram, the area that surrounds Rennes Les Chateau. This new work was born as a result of all we had been through together. We were beginning to feel that we now had something tangible, profound, and deeply meaningful to share with others who were feeling the call to meet their Beloved. We felt we had some priceless keys and maps we could share with people, flagging the possible challenges they might encounter along the way.

I was thrilled to offer this work in union with my Beloved, knowing it was my destiny to be used in this way during this lifetime. What a joy to be able to share with people how to love like never before, to offer my experiences and footsteps on the once forgotten path towards sacred union between man and woman. It had been my dream as a child to devote my life as a beacon that catalyzed love with others, and now this time was deliciously dawning.

Since Egypt, I had pretty much forgotten that I was still waiting for the results of my biopsy. I had become more settled, enjoying a relaxed outlook on life. Since I was feeling so at ease, it never occurred to me to chase after the results. That is, until we were having coffee at Masion Christina, our local coffee house in Rennes-les-Bains, one afternoon when my mobile rang.

"Bonjour, Scarlett, this is your doctor from Carcassonne Hospital, I have just received the results from the biopsy."

"Oh, hi."

In that moment, suddenly the whole scenario came flooding back. A wave of clammy sweat crept over my body, as I became aware of a heavy sinking feeling.

"Thank goodness… What are they?" I tentatively asked, as I mouthed to Sananda that it was the hospital on the phone. He abruptly stopped chatting with Christina, the owner of the Chambres d'hotes, as they both stared at me.

Christina knew I had been anxiously awaiting this call as we had been hanging out most of the summer at her place, drinking coffee, and using her Internet connection. She was our godsend, our local and organic Google search engine. She knew the answers to where everything was in the area, and was pretty clued in with who's who in the expanding conspiracy theorists circles, as most of them ended up staying at her place. It was quite normal to be sharing a table with a few wanna-be Indian Jones's or Mary Magdalene reincarnations.

As I waited for the doctor's response, I nervously stood up and began pacing around the table looking to find a quiet spot to have this rather sensitive conversation. I pressed my ear against the receiver to hear the answer.

"First of all I have to apologize for the delay in getting back to you. The reason it took so long was because the lab decided to test again and again, to make sure we really did have the right answer…"

Okay, fine. But get on with it! I impatiently waited for him to tell me the news.

"Because we found nothing, you are clear. Whatever was showing up as abnormal is now normal again. Your results are good, you have nothing wrong with you and there is nothing to worry about. However, we would still like to see you in six months to keep an eye on you, making sure you stay clear," he said.

A heavy wave of pent up tension left my body, as I exhaled the sigh that was keeping it all together. He continued to tell me that this was a medical mystery, a near impossibility that a grade four abnormality could disappear. The staff at the lab sent my sample to numerous other departments in the area so they could test with even more advanced and sophisticated microscopes. To the utter bewilderment of the doctors, the same result appeared again and again—negative, no abnormality detected. Basically, the entire gynecology department in Carcassonne was shaking their heads in disbelief.

Again another sigh, this time relief and gratitude, I had waited for this news all summer. My hand went up to my heart to try to steady its pounding, as tears began to brim in my eyes as I circled around the narrow streets repeating the words, "thank-you, thank-you, thank-you." My face was abloom with joy, gratitude, and sheer excitement as the layers of anxiety dissolved. I couldn't rush back to the café quickly enough to tell Sananda the news. I felt as if I was on fire with life, bursting with euphoria and ready, so ready, to live like I have never lived before. I felt like my global comeback tour was about to begin—watch out world!

Sananda was right all along, he had one hundred percent faith this would be healed, whereas I was more at the 88 percent mark. I knew it was possible, I never doubted that. What concerned me and made me question my faith the most was the excruciatingly long wait for the results. Just before I reached Sananda, I slowed down to take some time for myself to relish this moment and inwardly praise my immune and reproductive system. I smiled to myself, sending the warmth of my smile to those places, whispering another thank you. I knew why and how this had been achieved. Why? Because I had emptied, cleared, and healed all suppressed and unresolved sexual matters. How? By delving deep into painful places and memories, while surrendering and staying open and authentic. This result was an accumulation of the powerful depths of our love, prayer and combined efforts to strip away the past. Unwavering courage to stay true to love had been the healing medicine that reversed the disease, back into ease.

"I'm clear, I'm clear!" I gushed to Sananda, as he rushed towards me pulling me into his arms. He spun me around cheering and laughing at "our" news. He was overjoyed and sincerely jubilant. I didn't know whether I was going to laugh or cry, so instead I opted for a mixture of the two, a facial gesture that Sananda affectionately calls "scrunch face."

Christina crept out onto the street to be with us, cautiously approaching, gauging to see whether we needed some space. As soon as she heard the celebrations she knew what the results were. More and more people began to gather wondering what all the fuss was about, and within minutes the whole of Rennes Les Bains was privy to my results. To say I felt an enormous sense of relief would have been the understatement of the year. Quieter than my initial, obvious reaction, was a more humble recognition that a miracle had taken place. Side-stepping our unexpected group of well-wishers, I took Sananda's hand with my own as I placed it over my heart, tenderly thanking him for all he gave to me during this part of our journey together. My thank you was only a signpost towards a feeling that could not be described with any language. He was my sole inspiration.

"We did it, darling, we did it," I whispered.

"I never doubted it for a second," he replied. His eyes tenderly shone into mine, as he cupped my face with both his hands.

"I love you Scarlett, and I will always guard and protect you. You are my queen, and I will endeavor to support you to become all you are destined to be."

He drew himself closer towards me, as he slowly kissed my lips. We stayed in that unmoving kiss for what seemed like another lifetime—drawn into a world without time or space. Slowly, we became aware that we were in the middle of the street, and so resumed our cheer by accepting a shot of brandy from the region. Any good French man/woman will tell you this is *the* best way to celebrate—with the entire community present! I only wish the fabulous Miss Chloe (and Joan of Arc, being French and all) could have been there as well.

"Compliments of the house!" Christina cried as she raised her glass to announce a toast for continued good health.

We all chinked glasses and drank to continued health for all. Once out of earshot, Sananda and I vowed to continue where we left off with that kiss when we got back home. I snuck a surreptitious look at Sananda when he wasn't aware; he was too busy enjoying the merriment as he burst out laughing with Christina's husband. When Sananda laughs, the whole world knows about it. It is one of the loudest, heartiest, and infectious laughs I have ever heard. I realized in an even deeper way that Sananda never did doubt my full recovery; he held the intention in his heart, even though at certain times it looked as if I was losing my faith. He held steady, no matter what. I walked up behind him as I squeezed his hand resulting in a warm pang of gratitude in my heart.

This type of endurance was the hallmark of a best friend and Beloved. It is during the toughest hardships that the Beloved connection literally acts as another life support system. By becoming one being, they can fulfill, support, and give copious amounts of internal strength, healing, and insight to one another. In many ways their union amplifies all attributes, qualities, and talents within the two, which are then available for the other to 'borrow' and draw upon. All gifts and abilities become shared and accessible to the other. This was exactly what had happened between Sananda and me.

As soon as we gulped down a couple of celebratory brandies, I called mum and dad with the good news. In a semi-drunken, ridiculously happy voice I shared my good news as I spelled out all the details, making sure mum knew the facts and was settled that I was now officially healed. In the background I could hear dad cheering, calling out his praise as he at first negotiated, then resorted to tackling mum for the phone to get a chance speak with me. I laughed at their antics, after forty-five odd years you would have imagined they would have mellowed. But no, they always seem to remind me just how much life they have in them.

They were so overjoyed and relieved. God bless them, they had been tracking my progress every step of the way, especially mum ever since we shared the fateful call together. I loved sharing this superbly good news with everyone; it was amazing to hear the multitude of ways in with people responded. Chloe was over the moon when I told her, releasing a variety of squeals and a myriad ways of saying, "oh my god!" After a shockingly long time on the phone (long distance mobile—ouch!), she promised that later on in the night she would have a glass of champagne on me. She will as well, I thought to myself, as I imagined her out and about in the various members' bars of West London, rubbing shoulders with the rich and wanna-be-famous. She had just returned from seeing an old friend in New Zealand, so was back on the London radar. I imagined she no doubt had some serious catching up to do.

❧

With aggressive cancerous cells out of the way, Sananda and I were able to even more acutely focus on our path ahead as Beloveds. And before we knew it, we were hours away from teaching our new retreat together. We were calling this new work *The Wounds to Love*, deciding that our first 'birthed' creative venture was to be held in a beautiful old rustic farmhouse at the foot of Rennes Les Chateau. Thirty-five people were coming from all over the world— making up a healthy mixture of both men and women.

Over the course of seven days we shared openly the path we had forged together, explaining in detail the path of the beloved, and highlighting the five initiations that needed to be overcome and healed within. We took time to really be with the people who came to us to strengthen their capacity to deal with the resistance that would inevitably arise from being in relationship with their Beloved. We wanted to ensure they did everything possible to clear away any remaining heartbreak before their Beloved showed up in person.

The week was such a joyful experience full of laughter and tears, as those in attendance slowly opened up and intimately spoke to us about their fears and longings. This was such a new way in working for me. For far too long I had the feeling I was holding myself back over the years as I taught yoga. My heart's desire was to work way beyond physical postures and breathing techniques, and now this opportunity was here, inviting me to help others delve deeper into themselves. For the first time in my life I felt I was in the right place, being used in the way I was created for. I felt such a huge surge of gratitude for life, for Sananda, and for myself coming through this journey, with the know-how to guide others.

Seven days arose and fell away in what felt like a blink of an eye. Long enough for me to know I was now working within the field of my soul purpose. In hindsight, I knew that everything I had experienced since meeting Sananda was pushing me towards this place. It had been an intense journey—healing my cervix, cleaning away past guilt and regret, reawakening my sexuality in a clear and balanced way, learning to trust in intimate love again, purifying my shadow, and finally accepting the chaos of life. I had moved so much, shifted so many layers, and truly felt as if I could now drop into life and fully be myself. In a word, I was fearless.

As the end of October came around, Sananda decided to go back to England to record a new album. Since returning from Egypt he had been absorbed with creating a sonic soundtrack that guided others into deep transformative places, based upon five spirals of sound. He wisely relied upon the use of sound and mantra within his field of work, knowing the codes and frequencies that opened up other realms and dimensions within others and the Universe. He invited me to come, but I chose to stay in France, using this valuable time alone to prepare inwardly for our wedding that was only a month away. It was my intention to make sure there were no more lurking energies creating a veil between us. When I stood before that altar, I would be the fullness of my femininity; ready, willing, and able to make that commitment for my entire lifetime.

Once Sananda boarded the plane, I had ten clear and open days to spend time administering the loving care I planned to enjoy. I decided upon daily saunas, a couple of massages, and plenty of free time to walk and be in nature. I was guarding this precious time, making sure I did not see or meet up with anyone, conserving my energy, making sure not to waste it on talking or entertaining. It felt important to draw the curtains to a close around me, that I may travel around incognito to all the magical places that surrounded us for the last time before we returned to England to get married. It was a precious time to play catch up with myself, as I integrated all the warp speed experiences I had clocked over the last seven months. Every morning I bathed with rose petals, delicately fragrancing my body with essential oils from the local area, and enveloped myself in silken clothes, purposefully picking them by their color, feel, and expression. I was intentionally using this time to engage in 'goddess rituals,' (see Last Word for more details) to further embody the divine feminine, so I would be ready in more ways than one to claim Sananda as my husband.

I took my time wherever I went, walking slowly, driving carefully, and truly see and feel this legendary place I was living in. We only had a few more weeks left in France as the six-month period was nearly through. So I made sure I spent this last bit of time in the most delicious ways I knew how. This area in France was pulsating with conspiracy and paranoia, and was almost falling over itself with treasure hunters, reincarnations of Mary Magdalene, occultists, and filmmakers. Rennes Les Chateau had become the Mecca for the lost treasure of the Knights Templar, the Cathar heresy, secret societies, the Merovingian Kings, the Holy Grail, Mary Magdalene and the continuation of the bloodline from Jesus Christ. Everywhere you went, you would meet someone whose sole purpose was to solve the mystery.

Yet for me, the mystery was not the treasure or the esoteric power that went with it, my understanding was that the mystery was in the land, in the earth itself, and even more so, when the sun went down and the shadows began to form. With Sananda away, suddenly I was able to move around at my pace and flow to which I took great advantage. Late one night, like I had been planning to do for months, but never seemed to get around to; I pulled on my boots and headed down the hill towards our own secret hot springs waterfall. It was such a thrilling adventure to be walking around at midnight, in the dark with no torch sensing the road down towards the waterfall. Long before I got there, the unmistakable odor of sulfur filled my nose, confirming I was heading in the right direction. I loved playing outdoors, especially at night. This playful joy reminded me of when I was a child. I often wondered why people become so serious once they reached adulthood.

I was a little disappointed in myself for a moment, realizing that I had become so absorbed with Sananda and going with his flow that I had been ignoring the impulses of Shakti. Shakti represents the feminine impulse of life, also known as life force. I invited her to work through me so often on my journey because of her often wild, creative, impulsive, and imaginative ways. Her longings never make any sense to the mind, yet her voice pleases the heart and fills the soul. Shakti is fearlessness, not foolishness. Her confirming presence fills me with ecstatic goose bumps as soon as I step into her power. Her presence fills you with an almighty sense of 'I can do this,' which for some can be terrifying, resulting in them fearing Shakti, as this energy is hardly controllable. It is pure artistic endeavor and pursuit. I made a mental note to make sure that I wouldn't forget about Shakti again as her fearlessness and passion was far too precious—especially during a time like this. (Oh, and by the way—there is no need to fear Shakti—she is simply 'you' unleashed!)

However, my disappointment soon gave way the moment I heard the tumbling waters of the spring splash against the smoothed limestone rocks. All of a sudden the devic world opened up, bringing to life imaginary creatures and friends that appeared everywhere in my adventurous inner world. In my joy, I promised out loud that I would never overlook the impulses and longings of Shakti ever again. I threw off my clothes in wild abandon, knowing there was no one around and even if there was, no one could see my nakedness since it was pitch black. I was squealing with delight as my feet sunk into warm, gooey mud as I crossed the shallow stream to where the waterfall was. This made me giggle because of the hilarious sound of the squelch and surprising sensation of wet mud seeping through my toes.

My fingertips reached for the rocks to get my bearings as I climbed up the waterfall to reach the seat that had been formed over the years. First I had to step through all the foam and froth that had formed at the bottom where the water and silt was landing. I was laughing and giggling as the water splashed all over my face, causing me to spit out and occasionally swallowed the water. I reached my throne and gracefully sat down upon its seat in the middle of the waterfall while fluid torrents cascaded alongside each shoulder, pouring down the sides of my body like infinitely long watery hair.

I had become the Queen of the Fairy Kingdom and the Goddess Aphrodite, which means, "she who has risen from the foam," also known as the Goddess of Love. My body eased up under the pummeling weight of hot water that plunged to my neck and shoulders. It was just like receiving a full-on massage with a Maori Warrior, whose hands worked to find and release those deep and tense muscles. I sat there for a long time, warming and wondering under the water. With my eyes closed, I meandered into this world and in no time soon realized I had begun to softly murmur some kind of ballad.

Still singing to myself and the inhabitants of the spring, I stepped back over the stream and groped my way over towards a tree where I had hung my towel. I dried myself off under the moonlight, and invited the breeze to finish off the rest of the job. I felt so fresh and young, like a water nymph or sprite, as I pushed my damp feet back into my boots, and shook my hair free from my towel like a prowling lioness. This was what it meant to be alive— to be free to enjoy the simple delights of this earth and all of its wondrous creatures, real and imagined. As I began to walk back up the hill to our tiny hamlet, I felt I belonged to something spectacular and that I was part of everything. To me, worldly success did not touch this feeling of pure realized contentment. I had fought through the five wounds of love and beyond, fought for my Beloved and won. Of course fighting for one's Beloved actually means fighting for one's self. Who would have known it? I had opened to love, although painful, and felt my reward had well and truly arrived!

As I deliberately walked up the hill, I began to contemplate how I felt about our up and coming marriage. I realized my life as a single woman was about to come to an end. But what did that actually mean? Many of my friends were warning me about marriage, as too many disappointments and heartbreaks had made them cynical and suspicious. There were not many people I could turn to who could understand. I found that it was hard for people to understand the intensity of a Beloved relationship if they are not already in one, as it's an altogether different ball game. Beloveds are, in fact, "fighting" to heal the lifetimes of pain and wounds that have accumulated between them. Although the majority of these wounds are a result of previous lifetimes, there is also a sizable chunk of karma from their moments of separation. For a Beloved, these times of separation are the most painful. Their coming together won't always be smooth, but the lasting karmic implications and joy that arise are far worth the effort.

It felt as if the last seven months washed clean any remaining ideas around my sense of individuality. I was more than ready to go through with this. To finally release all that energy around 'finding the one.' Now that he was here, the idea of getting married filled me with a sense of freedom. By the time I walked through the front door and collapsed into bed, the silvery moon had sunk behind the low-slung clouds looming above the mountain of Bugarach. I pulled the pillow closer towards me, smiling in my sleep as I dreamt of Sananda.

The next day I awoke much later than usual, enjoying the feeling of being deeply rested after being pummeled by the sulfur waters from the night before. I padded upstairs to the kitchen in my dressing gown and prepared to fix myself some tea. There were only a few more days left before Sananda would return, I intuitively knew I had to clear any possibly remaining "ghosts" by performing a specific meditation (see meditation to clear the past and dissolve any ghosts in Last Word) before Sananda returned to France, as we had talked about embarking on a nine day practice where we would declare our vows to one another, speaking and sealing them into the subtlest layers of our being. So by the time our wedding day came, our vows would be tattooed into our psyches, not just said in one fleeting moment whilst drunk with wedding day bliss. No, they would be spoken with care and consideration for nine mornings in a row, embedded with loyalty and infused with intimacy.

According to a body of Egyptian esoteric teachings, we all have nine layers or bodies to our being. One of them is the physical body. The other eight include your shadow, Shakti (life force), heart, mind/memories, soul, name, light of consciousness, and the part of you that is fully seated within the godhead. So we would be addressing one 'body' at a time and speaking directly to that aspect.

Days later, I met Sananda at the airport. In a rapturous embrace we kissed again like we did a year ago outside L.A. Fitness in my old hometown. It was love at first sight again, as we spoke nine to the dozen of our adventures whilst apart. Sananda was so excited to be returning home, eager to get indoors, throw his clothes off, open up the doors to the view of the Pyrenees and of course climb into bed with his very soon-to-be wife. I was ecstatic he was home again, giving us the time together to reconnect before the big day arrived.

Every morning for nine consecutive days we sat side-by-side in meditation on the sofa in the lounge as we declared our vows to one another, spoken from the heart, and transmitted into the other in a way that mere words alone could only ever half bake. We planned it in such a way that on the final day these vows would be spoken aloud in front of all our guests at our wedding that we had created together. It was in this moment that our union would be sealed and sanctified for eternity.

It could be a lost hope to even imagine I could find the words to share how speaking and receiving these vows made us both feel. Perhaps if you close your eyes and imagine the breath of your Beloved speaking them to you, not only hearing, but feeling the vows of eternal love being spoken into you. The words reassured, soothed, and eased. All parts of us received the vows. We took our time to speak directly into the nine bodies, one body per day and found that every ghost that may have been lurking between us was laid to rest. There were no more obstacles, no more doubts, and absolutely no more fears. I was ready, eager to begin my life with him and so infinitely grateful for everything he was, is, and shall ever be.

The five wounds to love were a discovery that set me on a journey that rocked my world. I battled each wound to the core, and now I had arrived in a place where I was teaching others how to do the same. My Beloved and I were now on the other side of the five wounds and about to embark on a new chapter of this pilgrimage to love...

The Atomic Cry

My Beloved,
If you were to split the atoms of my heart
Still all my love could not be measured
God himself could not speak of this devotion I tend for you

My eyes open every morning to your being
Yet my heart remains open and playing
Tones of endless bhakti simply for you

My innocence comes from my trust in you and this love
I am the greatest lover of your life
I am first and last in the queue to kiss your feet
And Stroke your face

I pray to God to show me more love
So I may deliver it to your door
I am your post woman who brings you the Good News
That you Beloved shall never experience one minute without
    my love
In you, within you, around you I live
I am your Gift from God.

—ANAIYA AON PRAKASHA

CHAPTER TWENTY

DESTINATA

Parents house, England, December 7, 2009

M Y EYES opened to the familiar sight of light streaming through the windows of my parents conservatory, followed immediately by feeling a heavy lump at the bottom of my bed where my two cats lie sleeping. Peeking out from underneath my duvet, I found myself yet again in my trusted sofa bed, as I looked around my old bedroom, for the last time as a single woman. My destiny had arrived.

It had been ten weeks since my finale inside the sarcophagus in Egypt, yet it felt like it was only yesterday. A warm rush of gratitude floods my body every time I reminisce, reminding me that my connection with the Queen's Pyramid is eternal. And today was one of the days that I would bring that Queen energy through me. I rolled over in bed catching a glimpse of my champagne wedding dress hanging underneath its transparent, protective layers; longing to be worn along with my Christian Louboutin shoes that were begging me to step into them. I trembled with even more excitement when I noticed flowers everywhere, filling the house with their fragrance and beauty.

It looked as though mum crept in while I was sleeping and distributed them to every possible corner of my bedroom. All the surfaces in my soon-to-be ex-bedroom were covered with cards overflowing with well wishes and good luck for the big day ahead. Right next to me on my bedside table was a white satin case with a traditional set of Indian bridal jewelry made up of an abundant cluster of gold and emeralds that Sananda's mother had given me as a gift. A gift, which had been handed down from her ancestors. Could there be anything more divine?! There was also a necklace, pair of earrings, a bracelet and traditional Mang Tikka, which was a beautiful piece of dangling jewelry that dripped down from my hairline to just in-between my eyebrows.

Thinking about all the jewelry, instantly reminded me of the previous night before. I smiled as I remembered how Sananda's mother had arranged an Indian traditional hen party for me, complete with Bhangra dancers, Indian food, and an appointment with a henna tattooist who covered my hands and arms in the most intricate beautiful markings inspired by my hopes and wishes for an eternal and sacred marriage. Because it was a surprise party, Sananda had been the one in charge to invite a handful of joint friends to come over. Our merry gang consisted of a couple of friends from the States, another friend from England, along with Sananda and his best friend, to make six of us altogether.

Chloe would have been there but she was already in New Zealand with her best friend Sarah, who was just about to give birth for the first time, and she was destined to be the godmother. Chloe was beside herself with guilt for weeks before the wedding once she got news that Sarah wanted her to be there for the birth. She was in such a dilemma, not knowing what to do for fear of hurting or letting down her two most cherished friends. As soon as she told me, I gave her my blessing to go to New Zealand. I understood that the precious moment of giving birth far outweighed a marriage ceremony. I urged her to go, as I knew deep inside she would get so much out of the trip. So, the six of us headed off to the West End of London after the hen party to go clubbing together. But before we left, we decided to dress up and get a little wild. I sported a bright pink *Pulp Fiction* bobbed wig, an oriental crimson and gold silk corset, and 70's styled black and silver pinstripe flares. When I saw Sananda, my jaw dropped with admiration, he looked like a hip-hop pimp gangster drenched in an all white suit (except sexier!).

As we neared the entrance of the club, the pulsing throb of bass lines penetrated our chests, as the rhythm hooked us in. I remembered this old familiar feeling of awesomeness, excitement, and the thrill of entering the dance, not knowing or caring where it was all leading, just as long as I was part of it. I began to strut as we walked up to the door, enjoying the buildup, the mounting tension, before we burst into the main room heaving with music and sweat. By the time we entered the nightclub, there was no soul alive who would not agree that we looked like the King and Queen of Hollywood. It was two days before our wedding, and I wanted to dance. And dance, we did until the early hours of the morning.

We planned the party in such a way that the next day was a 'day off' before the wedding. And to make sure I felt absolutely wonderful on our big day, I only indulged in one glass of champers. I planned on spending the entire next day at the Bath Spa with Sananda and wanted to enjoy every ounce of it! After six hours of sweating, steaming, and massaging out any and all unwanted toxins we looked and felt ten years younger. I must say I was rather pleased with the results; we both were. I drove Sananda to a pub where he was staying, along with a whole bunch of guests. It was important to me that we slept in separate locations on the eve of our wedding, as I was banking on an unforgettably spectacular grand entrance.

I swam back into the present moment as I blushed and swelled with appreciation for all that was about to unfold. The day had finally arrived. The day I took the rite of passage from being a carefree young woman to entering the stage in life where I became a wife. I was about to live and be with my husband. This came with a huge sense of responsibility that I warmly welcomed. Now, there were two of us, we were a team, we considered and supported one another all the way. We held a powerful sacred circle, which was impenetrable by the world and its mechanics. There was nothing I would not do for this man, and I knew with every fiber of my being he felt the same way.

I could see how the path of the Beloved had insisted on us embodying the fullness of marriage. This was a choice that we both stepped into after recognizing our previous years of non-committed relationships. We needed to create a solid and trustworthy bond that lovingly held us together should we experience the old patterns of bailing out. Walking the path with the Beloved is an encounter that is given to those responsible and mature enough to handle the energy and the capacity of its yearnings. Mature in ways that are not limited to age, but rather of character.

With bare feet I wandered into the garden, touching the trees and breathing as I took my time to feel the enormity of the day that lay ahead. My God, just one week before my fortieth birthday and I am about to walk down the aisle. I giggled to myself as I would never have imagined I would have been doing this less than a year ago. I always knew I would one day find my Beloved, but I didn't foresee that we would actually marry. Perhaps in the haze of my wild hippy days the notion of marriage was cast out, along with a pension plan and a mortgage.

So, now hours before the big day, all I could do was laugh at my once treasured pious ideas. I reflected on the number of times I nearly considered not continuing on with this path, and laughed. I had used petty reasons and judgments to not fully step into this true commitment, a commitment that I longed for. I had to undo all those silly ideals of being 'free' and 'uncommitted.' It's amazing how much one can change when they really want to. I rolled my eyes in near disbelief as I remembered all the times I thought I had a choice in all this.

I had no choice. The moment I laid eyes on him, I knew, I simply knew. I felt relaxed and present, yet vitally aware that on this day many things would change. I did not know what, nor did I care, I was content to allow the whole day to unfold, and to cross any bridges if and as they should arise. An hour later I blissfully glided back to the house, ready to engage with life in a big way. Reflection time was over now that the 'big day' was about to begin!

Mum and dad were up and puttering around getting breakfast. As soon as they saw me they burst into life as our shared happiness and laughter rang throughout the house. Over breakfast I played all my favorite songs louder than usual, while they played theirs. We seemed to be the best of friends in that moment, outgrowing our ideas that they were my parents and I was their child. After forty years, finally the ties and bonds of being a daughter were stretching and widening, making way for the role of wife to now be included. I allowed that realization to settle into place, and uttered some excuse to walk out of the kitchen, as I was so moved and touched by the obvious glory filling the house. I stopped for a moment, leaned against a wall full of pictures from my childhood and felt tears of joy streaming down my face. It had happened. I had called him into my life on that mountain and since then everything had changed. Best of all I was sharing all of this joy with my parents—people I loved and treasured more than anything.

Suddenly, the loud ringing of the phone brought me back to the present moment. And once it started to ring, it didn't stop. I don't think the house has ever encountered so much activity. Friends from Hong Kong, Australia, America, and New Zealand called to say they were with me in spirit. There was really only one phone call I was waiting for, though, and that was from Chloe.

Just as I was thinking that, the phone rang—and I knew it was her. She squealed when I picked up the receiver. Within seconds we realized we had that annoying delay that happens when you call someone in New Zealand or Australia. This was a nearly impossible situation, as we were both so giddy with happiness we kept forgetting to pause in between sentences. Her reply would come back, just as I was launching into my next round of news. I was talking a mile a minute and so was she, when I finally got the message she was trying to convey to me. Sarah had given birth to a little girl that morning. Ah, another wave of excitable laughter and tearful words of congratulations.

Out of corner of my eye, I saw that mum was either trying to get my attention, or she had recently taken up mime acting as her second hobby. She was waving her arms around, miming that time was running out and I needed to get off the phone as my Godfather would soon be coming, and I hadn't even gotten my dress on. She still had to do my hair, and by the way, "come on you haven't eaten your breakfast yet." Phew, I was exhausted just watching her! Chloe and I said our goodbyes, on one side of the world to another, as truly joyful events were occurring for us both.

As every minute passed, I swelled with more radiance and brewing excitement. Mum came to help me put on my dress and fix all the undergarments, making sure my hair stayed in its rollers and that I didn't step on the cat in the process, as I could not see my feet at all once the dress was on. We kept shouting at dad in unison to, "Stay Out!" whenever he asked to come in to see how I looked, as I was in various states of undress and dishevelment. Finally, I was ready. I opened the door and stepped out into the hall.

He was unable to speak, as he became silenced by the vision of a woman who appeared at the doorway of the bedroom where he would once tucked in his little girl for bed. All he could do was wipe a tear away from his well-loved, weather-beaten, handsome face, and sob, "You look beautiful," taking out his handkerchief and blowing his nose in a way that only my dad does. Mum walked over to him to offer her support. I was the only daughter you see, so this was big for him. I walked over to them both with my arms outstretched, as we all hugged one another. Mum glanced at her watch reminding us it was time for her to go and that dad and I should follow in half an hour.

I took the bit of time left to fix the last minute touches on my dress and face, making sure that the moment Sananda saw me he would become entranced with rapture and devotion. It was my intention that I would be a true vision of natural beauty with a body ripe with love. I took one last glance in the mirror as I realized I had completed my task in becoming a true queen, whose presence was one of beauty, kindness, and strength. All of my experiences had made this day possible. I was about to marry my Beloved.

I leaned in closer to the mirror, turning around to scan for anything that might be amiss. Nope! I really did look exactly like the vision I wanted to present to Sananda. My strapless champagne silk wedding down was corseted to the hips, emphasizing my feminine curves and producing a waistline the Victorians would have died for—literally. My golden hair was piled on top of my head with barrel curls dropping to my shoulders, giving the look of a Grecian goddess, as a scattering of white and red roses flocked my tumbling tresses. My mother had handmade an incredible bouquet of twenty-two (date I climbed the mountain and a rose for each of the qualities of love) blood red roses that were bound with a golden ribbon that I held in my hands. Last but by no means least, underneath the gown I wore pure silk underwear, complete with my mother's baby blue ruche satin fifties style garter around my left thigh.

Now I was ready to leave my old childhood home and take the surreal journey with my father and Godfather to the venue where the ceremony was already beginning to give birth. As I climbed into the matrimonial car, it seemed that all of this was happening to someone else; yet when I looked down it was *my* hands folded in *my* lap, upon *my* wedding dress. I caught my reflection in the shop windows as we drove through Newbury High Street, windows I would often gaze into as a teenager and shops I had once worked in as a Saturday girl. We continued to drive past L.A. Fitness, the gym that was once my second home and the place known for "the Kiss" only months ago. My, how a life can change!

Finally, we arrived at the venue, which was an organic farm, nestled in the Lambourn Valley, famous for its racehorses. Oh God, now I felt nervous, or was it excitement, maybe I was thrilled, or was I shy? Ah... I didn't know the difference anymore. All I knew was I had to get out of the car and make it to the main hall, and in Christian Louboutin seven inch heels that could prove to be a slight problem considering it was December and raining cats and dogs. Luckily, dad appeared at the side of the car like a true Knight in shining armor, offering me his arm, which I graciously accepted.

Dad and I walked into the foyer together as we constantly squeezed each other's hands in support, knowing we were both entering into a day we would never forget. Everyone was already settled in the main room, awaiting our arrival. My heart was pounding as we stood outside the door, and dad gave the sign that the ceremony could now begin. Dad and I were both shivering with nerves, as I constantly reminded both of us to keep breathing. Talk about a tense moment—it was off the scale. I have no idea why, but I kept bursting out with laughter, at the most inopportune times. Like when I was supposed to be quiet because the ceremony was about to begin. I almost had to stuff a rose into my mouth to stop the giggles.

Then, from out of the silence came the first notes of the most heartfelt, powerful rendition of 'Nessun Dorma' I have ever heard, brought to life, or should I say love, by two special friends heralded for their angelic voices in the operatic world as well as the spiritual community. As I stood with dad in the doorway, our world fell silent. Clutching his arm, I looked out into the room that was welcoming me on my wedding day. I saw our friends singing directly into our hearts.

We were both so choked up; we did our best to hold back our

emotions. It was a hopeless attempt to try and remain composed or keep my make-up in check for that matter. Once the first note was sung, the lyrics and love could not override trying to keep it together. In fact it was rather wonderful to simply let go, and openly be moved and cleansed by the rawness of the moment. The Wedding Registrar was so moved by this performance he was actually physically moved back in his chair from the force of it, gasping, laughing, and openly clapping, before hurriedly clasping his hands over his mouth to silence the sacred moment.

Once they closed their opening song, dad and I proceeded to walk down the aisle towards where Sananda was waiting. I did speed up just a bit, in case dad had any last minute nerves and refused to let me go. But like a dream, he silently and gracefully pulled his arm from underneath my hand and offered it towards Sananda, the man that was moments away from becoming my husband. In that moment another friend began to sing the key sounds of an ancient Egyptian blessing, as Sananda and I laid eyes on each other for the very first time that day. I looked up at him with eyes filled with love and amazement, taking in every part of his face, feeling his presence as we stepped into each other. He looked so handsome in his all-black Indian Nehru suit buttoned up to his neck, with a jeweled gold shawl casually yet artfully slung over one shoulder. His face was shining with a haze of gentle sweetness as we smiled at each other, in a way that suggested a shared secret. I breathed him in, as his fragrance radiated throughout my brain and my shivering body.

Hand in hand, we climbed the steps and sat for the legal ceremony. Both of us could not stop smiling, constantly looking at each other like ecstatic children as we moved through the legal ceremony with ease. I don't know how, but we managed to say all the right words in the right places, sign papers, and repeat the marriage declaration, all delivered alongside bursting and overflowing smiles, the odd squeeze of each other's thigh, somehow managing the high that was threatening to peak too soon.

Luckily, the moment appeared just in the nick of time as we gazed into one another's eyes, steadily speaking out the words "I Do" as we silently, with baited breath, exchanged our rings (again) from the sacred union ceremony. There was a simultaneous inhale as everyone widened their eyes the moment we placed our rings onto our marriage fingers. A celestial atmosphere charged the room as we gazed into one another for what felt like an eternity, standing in pure presence, like a King and a Queen. From behind us, we heard the timeless words that declared our sacred union.

"I now pronounce you man and wife."

I felt that sentence plunge deep inside my being, the whole of me blossoming and flowering into a vision of boundless happiness and infectious love. We felt it was important to have a legal ceremony, as we wanted to ground and anchor our commitment. We would not be satisfied with some New Age hippy ceremony, or some form of hand fasting that lasted a year and a day. Oh no, we wanted a true, solid, and eternal bond that withstood the trials of time.

Once the legal part was complete, we moved into the best part of the ceremony that we felt moved to share. On bended knee, Sananda took my hand and whispered his vows for the last time in front of all our guests. Every word was alive as it became released from his mouth, infused and glittering with the essence of his heart and soul. His words were a transmission that lit me up from the inside as my radiance beamed through every pore of my body, targeted for him alone.

I asked him to stay on bended knee so I could pour into him my vows of eternal life and love, with him, in him, and beyond him. I shook with vital energy as the fires inside began to burn away any and all last minute ideas that I may have had about being single, or separate from him. In that moment I gave myself to him, body, heart, and soul. I witnessed inside me how a part of my 'self' died, to clear the way for the full rebirth of sacred union. I had to become empty, to become full. By the time all forty of my vows were spoken, one for every year that I had lived waiting for his return, I was complete. Now nothing, absolutely nothing, stood in our way.

To seal this heavenly moment, another dear friend of ours began to strum out the melody of *The Power of Love* by Frankie Goes to Hollywood on his guitar. We turned to face him as he began to sing the lyrics from a song that was obviously written by one drunk with love. His voice at first was almost a gentle whisper, meandering over the first verse, growing and growing until his voice and pounding strums filled the hall, as he cried out with the power, the velocity, and the heavenly charge of one hopelessly possessed by the eternal loving passion of the Beloved. He poured himself into that song, lit the match, and then exploded, and as a result there was not a dry eye left on that organic farm.

What a finale. But there was still more to come...

After the ceremony, we walked out of that room hand-in-hand as man and wife, and entered into an ocean of smiles, hugs, words, and tears of endearment. The foyer was a swirl of color, voices, and movement as we both climbed onboard the carousel, moving from one person to the next—it was much like being at the fun fair (although since it was my wedding day I would have to say much more spectacularly glamorous than a fair). One face blended into the other, as genders merged and skin colors blended until I found myself back in the arms of my husband, where we playfully kissed and twirled each other around. We took our chance and snatched a few precious moments for ourselves as we snuck outside to catch our breaths and get away from it all, for a fleeting moment.

When we were ready, we took a deep breath and dived back in. Our friends were a charismatic mixture of opera singers, fire-eaters, yoga teachers, spiritual teachers, snake charmers, children's authors, models, exotic performers, and dancers. All charmed together to witness the union of our love, along with our devoted families who were blissfully simple, normal everyday type of people. My parents were used to such antics as over the years I had introduced them to the artistic world, the fashion world, the gay world, then the spiritual world, and now on this day decided to throw it all together in one enormous fiesta. Personally, I think they secretly loved it! Well I know mum did, especially when the snake came out.

Yes, there was a snake at the wedding, a black asp to be precise, and my God, was she loved and adored on that day. This snake represented Shakti, our beloved wild force that animated us both with no threat of ever diminishing. Circling around my neck, slithering over bemused seventy-year-old grandmothers from sleepy English towns, coiled around Sananda and all who dared to hold it, it was our symbol of life force. Our snake belonged to a fire eating, angel wing wearing friend, who was performing our rites of love and blessings at various times of the day, until he passed out, unable to carry his giant seven foot wings any longer!

Our wedding was literally like being in another world, and everyone felt it, even the builders from our local village. Something indescribable was happening, and even the most jaded and cynical were transported into a magical world where love became reality, even if it was for just a few hours. Several people remarked that it was a highlight of their life, and that it was their soul purpose to feel and witness an event such as this: a Gift of love. As Beloveds, Sananda and I wanted to create this type of experience for our loved ones; we wanted them to see and feel the depth of fully opening to love. It is an important aspect on the path of the Beloved.

The wedding day continued to spin forward with so much happening, all the time, constantly changing, one minute here, one minute there, until everything became one undulating and writhing blur and then... Snap! The day was over in the blink of an eye. In one moment I was single, in another I was married. Suddenly, it was time to go. As we set to leave, our guests became magnetized yet again in a circus of kissing, hugging, waving, eyes, faces, words, names. In the middle of that action, I felt the protective arm of Sananda guiding me outside to where his brother was with the car and waiting to take us away. I collapsed in the back seat and for half an hour, I gazed ahead unblinking and barely breathing, while the rest of me caught up.

Sananda and his brother were busily chatting and laughing as they caught up on old times while I was comatose. As we sped down the motorway, it reminded me of how my life had recently speeded up, how everything had become a blur of faces, places, and spaces. Sananda kept turning around checking to see that I was okay, which I was. Before I knew it, we had arrived at Heathrow Airport where we had arranged to stay the night before we headed for Egypt the very next morning.

We checked into our relatively romantic bedroom—it was a hotel airport after all! Kicking my enormous seven-inch heels off I collapsed on the bed as roses and billowing netted underskirts filled the room. Sananda threw his clothes off as he launched himself into the shower singing all kinds of interesting sounding notes as I flipped up the screen of my laptop. Immediately, I opened up the "compose email" window to connect with the woman responsible for setting all of this in motion—Prudence. I had promised I would stay in touch after that fateful cold and wet evening in London two years ago. It was now time to share with her the full magnitude of what had transpired.

The words just poured out, in fact I had to consciously slow down as I seemed to be creating a new language then and there on the spot—due to my haste to get it all out before Sananda came out of the shower.

Twenty minutes later he appeared at the bathroom doorway in nothing but a fluffy white towel around his waist. I took my time as I gazed up at Sananda's dark and delicious form as we both drunkenly smiled at each other at the sheer beauty of it all—knowing we were aligned, on track, and in perfect harmony with every living thing, atom, and molecule around us.

His eyes glinted with teasing love as he seductively hooked one finger into this towel and pulled it free from its knot. Eh Viola—the body of my husband was awaiting me…

I gotta go now, I have some serious loving to do.

The question is: Do you?

This is where I have to leave my story, as I could go on forever as life continues to reveal exciting new insights into the mysterious ways of the Beloved. I began this journey to find "The One" and it worked. But, I wrote this book for a very different reason altogether. My wish is for you, the reader, to know what it's like to say yes, when in the past you may have said no. I used myself as an example of "a woman who said yes" to ignite you, to awaken you, and to impassion you for the next step on this journey.

Take time to honestly answer these questions before we begin:

- Do you or have you ever felt that you are destined to meet your Beloved or Soul Mate?
- Are you in a Mr./Mrs. he/she "will do" relationship?
- Are you ready to live?
- Will you chose love over fear?
- Are you ready to give everything, face every fear, and heal every single resistance that holds you back from love?

If the answer is yes, read on...

Because if you remember, over two years ago during January 2008, I met Prudence and she said:

"The legend continues to say that whoever climbs the mountain must tell one other of its existence, but only ever one. You have to know exactly who to tell, or the mountain will lose its power," Prudence looked down into her glass, slightly frowning.

"How do you know who is the right person to tell?" I asked.

"You have to know that the person you tell is ready to hear, and willing to climb within nine months of being told. If the story falls on deaf ears, then the legend is lost to story books and fireside magic" she said, brushing the stem of her glass as she looked sideways.

Are you prepared to climb Mont le Coeur? Are you adventurous and willing enough to meet 'The One' and follow the voice of love that lives within your heart?

If so, turn the page and find out how…

I have two ways of loving You:
A selfish one
And another way that is worthy of You.
In my selfish love, I remember You and You alone.
In that other love, You lift the veil
And let me feast my eyes on Your Living Face.

—RABI'A AL-ADAWIYYA, *DOORKEEPER OF THE HEART*

LAST WORD:

A HOW-TO LOVE AND LIVE WITH YOUR BELOVED

OW IT BEGINS… for you. This book is your book, your story, and your journey with *your* Beloved. Believe it or not, you have everything you need to embark on this path, to say YES to love no matter what: you've read my story, you know the landscape, you can even follow my footprints should you get lost. And there will be hundreds upon thousands, possibly even millions, of us supporting one another along the way. The path to the Beloved is aflame! As we near 2012, more and more of us will be drawn to our Beloveds like never before.

My last word is truly your beginning. And I want you to have everything you need to be successful. I've created this section to give you the roadmap, tools, and ways to prepare for your journey into the love that you deserve. It's out there—I know it—and everyone is included, everyone is invited on their very own pilgrimage of love.

But before I release you onto this path, we need to have a heart-to-heart about where you're at in your life:

- Are you already in a relationship? Is it working, do you feel fulfilled, do you help one another grow and become more of who you really are? If the answer is no, (remember that before I met Sananda my answer would have also been no) you have to create change. Ruthless, powerful change— NOW. You either have to create the action steps to bring the relationship back to life in a fulfilling way or end it. Ouch, right? Saying "yes!" to love in every moment also means not having a placeholder, blocking you from your Beloved.

- Have you had your heart broken and are holding back in case it happens again? I was once in this position and realized that my suffering was caused by the idea of never getting the chance to love again.. I came back to life once I said yes to love. This is your life, how are you going to spend it? In protection from love? Or in service to love? I know which one I chose. Make your choice now. Once you get a taste of it, you'll wonder why it took you so long to say yes!

- Have you not been in a relationship for some time and are wondering what it's all about? This is a great place to be— as you have empty space to fill! Welcome to life, in a big, enormous, incredible way. Once you've healed any past sexual and emotional interactions you will be ready and open to meet your one. Keep reading to find out how. What I've discovered from being in a deeply committed relationship is the wonderful opportunity to be a mirror for one another—whether it's in a subtle way, like with a Soul Mate, or in a more intense experience with the Beloved. Either way, the more you love, the more you see this mirror in action. When you have empty space to fill you are ready to experience all of this and more.

You see, love serves growth and authenticity. The deeper you fall/rise in love, the more you will be given the chance to dissolve and release all your shortcomings and ways of holding yourself back. It's ironic really, we think we see the other's flaws so clearly, but often have no idea about our own. Your Beloved will greatly assist you with this task of seeing and understanding your blind spots. A wonderful Rumi quote that I always keep close to remind me of the mirror is:

If you are irritated by every rub, how will you be polished?

All that's left is to decide how far you want to take your pilgrimage of love. Do you yearn to resurrect your current relationship into one that is open, honest, and fun? Or do you feel drawn to go all the way; that you're destined to meet your Beloved (and would pull the hind legs off a donkey to know what to expect and how to prepare)? Whichever camp you're in, I have useful guidance on how to make the journey together the greatest on Earth. As you've learned from my story, Sananda and I had plenty of time to develop these important navigational tools.

As with all journeys in life (and medical procedures and pharmaceutical drugs, etc.), I must include a disclaimer. The good news is, it won't make you feel bad!

This section has been created from the repertoire of my own personal practices that I studied, integrated, and now passionately teach. The subsequent practices/guidelines stem from a highly invaluable intuitive source that guided me on how to process all of this energy during my experience. These practices may not be true for everyone. So as is always the case, have a read through, take what rings true, and discard the rest. Remember, this is your path. And no one can dictate what that may look like for you.

Now that we've gotten that out of the way, let's get to it...

Finding and being in relationship with your Beloved, as you've probably gathered by now, is a full-body experience, which includes your mind, all your emotions, and soul. It's a huge work out, and I wholeheartedly congratulate those who have already met, and tremble with anticipation for those still to come.

So, are you ready? Below are the goods you need to jump on the (Be-Love-d) train!

First things first: How to find the mountain

The real name of the mountain is La Sainte Baume, and it is located in the south of France, near the town of Saint Maximin, which is well worth a visit. You can get there by flying to either Nice or Marseilles, then taking the highway to Aix en Provence to Saint Maximin and follow the clearly marked directions for La Sainte Baume.

Where to stay

The Hotellerie de la Sainte Baume is run by the Benedictine sisters and is a great lodging option. Every year, this hotel hosts hundreds of pilgrims willing to climb the trail up to "la Grotte." The old, beautiful hotel stands alone in the valley, and above one can see through the forest, the cliff, and the sanctuary carved in the mountain. It is an austere cliff, and has a very special feeling to it. Can you imagine that long ago, Mary Magdalene stood in this valley, searching for the same spot? Pure magic! www.saintebaume.dominicains.com

If you don't feel called to this locale, you can stay in Saint Maximin where there are plenty of additional lodging options.

What to do if you cannot get to the mountain

The truth is all around you are ancient natural places (also known as sacred sites) that were once used for fertility, love, and/or marriage ceremonies. If you cannot find one, then any sacred spot that awakens and arouses within you the urge to merge with your Beloved is ideal. The key to making this work is emotional charge! You have to create the desire and passion within to bring the Beloved to you. Based on my own experiences, below is a step-by-step process for calling in your one:

- Get yourself into an emotional state of gratitude, excitement, passion, and deep longing. This is a blend of Shakti (passion, power, and creation). I did this by playing powerful, evocative music on the way up to the cave. Music that brought to life my feelings of courage, victory, and purpose.

- Then, blend with the feelings of gratitude called Bhakti

(gratitude, devotion, and love). This combined magnetism of Shakti and Bhakti is what's needed to bring him/her towards you. I did this my playing incredibly tender and heartfelt music that reduced me to tears and opened my heart.

- Feel these powerful emotions in your heart, body, and soul. Blend the two together by imagining both of these aspects within you. Shakti, the warrior and red blooded being of desire and passion, and Bhakti the tender, compassionate being of devotional love. In your imagination see them merge into one being, and from that unified state, begin your prayer.

- Once you are connected to that feeling, begin to call to your Beloved. Praying, asking, inviting, and urging him/her to come into your life. Imagine him/her in front of you— what would you say, how would you feel? See and feel the love and longing in his/her own eyes and heart—remember they miss and yearn for you as much as you miss and yearn for them. It's a good idea to make sure you will not be disturbed during this, as you need to be fully present in this intimate connection with your Beloved. I spoke out loud to him, as if he was in the cave with me. I imagined us holding one another and feeling our two hearts together.

- Stay with this as long as it feels comfortable. Keep building the energy and emotion. Tears, heat, trembling, and powerful sensations in your heart chakra and throughout the rest of your body are all normal during this exercise. Welcome them.

- Once finished, say a silent blessing of "thank you." You've called your Beloved in. You can perform this practice on a New Moon for added potency. When I did this in the cave inside the mountain, it was a New Moon, a lunar eclipse, and a total eclipse of the sun. So, check your planetary alignments and go for the most powerful times that resonate with you. You are orchestrating the Universe with this prayer, so grab all the help you can get.

Now that you've called your Beloved in: how to find him/her

It starts here: pray and/or meditate daily—same thing really (one is listening and the other is speaking). It doesn't matter who or what you pray or meditate to (or for how long even!), just as long as that prayer is felt within you, as an ache or longing to find him/her. You simply *have to* create the desire and passion to meet. You are praying for the doors to open so that you can both meet and to dissolve any blocks or obstacles that are currently preventing you from doing so. Remember to listen and pay close attention to any bodily sensations as well as any inner wisdom that arises. Then, be absolutely sure to take action on any and everything that arises within you during these times of prayer/meditation. Shakti will tell you very clearly what you have to do to prepare and how to do it. When you start acting on this advice you will receive her support, and the chances of meeting your Beloved will grow and grow.

Simply put: your inner wisdom will guide you to your Beloved. Follow all guidance you receive during this time of prayer and meditation. It is wiser than you ever imagined!

If you're already dating or having casual relationships, pay close attention. If you do not feel the Beloved's presence, then keep the dating/relating to a minimum, so not to waste your time or theirs. I recommend just one date to meet and feel. Remember what I said; when you meet you know it! Do not waste any of your precious energy worrying about whether you will know or not—you will. It is something that is felt within the heart first. A powerful warm sensation that tells you, this is your one. Then the more you look into his/her eyes, the more you will see their love for you. It's so obvious. When you experience meeting your Beloved for the first time, please post your story on the website, as this is a question that is asked time and time again. The more the word gets out about the truly overwhelming knowingness, the more readers and lovers-to-be will have faith. Your motto at this time needs to be, "I am having so much fun dating on the quest to find my Beloved, but I will not get into any relationship *unless* it is with my Beloved." Enjoy this process! Your Beloved will be attracted to you (and vice versa), when you are your most authentic self, having so much fun in your life.

The Purpose of the Beloved

The purpose of coming together with your Beloved is to completely and utterly unify—leaving nothing for yourself. No more Miss Independent gals or Mr. Bachelor men. You will become two hearts and one soul. Please know that this is not merely a romantic dream or fairytale of meeting Mr. or Mrs. Right. This is absolutely what is possible. It is a divine marriage, where every moment is shared, drenched in trust and consciousness, and renders both parties in a profound sense of love, rest, and embrace with all of life everywhere.

In short, a life lived without fear.

Doesn't that sound delish? Trust me, it is.

The greater purpose of coming together with your Beloved is to then extend that loving fearlessness between the two of you in service to others. This can cover an entire spectrum of possibilities. The one common notion is that the union will be given to something greater, other than living happily ever after. You get to be madly in love with the person you are meant to be with *and* work together to transform the world in some capacity. It doesn't get any better than this!

One last hallmark is that this journey is full-time and devours every waking (and sleeping) moment. It's not something you do on the weekend when you spend time with each other. No, the moment you meet is the moment it begins. Your other will ache for your constant 100 percent presence, even when you are not there! You will not be able to be half-hearted or a part-timer about this. It is often intense, hot, passionate, challenging, and painful at times, yet paradoxically relaxing, nourishing in ways that were once forgotten, and magnificently healing.

I can also sincerely promise there is a way to work all this out whilst being part of the everyday modern world. You will find a way, as what you are is far greater than any culture or society. It's amazing to watch as the elements of your life that were once so rigid, bend and mold to your unified existence with your Beloved the more you journey together. You will have so much support from the cosmos, all you have to do is ask, and it is there. So when you meet a challenge, ask out loud for "help!" It will most certainly arrive.

Please note: from my experience, friends and family may not offer useful support, as they cannot usually comprehend what is going on, unless they are going through the same thing. You are going to have to go to the divine on this one! It's a true test to follow your soul, as this love brings in powerful, enlightening lessons on many levels. You saw it in my own journey with Sananda; I was virtually on my own, using my intuition to guide me. And that's why it is so important that I support *you* on your journey to the Beloved. You're not alone ever—you are always guided and supported!

When those feelings of loneliness or going at this journey alone do arise, offer a heartfelt prayer for help. When I experienced these sensations, I would often climb into bed (where possible), or find a private place to cry. This process opens your heart to such a profound depth, and so you will become increasingly sensitive— which is a beautiful gift. To love at this level, the heart has to be open and receivable. I had to remind myself that I was not alone; that others had traveled this path before me. I would always be aware of my feelings, openly crying when I had to, making sure that I was not denying any emotions. All emotions (positive and negative) come from the soul. As this was the place that we truly coming from, and making our way back to—I made damn sure I was doing my part with the housework! Every feeling that I had was acknowledged, felt and released. If ever I felt lonely and that no one understood me, I would absorb myself with the power of the Beloved by reading the incredible poetic words of love by Rumi or Hafiz. These two poets reminded me, that I was not alone.

Please remember you can (and I'm entreating you to do so!) take refuge in my story, knowing that I am walking beside you every step of the way. This is part of my service, to support and encourage those who are on the Path of Love. Reach into your heart and you will find me, amongst many others, waiting to assist you on your next step. Whenever faced with a situation you don't feel prepared for, ask yourself such questions as 'What would love do now?' or 'What would love say in this moment?' Say yes to love in every moment, letting it guide you to your other. Trust, as you are being perfectly led.

Another commonality of Beloveds is that they typically have two (usually polar opposite); highly individual unique ranges of experiences and lessons. For example, Sananda's life was one of profound consciousness and experiences of God in Samadhi (God realization). This resulted in his path being one of truth and clear seeing. Whereas with me, it was quite different. My life had revealed to me a Path of Love and Bhakti (devotion). In my 'moments' of God realization, my gift was love, genuine care, and kindness for all living beings.

In a word you could say that I was 'love,' while Sananda was 'truth.' We realized we had to share our understandings and experiences of love and truth with each other, so we could learn from one another in action. What do I mean by that? While we were dating and especially during the time when we were living together in France, I learned about truth and clear seeing from Sananda through deep and painfully long periods of time in meditation and stillness. He learned about love and kindness by watching me in action in our life, sharing my infectious joy and fun with all living beings.

These apparent 'differences' will appear both extremely interesting to your other, and potentially problematic as at first they may not fully comprehend why you chose to experience them, as it may seem to contradict their journey. They may feel your experiences are far too much in opposition to theirs. However, your Beloved will inevitably wish to address these experiences with you in various ways to a) understand what happened to you, b) feel your experiences deeply for themselves and then finally c) clear away the more darker aspects that could potentially pose as obstacles to the full union. For instance, with Sananda and me, we now share all of our combined aspects—power, Shakti, profound consciousness, Bhakti (love), Shakti, and compassion—as we have integrated and become one. Truly magical!

In short, the reason why you come together with your Beloved is to burn, pull down, dissolve, and heal all and any resistance that may be preventing you from truly becoming one with your other. For some reason, which I often call grace, you have been destined to find one another again on Earth. As you know, this is a priceless and rare blessing as it was once highly unusual for both Beloveds to be embodied on Earth at the same time. Both Sananda and I feel very strongly that the coming of 2012 is allowing for more Beloveds to be brought together than ever before. And as you read in my journey, the process can be ruthlessly fast and chaotic.

Why all the high-drama intensity, you might ask (as is often the case for Beloveds)? Beloveds were birthed together as one; therefore deep within them they know that exquisite oneness is possible—even if on a human level it seems as though it's been long forgotten. Because of the deep oneness they both feel drawn to; there will be an intense desire to return back to their original state of oneness as soon as possible. It could, of course, also be a slow, steady, and relatively smooth transition. Anything is possible in this magical world, right? But, even if the coming together is smooth, the purpose is the same. Once you merge with your Beloved (whether effortless or challenging)—please share your experiences with us on the Pilgrimage of Love website.

Three steps to prepare for the Beloved

As discussed in Chapter Six, there are three steps that must be taken to prepare your life for your Beloved. Following these steps sends powerful messages to the Universe, your higher self, and the energy of your Beloved that you are ready for this union.

First step: Create the vacuum.

There's one thing the Universe can't stand and that's an empty space. Please note, I don't mean a 'dead' space, like, "I can't find my Beloved, so in that case I will turn into a hermit." No, you must create an alive space that's teeming with Shakti (remember, life force). Your life should as stated before be more like, "I am having so much fun finding my Beloved, but there is no way that I will get serious until I know he's The One."

Second step: Begin to prepare

Embark on your own personal healing journey, paying special attention to healing all of your past relationships and attitudes towards sexuality. Spend time alone dissipating all energies that are not your own. And last, but by no means least, meditate daily and speak with your Beloved, even if you feel he/she is not there or listening. You may feel as if you are entering a dark night of the soul. Remember to trust the process; you are emptying out all the unnecessary junk from your emotions and subconscious mind. Stuff that will inevitably get in the way when you do finally meet your Beloved. Trust me; it's no good coming together with a wild variety of unhealed experiences. Get rid of as much past accumulation as possible.

Third step: Follow all impulses (Shakti urges) however unusual

Your Shakti will guide you both to collide with each other in a very *big* way! If you hear or feel guided to, "Be at the library at 3pm and wait on the steps," you better be there. At first, all these impulses may not lead to much. But I assure you, you are simply exercising an old intuitive muscle. The more you trust and respond to your inner guidance, the truer and deeper the wisdom will become.

The seven jewels of sacred union

The seven jewels of sacred union are: trust, passion, courage, forgiveness, communication, awareness, and faith—and were gleaned from my journey with Sananda. Using the traditional yogic knowledge of the seven chakras as a backdrop, I felt these words best described the ideal prescribed state of being on this sacred journey. I recommend meditating upon these qualities daily, gently placing them into the chakra locations within your body until the particular aspect becomes felt and integrated. As you practice this every day, the energy builds up so you can tune into them within a moment, if the need arises.

1. The first jewel is **Trust**. Place this blood red jewel in the first chakra, at the base of the spine. "Trust the Process" was one of my 'trusted' mantras throughout the entire journey with Sananda, and still is to this day. In times of trial, take a deep breath and repeat the mantra a couple of times until you feel stably situated within the base of your spine as you become centered again. When you trust the process, there is a natural letting go and willingness to go deeper despite any mind activity that may be suggesting otherwise. See Meditation to transform distrust, suspicion, and insecurity.

2. The second jewel is **Passion (Shakti)**. Place this sunset orange jewel in the second chakra, inside the womb for a woman, or hara for the man. This jewel is all about passion and hunger for union and oneness. You are creating a delicious appetite to give and take whatever is necessary in the moment to keep the momentum up within the partnership. You'll uncover an un-ending thirst for more and deeper, and a natural curiosity to discover and unveil each other through this jewel. Allow the warmth of passion to radiate from your second chakra. Refer to the Womb Breathing meditation to support this jewel.

3. The third jewel is **Courage**. Place this daffodil yellow jewel in your third chakra, deep inside the solar plexus. This jewel provides you with the bravery to keep going even when it hurts and the willpower to do something different rather than fall back into deep-seated patterns. It gives you

the courage of a lion to stand for love at all times even when you want to run. Again should you feel the impulse to abandon ship, take a deep breath and feel your resolve swirling in the power center of your navel (solar plexus).

4. The fourth jewel is **Forgiveness**. Place this emerald green jewel in your fourth chakra, inside the center of your heart. When you first come together there may be a lot of forgiving to do within yourself and with your partner. So keep the forgiveness flowing, and don't allow unresolved resentments to build up. Stay heart-centered, rather than staying in your head. This was the greatest challenge for me during my Pilgrimage. The power to go back to the mind was huge, but with the forgiveness jewel in my heart, I would always remember to return back to love. The yogic meditation for this is called the meditation to stay in your heart and get out of your head.

5. The fifth jewel is **Communication**. Place this sapphire blue jewel in your fifth chakra, inside your throat, particularly the space where you voices arises. This means being completely open, honest, and transparent in all communication (which includes listening). There can be no secrets between you whatsoever, as they will be felt within your field and will cause problems. I'm sure you've experienced this very thing any time you've shut down or withheld from a partner. Communicate openly through your throat chakra how you're feeling, any fears or anti-union thoughts you may be having, share your nightly

dreams (if they seem relevant), and stay vulnerable. One of your goals needs to be infinite intimacy, the unending desire to continue to grow closer. See meditation to solve communication problems.

6. The sixth jewel is **Awareness** (self-inquiry). Place this indigo purple jewel in your sixth chakra, at your third eye point, in between your eyes. You have to be aware of all that is going on within you. You will need to inwardly inquire as to what is being felt and why, and become vigilant of your actions, words, and deeds. You need to know why you do the things you do, and excavate for profound truths. Turn to your sixth chakra jewel to help you see and unveil the reasons why you are motivated to behave and act in certain ways. See meditation to develop intuitive guidance and sensitive awareness.

7. The seventh jewel is **Faith**. Place this golden white jewel in your seventh chakra, above the crown of your head. This is different from trust, as trust is an emotion that takes care of our human fragility, whereas faith is something far greater. Faith is sustenance for the soul, the absolute knowing and surrender to the intelligence (Universe, God, Allah, etc.) that all Beloveds experience to merge into full ecstatic union. Have faith and take refuge in the part of the Beloved that is already immaculately merged at the level of the soul and has never truly been separated from your human self.

Practicalities – How to prepare:

You need to be the owner of a relatively open and healed heart, and also have a clear and healthy approach to sexuality. It is usually these two areas that hold a backlog of past experiences. To enter into the sacred relationship of the Beloved, one needs to be without 'ghosts.' When I say ghosts, I am referring to past lovers, past tragic memories, or sexual trauma. It is a very good idea to do some work to clear the past first. Otherwise it will come up once you immediately merge with your Beloved, and if it is too intense too soon, you may ricochet off each other, and hurt one another further.

Authentic tantra can help with sexual healing, as well as meditation, and working with a trusted professional to clear any sexual blocks or broken hearts. Personally, yoga helped me tremendously with clearing my heart, which led me to find the most wonderful spiritual teacher, Gangaji, whose path was one of love and truth. What matters most for your individual path is to go deeply within and ask what you need to heal these past hurts so you can more fully open to your Beloved. When you do come together with your partner, both of you will be able to further heal and carve open the heart and the womb in the woman, and the heart and hara (navel power center) in the man.

You will also experience a natural impulse to explore new ways of making love. The old, tried and tested methods just won't satisfy the deep longing to enter each other's soul, and discover one another beyond bodies, names, and genders. It is possible to truly merge with one another, energetically, in a place that is pure love. As you can imagine this is a deeply profound healing process that brings so much gravitas and anchoring into the gender that you are in. For instance, a woman truly discovers her divine feminine essence and the man discovers his sacred masculine through full union love making. Naturally, within them both is the harmonious inner sacred union of their own inner feminine and masculine, the added joy being, it's there to share and experience on the outside too. Below is a way to expand this sexual union.

The Seven Gates

Please note: This practice should be performed with a partner you love and trust as your Beloved.

The Seven Gates are a set of energetic doors that form a channel from the yoni (vagina) lips to the g-spot or gratitude spot, to the clitoris, cervix, and then into the womb that contains the 5th, 6th, and 7th Gates. When healed, nourished, remembered, and honored as sacred, these Seven Gates become the keys to sacred love-making. Each gate opens as you progressively heal each part of the yoni and womb, making them sacred portals once again.

The gates start from the First Gate at the opening of the yoni lips, up into the Seventh Gate of the fully open womb. The gates become more like energetic veils of emotion and love when one reaches the Fourth Gate and beyond, which is the opening into the womb of pure space, and infinite potential. At this point, one starts to access the subtler energies of the womb, as well as those things that are not yet manifest. You know, the things you want to manifest but have not yet. The good stuff! One starts to make love in a different way on the subtle planes, and goes deeper into bliss. The man becomes swallowed in the infinite womb, and surrenders to the depths where all men wish to go, back to the source of life and original innocence. The man becomes humbled and empowered in a new manner, and the woman rests in ease and deep acknowledgment of her own divine nature, born from the deeper connecting and opening of the womb and heart. Divine Feminine and Divine Masculine are then born.

The inviting of the masculine essence to come deep into you requires that you become vulnerable; opening, embracing, surrendering, and receiving the male essence in its totality. When the Seven Gates are open, you are letting a man into your soul and your feminine essence, as well as fully into the womb consciousness, which holds enormous benefits for him.

This letting in, of course, can only happen through deep mutual intimacy, and surrender to the other. When enough sexual, emotional, and heart healing has been done by both partners, both alone, and in the mirror of relationship, then this penetration and surrender can occur, organically unfolding the gates. The level of mutual love, trust, commitment, and willingness to grow are key factors in this, as well as the ability of the man to be able to emotionally support the woman and be the safe pillar for her, therefore letting her go deeper into her own essential feminine nature, and deeper into the womb consciousness, taking the masculine with her. Since healing this before coming into conscious relationship doesn't always happen, the process of the Seven Gates can guide you both there.

The Seven Gates stir memories of the power that is within your soul. Integration of these memories is a key to opening and crossing each threshold. Allowing yourself to be penetrated by a male consciousness is the key to opening *all* of the gates *if* you are in a physical relationship. However, many female mystics have opened many of the gates through surrendering to God in a personal form, such as a lover of Krishna (a gopi) would, or like female Christian mystics who asked for, and were penetrated by, the Holy Spirit. In today's world of interconnection and the embodiment that only an intimate physical relationship can provide, the main way to access this is through committed relating between man and woman.

The power of a woman is deep inside her womb; all that is needed is a gentle reminder and a loving touch to begin the process of making sacred what is already innately within. The seven gates is a journey of reconnection from your (Bhakti) heart back to your (Shakti) sexuality. Usually these two energies have been withdrawn from one another for various reasons that I won't address here (but that I do address directly in my book *Womb Wisdom: Awakening the Creative and Forgotten Powers of the Feminine*). Yet with gentle focus on each gate, whether the man is inside the woman, or touching gently with his fingers or breath; feel inside the sparking presence of life force at each threshold. Love and bathe each gate with conscious presence, igniting and firing their re-awakening and their true purpose.

Side note: this practice can also be done while you are alone. Like a form of meditation you can inwardly focus on these intimate parts of yourself making sure that you start at gate one and move all the way up through to gate seven. In my earlier experiences, I wasn't able to make it to gate seven without falling asleep. It is relaxing and healing all at the same time.

*Portions taken from *The Power of Shakti* by Padma Aon Prakasha

The Five Wounds

We have already covered these earlier on in the book, but below is a recap. Remember, the wounds can occur in any order at any time. They will *always* show up in a relationship with the Beloved. It will be different for everyone, of course. Some wounds may take months to heal, while with intense work, it could take a couple of days.

For instance, betrayal was my most painful wound. The most turbulent charge was dealt with in the moment (when I first found out), yet it took four more months for every piece of the wound to be finally healed and completely dissolved. The other four wounds took on average three to five days to be completely worked through. Depending on your particular path, some of the wounds may have a stronger emotional charge or may be milder. Once you have cleared them, there is an incredible sense of freedom that surges throughout your whole body. You simply know that it is done. When I cleared the wound of betrayal I felt like laughing for days, the sense of freedom was so completely liberating.

One vital piece of the wound puzzle is powerful vigilance. When the wound opens up, there will be a strong inner dialogue surrounding the nature of the wound. How it was wrong, unfair, unjust, how that person was cruel, untrustworthy, etc. This is the voice of the wounded part of you, masquerading as either a victim or aggressor. It is easy to listen to these inner prompting's and launch into another cycle of building yet another layer over the wound by reacting as either victim or aggressor. In these moments, we must do something different, which is to drop the storyline surrounding the wound. As soon as the wound has been touched, simply deal with the energy and sensation within the body or emotions. Please steer clear of the mind—as your healing will not lie there. When you do this honestly, with no storyline present the healing can happen within a very short period of time. Prepare to be amazed, and set free!

Below is each wound and its subsequent antidote:

- **Betrayal – Trust the process.**
  Betrayal shows up in the stomach or third chakra. It is a dreaded feeling that twists and turns in your stomach, giving rise to nausea that suffocates and stifles your breath. Even the suspicion of betrayal has the power to trigger these feelings within the body and mind, causing one to react in a multitude of feelings from rage and revenge, to hopeless despair, hate, or depression. Betrayal is usually a two-fold wound. First is the act, words, or thoughts that take place behind another's back. Second is the concealment, and the purposeful ways to cover up the act.

- **Denial – Embrace the experience.**
  Denial occurs when you shut out the truth, sometimes even when you know better. It is located in the throat, or fifth chakra. To refuse to admit, recognize, or deal with an aspect of your life that blatantly exists, and is shown to you in many ways, is denial. Our first denial is always one of love. This leads to a betrayal of love, by escaping and running away from the issue and into the mind with its web of excuses, judgments, reasons, and rebuttals. The only way out is to confess, honestly and openly. Full disclosure is the key. Denial is a big, fat defense mechanism.

- **Judgment – Forgive deeply** (to heal the pain of being judged, and also the shame and guilt of being the judger). By forgiving you will immediately cancel out both. Your forgiveness will soothe or greatly reduce any arousal of shame/guilt in the other or self.

     Judgment arises from reason, logic, wounding, projection, self-criticism, belief, and assumed moral and emotional superiority over another. It is a veritable mélange of pride, anger, wounding, and punishment mixing together to create judgment over another, and therefore yourself. Judgment is always taken from a lofty, hierarchical, and separated position and resides in between the brows on the face or sixth chakra, otherwise known as the third-eye. It is the wound that fills and swims throughout the head, whether judging or being judged. It sits within the mind and projects out into the face of another.

     When being judged, it is the shadow within the corridors of the mind that picks up the energy of your persecutor and later when you are alone, starts to replay the tape. The voice of judgment takes the negativity it has received, turns it inward, and projects it back towards you. The wounds of judgment can then tease and belittle you, or wind you up with plans of revenge that eat at your self-esteem.

- **Separation – Surrender into the greatness of Love**, or the greatness that you have been graced to meet your Beloved in this lifetime.

Separation is a powerful shift of our energy when we choose to detach and stop feeling, and is located in the crown, or seventh chakra (our connection to love, god, source). Separation is one of the greatest methods of protection, as it means we do not get hurt. We create a box within ourselves, a place where we can view the world and others from a safe distance without feeling. Separation cuts off love in all ways—both in the giving and receiving. As soon you protect yourself from anything, then you are entering fear.

As soon as one enters separation, others around you will feel a prickly sensation in your auric field that fiercely bellows "Back Off." With most people, the natural response is to do the same, and it is here that many can enter a power struggle of who can cause the most harm, by various ways of being cruel and unkind to the other.

For Beloveds this is the most deadly of all wounds, as it is the most challenging to overcome. When you are in separation, its feels powerful and righteous, as you sit upon your icy high and mighty throne. The idea of becoming loving and warm repels you—which is completely at odds with creating a conscious relationship.

- **Abandonment – Reunify the abandoned piece of yourself** with that which your other loves most in the world. Bring the hurt part into the warmth of your courageous lion heart (which you clearly have as you wouldn't be on this journey if you didn't) and hold it there, observing it. By observing (making sure there are no veils between you and the wound) within yourself, bring all your compassion and love to its core. Allow the love to surge through the wound, healing ever aspect.

Abandonment is that secret feeling that surges through your veins charged with emotion, which screams "victim!" It is located in the first chakra, at the base of the spine. Abandonment is self-sabotage, self-pity, and has narcissistic tendencies that are cruel and punishing.

Abandonment is the voice of the shadow speaking and moving its way into your thoughts, speaking to your already low self-esteem of the reasons why you do not belong, why you are not good enough, and that you have nothing of value to say or give. It tells you that you are uninvited, you have not been chosen; you are the black sheep cast out.

Creating Balance

All work and zero play is no good for you and your Beloved! It is vital that all this powerful transformation becomes balanced with other activities such as fun and play. Why? It gets to be way too much (and adds to a sense of overwhelm) if balance is not brought in. Do not stay focused on serious transformation only. There is much joy and balance to find in your relationship with your Beloved. Follow the recommendations below on a regular, consistent basis. Trust me; this is critical to your success with your other!

- Bring in as much **laughter** as you both can handle. Meeting your Beloved is fantastically hilarious. You will often share the same sense of humor, enjoy each other's mischievous sides, and experience the best laughs ever! Allow the laughter to sink in, touching and healing all the parts of yourself that are rigid and serious. It's so much fun to enjoy life with your other, the more you laugh and relax with one another, the more you will experience life as it truly is—a gorgeous dream. Once that fearlessness kicks in; there is nothing that you cannot do together, as you simply enter into a world where you can love without fear.

- It's also imperative that both of you **rest** and integrate all that is happening within you. Sleep all weekend if you have to.

- Take plenty of time for **massages, spas**, and yes, more sleep. It's the physical body that takes the full brunt of the endless changes, so keep up the rest, stay healthy, and nourish yourselves well.

- Regular **exercise** is important to keep the energy moving through you. Hard and pumping cardiovascular exercise is perfect for when the heat is on and you're crazed with frustration, or try gentle yoga when you feel a little lost or displaced.

- **Meditation** is another lifesaver during this process. See the meditations below, and choose a meditation practice you feel drawn to and know you will be dedicated to maintaining.

Meditations

All of these meditations have been selected from my vast repertoire of yogic teachings that I studied over the years. Many of them I personally practiced over a long period of time, and others I have taught after trying them a few times in the build up before meeting Sananda. These meditations are powerful and simple in application, yet designed to seriously shift and clear any obstacles that may be preventing you from meeting your Beloved, or settling any disharmony during turbulent times. These meditations work on your vibration or your electromagnetic field also known as your aura. As the term suggests, electro is electrifying, and magnetic is attracting. With a powerful electromagnetic field, you will be able to attract and magnetize your Beloved, whereas with a weak electromagnetic field you will experience a pretty flat and uneventful existence. It all has to do with energy. Energy attracts your Beloved and energy keeps the Path of Love unfolding ever deeper.

You will love these life-transforming meditations! Even Chloe digs them.

All of the meditations below can be done in Easy Pose or sitting in a chair with a straight spine, making sure your feet are uncrossed and are placed on the ground.

Easy Pose is the typical yogic cross-legged position that is usually practiced on the floor with a cushion to support your buttocks. Make sure your spine is straight and long, and that the back of your neck is lengthened, by slightly lowering your chin towards your chest.

For the meditations featured below, choose one you feel most drawn to and do it once a day, for forty days straight, for at least eleven minutes. It takes eleven minutes to clear/heal your emotional body and forty days to break any habitual patterns or deep-seated issues. After that forty days, refer back to see which meditation you're drawn to next.

Meditation to transform distrust, suspicion and insecurity.

This meditation transforms the energies of distrust, suspicion, and insecurity by uplifting the frequency of the lower triangle or shadow self, into the all-forgiving realm of the heart and soul. When I experienced the above fear based energies, like when I felt I was never going to meet my Beloved, and also during the early days of dating Sananda (when my mind was doing overtime) this was the meditation I turned to. By directly turning fear into love, this meditation becomes an all out alchemical experience. It is best done the moment you feel any or all of the emotions of distrust, suspicion, and insecurity. If these feelings are a regular occurrence, you may well decide to do this meditation as a forty day practice.

Whether you have met him/her or not, the greatest gift you can give yourself is the healing from these energies of distrust, suspicion, and insecurity. The more you heal yourself, the smoother the journey with your Beloved will be. If these energies are strong within you, the meeting with your Beloved will be delayed. Those with a relatively open heart and healed sexuality will be blessed with meeting their Beloved. Like attracts like, love attracts love—it's so simple (in language anyway!). By doing this meditation, you will break the pattern within the motor neural pathways of your brain.

This is the realm of learned behavior and patterned responses.

1. Sit in Easy Pose with a straight spine and hold your right palm six to nine inches above the top of your head. The right palm faces down, blessing you. This self-blessing clears and expands the aura (this is the part that attracts!). The left elbow is bent with the upper arm near the rib cage. The forearm and hand point upward. The left palm faces forward and blesses the world. The eyes are closed and focus is at the lunar center in the middle of the chin. Breathe long, slow, and deep with a feeling of self-affection. Try to breathe only one breath per minute: Inhale 20 seconds – Hold 20 seconds – Exhale 20 seconds. Continue for 11 minutes. Inhale deeply and move slowly and directly into position for exercise two. You can extend this posture for up to 31 minutes.

    What this does: You are mentally and hypnotically blessing and forgiving yourself. This self-blessing affects and corrects the auric field—the part of you that attracts and leaves behind an impression. Doing this exercise could be uncomfortable as you transform the energy of distrust, suspicion, and insecurity. All these feelings are stored in your heart center, therefore by extending and lifting your right arm you are moving all that old, stuck energy.

2. Extend your arms straight out in front, parallel to the ground, palms facing down. Stretch out to your maximum. The eyes are focused at the lunar center in the middle of the chin, and the breath is long, slow, and deep for three

minutes. Inhale deeply, and move slowly and directly into position for exercise three.

What this does: Benefits and strengthens everything between the neck (communication) and the navel (courage). It gives strength to the heart and opens up the heart center (forgiveness).

3. Stretch your arms straight up with the palms facing forward. There is no bend in the elbows. The eyes are focused at the lunar center and the breath continues to be long, slow, and deep for three minutes. To finish; inhale, hold your breath for 10 seconds while you stretch your arms upward (try to stretch so much that your buttocks are lifted) and tighten all the muscles of your body. Exhale. Repeat this breath two more times.

    What this does: Creates a pure and transforming pillar of light that descends into your whole being. As it descends you open up to forgiveness, transformation, and healing.

After these three exercises, lie down in a comfortable position making sure you stay warm, as your body temperature will drop. This cooling of the body is the transmutation of the internal energies. Continue to rest or even sleep for as long as you need.

Meditation to stay in your heart and get out of your head

This meditation is for those times when you simply cannot get out of your head; when you're inundated with compulsive thinking and/or filled with doubts or confusion—trying to figure out "who" your Beloved is or if you're up to the task at hand, etc. By working with the glands in the brain (pineal and pituitary) you will begin to bring about balance by releasing the correct hormonal levels to open to the frequency and quality of the heart center by stimulating the thymus gland. Yes, it may sound confusing, but this is exactly what happens during this meditation—it's incredible! As the heart center opens, the potential for compassion, forgiveness, and humility extends into your reach. This meditation draws excessive mental (obsessive thinking) activity down into the heart where balance can be found. This can be a life saver! Remember the path of the Beloved is one of feeling and sensitivity, therefore we have to be centered in our hearts. Like most of us in the West, we have been taught to be more head centered (high achievers and all that), and we have to learn another way. When you find yourself consumed with thoughts, reach for this meditation and within eleven minutes you will be back in your heart.

Posture and Mudra: Sit in Easy Pose with a straight spine. Bring your hands onto your chest so that your thumbs are tucked into your armpits. The thumbs press against the ribs. Rest the palms and fingers of each hand against the chest. Relax the elbows down by the sides. Close your eyes and inwardly gaze down into your heart center (forth jewel). Allow sensations to be felt as you look into and reconnect with the innermost feelings of your heart.

Breath and Mantra: Pucker the lips and inhale and exhale deeply through the mouth with a whistle. Listen to the whistle sound of the inhalation as you continue. Continue for 11 minutes.

Meditation to develop intuitive guidance and sensitive awareness.

This meditation is for learning the invaluable tool of self-inquiry and/or self-awareness. If ever you want to know *why* you do the things you do—here's your key.

This meditation will bring about the clear, calm sensitivity that is greatly needed when in relation with your Beloved. You will also be able to develop the skillful art of subtly being able to sense the response and reaction in your Beloved, so that feelings and unresolved issues are out in the open and healed.

Additional benefits are:

a)   to maintain your youthfulness of mind and body;

b)   to bring health and healing ability;

c)   to fertilize the brain with its correct hormonal levels so you don't sink into depression; d) to eliminate fatigue and maintain a constant flow of energy; and e) to make you intuitive and universally sensitive.

Posture and Mudra: Sit in Easy Pose with a straight spine. Hold your hands at the solar plexus level in fists, except for the index fingers, which are straight. Hold the right hand palm down, left hand palm up. Put the right index finger on top of the left index finger, with fingers crossing exactly in the middle of the second segment (by each knuckle) so that a special meridian (energy line) contact will take place. Inhale deeply and very slowly (15 seconds) through the nose. Exhale through the puckered mouth (not whistling) forcefully and completely, directing the breath at the tips of the index fingers. (Never do this with a quick breath.) Feel the fingertips getting cold or vibrating. Close your eyes and inwardly focus at the third eye point.

You may yawn or stretch but keep breathing. Meditate on your own life force being carried by your breath. Continue for a maximum of 11 minutes. When you finish meditating, unlock the fingers and stretch the arms upwards.

Meditation to clear the past (and dissolve any 'ghosts')

Do you think about an old lover and want to be liberated from the grips of the past, releasing him or her from your aura? Then, this meditation is for you! There is nothing more powerful to release the auric pain we suffer when we break-up with a lover than this meditation. It will re-establish your aura as your own. It is truly a 'must-do' meditation for the path of the Beloved. As Westerners, we haven't been taught how to energetically clear ourselves before moving on to a new relationship. But have no fear—here is one of the primary ways to do so!

If there is a ghost lurking around, your Beloved will sense it and it will cause all sorts of problems. There is no problem 'sincerely loving' your old partners, that's natural. I am speaking of needy or unresolved energy, which is messy and sticky. We all know the difference between healed and completed relationships and those that are still bonded together due to some unresolved tension. They are the ones that have to be healed.

This meditation is also beneficial for everything from breaking habits to achieving emotional balance. It helps you focus and center yourself. It is a catalyst for change because it is a powerful spiritual cleanser. You may go through a lot of uncomfortable sensations;

physically, emotionally, and mentally because you will be releasing a lot. Be present to what you're experiencing and be willing to let it all go. If you are willing to change and welcome a new dimension of being into your life, this meditation is for you.

Meditation Process:

1. Sit in Easy Pose, closing your eyes as you bring your mental focus to the third eye point (sixth jewel).

2. Chant SA TA NA MA.

3. While chanting alternately press the thumb with the four fingers. Press hard enough to keep yourself awake and aware of the pressure. Keep repeating in a stable rhythm and keep the hand motion going throughout the entire meditation.
   - **SA:** press the thumb and the first or Jupiter finger together with pressure. The Jupiter finger brings in knowledge, expands our field of possibilities, and releases us from limitations.
   - **TA:** press the thumb and the middle or Saturn finger together. The Saturn finger gives us patience, wisdom, and purity.
   - **NA:** press the thumb and the ring or Sun finger together. The Sun finger gives us vitality and aliveness.
   - **MA:** press the thumb and the small or Mercury finger together. The Mercury finger aids in clear communication.

Each time you close a mudra by joining the thumb with a finger, your ego "seals" its effect in your consciousness.

4.   Visualize or feel each individual sound come into the crown chakra at the top of the head, down through the middle of the head and out to infinity through the third eye creating a 'L' shape movement. This is very important and must be done with each sound. It is an essential part of the cleansing process. If this part of the meditation is not done, you may experience a headache. Remember to keep the "L" going for love!

While doing this meditation, you may experience pictures of the past come up like on a movie screen in your mind. Let them dance in front of your eyes and release them with the mantra. This is part of the cleansing of the subconscious mind. If emotions come up, you can also incorporate them in the chanting (i.e. if you feel anger then chant out the anger). Whatever you experience is okay. Do not try to avoid or control your experiences. Simply be with what is going on and go through it. It is all part of the cleansing process. Use a timer to set the duration of the meditation.

Thirty-one minute version

- For the first 5 minutes chant out loud. (The voice of humans.)
- For the second 5 minutes chant in an audible whisper. (The language of lovers.)
- For the next 10 minutes chant silently. (The language of the

divine.) Keep the hands, L in the head, and tongue moving.

- Then 5 minutes whisper.
- End with 5 minutes out loud.
- The last minute, listen inside and hear the mantra and experience the L in the head. Do not do the finger movements.

Optimally, this meditation is done for 31 minutes. It can also be done for 62 minutes by doubling the process.

Eleven-minute version

It can also be done for a shorter amount of time. For the eleven minute version do:

- 2 minutes out loud
- 2 minutes in an audible whisper
- 3 minutes chant silently. Keep the hands, L in the head, and tongue moving.
- 2 minutes whisper.
- 2 minutes out loud.
- Then sit quietly and listen inside, hear the mantra, and experience the L in the head. Do not do the finger movements.

At the end, inhale deeply, raise the arms up in the air and vigorously shake the arms and fingers. You can involve the whole body and spine. Exhale. Repeat one or two more times if you desire. This is an important part of the meditation as it helps move and release the energy in the body. Relax for a few minutes before going about your day. Or relax on your back. If it is before bed time, simply go to sleep.

Meditation to solve communication problems

This meditation works on opening up the throat chakra and connecting to the heart, ensuring that all communication is coming from a heartfelt and truthful place. If you often experience a weak throat chakra, feeling unable to speak clearly or without a sense of power and self-authority, then this is the meditation for you. This powerful meditation activates the power of conscious communication so you are able to express clearly and openly, as well as being able to listen deeply and respond in loving clarity. Again, this was one that I often practiced whenever I found it difficult to express painful emotions to Sananda without bursting into tears. The glory of this meditation enabled me to stay emotionally calm, and to speak my truth with no sense of blame or victim mentally. Hallelujah!

Posture: Sit in Easy Pose with the spine straight. Eyes are closed and looking softly into the third eye point (sixth jewel).

Mudra: Touch the thumb and Mercury (pinkie) finger of one hand to the thumb and Mercury finger of the other hand, creating a lotus shape with the hands. Bend the Sun (ring) fingers in toward the palms, but do not let them touch the palms. Leave the Jupiter (index) and Saturn (middle) fingers pointing straight up, but not touching.

Music: Meditatively listen to a piece of instrumental music that heals and relaxes.

Time: Start with 11 minutes and work up to 31 minutes.

Womb Breathing

Ladies, your womb is the gateway to totally out-of-this-world experiences! By reconnecting with the womb, a woman discovers a huge missing piece of her puzzle. For the best part of fifteen years, I had been on the yogic path and spiritual journey and had bypassed the importance of the womb, because I did not know it was an important focal point. Strangely enough,it was Sananda who reintroduced me back to my true seat of female power and stillness. Since discovering this well of my creativity and essence, I can honestly say that to live in ignorance of the womb is a tragic loss for womankind.

Your womb is the doorway to the deepest meditations and inner journeys, and also to the path of the fullest, most juicy embodiments of womanhood. More importantly, the voice of the womb is your true inner guru. She knows exactly what is going on at any given moment. With practice you will be able to tune into any given situation and know exactly what to say, and how to handle any circumstance that life throws your way. When a woman reconnects with the vastness of her womb, her life deepens, and begins all over again. When she then shares that essence of her being with her Beloved—watch out!

The womb is the source of Shakti—need I say more? Let's just say you will have access to vast quantities of energy and endurance.

I have included a very simple, yet powerful practice that can bring about those first steps to becoming a fully authentic feminine being.

Womb breathing can bring clarity to any questions (including those about your Beloved!) that you are asking, so you can receive deeper answers and insights. Another important aspect of womb breathing is that it can open the door to sexual healing, and much like the seven gates reconnects Shakti with Bhakti. Womb breathing brings attention, breath, and light into the womb that energizes and cleanses, welcoming in inner focus and a sense of profound wisdom. Womb breathing requires patience (depending on your own connectivity, you may find it difficult to stay womb centered, as the 'norm' is often to return back to your head) and gentle presence from you, as it is done in a sacred manner with the clear intention to heal, soothe, and open the gateway into the womb.

To begin, find a place and time where you will be undisturbed and feel safe to make sound or rest in the silence. Be with this breath, and give it your undivided attention and focus. Feelings and emotions may begin to surface, so be in your allowing, open, receptive feminine nature, and go wherever the practice takes you. Most of all enjoy! This can be a pleasurable, sensual experience.

1. Lie on your back with your feet on the floor and knees bent openly, as if you were giving birth.

2. Make yourself comfortable with cushions to support your head.

3. Place both hands over the womb and make conscious connection with yourself, your womb, and your breath.

4. Begin to bring your focus to your PC muscles. (The area that controls your urine flow.) Take your time to find these muscles, and then contract them.

5. On a slow rhythmic inhale, squeeze the PC muscles together and suck the breath into the womb. Feel and see the breath as light coming into the womb. Treat the breath with a quality of preciousness. Imagine light flowing into the womb.

6. Hold the breath in the womb, whilst squeezing the PC muscles.

7. With your hands make slow large circles, clockwise and anti-clockwise. As you make circles, feel the light of the breath bathing and suffusing the whole womb.

8. On the exhale, relax the PC muscles, pushing the breath through the PC. As you release the breath, feel the subtlety of the light flowing out of the yoni.

9. Feel as if you are sensually delighting in yourself (to stimulate some Shakti), and cleansing your womb with golden light. Allow yourself to truly feel the energy deep inside. Some women experience this as a sexual experience, while others experience a sense of gratitude—again we are all different. Because we are dealing with Shakti, just allow that energy to guide your movements and responses.

10. Then again inhale; pulling in the PC, holding the breath in the womb, making circles with your hands.

11. Repeat this for 10 minutes.

*As taken from *Womb Wisdom: Awakening the forgotten and creative powers of the feminine* by Padma and Anaiya Aon Prakasha.

Goddess Water Rituals

Feeling and experiencing Goddess energy is paramount to both genders (as we embody both feminine and masculine energy) on the path to the Beloved. This spring water ritual will amplify your feminine Goddess energy—connecting you further to Mother Earth and your heart. Water amplifies and holds memory. So, whatever you do in water has tremendous power. Speaking out your prayers and words of intention—(great for opening up the throat chakra as well!) will charge the water and amplify your work. The water is already inherently magic, yet filled with your prayers and intentions, its power becomes tenfold.

Spring Water Goddess Ritual for Intentions, Connection

Locate a mountain or hillside spring to bathe in. Visiting natural hot springs is a wonderful option as well. This is ideal for setting your intentions for calling in your Beloved or amplifying your connection with him/her.

- Call forth the healing powers of the water by invoking a water goddess or deva that you feel closely connected to. I always call to Aquae Sulis (the Roman goddess of water), to amplify the healing qualities of the water to both restore and invigorate me or to cleanse and wash away certain energies.

- Step into the water or under the waterfall (if there is one).

- Feel the water on your body. The feminine embodies energies, so it's important to really feel (this means connecting to your body by closing your eyes, going within, and feeling what's there) the thrills and subtle movements of Shakti running through your body as you bathe and play under the water.

- Recite your prayer or intention as you're in the water. Continue to feel your divine feminine energy amplifying the water with your words.

- Spend as much time in the water as you intuitively sense what is perfect for you.

- Upon leaving, thank the water for its gift and thank your divine feminine for opening up the pathways to connect.

Spring Water Ritual for Prayers, Healing, and Restoration

If you're practicing a ritual to amplify your prayers or to call forth a healing or restoration, then try to collect some of the water from your spring wash. A healing water ritual may be perfect for when you are letting go of any 'ghosts' or want to heal something within you to attract your Beloved.

- Speak into the water your request for healing, restoration, and any prayers. Water holds your spoken words and feelings, and doing this magnetizes your request.

- Collect some water. You can do this by placing a bucket or any kind of container near your feet, so that the water can run off your body into the container.

- If the water is drinkable, ask the spring to bless it with its powers of healing and renewal so that you (and your pets/plants) may drink it.

- The collected water can be placed on your altar, or poured into your spiritual cleansing baths. You could also add some to your natural cleaning products for housecleaning.

- Sharing the collected spring water with the plants and animals in your home will connect all of you together in a more amplified way.

Frequently Asked Questions About Finding the Beloved

(I know, you've been tallying questions in your head—so without further adieu, here are the answers!)

1. **How do I know if I have met my Beloved?**

    You completely and utterly know! This knowingness is far stronger than the questioning mind, and wipes out all questions and doubts. If you are asking this question it most probably means you have not met them.

2. **I think I met my Beloved once, but we split up, does that mean we failed?**

    Beloveds never accidently meet; it is a planned and very precise affair. There are no accidents! Beloveds will burn through copious amounts of issues, bring tremendous healing to one another, and experience the most profound sense of undiluted oneness and intimacy that can never be matched again in this lifetime. If this doesn't happen, then it wasn't your Beloved. Both parties will do whatever is necessary to heal through and make this happen.

3. **What is the difference between a Soul Mate and Beloved?**

    A Soul Mate relationship (discussed in the Introduction in greater depth) is an instant knowingness that is felt at the beginning, the moment you come into contact. However shortly after this wondrous reunion, there tends to be a deep, immovable sense that this relationship is temporary and won't be forever. You will also have an accurate sense of how much time you will be together. With Danny, within weeks of meeting him I asked in meditation how long it would be and the answer appeared. Of course, I tried to fight that knowingness and hung on longer than I probably needed to—but the answer was still there. You can also ask your womb. Again you will simply know the answer. I often found that it came with a sorrow, as there was this tremendous love, which was interwoven with a thread of knowing that 'this is temporary.' With a Beloved, you know it's permanent. A Soul Mate also prepares, refines, and gets you ready for the Beloved, if it is your destiny to meet in this lifetime.

4. **How do I become the person my Beloved will instantly see/feel?**

You already *are* that person and no matter what he/she will see/feel it.

5. **Does Beloved recognition ever take longer than a split second?**

From personal experience, it was split second recognition. It is felt strongly. Perhaps you may deny it for a short while, but eventually it will draw you back together. You cannot miss each other, it is not possible. Now, what you do after you meet is up to you—which is why you now have this book as your guide!

6. **What if I'm not here in this lifetime to meet my Beloved?**

If you're reading this book, then I feel you are on the path of meeting your Soul Mate—at the very least. You would not be reading this book otherwise.

7. **How do I know if I am meant to meet my Beloved?**

You either know it, or you don't. It is as simple as that. If you don't feel drawn to having a Beloved experience, then you're not here for that; if you are, then you will no doubt experience it.

8. **I have met my Beloved, but he/she doesn't know it. What shall I do?**

Beloveds recognize one another. They are vital, they are awake, and they know. What may be going on here is a huge projection on your part, hoping, wishing that this person was your Beloved. I guarantee you, it's a two-way affair. Beloveds are on the lookout for their other their entire life—consumed with this passion they recognize each other the moment their eyes meet (maybe that's where that classic old cliché of love at first sight comes from).

9. **I have been married 20 years, and have recently found my Beloved outside of my marriage. What shall I do?**

Ah, yes, we are seeing more of this than ever before! First off, Beloveds will not push, demand, or expect any untoward behavior. Yes, there will be a powerful magnetism, but it won't necessarily be to get each other in bed. Of course that will be present, but it may not be the main impulse. It more often than not is to look at one another, talk, and make concrete that what you're both feeling is real.

If, your husband/wife is clearly a Soul Mate, then you must treasure his/her heart as you gently handle the breaking up process with care, consideration, and kindness, as he/she may have fallen into amnesia and forgotten that it was once his/her job to hand you over. If this man/woman is obviously not a Soul Mate, (i.e., a pain in the ass, obviously asleep, and/or lazily living) then ruthlessly get out of the relationship being honest, open, and resolute.

For a woman, it can be easy to get pulled back in with emotional blackmail. My advice is to get on with the task at hand, remembering of course that all human beings deserve care and kindness when going through a break-up. Just don't get sucked back in, if you know your Beloved has shown up. (Was that a politically and spiritually incorrect piece of advice? So sorry, but my purpose is to support Beloveds in coming together—no other way will do!) Besides, Beloveds are not usually politically or spiritually correct whatsoever. You can throw that hope right out. This is soul work at the deepest level, so tact is not always the order of the day. Together you will be a law unto yourselves, free from fear, and resting in the eternal.

❧

My last, last word—no really

And now, for what you've no doubt been waiting for (well, beyond meeting your Beloved)—my last, last words (in this book anyway!).

I wrote this book to declare to the world that meeting one's Beloved is not a false 'love story.' It does still happen, it is real, and it has nothing to do with fairytales and Knights/Maidens in shining armor. It is a result of two people joining together fully, sharing their lives completely, and revealing their light and dark sides, leaving nothing hidden or secret.

My final words are to touch that receiving place within you, to implore you to make a stand, to give your life to something that is real and incredibly rewarding. To say an enthusiastic YES to love, no matter how hard, no matter how terrifying. By opening to love with your Beloved your life will shift in many miraculous, unexpected ways, revealing the chance to live free from all fear.

I promise you this is the truth.

Within the tapestry of my life experiences, nothing has ever come close to matching, let alone surpassing, the absolute contentment that is the result of becoming open and devoted to love. I believe that pure love is the one thing all of us can share, as it gives us a glimpse of what life is all about. This glimpse catapults us into a thriving world outside the boundaries of 'me and my problems,' and reveals to us a place where there are no problems, nor ever will be. In other words, a true soul connection with yourself and your other.

So, how will you spend your life? What does it stand for? What has your life been in service to?

I know that my life has been in service to love, and with that I can depart in peace, knowing I gave and received fully. In my heart, I wish for us all to be able to say and feel this within us, in every moment. As it is in this spirit that life is worth living.

In this place, deep within the cave of the heart—this is where I will meet you.

I am awaiting your "yes!" to come and join me on the Pilgrimage of Love. Will you?

Anaiya Aon Prakasha
Thanks Giving Day 2010
London, England

I have loved in life
and I have been loved.
I have drunk the bowl of poison
from the hands of love as nectar,
and have been raised above life's joy and sorrow.

My heart, aflame in love,
set afire every heart that came in touch with it.
My heart has been rent
and joined again;
My heart has been broken
and again made whole;
My heart has been wounded
and healed again;
A thousand deaths my heart has died,
and thanks be to love,
it lives yet.

I bowed my head low in humility,
and on my knees I begged of love,
"Disclose to me, I pray thee, O love, thy secret."
She took me gently by my arms and lifted me above the earth,
and spoke softly in my ear,
"My dear one,
thou thyself art love, art lover, and thyself art the beloved
whom thou hast adored."

—Hazrat Inayat Khan

Sources and Resources

Make sure you catch up with Anaiya's continuous Pilgrimage of Love on her website, where you'll find her "Pilgrimage to love" world-wide teaching events, seminars, and on-line courses that prepare you to find "The One" as well as her on-going discoveries on How to Live/Love with your Beloved.

http://www.pilgrimageoflove.com

For those who wish to know more of the in-depth process into Anaiya's womb healing, along with all the tools and practices for opening and clearing the womb please read *Womb Wisdom: Awakening the Creative and Forgotten Powers of the Feminine*, by Anaiya and Padma Aon Prakasha (Inner Traditions). Together, the pair wrote this book as they ventured through the process.

For information on The Seven Gates, read *The Power of Shakti*, by Padma Aon Prakasha (Inner Traditions)

You can find both these books and a host of others, including music at http://www.wombwisdom.me

Also, you will find a list of events for Pilgrimage of Love, Power of Shakti and Womb Wisdom, as well as other related workshops.